FIRST RANCH IN MONTANA

BY: GENNARO ROSETTI

Available as an ebook

ISBN 979-8-9928998-6-3 (paperback)

ISBN 979-8-2859459-8-7 (hardcover)

Publify Publishing

Lampasas, TX 76550

contact@publifypublishing.com

To my Posse:

Maria, Jake, and Leo

CONTENTS

Chapter I

THE HEARTH

He was born in St. Louie, his Pap a tradesman, a gunsmithy, an' a good one to hear tell. If you was headin west, the one thing you'd best bring was a good piece, an' they didn't come cheap. T'was a fine livin. Till the war come and got everybody all riled up.

Jacob McCune

St. Louis, Missouri

The shop sat squat on the corner of Cumberland and Main, a few blocks from the river near the East Quay. It was plain ugly, made of grey Mississippi mud brick, utterly without ornamentation of any kind, not even a window. When he first came to this country, Johann made do with a log and thatch cabin, but he squeezed every nickel and saved enough to build a proper work room. He couldn't risk the wind blowing though the chinks and spreading fire to the powder.

It was his father who taught him how to forge steel and make guns. He was a brutal taskmaster, not easily pleased. And Johann learned his trade well, but there were too many gunsmiths in the old country. Johann came across to the new world.

There was a sizeable German community in St. Louis. They had been moving down the Ohio from Pennsylvania for a generation now. Johann loved the wide-open spaces, the big river, the rough and colorful characters that would never have been tolerated in the old country. Here he could work without having to ask anyone's permission and it was here he met his Anna, a good Deutschfrau as strong as most men. Even amongst their hard-working German neighbors, the two of them were known to be particularly industrious.

St. Louis grew up around them. It'd been nothing but a den of thieves and drunken scoundrels when Johann first arrived, another reason for strong walls and a thick door. And now Johann was teaching his own son, Leopold, the trade. Johann enjoyed showing him new techniques, presenting them with the enthusiasm of a magician performing a favorite trick. The boy was already a full head taller than his father, and his shoulders were wide and coming into muscle, even if his face was still soft and hairless. If his attention wandered from time to time, or he spent too much time running an errand down along the docks, it was to be expected.

The workshop was warmed by a brick forge built into the corner. The floor was dirt but hard packed. Mounted on the walls were barrel molds and the seasoned blanks of walnut and hickory used to make his stocks. In front of the forge sat a heavy, elongated anvil. Unlike a blacksmith's anvil, it was ground perfectly flat and had a channel running along its length. A rifle barrel could be clamped into the channel to be straightened or polished. Oil lamps hung from the rafters, casting a serviceable light on the large workbench that dominated the room. The oak bench was thick and solid, worn smooth and of a rich patina darkened by gun oil, powder and sweat. It served as a barrier to keep people from entering the work area and on its side small wooden drawers were filled with triggers, springs, gun sights and other small parts. Hung along the wall behind the bench were metal files, spoke shaves, drawknives and polishing wheels. A few staved barrels stood by the wall, filled with oil and polishing powder.

The rear door was narrower than the front but just as sturdy, and across its stanchions slid a wood stave that locked it tight against the frame. The door led to a yard where a few stacks of rough lumber were stickered and covered with tarpaulins. The rest of the yard grew thick with grass and wildflowers. A dirt path wound through the yard to the small clapboard cabin that sat beneath the shade of two enormous cottonwood trees.

The yard between the house and the workshop was Leopold's. He knew every inch of it. He had played there as a child and now he worked there, cutting wood for the fire, shoveling coal for the forge, shaping the rough lumber for stocks and keeping everything in order the way his father demanded. Leopold liked to come outside whenever he needed to see the sky. The sounds drifted in from the waterfront and he could see the smokestacks of the riverboats. He dreamed of stowing away and heading west, towards the distant mountains. The fur trappers, his father's customers, were always talking about the mountains.

Leopold had his own bench against the wall. He'd made the bench himself and was exceedingly proud of it. A long octagonal rifle barrel was clamped down and Leopold leaned into his work with the polishing block. He dipped a thick leather pad into a barrel of rubbing compound and, using both hands, applied as much muscle as he could, working himself into a flowing sweat. Johann looked over at his son with a smile and a slight shake of his head.

"Come," Johann called. "Watch."

Leopold wiped his brow with a handkerchief, laid the block aside and walked around behind his father. He was tall enough to see clearly over Johann's shoulder. The old man positioned a Kentucky long rifle on the bench in front of him.

"It's a fine rifle, though it's not been cared for like it ought."

Johann laid the rifle on its side, took a small screwdriver and removed the firing mechanism.

"Look at the rust! The chamber is almost completely choked off."

With a few deft motions he had the entire rifle laid out in pieces on the bench. As Leopold watched he dropped some of the parts into an earthenware jar filled with strong solution. He removed the barrel from the stock and sighted down its length, then held it up so his son could see. Johann dipped a coarse steel brush into another jar of compound and ran it though the barrel. The brush came away black with soot and powder.

Taking out a small file, Johann worked the firing mechanism, first to remove all the corrosion that had built up along the outside and then to clean and polish it, smoothing the two halves of the pivot.

"It must be perfect, no pits, no rust. It must be adjusted precisely so that always the same pressure is required. This trigger is too tight. What happens when the trigger's too tight?" he asked.

"It jerks," Leopold answered. "You miss."

Johann nodded. "If it were my rifle, I'd fix it so that only the slightest touch was needed. But since Herr Walker did not ask, I will not fool with it. Never change the pressure on a trigger without asking. The man might shoot his foot off," Johann laughed. "That would be bad for business!"

"You like your work, eh Papa?" Leopold asked.

Johann stopped, as though he had never considered this question before.

"Work is work. You want to eat, you work. But Ya, I suppose I do. Especially working on a fine old fellow like this," he said, patting the gun.

"But didn't you ever want to do nothing else? Leopold asked.

"This is what my father did. What he taught me to do. I never thought on nothing else."

Johann took another brush from the drawer and worked it into the corners of the casing.

"I am lucky to have such a skill. I don't have to worry about the rain falling too hard or not falling hard enough. I don't have to worry about my back giving out or my goods going out of fashion."

Johann stopped what he was doing and looked up at his son, as though something had just occurred to him.

"You don't want this work?" he asked.

Leopold shook his head "No, no. I like it well enough."

Lee hesitated, not wanting to hurt his father's feelings.

"But sometimes, I think I don't want to be cooped up. Might want to work at something outside. Like the trappers who come down the river."

Johann continued with his task. And just when Leopold thought the conversation was over, his father started again.

"We think we can do anything when we're young. And sure, it does get hot in here. But that's not so bad when it's blowing snow outside! You got some skills now. I think you have the talent. Not everybody can figure out how things go together, but you pick it up fast enough. We have the war now. After that, people will come through here heading west. They will be needing a good rifle. It is a good living you stand to make. I'm old. I'm not going to live forever."

"You're not old."

Johann removed the stock from the rifle and handed it to Leopold, "Sand it down till all the scratches are gone."

Johann turned back to his work, and then stopped and looked up at his son.

"I don't know," Johann said. "I think, sometimes, that all I want is to live long enough to see you married. And to meet my grandson. That would be nice."

Johann went back to his work. Leopold put his big hand on the old man's shoulder. Usually, his father didn't talk much, except to tell him what to do.

"This kind of weapon is still useful," Johann changed the subject.

"Though it won't be long before everyone is using the new breach loads and cartridges."

They were interrupted by the sound of boots on the street outside and suddenly the door was thrown open, a burst of brilliant sunlight momentarily flooding the workshop, silhouetting a group of Union officers. One of the young officers held the door as his superior stepped inside. The General was tall, his back straight as a rod, his beard trimmed close and gone to gray. His eyes were alert and piercing. There was neither warmth nor levity to his demeanor. Johann smiled politely and wiped his hands on his apron.

"General Thomas Ewing," the officer said, introducing himself.

Johann stepped forward, holding up his hands to indicate that they were dirty. The General nodded imperceptibly.

"I'm sorry, there's nowhere to sit. Leopold, bring the General your stool."

"Not necessary," Ewing replied. He turned to his adjutant, a thin man with bad skin, who handed the General a finely decorated mahogany box. Ewing opened it, revealing a pair of matching pistols. The box was lined in velvet, the steel engraved in a delicate filigree and the ivory handles were beautifully ambered from age and use.

"I've heard you do careful work. These are in need of some attention. They've been bounced around quite a lot lately."

Johann reached down and picked up one of the pistols, testing its weight and examining the action. He nodded his approval.

"I will take good care of them."

"See that you do," The General replied. "How long will you require?"

"You can come for them on Friday, General."

Ewing nodded, looked down and examined the rifle laid out on the work bench.

"Handsome piece. Who does it belong to?"

"Herr Walker," Johann said proudly. "He brings all his work here."

Unexpectedly, Ewing frowned, glancing toward his adjutant, "Hyram Walker?"

"Ya," Johann said.

The Adjutant leaned forward. "He has a farm down along the stage road. A suspected sympathizer."

"Oh, I wouldn't know about that," Johann stammered. "I am just a shop keeper."

Ewing nodded to his adjutant who quickly scribbled something in his notebook. "Until Friday then," he said, stepping back out through the door.

Fort Laramie, Wyoming Territory

Elizabeth Cain stood in front of the rickety easel the fort's carpenter had fashioned for her. She had never owned an easel, and Elizabeth wasn't sure what went into one, so the result was unstable and barely serviceable. She was situated on a low hill with a good view over the river to the western hills. It was only a quarter mile from the fort, but her father sent two troopers to accompany her. One was spread out on the tall grass behind her, sound asleep. The other leaned on his rifle, staring off into the distance. Elizabeth had the uncomfortable feeling, whenever she turned her back, that he was staring at her. She was not accustomed to the way men looked at her. Though she was careful to dress modestly, there was no hiding her shape.

The sun was just beginning to set. The Laramie River caught the flat light of the low sun, the moving water sparkling through the shifting leaves of the cottonwoods. Elizabeth spread her paints out on the tray. She wanted to capture some of the depth and subtlety of the colors she saw but her skills were simply not up to the task. If she could capture just one of the elements, the trees, the sky, the hills or the long yellow grass swaying gently in the breeze, then that would be enough. It was too much to expect to capture them all in a single painting, not yet. At seventeen years old she was a competent artist. But being merely competent was not enough for Elizabeth. It never occurred to her that merely enjoying a thing was enough, in and of itself.

She brushed her long black hair away from her face and retied the ribbon that held it in place. Her hair was a problem. She wished there was somebody she could trust to cut it for her, like her mother used to. Her father, Lieutenant Colonel Avery Billings Cain, had recently been appointed the commandant of Fort Laramie. Up until last year, she hadn't seen much of him. Cain was a graduate of West Point, a career officer who had risen quickly through the ranks. At the outbreak of the war, he was given command of the 3rd Massachusetts infantry. At the battle of Williamsburg, he was shot through the shoulder while leading a charge against a line of fixed Confederate defenders. The ball passed straight through, tearing muscle and tendon, and he was laid up for a month.

In August he took part in the battle of Bull Run, a fiasco in which the commanders on both sides showed their inexperience and poor judgment. Union forces suffered almost three thousand casualties. Cain was blown off his horse by a canon blast and knocked unconscious, his body riddled with shrapnel. He lay senseless while the bloodbath continued to rage around him, awakening in the dead of night in an open field with the bodies of the dead and dying strewn all around him. It was Dante's hell on earth. He was soaked in blood, too weak to move and dared not call for help lest he be picked off by rebel sharpshooters.

When they finally got him to a field hospital, he was close to death. The Surgeon removed more than thirty fragments from his back and neck, but a few were so deeply imbedded that they were stitched over and left.

Elizabeth's mother, back in Plainfield, had not yet even heard that her husband had been wounded when she herself was struck down with influenza and was dead within a week. Until then, Elizabeth had been a happy young girl, sheltered, without a care in the world. Suddenly her world was cast upside down. She had no brothers or sisters; her mama had been everything to her.

Her father's family had been unable to get word to the Colonel, so Elizabeth was taken in and cared for by her aunt. It was another two weeks before the news finally reached them that her father had been wounded and was himself near death. The weeks that followed were the worst of her life. She cried herself to sleep every night, wondering what would become of her and trying to come to grips with the thought that she would never again see her dear mother and that she would, most likely, lose her father as well. Gradually, she began to harden herself to her circumstances. She had been naive to think life was so simple and benign. Families everywhere, north and south, were being torn apart. The evidence had been there, and she had blithely chosen to ignore it. Never again would she be caught so unprepared.

Weeks passed without news. In late September she was helping her aunt gather the last of their summer vegetables when she noticed an old man with a cane limping slowly down the lane. At first, she didn't recognize him, he had grown so thin and frail, but then she threw off her work gloves and ran to meet him, throwing her arms around her father's neck and looking up into his sad blue eyes. For the next few weeks Elizabeth took care of him, talking with him about the war and the friends he had lost. He patiently answered her questions, but he preferred to learn about the things that were important in her life, the books she was reading, her friends, her dreams. It was as if they were getting to know each other for the first time and discovering that they liked each other. As a young girl, she had found her father aloof, stern and impatient, but the war had softened him in some fundamental way. Now, it was not unusual for him to spend the whole afternoon sitting on the porch talking to neighbors and watching her work in the garden. In the back of Elizabeth's mind was the constant fear that he would be ordered to report back to the war and that, this time, she'd lose him for good.

In due course he did receive his orders. But in deference to the fact that he had already been seriously wounded twice, he was not ordered South, as expected, but West, to command the tenth infantry at Fort Laramie on the Wyoming frontier. He was to leave immediately and report without further delay. Cain assured his daughter that he would make arrangements for her to stay with her aunt, but no sooner had he spoken the words than the fighting began.

She refused to be left behind. Elizabeth could accept that she could not accompany him to a war, but she was not about to stay home if he was stationed out West. She had read everything about the frontier and dreamed of seeing it. She would be a great help, she argued, maintaining his home and helping him entertain. At first Cain wouldn't hear of it and they went to sleep that night with the matter unresolved, both of them upset that the argument had created such an unexpected rift. The next morning, she dug in deeper. Every argument he came up with she summarily dismissed. Cain himself did not relish the thought of leaving her behind, but a military base was no place for a young woman. In the back of his mind, he realized that, if he left her behind, she would probably marry and be lost to him forever. For three days the battle raged between them, but Elizabeth steadily wore him down. He, at last, relented.

She'd been captivated by the terrible beauty of the open prairie as they traveled west, first by rail, and then on horseback with a Cavalry escort. It was a long and difficult journey. The Great Plains, vast and hard and colorful, were so different from the pastel countryside of Massachusetts. From the soot darkened windows of the train car, she saw antelopes, eagles, coyotes and great herds of buffalo, and she recorded the experiences dutifully in her journal. Only the Indians proved a disappointment. Those she saw in the towns they passed were not the fierce and noble warriors of literature, but poor, downcast beggars and drunkards who hung near the platform looking for handouts. She pitied them and went out of her way to avoid them.

Fort Laramie itself was not at all what she expected. There was no palisade, no ponderous wooden gate requiring half a dozen men to open. Instead, it was a beautifully situated collection of buildings on an almost level site entirely encircled by the river. Tall grass spread in all directions and cows grazed in the open parade ground. There were deer along the river bottom and the occasional buffalo on the hills in the distance. The fort's only security lay in its isolation and the size of the garrison. The buildings themselves were mostly rough-hewn log, but a few had already been replaced by brick and mortar, complete with glass windows, wood trim and even curtains. Construction had stopped for the duration and piles of building material lay scattered about. The very air delighted, a prairie wind blowing the smell of freshly baked bread from the cookhouse. Elizabeth loved everything about the land, every grove of trees seemed to promise adventure, beyond every hill lurked danger and excitement.

But life was not easy. Far from it. Even planting a vegetable garden took many times the effort it had in Massachusetts. She had to break the hard clods into something resembling soil, mix in as much manure as she could cart from the stable and work it with a hoe till her palms blistered. In the spring, after planting the precious seeds carried from the East, she had to scurry when one thunderstorm after another threatened to wash everything into the river. Then the rain stopped, and the new shoots had to be watered by hand lest they shrivel up and die. Every jackrabbit, deer, prairie dog and crow on the Plains came in for a taste. A proper fence had to be built to keep the critters out. There was work upon work, but there was beauty too, and the satisfaction of knowing that what you had was hard earned.

Elizabeth looked up at the western sky. The clouds were at the peak of their color now, a violent crimson trimmed in grey and white, rising thousands of feet into the summer sky. She hurried to mix her colors, washing them onto the paper with light strokes, watching them spread and blend and slowly dry. One of the troopers came up behind her and told her it was time to head back. He was so close she could smell the stale tobacco on his breath. She ignored him, working quickly now before the color bled from the sky. When she finished she put down her brush and watched a hawk ride the thermals over the hills to the north, drifting effortlessly on the breeze, watching, waiting for movement from below.

Chapter II

PIEGAN

When I was layin trap, them Blackfoot was the most feared of any tribe, bar none. They were good riders and had plenty of grit in a fight. An you couldn't buy em off like other Injuns. Didn't care much for your beads and baubles.

Jacob McCune

Marias River, Blackfoot Territory

Butte Bull's band consisted of ten lodges: twelve men, five young bucks, and an assortment women and children, about forty all told. It was a manageable number who could move quickly, hunt what they needed without straining the resources and live in relative harmony. There were bigger bands, but with too many braves there were bound to be disagreements. They would join other bands on occasion, when it was time to hunt buffalo, or to celebrate the Dance of the Sun. Occasionally, a young man would go off to live with a new wife or a squaw would come to join their band. A brave might get in an argument with a family member and leave. That sort of thing was to be expected.

It was cool in the hills this time of year with plenty of water flowing down from the mountains. There was no shortage of game: deer, elk, goats, sheep, plenty of birds, beaver and bear. When his people got restless, they might move deeper into the mountains. Later in the summer, when food got scarce, they'd move out onto the plains to hunt buffalo.

Butte Bull's position wasn't something handed to him. He'd earned it by virtue of his skill in raiding, his prowess in the hunt and, most importantly, his calmness and wisdom in dealing with the many problems that arose. Somebody was always making trouble. A husband might mistreat his wife. A young brave might rush off and steal horses when none were needed. You couldn't tell another man what to do. You could only talk calmly, smoke the pipe and make clear the course. Usually, the others went along. Butte Bull was tall for his people and thick in the legs and chest with no fat creeping on the way it sometimes did with men his age. With forty summers behind him, he wasn't the young buck he had once been, but he was still strong. His hair was black and straight, tied back and well-greased. His eyes were an intense shade of darkest brown. He was not a man you crossed on a whim, but he worked hard to keep his temper, even when those around him tried his patience.

The long days were upon them, the easiest months of the year for his people. The band had set their camp along a swift moving stream that tumbled down out of the mountains, the water deep and as cold as the snow it had lately been. The grass on the hillside was still thick; if the game held out they could remain here till they moved down to the Missouri for the gathering.

Butte Bull was up early and in a good mood. His wife, Raven, had reached out for him last night, something she didn't do that often anymore. When he stepped out of the lodge the sun had not even cleared the low ridge to the east. He decided to take his son, Mountain Sun, on a hunt up on the high meadow. He was the last of his three sons, and the youngest. The others had died of the pox that had decimated his people. But he did not like to think of his sons or of the daughter he had lost. He went back into the lodge to wake his son and had to shake him three times before the boy crawled out from under his blanket. The third time, he'd been none to gentle about it. Raven put together some food while Mountain Sun went to collect their ponies.

The village was still quiet, only a few squaws up and about their chores. As they followed the trail that wound up out of the valley, Butte Bull enjoyed the cool breeze blowing down from the mountains and the feel of his good pony beneath him. There were many places to hunt at this time of year, but Butte Bull loved going into the mountains. Maybe they could take one of the big sheep before the animals headed into the high country. They were especially delicious.

Butte Bull made his son ride ahead and told him to be alert and keep his eyes on the trail. He was already as tall as his father with more muscle than most boys his age. He would be a powerful warrior, Butte Bull hoped. And he was brave almost to the point of recklessness.

They rode for two hours, climbing steadily into the mountains. When they came to the first of the lakes, Butte Bull signaled his son to head for the meadow at the inlet. There was a faint trail just inside the tree-line and they followed it to the head of the lake. The reeds were thick here and as they approached the meadow Mountain Sun stopped, signaling that he had picked up sign. He slid down off his horse and knelt in the grass. The boy pointed to a spot a few hundred yards ahead where a stand of young aspen bordered the meadow.

"I'll look," he signed.

Butte Bull tied the horses to a tree, sat down and leaned against a rock, content to let his son move on alone. He could see the boy circling the meadow, keeping just inside the trees, his bow in hand but no arrow yet notched. At this time of year there was no need to use rifles except to fight. It was important to maintain the old skills. As the boy approached the Aspen he peered into the shadows, looking to see if the game was still bedded down. Butte Bull watched as his son slowly eased himself down in the high grass. He was going to wait them out, he thought, smiling. He'd been afraid the boy would go thrashing through the brush, flushing the game out ahead of him. He had patience, this one, he thought, not like I was at his age.

The sun climbed above the trees and the chill began to lift from the air. Butte Bull lay with his back against a rock and looked up. The sky was a soft pastel blue. The few clouds that floated overhead were not storm dark or threatening; it would take hours for a storm to build with such a slight breeze. There was still snow on the peaks, though most of it would soon be gone. He put his hands behind his head and stretched his legs, though he knew he should be more alert. There were plenty of bears in the area and it wouldn't do to let one sneak up on him. But he soon closed his eyes. Maybe just a minute, he thought.

Butte Bull jumped at the sound of the carcass thumping down on the grass beside him. He leapt up, momentarily disoriented, only to see his son standing over him, a fat grin on his face. Butte Bull was about to berate him for his insolence when he looked down and saw the doe, nice and plump from spring grass, a trickle of blood indicating a clean shot through the heart. He glanced up at the sun; he'd been asleep for an hour he guessed. Mountain Sun was already at work with his knife, gutting the doe and telling his father about how he had waited till the deer was only twenty yards away before taking the shot. His father let him brag; it wasn't a bad thing. That's how reputations grew; how boys summoned the courage to do more dangerous things. In a short time, they had the deer quartered and tied onto the horses and were starting down the mountain. When they were within a quarter mile of camp the dogs started barking, running out to meet them. Butte Bull kicked his horse abreast of his son's.

"Don't tell your mother I fell asleep," he warned.

St. Louis, Missouri

The house itself was small. Johann was still working in the gunshop, but Leopold quit early to put time in on his schoolwork. Of course, there was no sparing him to attend a proper school. What education he received would be scratched out on his own or with the help of books his mother borrowed. He sat at the kitchen table struggling over a book while his mother stirred a thick stew over the hearth. He was hungry, and the smell was distracting.

"That smells good. I'm getting hungry."

"You're always hungry," his mother answered.

"I know. Why is that?" he asked.

"Still growing, I suppose."

His mother swung the iron hook away from the fire and lifted the heavy kettle without strain, carrying it to the table.

"Go wash your hands. You smell like bear grease."

When they were seated at the table, Mrs. Stemmler nodded to her husband, who thanked God for the food. Leopold's mother filled a plate and passed it to her son.

"Thank you, Mama."

She handed a plate to her husband, and then served herself.

"General Ewing came into the workshop today," Leopold told his mother. "Said he'd heard Papa was the best gunsmith in St. Louis."

"He said no such thing," Johann corrected.

"Is this something good? For business?" his wife asked.

"It's never good to be noticed by powerful men," he answered.

"Things are just fine the way they are. I hope Herr General forgets about me as soon as possible."

"Nonsense," she argued. "The army could keep you in work forever".

On Friday afternoon they were hard at work, as usual. Johann had done an especially thorough job on the pistols for General Ewing. Though he did not want to draw undue attention to himself, neither did he wish to displease the General. Johann was concluding a transaction with Mr. Truman, a wealthy landowner whose farm lay just across the river, when General Ewing and his entourage entered. Ewing and Truman nodded to one another. They were acquainted.

"Ah, General," Johann greeted him. "How good to see you. I have your pistols ready."

The General ignored him. "Mr. Truman. We haven't had the pleasure of seeing you in town lately."

"Good afternoon, General." Truman nodded, "I come when business brings me."

"What business is that?" the General inquired.

"My own," Truman replied coolly.

Ewing glared at Truman, glanced toward the rifle in his hands.

"I've heard rumors that your sons have gone south and are fighting with the rebels?"

Truman hesitated.

"That's right," Truman said. "Though it was against my wishes, I can tell you that."

The General shook his head. "What's it coming to, when a man can't even control his own family?"

Truman glared at the general. He was not a man used to being spoken to in such a manner. Johann watched nervously. The General had not, as yet, even acknowledged his presence. Truman waited, and then shrugged.

"They're young men," he said. "Get all sorts of ideas in their heads."

Ewing reached out for the rifle and Truman handed it to him. "Now why would a farmer like you need a weapon like this?"

"Country's grown dangerous. If there was ever a time a man needed to protect himself, it's now."

"You don't have to worry about that. That's why we're here. And I'm sure you stand in good stead with the Rebs, now that your boys have gone south. I suppose we should hold onto this for you."

Ewing turned and handed the rifle to his subordinate. Truman started to reach for the gun, the red in his face rising, but the look in Ewing's eyes made him reconsider. Truman was a prominent member of the community, but Ewing was the commander of a city at war with itself. The city was split by the war, more so than any other. There were no practical limits to the General's authority. Truman gave a general a foul look and walked out.

Johann and Leopold had been quietly watching the scene unfold.

"My guns are ready?" Ewing asked curtly.

Johann had the box in his hands and laid it down on the counter. Ewing opened it, lifting one of the guns to examine it. He nodded, clearly impressed by the work.

"Very nice, Mr. Stemmler. How much do I owe you?"

Johann handed the general an invoice and Ewing passed it to his adjutant, who quickly produced the money.

"Didn't we have a conversation," Ewing asked, leveling his gaze at the old man, "About being careful who you produce arms for?

"Mr. Truman is an old friend," Johann sputtered.

"Mr. Truman is a liar and a traitor. His sons will be killed and his family ruined. And you, Herr Stemmler, will have to decide where your loyalties lie."

The General looked over at Leopold, who was watching him with ill-disguised contempt. Ewing smiled and handed the box to his assistant. The General noddled, turned and left without another word.

The next morning Johann was at the workshop early. There wasn't a cloud in the sky and it looked to be another hot and humid day. Leopold had already cleaned the shop and laid his work out on the bench. Since it was Saturday, Johann took a few minutes to oil his workbench, admiring the way the oak soaked up the oil, enjoying the smell and feel of the wood. They had just settled into the meat of their tasks when a contingent of Union soldiers burst through the doorway.

Leopold recognized one of the officers who had come in with Ewing the day before.

"Johann Stemmler," the Captain said, stepping forward. "We have an order to search the premises. Please produce documents pertaining to the ownership of all firearms currently under repair and construction. "

"Documents?" Johann stuttered.

"Who does this belong to?" The Captain asked, grabbing the rifle off the bench before him.

Johann showed him the tag tied to the barrel of the rifle. The Captain examined every rifle either completed or awaiting repair. When he was done, he compared the list to a sheet of paper he pulled from the pocket of his coat and checked off several names. Johann had taken a position in front of his son, as though to shield him.

"Mr. Stemmler, you are under arrest for aiding and abetting the enemy in time of war."

"But we are only trades-people," Johann complained.

The Captain turned to his men. "Load up the weapons. Lock everything up. Post the sign on the door."

As they were led away, the Captain pushed Leopold roughly through the doorway and the young man turned, hatred burning in his eyes. The Captain laughed, wanting only an excuse, and then signaled for his men to take them away.

Yellowstone River Valley

It had been a hard year. Smallpox had ravaged the Absaroka, killing many of their strongest warriors, reducing their once formidable numbers at a time when they were beset on all sides. Then the winter came and it had been long and severe, killing off the weak who might have recovered if they could have held on till spring. To make matters worse, they were forced to keep moving. The Lakota, their traditional enemy, had been pushed south and west out of the Dakotas onto

Absaroka land, forcing them, in turn, to move further west, encroaching on lands already occupied by the Cheyenne and Blackfoot. So many ponies had died during the long winter that full grown men were forced to walk. To a Plains Indian, risking death stealing a horse was preferable to walking.

All through the spring the people waited for the buffalo. Spring turned to summer, usually a time of plenty, and the Absaroka went hungry. Marchabeau, the head man, sent one group after another in the four directions in search of the herd. They'd found no more than a few stray animals. There was nothing to do but keep trying. On the longest day of the year there was a great council. Seven braves were chosen to head out to locate the buffalo and steal horses. It was made clear to them that they were not to return until they had succeeded.

The seven hunters set out on the best of the remaining mounts, and among them was White Hawk, a warrior who made up in cleverness what he lacked in stature. He was only a little over five feet tall and rail thin even in fat times. But he was quick, deceptively strong and seemed to never need to sleep or eat. White Hawk was a good man to have on a war party.

The warriors were relieved to be out riding the prairie. It was hard to be stuck in the village when everybody was so gloomy. But, from the first, luck turned against them. A storm swept in and a stinging rain blew in their face. The cold rain froze fingers and toes, making life miserable for the men and the footing treacherous for their ponies.

They traveled for three days without finding game. Finally, they came across the carcass of an old black bear in a ravine along the river bottom. It appeared he had simply dropped dead; there wasn't a mark on him. But meat was meat, even if it was stringy and tasteless. They made camp along the river and ate till their stomachs hurt. Later that night White Hawk and the others fell violently ill, so sick that they lost most of what they'd eaten and felt even weaker the next morning. Surely their luck must improve. White Hawk was sure they'd find buffalo if they continued south. A few buffalo would do much to lift their spirits.

The weather did not improve. The freezing rain turned to a steady drizzle, not enough to even notice except that it kept the game bedded low and the warriors' moods even lower. They knew they were moving into Lakota territory but White Hawk thought it worth the risk. They should be able to avoid the big camps and might even stumble onto a small hunting party whose horses they could steal. White Hawk was known to be an excellent horse thief. His small frame allowed him to move lightly across the ground, so quietly that even the horses couldn't hear him approach. Before they could rear their heads in warning, he'd be stroking their neck, lulling them into a trance and leading them away without making a sound. But first, he had to find them.

White Hawk didn't like riding out in the open without even a line of hills or trees to escape to, but he had never been through this country before. What choice did he have?

They did not spot the Lakota; the Lakota spotted them. The war party was almost on them by the time he heard the sound of horses galloping toward them. The Absaroka took off with their enemies right behind them. It was late in the day and White Hawk hoped they could stay out of range until it was too dark for the Lakota to continue the pursuit. White Hawk, with his light frame and strong pony, was out in front, scouting the land ahead for some type of shelter, a creek bed or a line of boulders big enough to provide cover. They had four muskets between them, accurate enough but slow to load. They started a run up a long slope that allowed the Lakota to gain on them. White Hawk heard a grunt and saw one of his comrades drop off his horse and tumble across the hard prairie. Before they got to the top, another went down.

White Hawk and the four remaining men reached the crest and started down the other side. He took a quick look behind and saw that the Lakota were no longer following. They must have stopped to finish off the two who had fallen and to take scalps. The Absaroka pushed their ponies at as fast a pace as they dared maintain. They rode till well after dark, stopping at every rise to see if they were being followed. The thick clouds made for a lightless night. They found grass for their horses and slept without nourishment, taking turns keeping guard, wondering what they had done to turn the Spirits against them.

Chapter III

WAR

They sent Lee's Pap to a Union prison and Lee were given the choice: jail or fight for the North. He struggled mightily, but in the end, he figured things might go easier for his old man if he signed up.

Jacob McCune

Portsmouth, Ohio

The camp sprawled over hundreds of acres of rolling farmland, a small city of canvas and blue wool. The weak morning sun struggled to break through the fog and bring what heat it could to the chill autumn fields. Leopold rose from his tent and pulled on his pants. His face and hands were dirty and his lips so cracked that it hurt when he yawned. His thick blond hair was long and greasy and his clothes disheveled. He scratched at the bug bites that covered his legs.

"What I wouldn't give for some bacon and biscuits", he said to himself.

He was camped in a small circle of tents with the other men from his company, all of whom were hurrying to get dressed and keep warm.

"Get the fire going, Brancy," Jed called out. He was tall and thin, all elbows and angles.

Brancy scratched his thick red beard, bent over the wood pile and shook his head. "I will, if you go rustle up some dry wood."

"Where am I gonna find dry wood, it's been raining for a dammed week."

Leopold buttoned his shirt up tight and pulled his boots on. He was about to join his friends when the Lieutenant walked up.

"Stemmler, grab your gear and head up to the command tent."

"What'd I do now?" he asked.

"Didn't say you did nothing," said the Lieutenant, "Leave your rifle."

Captain McCurland's command tent occupied a prominent place at the top of a hill overlooking the sea of men and materiel cast across the land in all directions. Leopold tried to pull himself together as best he could, tucked in his shirt, flattened down his hair and wiped the crust out of the corners of his eyes. At the command tent a young corporal greeted him in friendly fashion, only adding to Leopold's confusion. He gave the corporal his name.

"Stemmler," the corporal echoed, checking it off a list. "Go on over there with them boys and get yourself some coffee."

Lee recognized a few of the men from the battalion. They were all young; country boys for the most part. He grabbed a tin cup and poured the thick black coffee, enjoying the warmth of it in his hands. There were about twenty of them, milling around restlessly and wondering why they were there.

"What's going on?" Leopold asked the man standing next to him.

"Hell if I know. We was woke and told to report."

"Rekon we're in some kind of trouble?" he asked.

The man shrugged and took another sip of coffee.

They sat for an hour, trying to stay warm and figure out what they'd done wrong. Finally, the captain emerged from the tent. McCurland was a small man with the ready look of an athlete, his eyes alert and intelligent. Following him was a tough old sergeant half a head taller, with a thick neck, long grey hair and wiry red whiskers. The Captain had a friendly smile; the Sergeant looked like he never once smiled and never would. The men scattered, looking for a place to set their cups, spilling coffee on their boots but eventually managing to form a pathetic uneven line. The Captain walked over, taking no notice of their disarray.

"Good morning, men," he said. "Young bunch, eh?" he said, glancing at the Sergeant.

"Pups," The sergeant said gruffly.

"I'm sure you're wondering why you're here," the Captain continued, walking along the line. "You boys have been singled out as being among the best marksmen in the battalion. We are forming a special squadron. Congratulations. You men have volunteered."

The Captain waited a few seconds for this sink in, then continued.

"Sergeant Parker, here, will be in charge of your training and deployment. You will be issued new equipment and supplies and will leave immediately for your new bivouac. I think you'll find this new assignment comes with a few perquisites you might enjoy."

The Captain examined his new squad. Most were mere boys with only the beginnings of a beard. They looked too skinny and too scared to be dangerous. He smiled at their discomfiture and shook his head.

"Cheer up boys, you're gonna get the chance to kill some Rebs."

A half hour later they were marching toward the outskirts of the camp and down into a hollow formed by the broad lee of low hills. Sergeant Parker called them in closer.

"Listen boys, I ain't one of them hard types. I'm easy nuf to get along with, less you buck me."

The first thing Parker did was bring them in for grub, bowls full of lumpy porridge and brown rolls, but they were happy to have it. There were tree stumps scattered across the clearing and the men took their plates and sat down wherever they could. Parker sat with them, holding his tin plate in one hand and eating with gusto. One of the recruits, an Ohio boy named Joby, with the browned skin of someone who spent most of his time outside, looked up from his food. He didn't look old enough to have ventured away from home, let alone be thrown into the midst of an army poised for battle.

"What's this about, Sergeant? What's this got to do with us being able to shoot?" he asked.

"You boy's gonna learn to be snipers," he said.

"What's a sniper?" Joby asked.

Parker laughed. "Ever hole up waiting for a fat buck to come out of the trees into your line of fire so's you could make the shot?" he asked.

"Shore, plenty a times."

"Well, that's what a sniper does, cept with men. We hide in the trees and pick off the enemy, then slip away afore they know what hit em."

"No marching in a straight line right at em?" Joby asked.

"Nope," Parked answered between bites of food.

"Bout time someone figured that out," Leopold said beneath his breath.

Later that morning they hiked over to the supply depot and the Sergeant led them to a stack of boxes under the guard of two armed troopers. They loaded the boxes onto a wagon and Parker kicked the old mules into gear. The recruits fell in behind, heading away from the main body of the encampment. Parker found a spot he liked and the men threw down their duffels and gathered round. Parker started distributing the gear. Everything was brand new, the boots, the clothes, the packs. The Sergeant had something to say about each item, none of it standard issue. The packs were smaller and lighter than what they were used to and Leopold wondered how he'd ever pack all his equipment into such a small sack.

Parked uncrated a box and tossed a bar of soap to each man.

"All right, boys. Head on down to the river and take a thorough bath," he said, throwing them each a bar of soap. "I don't want you soiling my new uniforms."

They tried on their new clothes. The shirts and pants were forest green, not blue. The clothes were warm but without metal buckles, braid or insignia of any kind. Parker checked each man to make sure that the clothes fit properly, neither tight nor loose. The boots were soft-soled and fur lined without a heel or hobnail. The gloves were buckskin, dark and tight fitting. The whole process took several hours.

Once the uniforms were squared away Parker directed the boys to set up camp, showing them how far apart he wanted the tents, how he wanted them oriented, how tight he wanted the lines and how to stow their personal baggage; The tents were brand new and, for the time being at least, free of lice and vermin. Several times Parker walked by and had them move a tent or straighten a line, always in a calm voice, but in a tone that invited no argument. By the time they had adjusted the tents for the third time, they knew that the Sergeant was more exacting than any NCO they'd run across before. He had a way of giving an order that was direct and personal. He looked you in the eye as though he assumed you were intelligent enough to understand the reason and importance of doing it right. If he had to tell you a second time, there was just the right amount of disappointment in his voice. No one wanted to be told a third time.

The next morning dawned cold and still with a thick fog settling in over the fields. The Sergeant moved along the line of tents waking the men. There was no blare of bugles or shouting. The Sergeant hardly spoke above a whisper, loud enough to be heard clearly, but no louder. The men hurriedly crawled into their new uniforms, pulled on their soft-soled boots and splashed water onto their faces. A separate mess tent had been assembled for them and they stumbled in, ate a hurried breakfast and reported to the field.

"Noise," The sergeant said. "Noise is the enemy. I ain't gonna raise my voice above a whisper, most times. That don't mean I ain't serious."

From force of habit, they fell into a ragged line, shoulder to shoulder. Parker waved them in and gathered them around.

"When I want you to line up, I'll tell you to. You're not regular soldiers no more. You've got to unlearn what they taught you and remember what you all knew back when you were boys. When you were out hunting in whatever god forsaken part of the country you came from, you didn't go thrashing through the brush singing and shouting. You moved quiet, with your eyes open and your ears tuned. That's what you're gonna do here. Even when you're just sitting around talking amongst yourselves, you're gonna do it quiet. You head in for mess, you move quiet. You take a crap, you crap quiet. Some of you won't be able to. Might be the type that's always stumbling over rocks or breaking branches, might be a snorer, or a big talker who can't keep his mouth shut. We'll send you on back, no shame."

The Sergeant looked around to be sure that his meaning was understood.

"You need to be thinking there's a Reb out there, somewhere in the tree-line, looking for a target, listening for the slightest sound. And believe you me, them Rebs can shoot."

He had their attention now.

"Afore the war, I was stationed out west. Out on patrol, we never once heard the injuns coming. Not once. If a fight started, it sprung up from nothing and was on us afore we knew it. When we camped at night, we hobbled the horses and staked a guard. They still managed to slip in and steal them, even with a troop of men camped nearby and men standing guard. We're gonna be like them injuns, moving about without disturbing a single leaf or blade of grass. We're gonna learn to communicate without raising our voices. We're gonna do our damage before the Rebs even know we're there, then we're gonna slip away before they know where we went. Any man who can't cut it puts the rest in danger. I won't have that; you mark me well."

Once he was sure his words had sunk in, Parker instructed them to unload two wooden crates from the back of the wagon and pry off the lids.

"This here's what's gonna make the difference." he said, pulling a new rifle out of the crate.

"A rifle?" one of the boys asked.

"Yep, it's a rifle. But it ain't like any rifle you seen before. This here's a brand new Spencer company carbine repeating rifle."

He held the rifle out at arm's length for them to see.

"Gather round, now. What's your name, boy?" he asked Leopold.

"Stemler, sir."

"Don't sir me, boy. Open that box there," he pointed

Lee opened a wooden box lying on the bed of the wagon.

"Know what that is, Stemler?"

"Yes, sir, those is cartridges."

"That's right. Cartridges. Meaning the powder and ball is all contained in a single package." He turned back to the others.

"This is a stock loading seven shot repeatin rifle." He worked the lever.

"Seven shots without reloading. Seven. Each a fifty-two caliber bullet with enough punch to drop a bear. You're gonna learn to get off seven accurate shots at a hundred fifty yards without pausing for breath. And you'll do it fast as you can work the lever. You're gonna get so good with this rifle that you'll knock seven rebs clear to hell afore the first one hits the ground."

The Irregulars, as they came to be called, put in hour after hour of practice. Most had honed their skill hunting small game back on the farm and, as the Sergeant suspected, they already knew how to stay hidden and move silently through the forest. But they learned more. They learned how to communicate in sign and with bird calls to encircle an enemy without giving away their position. They were expected to move about the camp as quietly as possible and to not talk if it wasn't necessary. They learned to listen, picking up small sounds most would have missed. Not all of them could do it; a few were sent packing. There was never a big scene; Sergeant Parker simply sent them back to Command for reassignment.

Their Spencer rifles became a part of them. They ate with them, slept with them and kept better care of them than any object they'd laid their hands on until then. They learned how to load and reload without having to look at their rifles, in the pitch dark and the pouring rain. They learned what might jam a Spencer and how to free it, how to move away from the smoke of a fusillade to get off another clear shot and how the wind might affect the flight of a bullet. They learned how high to aim at a hundred yards, at one fifty and at two hundred.

"After your first shot, some of the Rebs will duck for cover," Sergeant Parker instructed. "Don't hang on them. But there'll be others wants to come after you. They're your target. Look for the open places between cover. They'll need to cross and thar's your chance. Lead em just like you would a buck and squeeze it slow and steady."

It wasn't only drilling with a rifle. They marched; long, fast marches with full gear. They ran full out for three miles with their rifles, stopping every quarter mile to hit a target before running to the next. They learned how to sneak up on a man and kill with a knife, how to fight at close quarters with their bare hands and how to sit motionless for hours waiting for a target to appear. They had been hand chosen for this job and, as good as they were when they started, they were soon a damn sight better; and of them all Lee was the best. He had no need to talk and nothing to say. He liked being alone in the forest and found it easy to disappear. He knew guns and learned to fire his seven cartridges in rhythm without hurrying, quietly reloaded and continued firing in an almost uninterrupted sequence.

"Before you squeeze off your first shot, pick your next firing position so you can move there without thinking," Parker told them. "Smoke from the powder will get so thick you can't see a damn thing. You'll need to move away, never losing sight of your target."

The Irregulars learned how to coordinate their fire, so they could lay ambush over an entire field without allowing any avenues of escape. They learned how to provide cover in sequence, moving forward each in turn, to capitalize on the enemy's retreat. They learned to aim for the chest and torso, not the head; a serious wound was as good as a kill. Most of them had never been on a real battlefield, but they were as ready as Sergeant Parker could make them.

Powder River, Montana

White Hawk and the four remaining Absaroka finally slept, or tried to sleep, in the modest cover of the Cottonwoods lining the river. There was no fire and no food. Long Shadow, the youngest member of the group, wanted to kill one of the horses for food and the others were all for it, as long it was Long Shadow's horse that was eaten. They had no extra mounts and nobody wanted to double up, not if they had to make a run for it. The rain started again during the night and came down hard. All they could do was pull their buffalo hides over their heads and lie still. It was a restless night and they were up again with the cold grey dawn. White Hawk went down to the river with a sharpened stick. His people didn't usually fish, but he was hungry. He thought it would not be too difficult to spear a trout, but the water was deep and the current fast. He headed downstream to find a quiet pool and walked a quarter mile before he found a good spot.

White Hawk spotted a fat brook trout and was maneuvering towards it when he heard the first shots. His immediate instinct was to grab his rifle, but he had left it at camp. He had nothing but his sharpened stick and an old knife. By the shouts raised, he knew that the Lakota had tracked them to the river. He ducked behind a rock and tried to figure out what to do. They should have left before sunrise, he thought to himself.

The fight didn't last long. White Hawk felt like a coward hiding behind the rocks like a woman while his friends were dying. But he knew they stood no chance against the large band of Lakota and he didn't even have a weapon. Eventually the firing stopped. Only the shouts reached him. He could imagine the scene playing out; he'd seen it before. He waited more than an hour, alert for any sound or shout of alarm, and then slowly made his way back. His friends were dead; scalped and mutilated, stripped of everything of value. The horses too were gone. He saw the tracks heading north. White Hawk dropped to the ground; even the buffalo hides had been taken. He looked over to where his friend Long Shadow lay sprawled in the dirt. He was hardly more than a boy and this was his first long raid away from home. His throat had been slashed and blood pooled on the ground beneath him. His other friends had fared no better.

White Hawk sang a death song, closing his eyes and willing the spirits to accept his plea. There was not much he could do with the bodies. There wasn't enough wood to tie a decent scaffold. He dragged the bodies to a high ledge overlooking the river and faced them toward the rising sun. He straightened their legs and arms, imposing as much dignity as possible on the mutilated corpses. He carried stones and laid a border to mark the place. It would not keep the animals away but at least it was something. When he was finished, the clouds began to lift and the sun came out. He took that to mean the Spirits were pleased with his efforts.

Chapter IV

WARRIORS

Month after month, battle after battle, Lee lost track of how many men he kilt. Figured the Lord would never forgive him such trespass, orders or no. The boy in him was gone and it weren't never coming back. He got mighty good at his job, but the piss rose in him, madder with each friend he lost n each rebel he kilt. Seemed like it would go on forever, wit neither side making much headway.

Then his Ma's letter come, sayin his Pap had passed. Got pnumony in that dank pit of a Union prison.

Jacob McCune

Guyandotte River, Virginia

The dawn was slowly rising, but it was completely dark on the forest floor. The sky beyond the tree branches was lightening and birds were beginning to sing, stirring with first light. They spread out along a rocky precipice overlooking a freshly harvested field. A line of Ash trees on the slope rose in front of Lee, but the branches spread well over his head and his line of fire was unimpeded. Sergeant Parker had laid the ambush with care. The blued barrels of the Spencers blended into the background; the dark form of their bodies were visible only when they moved. It was hard to hunker down stock still for so long on a cold wet morning. But that was what they'd been trained to do.

He heard them before he could see them; Confederate infantry moving across the field in their direction. Lee knew there was no danger of his comrades firing prematurely. They were too well trained. Sergeant Parker and his men were outnumbered, as they always were, as he knew they would be.

Straining to look into the darkness, Lee saw the first of the enemy infantrymen move into view. The Rebels moved cautiously, ill at ease crossing the open field but trusting the early hour to protect them. It was beginning to grow light in the valley below. Out in the open, the Confederates were back lit and clearly visible while Parker and his men could not be seen crouching in the darkened recesses of the hillside. Lee checked his rifle, took a deep breath and tried to still his trembling hands. He selected his first target, then a second and finally a third, so that he could move on each in sequence. He selected his second firing position; one he could move to while staying under cover.

The enemy continued to advance across the field. They were moving slowly, spread out. At last Parker gave a shout and the Irregulars opened fire. The front line of rebels went down and, in the time it took them to figure out where the barrage was coming from, even more were cut to pieces. Those who were smart hit the dirt and kept their heads down. Most ran, or tried to run. They were cut down mercilessly, almost every shot a kill. A few made it to the tree line but when they poked their heads out to see where the shots were coming from, the Irregulars were waiting and the heavy caliber bullets found them.

Eventually the Confederate officers located the line of snipers, but by then the Irregulars were already slipping away. And then the Union Cavalry attacked. The Rebels had been busy setting up their artillery to fire on the tree line and were not prepared for a Cavalry attack from the flank. By the time the sun was fully up the battle was over. Smoke mixed with the morning mist rising from the ground. The dead lay scattered across the field and the moans of the wounded floated on the still air.

Once they regrouped, Parker directed his men forward to mop up and to look for rebel officers who were still alive. They spread out in a skirmish line two hundred yards wide and started down the slope. Now, for the first time, Lee was scared. The sounds of moaning and the low-lying mist made for an eerie scene. The thought of some wounded rebel lying in wait with his finger on the trigger set the boy's nerves on edge and brought his stomach up into his chest. So intent was he on the ground ahead that he soon lost sight of his comrades and was suddenly alone, walking slowly, his rifle ready, searching. He passed a body lying face up, eyes open, staring lifelessly at the sky. The bullet had hit him in the chest and the amount of blood spilt over his tunic was startling. Other bodies lay scattered, some missing a limb, others a jaw and some who seemed to be merely asleep, without a visible injury of any kind in evidence. Lee held his rifle on each just long enough to be sure they were dead, then continued forward, alert and soundless.

He heard moaning. At first, he couldn't tell where it came from. He stopped and looked around for his comrades, but none were in sight. Inching forward, he spotted a rebel soldier lying in a thick pile of leaves at the base of the tree, his musket just out of reach. Lee raised his rifle. The young man was watching him, both hands held over his stomach, blood soaking through his fingers. Lee saw the fear on his face and the look of utter surprise. He was just a boy. Lee looked around quickly and then lowered his rifle. He knew he should keep moving but took a few steps forward and then stopped. The dying man tried to speak but Lee could not make out the words.

Lee knelt next to him, removed his canteen and brought it up to the wounded soldier's mouth. The boy tried to drink but then slumped back down and moaned in pain. Lee looked away, glanced down. There was nothing to be done. The wound was mortal; he had lost too much blood. Lee tried to rise and move away but hesitated. He put a hand on the boy's short red hair and watched as his eyes closed in a spasm of pain. Lee looked at the wound again and all the blood, thinking it might have been his Spencer that did this, the hole was big enough. This was the kind of damage it was designed to do. The moaning ceased. If there was life left it was fading fast. Lee felt the guilt like a heavy yoke and pushed against it, willing his legs to rise and walk, taking one step and then another, moving away.

Not all the Union officers liked the idea of an Irregular force. To some, it was an affront to the honor of warfare as they had subscribed to it at the Point. But that didn't keep them from using the squad, moving them up and down the front. The Irregulars saw action in every skirmish that took place in their theater of conflict. Sergeant Parker had come to realize that Stemler was a man who could be counted on. He moved without detection and was more accurate with a rifle than any one he'd ever seen. The rifle was like a part of him. Between engagements, Lee was called on to scout behind enemy lines, to locate the position of rebel forces and slip back to report. He did this without complaint. He was all but invisible, but Parker knew that, if he were ever caught, he would be shot as a spy. The Sergeant tried to engage him in conversation. Stemler was polite and respectful, but Parker never penetrated the barriers the lad had erected around him. Parker sensed the anger in him, but he had no idea who or what it was directed towards.

The Irregulars inflicted heavy casualties. They honed their deadly skills at the expense of their former countrymen. The numbers were impressive, as even the most reluctant Union officers had to acknowledge. The Confederate officers were now aware of their existence and steps were taken to eliminate the threat. Parker would have liked to cease operations for a while, to lay low until their movements were less predictable, but that decision wasn't his to make.

Sergeant Parker was directed to plan their next ambush. The battalion had moved south in a broad swing to cut off rebel access to the river. He positioned the men carefully. Confederate troops were marching toward them. The afternoon sunlight flooded over their shoulders and the Rebs were squinting up into the sunlight pouring through the trees. When Parker gave the signal, the snipers began firing and the Rebel column started dying with frightening speed. The Rebs couldn't see the shooters in the blinding sunlight. Lee fired from cover and needed only to move the sights of his rifle from side to side to find a new target and take him down. Some of his comrades were already moving forward, anticipating a headlong retreat by the trapped enemy. Lee did not want to think, did not want to acknowledge any reality but the two-inch square target in the center of a man's chest. To do otherwise would be intolerable.

A deafening blast tore the earth in front of him. The Irregulars who had moved ahead were blown into the air. Lee could not see where they landed but knew it was probably not in one place or in one piece. He looked to see where the blast had come from. Rebel artillery had set up on the ridge overlooking their position. He could see the puffs of smoke, followed a second later by the sound of cannon echoing across the valley. Dirt flew up around him. More men fell. Lee moved away from the pattern of craters blistering the tree line, but the smoke and dust hung so heavily that he couldn't see where he was going. He had taken barely a dozen steps when a blast wave hit him with crushing force and he flew through the air. By the time he landed, he felt nothing at all.

Fort Laramie, Wyoming Territory

Elizabeth loved living in the West, but there were days when she wished there were someone she could talk to. There were no girls her own age and her father absolutely forbade her to talk to soldiers except in his company. Her days were spent gardening, reading, taking care of their quarters and writing letters back home. But what she really wanted was to get out onto the prairie and explore, and there was no way her father was going to allow her to do that.

The Tribes of the western plains had grown bold during the protracted struggle back east. The Army been able to post only a token garrison at the thin line of forts on the frontier. She'd heard stories about what the Indians did to their captives. She didn't know if she believed the stories, but even if they were true, she was too smart to let herself be captured. She began to wear her father down. She asked him to describe the country, to tell her about the wagon trains passing through on the Oregon Trail, which crossed the North Platte just east of the fort. The flow of emigrants had slowed to a trickle; but safeguarding the trail was still the most important duty of the garrison.

Her father had developed his own attachment to the territory. A Massachusetts man, born and bred, he was surprised by how he had taken to the Rocky Mountains and the wind-swept plains. He'd talk to Elizabeth about what he'd seen on patrol, but his descriptions did little to satiate her desire to get out and see things for herself. At last, he agreed to take her with him, but only if she promised to follow his instructions without whining or calling attention to herself. Of course, that didn't last long. She absolutely refused to ride in a wagon. She wanted a horse, despite the fact that, being from the civilized countryside of Massachusetts, she had never learned to ride. Rather than make a scene, Cain had a horse brought out from the stable. He instructed his wrangler to make sure it was gentle, but as thin and bony a nag as he could locate. He meant to ensure it was an uncomfortable experience. It was a can of worms he should never have opened. She loved riding. After the first trip, which she had to admit was rather painful; she spent all her free time at the stables. She watched the broncs being broken, talked to the stable-master and was allowed to help with the foals. She rode every chance she could, at first with her father and then within the parade ground on any horse she could beg, steal or borrow.

She loved watching the Cheyenne ride across the hills on their sturdy little ponies. They were superb horsemen. She was amazed at how comfortable they looked, riding bareback, seldom even holding the reins. One day the Colonel came out of his office and was surprised to see her racing a young Cheyenne boy across the parade ground. Races were held from time to time and were a popular diversion. It was what passed for entertainment on the frontier. There was a track that ran from the stable, down to the river, along the lower field and back. It was no more than a mile. But Elizabeth and the Indian boy were running their horses full out. Folks stopped what they were doing and were cheering and shouting. Cain suddenly realized that Elizabeth was not riding side saddle, the way a proper lady was expected to. She even had on a pair of worn leather boots complete with spurs, which she was not afraid to use. So much for not calling attention to herself, Cain thought, holding his breath as his daughter and the boy rounded the old willow that marked the turn. Then he forgot himself and cheered as Elizabeth spurred her horse across the field. Little by little the boy began to pull ahead and crossed the finish line well in front, but the whole camp let up a big cheer when Elizabeth crossed the finish line.

Elizabeth was fascinated with the local Indians and sought out every bit of information she could gather about them. Many of the officers and men had nothing but scorn and hatred for them, considering them less than human. But the men who knew them best, the old traders and trappers who passed through, had a great deal of respect for them. Some of these old timers seemed almost native themselves; and had Indian wives or had adopted Indian ways of living and thinking. The fort was situated at the foothills of the Rockies on the last stretch of the great plains. The Laramie River flowed east to the North Platte, which joined the Platte proper, finally flowing into the Missouri River itself. A number of tribes traditionally hunted and camped in the area, among them the Cheyenne, Shoshone and Arapaho. Indians seldom got to see a White woman, especially a beauty like Elizabeth. More than once the translators had to explain that the White soldiers did not trade their daughters for horses, though Cain told Elizabeth he was curious to know how many she would fetch.

Despite her short time on the plains, Elizabeth had an intuitive understanding of native sensibilities and proved useful to her father in suggesting circuitous solutions to problems. Perhaps it was just the non-confrontational nature of feminine logic that enabled her to suggest resolutions that hadn't occurred to the men.

Over the course of the last few years, White hunters had begun to come west and systematically kill the buffalo for the value of their hides. There was nothing illegal about it. In fact, it was the army's job to protect these hunters from Indian attack. But it was a bad business.

Cain knew the Indians depended on the buffalo, taking what they needed and wasting nothing. The hunters, on the other hand, left the meat and bones to rot in the sun.

the Shoshone had come across a group of these hunters a few days earlier. The White hunters claimed they were attacked without provocation. Blue Wolf, their chief, claimed they were fired on first. Either story might be true, but the result was the same. One of the hunters had been killed and another wounded. An unknown number of Shoshone were killed. The Colonel ordered the hunters out of the territory on the grounds that they were instigating trouble, but it was also his job to come out and make clear to Blue Wolf that they could not attack the Whites, no matter the provocation. The Colonel had met Blue Wolf on numerous occasions. He knew the chief to be a reasonable man and the tribe had not been hostile during his tenure at the fort.

The Colonel, Elizabeth and a group of hand-picked officers were greeted warmly when they arrived at the village. They were invited to sit and Blue Wolf filled his best pipe with the tobacco the Colonel offered as a gift. Elizabeth was fascinated, but kept her head bowed respectfully and sat quietly beside her father. Cain asked the chief for his version of what happened. Blue Wolf explained that the White men had killed more than thirty buffalo on the plain just north of the village and, when the Shoshone rode in to investigate, the hunters opened up with their big Henry rifles and killed two of their best young warriors. Blue Wolf was trying to be reasonable. Could this White Chief understand that they had to protect their hunting ground? That they had to protect themselves?

The Colonel was also trying to be patient, but the impasse was wearing on his nerves. If the Shoshone attacked another hunting party, he would be forced to use his cavalry to retaliate. He didn't want to put it so bluntly to the Chief, but the message was not getting across. Just as tempers were starting to rise, Elizabeth leaned over and whispered something in his ear. In his agitation he shook his head, but Elizabeth patted him on the knee, leaned forward and pulled out a box of sugar taffy she had brought along to give to the children. She held it out to Blue Wolf, who was annoyed by the interruption.

Elizabeth ignored his discomfiture, unwrapped a piece of taffy and put it in his hand. Blue Wolf was known to have a sweet tooth. He put the taffy in his mouth and began chewing with gusto. His previously intractable expression softened. Elizabeth passed the candy to the other elders. It was a comical sight, the stern and imperious Indians smacking their lips loudly as the struggled to chew. It's impossible to look intimidating while you're chewing sticky taffy. Cain laughed, despite himself, and took a piece of the candy.

"My daughter, who is very rude to have interrupted us, suggests that instead of fighting each other, we work together to solve this problem."

Blue Wolf continued chewing but nodded his head for the Colonel to continue.

"I will agree to prohibit hunting within three days ride of the Fort. But you will have to help me."

Blue Wolf nodded.

"If you see White hunters entering the area you must not confront them. You can run the buffalo off and send your fastest rider to the fort. I promise to send my soldiers out to stop them."

Blue Wolf stopped chewing, leaned over and spoke with the others sharing the council. He glanced quickly at Elizabeth and then back to the Colonel.

"And you will send the horse soldiers before the White hunters slaughter the herd?"

"Right away,

Again, Blue Wolf whispered with his advisors, and then turned to Cain.

"We will try it this way," he said.

After they finished smoking the pipe and discussing other matters of concern Cain thanked Blue Wolf and told him it was time for them to start back to the fort. They emerged from the lodge into the bright light of a sunny afternoon and the Chief walked with them toward their escort.

Blue Wolf said, "I would like to show you something."

He walked them to the edge of the camp where the horses were grazing on the open prairie. He called to one of the boys, said a few words and the boy ran off.

"I have heard that you like to ride," Blue Wolf said to Elizabeth. "That you like to ride fast".

Elizabeth smiled. "I do," she said.

The Indian boy came back leading a yearling colt. He was a magnificent animal, small and compact like most Plains ponies but with powerful legs and a wide chest. He was almost pure white except for black "socks" on all four feet. The boy was having trouble holding onto him. The colt was strong and had spirit and intelligence.

"I was planning to keep this one." Blue Wolf said, "But I am getting too old for such animal."

"I am sure that's not true," Elizabeth said, approaching the animal slowly and reaching out to stroke the horse's neck. The colt settled down at Elizabeth's touch and pushed its nose down into her hand.

"Even so, I would like you to have him. He will be a good horse for you; and will remind you of your friends here."

Elizabeth looked at the old Indian in surprise. It was far too valuable and unexpected a gift. As delighted as she was, she was unsure of what to do.

"Blue Wolf's generosity is very great. But I have nothing to offer you in return."

"Your friendship is enough," the old man smiled. "And I'll take the rest of that candy."

Chapter V

THE MOUNTAIN MAN

I have been driven many times upon my knees by the overwhelming conviction that I had nowhere else to go.

Abraham Lincoln

It was dark. Lee didn't know where he was. His head pounded within his skull. His vision was blurred and he was unable to make out more than the vague shapes of the trees. The sounds of the battle could be heard, but they were muffled and indistinct. He felt in the darkness for his rifle and felt the stab of panic when he was unable to locate it. His hands found the warm viscous mound of bloody entrails attached to a headless torso. He recoiled in horror, fighting hard to control his breathing. He crawled forward. His fingers touched the cold steel of a rifle barrel and he grabbed at it, examining it more with his hands than his eyes, relieved when he realized it was undamaged. He struggled to his knees and tried to orient himself, but quickly realized he didn't know where he was. The landscape was dream-like, surreal; broken limbs hung unnaturally from the trunks of trees and gapping craters of raw earth lay between them. He wasn't sure where the Union lines were, where north or south was, where safety or danger lay. He leaned against a tree. He didn't think he was hurt but was too disoriented to tell. He stood, took a few steps and tripped over the tangled roots of a tree, landing hard. The pain in his head blossomed with the impact and he closed his eyes, seeking whatever relief he could find, but there was none to be had. He brought his hands to his head and held them there, sure that his skull was breaking apart, and then he collapsed onto the ground and passed out.

When he next awoke the sun was filtering through the broken forest. There were no sounds of battle, only the lilting song of birds in the twisted branches above him. He rolled onto his back and looked up at the sky. Dark clouds moved slowly in and out of view. A stabbing pain still beat steadily in his skull and he took a slow breath to try to gain a measure of power over it, to see if he could control it. His hands still clutched the rifle.

He tried to remember how he'd gotten here, but it hurt too much to burden his mind. The pain was manageable only when he lay still and didn't move. He fought to remember and gradually it came, but only parts of it, bits and pieces, arbitrary and unconnected. He remembered his father and a great sadness washed over him. He envisioned the darkened form of a sniper crouching silently in darkness, darkness suddenly brought to light by the flash of fire thrown forth from his gun. He knew he had killed, and killed and killed again, more men than he could remember, more boys than he could remember. He was weak and didn't want to move, wasn't sure if he could move. He didn't know how many hours he lay there, flat on his back, fighting for the strength to return to his mind and body. By the time he stumbled to his feet the sun was going down. He began to walk.

The thick forests were his shelter and his sustenance. The land rose up towards the mountains. Lee moved west, avoiding roads, moving where the cover was thick and the way free of people. He lived on wild fruit and small game, never using his rifle even if his belly ached with hunger. The forest floor was thick with leaves and the weather wet. He left no trail; of that he was certain. He tried to tell himself that he was searching for his unit, but as his senses cleared he knew that it was unlikely they'd have moved this deep into the western mountains. He dimly understood that leaving was an act that would follow him all his life. He wondered if he'd done the right thing, but it did him no good to dwell on it now. There was plenty of land left where there was no government, no law, no army; and he meant to find it. He felt no loyalty to the men who'd killed his father. He felt no part of any of it. He wanted to find a place where he'd be left to himself. A place where no one would find him. He knew how to move without making noise, without being seen or heard. He lay down each night under the canopy of trees and didn't care that he was cold and hungry. The emptiness he felt seemed a fitting punishment for all the death he'd dealt. Loneliness crept upon him like an insidious whisper whose voice he couldn't silence, an echo from a void whose precipice he shied away from.

West. He crossed the Kentucky, skirting the scenes of other battles long since fought, the land rough and heavily forested. He moved slowly, doubled back on his own trail, reluctant to move forward too fast but unwilling to stay put. He did a thousand little things. He spent most of one day setting a snare to catch squirrels. He ate wild apples and blackberries. He stole clothes, a pair of boots and an old hat, but usually, when he saw a farm or a settlement he went around it. Occasionally he'd see soldiers in the distance, but he was too far up in the hills to be spotted. He kept his rifle handy and a mind to his back trail, prepared to slip away if the need arose.

Eventually he came down out of the hills, crossing the Mississippi below its confluence with the Ohio, still heading west, but without any particular destination in mind. Though he was close, he couldn't go home, as much as he wanted to. They'd hang him without a question asked. He missed his Mama, but would have to wait a while till he could get word to her. And anyway, that world seemed far away, a lifetime away.

He headed out over the plains, week after week, traveling at night or when he felt sure the country would hide him. He ate whatever he came across or could steal. He wasn't sure where he was and cared less; he only knew what he wasn't going to do and who he wasn't going to be. The towns grew farther apart. The world wasn't at war out here, at least not that he could see.

Late one afternoon Lee climbed up out of a deep arroyo. The old man sat astride a stick thin mare, smoking a rough-hewn pipe and balancing an old rifle across his lap. Twenty long horned and emaciated cattle were grazing on the dry grass. Lee froze, angry with himself for gettin careless. He continued walking, prepared to give the stranger a wide berth, but the old man lifted his arm and waved him over. In such open country, Lee thought, it'd be peculiar to ignore him. He headed over, checking his Spencer as he went.

"Howdy," the old man called out. "Don't see many folks out here, might as well be neighborly."

Lee nodded. He tried to return the greeting, but it'd been so long since he'd spoken to anyone that the words died in his mouth.

"You lost?"

"No, sir," Lee answered. "I ain't lost."

The old man swung slowly down off the horse. He hobbled its legs, untied his saddle bag and started toward the creek without looking back.

"Come on, then," he said. "Spect you're hungry."

The old man found a flat spot where he could watch the cattle and laid the saddle bag down on the grass.

"Gather some of them sticks and dried pies. We'll see if we can strike a fire."

Lee did as he was told. He was hungry and the old timer seemed harmless enough. Upon a closer inspection, maybe he wasn't so old. More precisely, he could have been any age from forty to eighty, so grizzled and leathery was his appearance. He walked with a slight limp, but moved quickly just the same. The fringe on his buckskins was worn to nothing and his moccasins were soiled and black. Thin grey hair hung to his shoulders and framed a long grey beard. But his eyes were soft and green, with a ready humor in them.

Lee piled the kindling and the old man started a fire with flint and steel. It was getting on in the evening and the air was growing cold. It was always surprising how quickly the heat of the day faded into the chill of night. The old man took a pot out of his saddle bag and handed it to Lee.

"Mind fillin that up, boy?" he asked.

Lee headed for the creek, rifle still in hand.

By the time he came back the fire was burning strong and the old timer had banked rocks against the breeze. He cleared a space and unpacked his supplies. He threw coffee into the old pot and laid it aside, waiting for the coals to burn down, then pulled out a frying pan and mixed up flour and water to a thick paste. When the fire was hot enough, he pulled some coals to the side with a long stick, unrolled a cloth and flicked a finger full of bacon grease into the pan. The smell of the frying grease set Lee's stomach to growling. He watched as the old man formed biscuits with his dirty hands and laid them into the pan. Then he unrolled an oil cloth and pulled out a dozen thick strips of bacon. These he laid carefully down the center of the pan.

"Ain't much," he said. "But it'll have to do."

"I'm much obliged, Mister. Sure smells good."

"Have a seat, boy."

Lee sat next to the fire, laying his Spencer across his lap.

"I ain't gonna bite, boy. You can lighten your hold on that," he said, nodding at the rifle.

"Been with me too long, I suppose. Ain't comfortable without it."

"I know the feeling," he said, fiddling with the coffee. "What's your name, Son?"

Lee hesitated, looking down at his lap. "Joe."

The old man nodded, "Joe what?" he asked.

"Joe Brown."

"Where you from, Joe Brown?"

Lee looked down, staring defiantly across the fire.

"Why you asking so many questions?"

The old man laughed, pulled a plate from the saddle bag, dished some biscuits and bacon onto it and handed it across to Lee. He picked a biscuit out of the fry pan with his fingers, opened it, laid a strip of bacon across it and then lifted it to his mouth for a bite. Lee laid into the grub. He swore it was the best he'd ever tasted.

"Let's set something straight," the old man said. "I rekon I don't really care what yor name be or even where you hail from. But I'm guessin there's some out there who do, so you better decide who the hell you are, boy, and make it sound convincing."

Lee looked up from his food, reluctantly nodding his head in agreement.

"Now what's your real name, boy? An no bull."

"Leopold," he muttered.

"Leopold, humph? I'll call you Lee. No sense straying too far from the truth. Too hard to recollect in a pinch."

"Now where you from, Lee?" he asked.

Lee shrugged.

"Not down south. North neither, not with that accent. My guess would be Missoura."

Lee stared across at the old man.

"So, let's see." The old timer continued. "What neighbors on Misoura. Indianee? That suit you?"

"Indiana?" Lee asked.

"That's right. You're an Orphan. Parents died years ago. . ." He scratched his head. "Smallpox. Wiped out the whole dern bunch."

"I ain't no orphan," Lee said.

"You sure? Folks feel sorry for orphans. Might get a free meal."

"I'll take my chances."

"That's a mighty fine rifle for a young pup like you. How'n you come by it?"

Lee looked up in anger, his hand unconsciously reaching toward the gun.

"It's mine, alright. And I can use it, too."

"No doubt, but how'd you come by it, young Lee from Indianee. That's what we're trying to figure. Can't go shooting everyone who asks, and they's gonna ask. That's Army through and through."

Lee shrugged. "You got a notion, I suspect."

The old man scratched his head again. "Let's see. . . A contest. You say you can shoot?"

"I can shoot"

"Really shoot?"

"I spose so."

"There was this contest, see. First prize was that there gun. An you won it fair and square."

"Sounds good."

"A corse it's good.

Lee smiled at the old man's bravado.

"Now, ain't you interested in who I be?" the old timer asked.

"Truth, or another tall tale?" Lee asked.

"Whatever makes for the better story. I been known to dress up a yarn from time to time. Name's Jacob. Jacob McCune. And I seen more of this damn country than any man alive and most who's dead."

"Pleased to make your acquaintance, Mr. McCune."

"And the boy's got manners too. Rare nuf thing in these parts. But don't make a habit of it. People'll think yor uppity."

Lee reached for the cup and took a long slow sip. They drank coffee til the last light drained from the western sky and stars began to fill the night. Lee reached across, took the pan and plates and headed to the creek. He dipped them in the water, using the soft sand along the shore to scrub them clean. The water was cold and quickly numbed his fingers and by the time he got back to the fire Jacob had spread his bed roll. An old wool blanket lay on the other side of the fire for Lee.

"Know how I know?" Jacob asked.

"Know what?"

"Know you and me is gonna be pards?"

"How's that?" Lee asked.

"You didn't take that gun down to the creek with you."

Lee turned; the Spencer was right where he left it.

He took off his boots, spread out on the ground and put his sack down for a pillow. He looked up at the stars and pulled the blanket to his chest. It smelled of horse sweat and mildew, but at least it was warm. All he could hear was the crackling of the fire and the sound of the creek.

"Lit out?" Jacob asked, almost a whisper.

Lee didn't answer, but he understood the question.

"Don't make me no nevermind. Got no stake in the war. Just trying to steer clear of it. You just gotta go careful."

Lee started to talk, but couldn't.

"Memories dim," McCune said. "The pain fades. Whether you want it to or not."

Missouri River, Blackfoot Territory

Mountain Sun was eighteen years old that summer. Though he still enjoyed the easy life that came with living in his father's lodge, he was nearly a man in every way, over six feet tall with broad shoulders and long muscled legs. He still ran with the lightness of youth; not the heavy body of a mature buck. As the only son of the great Butte Bull, he had been taught to ride and shoot both bow and rifle. He was an excellent tracker for his age and already an accomplished hunter.

Butte Bull's band of the Piegan Blackfoot had just arrived on the banks of the Missouri for the yearly gathering. There were more than forty bands. Lodges stretched up and down the river for over a mile. Hundreds of horses grazed on the opposite shore and children ran wildly across the fields or played in the river. Despite the festive nature, it was an important time for the People, a time when plans were made and councils formed that would affect not only his own clan, the Piegans, but the Bloods and the Northern Blackfeet as well. It was the time of the Sun Dance, their most sacred ritual. Sweat lodges were erected along the river and fires banked in preparation. It was the time war parties were organized and martial skills tested. And it was a time when young men took squaws in marriage. Mountain Sun was not averse to meeting a few nice looking girls, but he'd made it clear to his mother not to engage in any match making. Not that she'd listen.

Mountain Sun walked with his father, stopping to talk to old friends. Everybody commented on the change in the young man. Just a few summers ago he was out playing with the other children and now look at him. More than one family trotted out their marriageable daughters. By the time he and his father got back to camp, the women had the food prepared. Mountain Sun was hungry after so much talking but all his mother wanted to know was if he had met any girls, though when he told her who he had met she didn't have a single nice thing to say about any of them or their families.

Mountain Sun asked his father questions about the people they'd met, who they were, what they had done in battle and how many horses and rifles they owned. The young man listened attentively and was ready to head back out after dinner and continue the rounds of visiting. But his father was tired, content to sit outside in the moonlight and watch from the comfort of his old rug. There'd be plenty of time, he assured his son. Better to start slowly and finish strong.

The week passed in much this fashion. There was serious talk amongst the elders about the White man and the scarcity of game. There were reports on the strength and weakness of their enemies. Mountain Sun was selected to join a hunting party that went out in the morning in search of game. It was a casual thing but an honor, nonetheless. The hunt was successful and Mountain Sun brought down a doe with one shot. It wasn't much to brag about, but he would embellish the story as best he could.

On the morning of the fifth day Mountain Sun's mother woke him and his father and called them outside. There was a note of excitement in her voice. The two of them stumbled out to a bright summer's morning. Tied to the rawhide strap of the tent was a large white eagle feather. Mountain Sun looked at his father, who nodded, as though he had been expecting this. The feather indicated that Mountain Sun was invited to join the White Eagle society, a great honor. The White Eagles were one of the most prestigious military organizations among his people. Such groups were entirely separate from the traditional leadership structure of the tribe and their membership was select. Their rites and the identity of their members were supposed to be a closely guarded secret, though everybody knew who belonged. The society crossed clan lines. The White Eagles included members from all three clans and was a one of the institutions that unified the far-flung bands.

Mountain Sun had been hoping this would happen but had not voiced this hope, even to his father. The warrior societies performed various roles. Politically they tried to advance their own members to the senior councils in order to influence the policy of the tribe. They also performed a kind of police function and would discipline a tribal member who was habitually drunk or who took advantage of an older or weaker neighbor. This discipline might include a stern warning, a simple beating or even death, though this was rare. At the end of the summer gathering, when the people spread out across the plains in search of buffalo, the societies would organize for raids into enemy territory to count coup and steal horses, after which they would separate again and return to their individual bands.

"Are you pleased?" Butte Bull asked his son.

"Yes," Mountain Sun said. "I had hoped to be asked but. . ."

Mountain Sun stopped. He could see that his father was happy for him, but he detected some hesitation, as though he wanted to give voice to a warning but had decided not to. Perhaps his father was concerned with the ordeal of initiation? As boys, Mountain Sun and his friends shared stories they'd heard about these initiations. There was no shortage of rumors. It was said some did not survive. His father needn't worry, Mountain Sun thought, if others could bear it, then so could he.

The White Eagle society's camp was a mile away. No lodges. It was only for meetings and the initiation of new members. Mountain Sun was ordered to fast and arrived at sunset, as instructed. They brought him to the center of a large stone circle and tied him to a post that'd been sunk into the ground facing the fire. Three other young men his age were already there. He recognized them, knew one, Red Dawn, from years playing down by the river as children. When the sun finally set, logs were thrown onto the fire until the flames leaped high into the night.

A warrior walked to the center of the circle. He was a head taller than everyone else and heavy with muscle. He was called Omak and he wore a robe covered with feathers and an elaborate headdress in the shape of a beak with precious stones for eyes. As he walked toward the captives, Mountain Sun looked up at him. There were not many warriors his size among the People.

"Why are you here?" he asked the four young men.

After a pause, he continued. "Not because of who your fathers are. Not because your grandfather owns more horses than anyone in his band. There is only one reason.

Omak took a step forward and glared at the young men.

You are here because it is up to you to save your People."

Omak signaled for the other warriors to move forward. Mountain Sun recognized some of them; one was even from his own band. The older men walked up to the boys and, on a signal, began to beat them with their fists, chanting loudly as they rained blows down on the initiates. Unable to protect themselves, the young men had no choice but to absorb the blows as best they could. Neither Mountain Sun nor the other three cried out, though the blows continued for many minutes and blood flowed freely from their lips and noses.

Omak picked up a flaming brand from the fire and walked toward the boys. He stared into their eyes, searching for any sign of fear or weakness. He jabbed the stick into Mountain Sun's thigh and held it there. Mountain Sun clenched his teeth but did not cry out. The big warrior moved down the line, inflicting similar wounds.

"The People grow weak," Omak continued. "It is up to us. We must protect our lands and do it with such ferocity that none will dare enter our territory. It must be a forbidden land; a place the Whites know they can expect no mercy."

Mountain Sun was mesmerized. He'd imagined that membership in the society was a small honor and that some hunting and minor raiding would be involved. But this was a tribe within a tribe. His people were in danger and only the greatest resolve and most ruthless dedication could protect them. A generation ago, no trapper dared set foot on Blackfoot land. Now they were beset on all sides and forced to move north, away from the constant flow of immigrants.

Throughout the night it continued; beatings, followed by mystical ceremonies whose meaning Mountain Sun didn't understand, followed by the lionization of great deeds done by the White Eagles on behalf of the people. When first light rose on the horizon the four initiates were carried down to the creek and washed by the very men who had beaten them, then wrapped in blankets and given food to eat. Each was presented with the claw of a great eagle to wear around his neck. Mountain Sun came away eager for the chance to fight; certain that his own greatness, his own destiny, was that of a mighty warrior.

His father did not ask him any questions when he returned to the lodge. Mountain Sun, feeling newly self-important, did not greet his father or volunteer any information. Raven screeched at the burns and bruises that covered his body and chattered on about the hot-headed troublemakers who would do such a thing. She applied ointment to the worst of his cuts. The gathering was almost over. People were already beginning to pack up their lodges and head out onto the plains in search of buffalo. Butte Bull announced that they would be leaving the next morning and went off to inform the rest of the band. Mountain Sun looked at his mother, who shook her head as she cleaned a cut on his arm.

The following morning twenty riders rode east toward the rising sun. The four initiates wore simple loincloths with no other adornment, but the other White Eagles were magnificently attired in full war regalia. Their horses were elaborately painted, their lances decorated with feathers and their chest plates beaded and polished. They had earned the right to these costumes by killing the enemies of the People. The main purpose of this raid was to give the young bucks a chance to earn the same right. But until then, they were treated badly. They had to do the women's work in camp, carry water, cook food and tend to the horses. They were given demeaning and silly names. They'd have to earn their new names in battle. The older warriors never tired of making emasculating jokes. It didn't matter. None of the four young fighters doubted that in a few days their knives would lift hair. They could put up with a few days of childish torment.

Absaroka Camp, Yellowstone River Valley

Marchabeau's village was quiet in the hour before sunrise. White Hawk and his six companions had left the valley nearly two moons ago. In their absence, things had not improved for the Absaroka. Each day they struggled to find what food they could but, without horses, finding food was difficult; there seemed to be little or no game on the prairie that summer. Most assumed White Hawk and the rest of his party had been killed, but a few held out hope that they would return with a large cache of meat and fresh horses.

Every day the women spent time along the river, collecting berries and digging edible roots from the earth, but this was not enough to feed so many mouths. There was little activity in the village. The people were reluctant to rise early to another day of hunger. They might as well sleep and forget the emptiness in their bellies. The chief, lying under his robe, was just about to roll over and go back to sleep when he heard the sound of horses. He leaned on his elbows, listening. The beat of the hooves increased until there was no doubt. Excited, he reached over and shook his wife.

"Crow Feather," he said. "Listen. I can hear them. They've come back."

Without waiting for her to answer he lifted the flap and stepped outside. The point of the lance pierced his belly, projecting through his back. He heard Crow Feather scream and saw people running in confusion. He fell back, almost in slow motion, onto the hard-packed earth.

Omak and the White Eagles rode into the heart of the village. Mountain Sun saw his friend Red Dawn, riding close beside him, leap from his pony onto the back of an Absaroka and, with a single motion, Red Dawn drove his knife deep into his enemy's back. He flipped his victim over and Mountain Sun saw that it was no more than thirteen years old. The boy was gasping for breath, fear and shock on his face, but Red Dawn had him by the hair. With a sharp sawing motion, he cut a large swath of hair and scalp and ripped it free. Mountain Sun saw the light fade from the young boy's eyes as Red Dawn held the bloody scalp high air and gave a loud cry. Other White Eagles took up the cry. Without horses, the Absaroka were unable to mount any kind of defense.

Mountain Sun turned his horse in circles, searching for an enemy to engage, but all around him were only women, children and old men. He was anxious to make a kill before everyone had been slaughtered. He turned to rejoin the main party but was suddenly knocked off his horse. He hit the ground flat on his back, the wind pounded out of him. He rolled onto his knees, trying to suck air back into his lungs, when another blow landed across his shoulders. He looked up just in time to see a thick wooden stave descending toward him and rolled away just in time to deflect the worst of it, but even so it cut a deep gash on his forehead above his eye.

Mountain Sun looked up. The man who wielded the club was old, older even than his own father, but Mountain Sun had never seen such hatred in a man's eyes. The old man swung again and Mountain Sun heard the wind brush past as he jumped back, barely avoiding the blow. Mountain Sun pulled his knife and jumped to his feet. The old man must have been a formidable warrior in his day; Mountain Sun could find no opening to reach him. When Mountain Sun tried to close the gap, he was jabbed sharply in the chest or rapped on the arm. The screams of women and the bloody cries of the raiding party swirled around them but neither dared take his eyes off the other. The old man struggled for breath; he knew he could not outlast the younger warrior. Suddenly, he feinted to the left and raised the club for a strike that would have smashed Mountain Sun's skull like a serpent's egg, but the boy saw it coming and jumped in below the strike, driving his blade deep into the solar plexus and lifting with such force that the old man's feet left the ground. A few words Mountain Sun did not understand sputtered from his enemy's mouth as he fell back, the life in his eyes fading to death in seamless, silent transit. Mountain Sun pulled the knife away and looked down, unable to escape the haunting curse of the dead man's gaze. He knelt and turned the old man over so that he didn't have to see his face. With a half-hearted gesture, he pulled the old man's hair back, cutting a few inches of scalp away in his fist.

By the time Mountain Sun stood up and gathered himself, it was over. His chest and face were covered with blood. Dead Absaroka, mostly women, young boys and old men, lay scattered around him. Mountain Sun watched as the few women and children who survived huddled together, their arms wrapped around one another, kneeling on the ground and begging for mercy. Mountain Sun watched Red Dawn draw his bow and fire, point blank, into the huddled women, his arrow piercing an old grandmother's neck, belching a geyser of blood that soon covered those around her. The young Blackfoot notched another and was about to let it fly when Omak yelled at him to lower his bow and leave the women alone. Instead, Red Dawn grabbed a young girl by the arm and pulled her away from the rest, tearing off her clothes and raping her in full view of the others.

Those warriors who were not pulling women into the abandoned lodges were going through the village, taking scalps and searching for anything of value. It was remarkably slim pickings: a few old rifles, some tools, and a little tobacco, hardly worth the long ride across the prairie. But the journey had served its purpose. Each of the young men had made their kills and earned their names. In less than an hour it was over. The trophies were tied to their lances, the loot stowed and the Blackfoot started back toward home.

Mountain Sun rode in silence. The older men had smacked him on the back, acknowledging his kill. Each of his fellow initiates had raised their trophies as though they were won in fierce combat against a dangerous foe. This was not how Mountain Sun had imagined it. He felt no relief in finally having made a kill, no glory in slaughtering women and old men. Even the animals they hunted for food were treated with more respect. Mountain Sun felt trapped. Was he now bound to this band? Were they to decide who his enemies were? These were not questions he'd ever thought to ask. He understood, now, the look he'd seen in his father's eyes.

Chapter VI

THE DOUBLE EAGLE

I don't believe there ever was any life more attractive to a vigorous young fellow than life on a cattle ranch in those days. It was a fine healthy life too; it taught a man self-reliance, hardihood, and the value of instant decision- in short, the virtues that ought to come from life in the open country.

Theodore Roosevelt

Republican River, Kansas

The morning dawned wide and clear with the cold bite of autumn in the air. Lee shook himself awake and saw that Jacob already had the fire going and a pot brewing. It was the best night's sleep he'd had in a while. It'd been weeks since he woke without the dull ache of hunger gnawing at his belly.

"Morning, Lad," Jacob said. "Slept well, did ya?"

"Yes, sir," Lee replied, pulling on his boots.

"Can't barely remember last time I woke without being stiff as a board. Guess I should be grateful I'm getting up at'all. Pour yourself some coffee. I gotta be movin these beeves back to the ranch."

Lee nodded, poured himself a cup and sat back to drink.

"Where you headed, Son?"

"West," Lee answered.

"Anywhere's in particular?"

"Just west."

"It's coming on winter. Not a good time to be wandering the prairie without any particular 'where to' in mind."

"I'll be alright," Lee answered.

"They could use some help on this ranch where I'm aworking. Why don't you hole up there till spring. Put a few coins in your pocket and some meat on your bones."

Lee shook his head.

"It's a sorry outfit." Jacob continued. "Feller from back East. Don't know his ass from a handbag. But they don't ask no questions and we get paid, most weeks. Here's the tale we tell. You came looking for me. Town folks told you I was out here, so you tracked me down."

"Thanks, but I'll keep moving, just the same."

"Listen, Son. I know you've a mind to set out on your own and ain't too partial to folks. I feel like that myself, most times. But you got to recognize good advice when you hear it. You head west right now, yor good as dead. If the snows don't get ya the Injuns sure as hell will. Now finish that coffee and help me push these sons a bitching cows back to the ranch."

McCune was right about one thing; the Double Eagle was a sorry outfit. There were those who were gambling that the railroad would make it possible to bring western beef to the soldiers and cities back east. There was money to be made if the beeves could be raised and the meat shipped to slaughterhouses further east. But there was a shortage of manpower while the war was on. Those who were available were either too old or too green to be of much use. Lee was green as they came, but at least he was young and strong.

The bunk house was a low, sow backed shack on the verge of collapse. The wind whipped though gaps in the rough boards and the dust blew in one side and continued right on out the other, giving everything a good coat. Lee found a bunk off by himself and settled in, though all he had to his name was his rifle and a small cloth sack. They hired him on like Jacob said and the old man kept an eye on him. Lee wasn't afraid to work and didn't mind getting stuck with the jobs none of the other hands wanted. They took to passing the buck down to him and figured he must be addled if he didn't mind shoveling cow shit and washing down stalls.

Despite the fact that he'd spent little time in the saddle, Lee took to riding like he was born to it. The horses were in only slightly better shape than the cattle, but they were there to be ridden. Jake figured Lee would be more comfortable out on the range and told the foreman he'd take the boy out and show him the ropes. Being out on the open prairie suited Lee just fine. He tried to get the horses to run and, every once in a while, they'd oblige. He took a few tumbles, but before long he looked natural in the saddle. If there was a short count or a stray he'd volunteer to go after it. With winter coming, the stock had to be moved in off the plains and, as the first snows began to fall, there were still plenty of beeves that needed to be found. Some had worked themselves down into arroyos and had found comfortable spots they were reluctant to leave. There was so much open range that some of the cattle hadn't seen a man all summer and were almost wild. Long Horns were ornery and their horns could rip a horse wide open, so you needed to stay alert and move quickly. All the Hands had stories about the damage a Long Horn could do.

Jacob and Lee kept to themselves. Lee liked the old man and came to trust him. He felt no need to talk to the other hands and before long the boss got used to sending them out together. One old man with experience and one young pup with muscle and guts made as good a team as he had on hand. Lee wasn't much for conversation, but Jacob more than made up for it. Working hard in the saddle all day, Lee found himself looking forward to a warm fire and some of the old man's stories. Stories about the trapping days, about heading up into the Rocky Mountains in the dead of winter to set a line of traps. And come spring, a packhorse loaded with plews to bring down to Rendezvous for whiskey, supplies and a squaw. Back in St. Louis, Lee had heard these tales since he was old enough to sneak into the back of a tap-room, but no one made them come alive the way Jake McCune did.

Washington D.C.

The stalemate continued. Thousands died in regimented movements against fixed positions while the Generals seemed unable to grasp the fact that war had fundamentally changed. Guns and materiel moved more quickly to the front lines than ever before, borne on good roads or on the tireless backs of steam locomotives. Artillery was larger, easier to use and more accurate. Whole columns were laid waste before they got close enough to fire a shot. Rifles were faster to load and more accurate and lead balls were mass produced by the millions in factories well behind the lines.

Fredrick March was in the First battalion of Connecticut volunteers. He had been appointed a lieutenant. The son of a local merchant of modest means, he was not rich enough to buy himself a substitute, but at least he didn't have to fight the war as an enlisted man. He'd had a little schooling. He could read and write and had learned to read maps and use a compass. He was part of a battalion that was massed along the Potomac west of the capital. The rebels had been threatening to cross but, as reinforcements began to arrive, the threat subsided. After weeks of inactivity, the Union Generals had finally gotten up the guts to push back and give President Lincoln some breathing room.

The men stood around all morning waiting for the order but now, at last, they were on the march, heading for the pontoon bridges the corps of engineers had erected overnight. The troops moved in orderly fashion. They had little choice. Large NCOs with bayoneted rifles lined the path to make sure nobody got out of line. Every once in a while a puff of dirt would flare at their feet as rebel sharpshooters across the river took pot shots at them. Less often, a man would actually be hit. He'd be pushed out of line and a litter would be brought up from the rear. The column was too far away to hear the shot and couldn't even tell where it came from. They had no choice but to keep marching.

By afternoon, March's company reached its position on the fields above the river. He could now hear the sounds of battle, but the field in front of him was calm. The Captain came down the line telling them to be ready to move against the enemy's left flank. March felt little fear and was surprised and more than a little proud of himself.

He waved to his corporal. Michael Shay was his own age and had not been in America a full week before he found himself in the army. There were thousands of Irish in the front line. For them, it was work and three square meals a day. Better than they were used to, March thought to himself. Better than most of them deserved.

"Take half the men and move over to the fence line," March said. "We're supposed to provide cover if the Rebs launch a counterattack and try to drive us back toward the river."

"Aye, will do Lieutenant," Shay answered.

March watched as the corporal pulled twelve men from the line and positioned them behind a moss-covered stone wall at the edge of the field. The sounds of battle raged around them, sometimes distant and indistinct, at other times more insistent. March strained to see across the field but the smoke had thickened, making it difficult to tell what was happening. The sound of rifle fire grew louder; the battle was swinging towards them. Suddenly he saw a Union soldier running toward them, then another, and then a whole line of them. One fell headlong, arms flung in front of him, his rifle flying from his grip. Bullets thudded into the trees above them and March yelled to his men to stay down.

The trickle turned to a flood as the main line of the Union advance was turned. March watched as officers tried to rally the men, shouting at them to turn and fire on the enemy. A few, loading their rifles as they ran, did turn and fire, but most never looked back. Suddenly March saw the Rebs break through the trees no more than three hundred yards distant. It was the first time he'd ever seen the enemy.

"Whadda we do, Lieutenant?" the man closest to him asked.

"Wait till they're within range, then I'll give the order to fire."

The grey line moved across the field, taking time to aim and shoot. One Union soldier after another was hit in the back as he retreated toward the river. March crouched behind a tree, waiting to give the order to fire. Then, out of the corner of his eye, he saw Shay. The Corporal was yelling at the top of his lungs and leading his men over the stone fence. March was dumbfounded. He hadn't told the fool to run onto the field, just to lay down fire from behind the wall. Shay's men were thirty yards from the enemy when they fired their first volley, catching the rebel flank unaware and slowing its advance. The retreating soldiers saw the rebels falter, turned and joined in the counter-attack. Other companies along the line followed Shay onto the field and drove the rebels back. Within minutes the Rebs had been halted. March was astounded. By this point, even the men who'd stayed with him behind the cover of the trees were racing across the field to join the fight.

By the end of the day the Union army had advanced all the way to Middleburg. The south bank of the Potomac, and the Capitol itself, were safe. But things had not worked out the way March imagined they would. He had not received a commendation, even though it was his company that beat back the Confederate. He hadn't even been noticed. Instead, it was Shay who had been given a medal and a battlefield promotion. Now he was March's own superior officer. And the ass hadn't even done what he'd been told to do. March had ordered him to stay behind the fence and provide cover. That's all. What if they had all been wiped out? March would have caught the blame.

Belleville, Kansas

The town of Belleville lay ten miles west of the ranch. It was nothing but a store, a stable and a saloon with some passable whores.

It was too small to have a sheriff, much less a mayor. Jacob McCune headed there most paydays. After all the years alone in the mountains he didn't mind a little company and it wasn't often he had cash money in his pocket. For the first few weeks he tried to get Lee to come along but the young man refused, happy to stay behind to relax or read one of the boss man's books. So, he was surprised, one Saturday afternoon, when Lee finally accepted his invitation.

They had saddled their horses, wrapped their coats tightly around them and started down the trail toward the river. The dark sky pressed low over the prairie. The two of them rode hunched over against the bitter wind. They kept their faces down; all they could see was the grass shorn close and brown with, here and there, snow clinging to the rocks and hollows. It wouldn't be long now till winter settled in earnest. As they rode into town Jacob pointed toward the livery and they swung down off their horses.

"We's stayin the night," Jacob declared.

The main street was nothing but mud and the boardwalk one plank wide. The town gave the general appearance of being abandoned. Only the occasional glow of an oil lamp in a dark window gave any evidence of life. At least until they entered the Saloon.

The Marseille was a crudely constructed clapboard building. Bare boards, rotting and unpainted, planked its rickety frame. But the oil lamps were blazing, the tables were crowded and the bar was lined with farmers and cowhands. The interior was slathered in gold paint and, on the wall above the bar, a half-finished nude smiled down at the patrons. She looked down on the proceedings with a strangely twisted grin, as though not entirely thrilled to be there. A piano beat a lively tune and, scattered here and there around the room, there were women. Lee hadn't seen a woman in months. He'd forgotten how pretty a woman could be. How good they smelled. And how jumbled up he got when he tried to talk to one. Jacob headed for the bar and Lee followed; nodding at some of the hands he knew from the ranch. A few of them called out his name and slapped him on the back, happy to see he'd finally made the trip into town. Lee glanced up at the bawdy painting and quickly looked away. He didn't want anyone to catch him staring. Jacob handed him a glass of whiskey, tapped it against his own and tossed it back. Lee felt the burn. Tears welled up in his eyes and he kept his lips clamped shut. He tried not to cough, but the alcohol sucked the breath right out of him.

The night settled in just fine. Lee got used to the whiskey. The more he drank, the more the weight of his memories lifted away. The ladies were friendly, wore a little too much rouge and the heaviness of their perfume made his head spin, but there was always one that had her arm around him. He breathed the smell of them deeply. He liked the soft feel of them and the way they pushed up against him. They snuggled deep into his lap. He was happy to buy a drink or two.

Lucinda was fifteen years older and outweighed him by thirty pounds, but she had a healthy swell of bosom and most of her teeth. Her long brown ringlets fell wildly in front of her face and she spoke with the slow drawl of the deep South. Her eyes were a soft blue and her lips were soft. Before he got too drunk, she leaned over, gave him a long kiss full on the lips and whispered something in his ear. A smile spread across his face.

"Wait here," he said. "I'll be right back."

Lee made his way over to the card table. Jacob was losing.

"Don't you know not to be botherin a man when he's playin poker," Jacob said, annoyed.

"Sorry," Lee said.

Jake threw another two bits onto the table and looked at his cards. Lee waited, standing none too steadily, watching.

"You still here?" Jacob asked.

"I'm headin upstairs. Didn't want you wondering where I'd got to."

"Good idea," Jacob said without looking up. Then, as Lee headed away, Jacob grabbed his sleeve and pulled him back.

"No more than a dollar. And hide the rest."

Lee smiled, nodded and then went back to look for the girl.

"Lucinda's gonna teach the lad a thing or two," Jacob said to the men at the table.

Lee heard them laughing and guessed it was at his expense, but then Lucinda had him by the hand and she wasn't letting go. The room was at the top of the stairs. It was small and somewhat clean and there were white linen sheets on the bed. An oil lamp with pink glass cast a rosy warm glow.

"You ever been with a woman?" Lucinda asked as she sat on the edge of the bed. Lee stood facing her, watching, not making a move.

"I've had sweethearts," he said.

"Sweethearts," she said. "they don't. . ."

"No, guess not," Lee said, looking down.

"It's alright, Sweetie. That's their loss."

"They weren't as pretty as you," Lee said, blushing.

She grabbed Lee by the belt and pulled him toward her, then she had his belt off and his pants down and her hand felt warm and small and owned him outright. She let him take her clothes off and he fumbled a little but soon found more places that were soft and warm and more wonderful than anything he could imagine. Lee shivered himself awake. He was half buried in a mound of hay piled behind the stable. He had no memory of how he'd gotten there and trying to remember only made his head hurt. His stomach didn't feel so good either. He couldn't remember everything that happened, but he smiled thinking back to the parts he could. He brushed the straw off his clothes and tried to stand up. There was a thin layer of snow on the road and the mud had frozen solid. A thick layer of cloud hunkered over the prairie and Lee couldn't guess what time it was, though he suspected it was still early, not a creature was astir. Lee staggered up the street looking for Jacob and kicked his boots clean before heading back into the Marseille. A young girl in a torn brown dress was sweeping the floor with an old broom. She smiled at him and Lee smiled back, but the smell of stale liquor brought his stomach up. He climbed the stairs to Jacob's room and knocked. He slowly pushed the door open and saw Jacob lying on the bed, mouth wide open, sound asleep and snoring loudly. Lee rousted him out of bed. Jake wasn't generally cheerful in the morning. There was some cursing and a lot of grumbling. Jake pissed in an old pot by the bed and started the slow process of finding his clothes and pulling them on. Lee sat by the door and closed his eyes, waiting for the hammering in his head to ease.

The two of them headed down to the kitchen. A few of the hands had stumbled in for breakfast. The smell of strong coffee and bacon brought some of the life back to him. They stumbled to a table and the girl brought them coffee. Halfway through the hotcakes Lee's stomach began to settle. Jacob complained that his head felt like he'd been kicked by a mule and, for once, they ate mostly in silence. But the complete absence of conversation was not natural to the old man.

"Everything work out all right, last night?" he asked.

"Just fine."

"Figured out how everything worked and where to put it?"

"Eventually," Lee replied.

"Well, let's just hope you don't catch the clap or they'll be sending your pecker home in a jar," Jacob said, taking a big mouthful of food.

After Breakfast they headed back to the stable. The town was beginning to wake up. Lee stopped in front of the general store.

"Hold up."

Jacob rolled himself a smoke, lit it and leaned against the wall, looking out at the sorry collection of buildings. A few minutes later Lee came out holding a wide brim felt hat with a black leather band. Up till then he'd been without a lid. He tried it on and showed Jacob, who was unable to keep the grin from spreading across his face. The old man just shook his head and headed toward the Livery.

Fat Creek, Nebraska Territory

White Hawk knew he'd never catch any fish like this. The water was too deep and too fast. He carried rocks over and dumped them in the stream, forming a sluice to divert some of the water. It was humiliating. This was work for squaws and children. But when he'd completed the channel and herded a few fish into the pond he was able to spear a good size trout. White Hawk was not one to complain about the cold, but his hands and feet were freezing and his clothes were soaked. He found a sheltered spot and built a fire. He cooked and ate the trout and dried his clothes out by the fire. Then he found a good straight stick and took the time to sharpen its point, hardening its tip in the fire. Besides his knife, it was the only weapon he had. He looked up and saw that the clouds were building. Another storm was blowing in. If he followed the river he might spot some White men and steal a horse. The Whites were stupid with their property when they thought they were safe. By late afternoon the rain started again. It was a cold hard rain but, at least, it would cover his tracks.

The first settlement he came too wasn't White. It was a Pawnee village and, from the look of it, a sizeable one. He knew of the Pawnee, they'd been one of the great tribes of the northern plains but had fallen on hard times, much like his own people. They were said to be good warriors, mediocre hunters and worse yet, farmers.

White Hawk saw the freshly harvested fields along the river. North of the village he spotted a herd of horses grazing on the prairie. It was already late afternoon, with a dark and lowering sky and a steady rain. White Hawk would normally have avoided an Indian village, especially since he was alone and practically unarmed, but the night would be dark with heavy cloud cover and the sound of the rain would cover his steps and deaden his scent. He could see dogs. There were always plenty of dogs in a village this big.

White Hawk moved back up the river. He rubbed mud on his face and neck and tried to find a dry place to wait. He slept for an hour and, once darkness fell, he moved across open ground to the other side of the herd, away from the village. There wasn't much cover and White Hawk crawled to stay hidden in the grass. The rain continued. He waited till all sounds of activity in the village died away. He was good at waiting. He wasn't some young buck who ran in the moment the sun went down.

Well after the time when everybody should be asleep, he shook the stiffness from his limbs and moved toward the horses. It was too dark to tell if they had set a guard. He crept to within thirty yards without making a sound. Even the ponies gave no sign they were aware of his presence. Picking out the right horse was important. He needed to pick one that was gentle, that wouldn't shy away. And if he picked out a horse that was unbroken he'd have a fight on his hands. He spotted a fat little mare but, as he approached, the horses got wind of something and unexpectedly bolted away. Right away, a dog began to bark. White Hawk crouched in the grass, hoping the alarm would die down. Then he heard the sound of hooves bearing down on him and knew that there was a guard and that they were coming his way. He froze, unsure if he was better served to lie still or run. Running would give away his position. He was one of the best runners in his village, but he couldn't outrun horses on the open plain. By then one of the dogs had his scent. He could see two braves with rifles riding straight for him. He stood up and waved to let them know he was alone and unarmed. The riders slowed and White Hawk was relieved that, for the moment at least, they hadn't raised their rifles. Then the dog was on him. It wasn't big, but it was mean and persistent. It bit down hard on his leg and White Hawk leaned over to slap it out of the way when one of the guards knocked him over the head with the butt of his rifle.

He awoke the next morning tied to a post in the center of the village. His head hurt and he was wet and cold. A woman cut the thongs that tied his hands and White Hawk saw the scratches and bites on his wrist and hands. The dog must have had quite a time with him. White Hawk said a few words of greeting in the Absaroka tongue, but the Pawnee gave no indication that she understood. He stood unsteadily and walked over to a group of women cooking porridge in an iron pot. One of the women handed him a wooden bowl, saying something to the others that they all thought very funny. White Hawk ate the porridge with as much dignity as he could manage. It was awful, though the women seemed to enjoy it. When they were done, a group of them stood, picked up hoes and rakes and started walking to the fields. A large squaw, easily twice his own weight, reached down and grabbed him by the hair, pulling him roughly to his feet. White Hawk went white with rage, balled his fist and was ready to teach the woman some manners, but then he looked around and noticed that the other women had surrounded him. It seemed that they would love nothing better than to beat him to death with their farm implements. White Hawk couldn't imagine a more humiliating way to die.

The Republican band of the Pawnee tribe was being pushed from all sides, by the Lakota from the north, the Cheyenne from the west, and the Whites from the south and east. Over the course of the last thirty years their once great numbers had dwindled to only four hundred, the entire Pawnee tribe to a few thousand. Like most tribes in need of man-power, they were not adverse to adopting captives or strays into the band. Prisoners taken in battle were usually forced to work as slaves in the fields. Though it was sometimes possible to advance one's status from slave to a member of the tribe. White Hawk aspired to neither station. His spirit was very nearly broken. He was convinced that he'd done something fundamentally offensive to the Spirits to earn their serious and ongoing animosity. What that was he could not imagine but he resolved to lay low and bide his time until he figured out what he had done so he could make restitution. Barring that, any course of action he embarked upon was doomed to failure.

His days were unfailingly the same. The fact that he was slight of stature gave these fat Pawnee squaws special delight. They'd reach under his breechcloth and grab his manhood, yanking and twisting, and then laugh and make crude jokes. When they were finished with their abuse they'd go to work in the fields. If one of them felt that he was not working hard enough, or if she was in a bad mood, she'd whack him with a hoe. White Hawk dreamt of splitting their skulls with a rock and pissing on their brains.

At night he was tied to his post. The men, strangely enough, were seldom cruel or even rude to him. For the most part, they ignored him. Perhaps they could imagine themselves in his position. But if they harbored any secret urge to free him from the clutches of the squaws they restrained themselves; they'd be foolish indeed to deprive the women of their plaything.

The turning point came one day when White Hawk was given a large bladder and told to fill it from the river. Two Mother, a fat old Pawnee with a sadistic disposition, tossed the buffalo bladder to him and hit him with the blackened stick she was using to stir the embers of the fire. White Hawk did as he was told, taking his time. There was no pleasing Two Mother. He'd suffer her wrath whether he was quick or slow. Doing a task quickly just gave her more time to beat him. A full bladder full of water was heavy and, when he brought it back to the fire, it snagged on a sharp rock and tore. The water soaked Two Mother's already filthy buckskin skirt and doused the fire. For a big woman she was quick. She jumped up, cursing and hitting White Hawk with the stick. Again and again, she whipped him, slashing at his head and shoulders. White Hawk wouldn't give her the satisfaction of crying out or even protecting himself. He took the blows, though he well knew he might be dead before the old woman's venom drained away.

Ku-Sox, the village chief, watched from a few yards away. He'd never liked Two Mother. She was always in a bad mood. He had noticed White Hawk working with the women or tied to his post but had never paid him any mind. He assumed he was a eunuch taken in battle. Young captives were often castrated to keep them docile, but luckily no one had thought to do this to White Hawk. But, seedless or not, no one should have to suffer such abuse, and the Chief admired the way the fellow stood there without flinching, a look of such pure hatred in his eyes that Ku-Sox was actually impressed. The Chief walked up to Two Mother, grabbed the stick out of her hand and beat her across the back with it, then he led White Hawk away to his own lodge. He pushed him in ahead and called for one of his daughters to take the captive and apply salve to his cuts. He was covered in blood; none of the cuts were very deep, but the rough stick had made a mess of him. Ku-sox went off to the other end of the lodge while the young girl clucked her tongue at him in sympathy and began to clean his wounds.

Things began to improve. He was allowed to sleep in Ku-Sox's lodge, at first still securely tied but, after a while, without restraint. He might have slipped away but somehow felt that it would be a betrayal of trust to do so. The Lodge itself was very different from the buffalo skin structures of his own people. For one thing, it was huge, the biggest structure White Hawk had ever been in. It consisted of a framework of logs and branches covered with dirt and sod. From a distance the lodges looked like small hills. Forty people slept there, most of them the family or extended family of Ku-sox. It was dark inside and the smell of huddled bodies and burnt food permeated the walls. An Absaroka lodge was light and portable and well ventilated. In here the air was stifling, but it was still better than sleeping in the rain.

At the center of the lodge was the fire pit. The smoke exited, most of it anyway, through a hole in the roof. This was also the only source of natural light. People were always stepping on one another in the dark but most were too polite to call out. If you were a person of some rank you slept in the middle, near the fire. Those of lesser consequence slept against the wall.

During the day he still went out with the women to tend the fields. He was given the heavy jobs of hauling water and moving rocks, but if he came back at the end of the day with bruises Ku-Sox raised hell. The physical abuse soon stopped. Of course, it was humiliating to have to be protected from a bunch of women, but he knew he couldn't raise a hand against them himself. Sometimes he and Ku-Sox would try to talk together. He spoke no Pawnee and Ku-Sox no Absaroka, so the going was slow at first, but White Hawk discovered he had a natural talent for language and was soon conversing in a rudimentary way.

Ku-Sox wanted to hear about the West. He had never been to the snow- covered mountains. He wanted to know about the animals and if there were still plenty of buffalo. Most of all he wanted to know if the White man was there yet. Ku-Sox knew the Pawnee could not hold out much longer between the rivers. Already the buffalo here were nearly gone. White settlers passed through their land every day, usually without giving them so much as a pouch of tobacco or a jug of whiskey in toll. White Hawk informed Ku-Sox that the Whites were everywhere and, worse yet, the Blackfeet were apt to massacre anybody who crossed into their territory. Ku-Sox shook his head. He'd already heard something of this and was disappointed that it was true.

Autumn passed in this manner and White Hawk recovered his strength. It seemed like years since he'd left his village in search of horses and buffalo and he missed his wife and his family. But when the first snows began to fall he knew he'd have to stay the winter. He would think about escaping in the spring. With any luck Ku-Sox would give him a horse and let him go.

Double Eagle Ranch, Kansas

The Hands that signed on to stay the winter spent most of their time around the ranch house. There was feed to lay out for the stock, fences to check, and sometimes even calves to be birthed, but mostly there were long hours spent cooped up in the bunkhouse.

Jordan Birch was a mean and humorless man. He was short but solidly built with a barrel chest and thick legs. Birch was purposefully lazy and would curse a man if he was working too hard, claiming it made him look bad. The problem was that Lee liked to stay busy and, being the youngest, he became a natural target. Birch was always trying to ridicule Lee into joining the card games, hoping to lighten him of his wages. Lee refused, preferring to lie in his bunk, sleeping or reading books borrowed from the ranch house. Birch found this especially aggravating.

Truth was, Lee didn't really know the games and didn't want to appear ignorant. Besides, he had plans for the money he was making. To make matters worse, Jacob was quick to tease Birch. He was the type of man who took himself too seriously and this presented opportunities too rich for McCune to pass up. Birch didn't quite dare whoop on an old man, though he threatened to from time to time. But an uppity youngster like Lee was fair game.

In late January they were kept indoors by a three-day blow. Only the minimum watch was kept on the stock, rotating every few hours on account of the cold. There wasn't much that could be done for them anyway; some would make it, some wouldn't. Whenever Birch's turn rolled around, he came up with some excuse and told Lee to go in his place. The first couple of times Lee obliged; he was only too glad to get some fresh air. On the fourth day the storm finally let up and the morning dawned with patches of blue peeking through the cloud cover. The men pulled on their boots, preparing to head out into the drifts. There'd be some loss after a big blizzard and the foreman needed to assess the damage. They were heading out the door, Lee a step ahead of Birch. Lee was trying to button his coat and walk at the same time; not quite fast enough for the older man.

"Move it, boy," he said, giving Lee a hard shove from behind.

It was the unexpected indignity of the shove that set him off. He turned and pushed Birch back through the bunkhouse door and sent him sprawling across the floor. Lee knew he was in for a fight now, knew it from the look in the older man's eyes. Lee struggled to pull off his coat but managed only to tie his hands up in the sleeves when Birch landed the first blow. It felt like he'd been hit with a lead pipe. Birch hit him two more times before Lee fell to the snow. His head was spinning and his hands were still trapped. He tried to get up but Birch kicked him in the back of the head before he got to his feet.

By now, all the men had gathered, encouraging Lee to get up. Some just wanted to see a good fight, but most were none too fond of Birch and wouldn't mind seeing him get a comeuppance. Lee pulled one arm free and used the other, still in the coat sleeve, to fend off the attack. He tried to scramble to his feet but his boots found no purchase on the snow. The best he could do was keep rolling away. He took a kick in the gut and felt the air go out of him and, hard as he tried, he couldn't catch his breath. Another kick caught him in the ribs and hurt like hell. Finally, he'd had enough. He forgot about breathing and pain and even stopped worrying about protecting himself. He stood up just in time to catch a fist to the mouth, splitting his lip in three places. Lee swung wildly, missing badly. Birch stepped back and let fly again but Lee leaned away and only caught the blunt end on his ear. Lee dug his heels and charged forward. He had four inches on Birch but they weighed the same, except that Lee was all sinew and muscle without an ounce of fat on his frame. They rolled around in the snow, pulling each other's hair, groping for eyes, using knees, elbows and even teeth but Lee was still getting the worst of it. Birch got Lee's hand in his mouth and bit down hard. Bones would have broken if Lee hadn't buried his thumb deep into the other man's eye socket. The boy was covered with blood, but so was Birch, most of it Lee's.

They separated. Lee heard the shouts around him but paid them no mind. They circled. It was tough footing in the deep snow, and tiring too. Birch threw a round-house but Lee ducked it. The older man was sucking wind now. A minute or two of hard fighting will sap a man. Birch's big gut and lazy ways were catching up to him. Lee got in a punch, then a few more and finally, in a frenzy of anger and adrenaline, had Birch down and was beating him mercilessly. It was pure uncontrolled rage. Birch's nose and teeth were a mass of blood. Lee dropped his weight into each punch and the older man wasn't even able to raise his arms to protect himself. There's no doubt Lee would have killed him if the men hadn't jumped in and pulled him off and, even then, it took four of them to do it. Lee looked down, breathing deeply himself now. He glared down at Birch, who was out cold, his blood staining the white snow red.

Jacob led Lee to the barn and sat him down on a rickety old bench. The barn was dark and smelled of horse piss and wet hay, but the body heat from the livestock kept it warm compared to outside. Even so, there was a thin layer of ice on the water trough. Jacob broke it with the side of his hand and dipped a rag into the cold water. He examined Lee's face and shook his head.

"By tomorrow, your own Ma won't recognize you. Gonna be black as a lump o' coal and swolled up something awful."

Lee jerked away at the touch, then settled down and let Jacob attend to him. He could see blood rinse off the cloth but nothing hurt too badly, at least not yet. His chest still heaved; heaved with adrenaline and hatred and a little relief. Jacob broke off an icicle hanging from the doorway and held it to Lee's eye, switching hands when one got too cold. Then he examined the bite marks on Lee's hand.

"You better wash that good. Nothing worse than a Man bite. Specially from them nasty old teeth. Don't want no gangrene to set. I'd have to chop your arm off at the elbow."

Usually, after a fight, men who have to work together will patch things up, maybe even become friends, but Birch's grudge was bitter. Lee tried to spend as much time out of the way as possible. He'd take any job, just to get out of the bunkhouse. It wasn't that he was afraid of Birch. He just considered it prudent. The Foreman, on the other hand, noticed how hard Lee was working and told him he had the makings of a top Hand. He began to teach Lee a trick or two when he could spare the time. He taught him how to use a rope and how to ease up to a wild horse. Lee had the strength to drop a cow and worked in the branding yard when they needed him. He got kicked by mules and bit by horses.

He learned how to dig a post hole and learned just how hard the Kansas prairie got when it was frozen solid.

The snows weren't half melted before Birch saddled up and rode off. Lee came in one evening and was told he had gone. Lee nodded quietly, as though it didn't concern him. Winter was loosening its grip and the stock needed to get out and forage for whatever shoots of green managed to poke through the snow. The cattle were thin and weak and wouldn't last long without nourishment. One afternoon he was out on the prairie with Jacob, riding herd over thirty head. Jacob stopped to brew a pot of coffee to take the chill off.

"You know," the old man said. "If'n yor gonna survive out here, you gonna need to learn how to shoot."

"I can shoot," Lee said.

"With a long gun, maybe," Jacob said, reaching into his pack and pulling out a small bundle wrapped in cloth. He handed it to Lee.

"What's this?" Lee asked

"Go on, then," Jacob said, going back to his coffee.

Lee peeled the cloth away to reveal a Colt 44 caliber revolver. It was deep blue, slightly rusted and surprisingly heavy in his hand. He tested the heft of it.

"I got no need for it," Jacob said. "Can't hit a damn thing. It's a young man's piece. Figured you could use it. You won't survive winning too many more fistfights."

Lee headed for the tool shop next to the barn. The tools were crude, but Lee made do. He'd worked on handguns before. He filed the sights, cleaned the bore and adjusted the trigger and loading lever. The gun was as good as new by the time he was finished with it. The next trip into town Lee bought balls, powder and caps. Loading the Colt took some experience and finesse. First you measured the black powder and poured it down the chamber, then stuffed in the lead ball. The fit was tight. It had to be to prevent the ball from rolling out when the gun was tilted. Once the ball was most of the way down, you pulled the loading lever to drive it the rest of the way home. Jacob showed him a little trick of putting a dab of bacon grease on the ball to help slide it down and to seal the chamber, a handy thing if you didn't want all your chambers blowing off at once. Finally, you loaded the percussion caps into the cylinder. If you did everything right, you had six shots. There were often one or two misfires per cylinder, but Lee had loaded cylinders for his father's customers and had gotten good at it. Many men carried four or five cylinders for the same gun. When one was used up they would remove the cylinder, pop in a new one and have another six shots.

Shooting it was another matter. It was surprisingly hard to hit anything. You had to hold it with both hands and take careful aim, and that was hardly the point of a handgun. Lee practiced, and Jacob laughed.

"Hell, I oughta take that thing back. You ain't no better at it n' I were"

But eventually Lee started hitting his marks, a wood board stuck in the ground at twenty paces, a bottle at thirty, a tree at forty yards. Then back to town for more ammo. He practiced pulling the colt from his belt and firing in one motion. He didn't have a holster and Jacob told him to tuck the gun behind his back.

"Don't wanna shoot your pecker off," he warned.

By spring Lee was pretty handy with the Colt.

Chapter VII

A FINE WALK

I have never been lost, but I will admit to being confused for several weeks.

Daniel Boone

Republican River, Kansas

Lee felt bad leaving. The boss had been good to him and made it clear he wanted him to stay on. But once spring came Jacob and Lee collected their wages and headed out. Lee had an itch to see the West and felt that Kansas was still a little too close to the war. Jacob had his own reasons. He'd been on the Double Eagle for more than a year and he didn't like being stuck in one place for too long. He and the boy had kind of partnered up and the old man thought it might be a good idea to keep an eye on him for a little longer. They headed out on foot since they didn't own any horses of their own. But Jacob insisted that they buy a mule to carry the gear. They made for a reliable beast of burden, and you could eat one if you had to.

There was no map, just a general plan to head north till they hit the Platte. They'd head west, trying to skirt the tribes where Jacob thought them to be. It was still cold, but Lee could see that winter's grip was loosening. An occasional gust of warm air would sweep across the prairie, or a dandelion could be seen poking through the snow. Jacob's store of old aches, pains and broken bones kept the pace slow but the old man could walk from morning till night without stopping. For a week they didn't see a soul, nor even a sign that folks had ever passed that way before. But as they got closer to the Platte they crossed a wagon track or two, mostly old, some deep and rutted, left by folks heading to California in the big rush before the war. The pace of emigration had slowed considerably, but it'd pick up again once the war was over.

Lee was intrigued by the prairie, gentle hills rolling away for as far as the eye could see, a landscape so vast that you began to wonder if there'd ever be an end to it. From the crest of a hill, you could see for miles, but once you walked down into the trough you were blind. It was easy to lapse. Jacob kept in on Lee to be alert and move quietly, but he needn't have. Lee had been trained to stay alert and move without making a sound, almost as well as Jake did himself. Food wasn't a problem, at least not yet. There were deer and fowl along the creek bottoms.

Late one afternoon the sun began its long slide into the haze on the horizon. They'd been walking since sunup and Lee thought it was about time to start looking for a place to bed down. The wind bit with a stinging chill and Lee found himself day-dreaming about a warm fire and hot food. Jacob pointed to a line of cottonwood about a mile off, a likely sign of water. As they approached the trees they stepped ever more carefully, keeping low and looking for sign. A creek flowed out of the copse of brush that crowded both banks. The prairie cut away and dropped thirty feet to the water so that only the tops of the trees were visible from the bank above. Lee heard birdsong, which he took to be a good sign that they were alone. They slowly approached the edge of the break but, rather than head right down into, it Jacob walked along the edge, peering down the slope, trying to see into the already darkening shadows. Gradually the creek bed widened, creating a gently sloping bank. Jacob slid down with Lee right behind. Even before they spotted them, they could hear the wild turkeys. Lee smiled. These weren't like deer. They were a lot slower to react to danger.

They crept within range and Lee raised his rifle. A fat Tom stepped out into the clearing and Lee dropped him with one shot. Jacob reached down and grabbed the bird by the neck.

"That gun made a mess of him," he said.

"Least I hit it," Lee shrugged.

"Start in on this," Jacob said. "I'm gonna check things out."

Lee took the bird and walked down to the creek, leaned his rifle against the rocks and watched as Jacob disappeared into the trees. Lee tied the mule to a tree with enough slack in the line so it could graze. Then he started in cleaning and gutting the turkey, making sloppy work of it. He hated plucking fowl. His mother made him pluck the chickens and he'd never liked it. The feathers made his nose itch and the damn things had fleas. Some of the quills broke when he tried to pull them out but he didn't care. He was hungry.

Once the bird was cleaned, Lee walked up the bank and looked around. He knew better than to make camp out in the open. He looked for a place that'd be sheltered from the wind but still had good sightlines up and down the creek. He came to a group of head high boulders backed up against the slope of the hill, with trees on each side. He gathered some dead fall, as dry as he was likely to find amidst the patches of melting snow, and laid in a good stack. Then he collected a few rocks and shaped a ring two levels high, packing dirt against the sides and leaving the open end facing the boulders so that their exposure would be minimal. He broke kindling, prepared a fire and soon had it ready to light, but decided he'd wait till Jacob came back. In the meantime, he walked to the creek and filled a pot with water. After a few minutes, he saw Jacob heading back.

Darkness fell quickly within the shelter of the trees, but they had the fire blazing in its earthen bed, throwing its warmth out at them. Hardly a wisp of smoke escaped, and what little there was lost itself in the bare branches overhead. The turkey was skewered and roasted on a crude spit. The skin was burnt black in places, but the meat was delicious. They ate till their bellies were full. When he finished eating Lee rose up off the ground and walked down to the water to clean up. Jacob was content to wipe his greasy hands on his pants and leave it at that. Walking back to the fire, Lee realized he'd gone from ravenously hungry to dead tired in no time at all. Jacob was already lying under his bedroll, his head on his sack, sending smoke rings from an old hickory pipe up into the sky. Lee got his blanket and spread it out on the other side of the fire; pulling a pile of wood near to hand so he could reach it without getting out from under. He pulled off his boots and rubbed his feet. The boots were too small for him and his heels had blistered. Maybe his feet were still growing.

"Where we headed?" Lee asked in a quiet voice.

"To the mountains, Boy. To the mountains," Jake said, as though it were odd to think there'd be anyplace else worth going.

The days grew steadily warmer and the snow disappeared from all but dark and shaded places. Jacob and Lee continued to walk at their own methodical pace, covering close to twenty miles a day. One morning they crested a hill and there it was: the Platte, wide, flat and mud-brown. They found a place to ford and slogged across. Once on the other side they elected not to walk along its bank for fear of being spotted. Instead, they paralleled the river, ranging from a quarter to a half mile north of it. That way they could double back if they needed water or wanted to ambush the game that came to drink. The prairie grass was beginning to grow again, their brown world becoming a little greener every day. Lee took a shot at a prairie dog with the pistol Jacob had given him and came close to hitting it.

"Don't go shooting that thing," Jake said. "This is injun territory and you might catch more n you bargained for."

Sure enough, the next afternoon they found their first sign of Indians. Jacob made it out to be about twenty ponies, unshod, heading toward the river, north to south. The tracks were at least two days old, meaning they could be miles away by now, or just over the next hill.

The following day they found more tracks and Jacob thought they might need to detour south, though it would be a nuisance. The weather was clear and the ground firm underfoot. They were making good time and there was game along the river. Lee was out in front and had just cleared a rise when he spotted something in the distance. He waved Jacob up and pointed ahead.

"Injun village," Jacob said. "And a big un, by the looks."

"What do we do, now?" Lee asked.

"Let's get a little closer," Jacob said.

For the next hour they kept to the low ground, stopping occasionally to listen for riders. They climbed another rise and Jacob could make out the long earthen lodges and the crops beyond.

"Pawnee," he declared.

"They friendly?" Lee asked.

"There's worse," Jacob answered.

"What's that spose to mean?"

"Well now. We could try and slink round them. But it'd be a coupla days skirt and, seeing how there's a mess of them, we're likely to be running into their hunting parties for the next week or so. Pawnees catch you on the open prairie they ain't likely to embrace you."

"So?" Lee asked. Jake had a way of rambling around a question.

"For the most part, you walk into a Pawnee village and announce yourself proper, they're duty bound to be hospitable."

"So that's what we're doing?"

"I rekon," Jake said, starting toward the village. "At least, I think it were the Pawnee kept that custom."

The Pawnee took little notice of them as they walked up the trail to the center of the village. One old timer and a boy leading a mule wasn't exactly the Seventh Cavalry. They were neither threatening nor particularly interesting, except to the pack of children who followed them, laughing and calling them names. In fact, such little notice was taken that they had to ask three different people where the head lodge was. Pawnee was one of the Indian tongues with which Jacob wasn't conversant, but with the help of a little sign language Jacob got his message across and they were led to the lodge and told to wait.

A few moments later Ku-Sox emerged, his mouth still greasy from the dinner they'd interrupted. The chief looked none too happy about it either but, as Jacob had guessed, his natural courtesy guaranteed them a cordial reception. Ku-Sox called a boy over to take care of the mule and led the guests inside, where they were given a place by the fire across from the chief. Bowls of meat and corn were brought to them and without too much in the way of introduction they were bade to eat. The foot was good and Lee was hungry. He was always hungry and walking the prairie didn't make for regular meals. The Pawnee sat in small circles, eating, talking and laughing. Children ran in and out as their mothers yelled and their fathers ignored them. There was so much noise inside the darkened lodge that Lee could hardly hear himself think. Ku-Sox himself looked the picture of a wise chieftain, upright in dignity and tolerant of all the commotion around him. Privacy was not something the Pawnee had a lot of use for.

When dinner was over a bowl was brought so they could wash their fingers. When Jacob dried his hands on his shirt the chief looked away, obviously embarrassed for him. Ku-Sox opened the conversation with a few words, but Jacob quickly signed that he did not understand. Jacob's English fared no better. Hoping the chief might be fluent in one of the languages of the Plains, Jacob posed a question in Lakota and then in Shawnee. It wasn't until he tried a few words in the Absaroka tongue that Ku-Sox's eyes lit up. He called across the room. A small, handsome Indian walked over from his place by the wall and sat next to the chief. He was distinctly different in appearance from the rest of them. Ku-Sox said a few words to him and gestured to the White man.

"I am White Hawk. I am Absaroka," he said in the language of his people.

"I'm Jacob McCune," Jake answered in the man's language, "and this is Lee," he said, patting Lee on the back. "Thank Ku-Sox for his hospitality. It's been weeks since we had a good meal."

White Hawk nodded, and then translated this to the Chief, who indicated with a nod of his head that they were welcome. Ku-Sox gestured for a pipe to be brought forward and untied the small tobacco pouch tied to his belt. Jacob anticipated this and handed Ku-Sox his own pouch, offering it to the chief as a gift. Ku-Sox smiled, packed the pipe and lit it, passing it across to Jacob.

"What brings you to our village?" Ku-Sox asked through his interpreter.

"For many years I have lived up in the shining mountains. Now that I am old, I wish to return," Jacob said.

"It is a long way," Ku-Sox said.

"We are in no hurry," Jacob returned.

"I hear there are many bear in those mountains?"

"There are. But not so many as once was."

"You ever kill one of the great bears?" he asked.

"You bet, and a coupla them almost kilt me."

"I would like to kill one of the great bears. But they do not come this far down river any longer."

"Maybe you should come along?" Jacob said.

Ku-Sox considered this, took a long slow draw on the pipe and handed it back.

"Someday," he said. "When the river gets too crowded with White men."

Jacob told Ku-Sox of all the places he'd been and about the endless water many weeks travel beyond the mountains. Ku-Sox had heard of the great water but did not really believe it existed. Jacob told him about a wide land to the south. Land so dry you could ride for weeks in any direction and not see a tree or another living thing, the land of the Comanche and the Apache. Jacob talked about the wives he'd married and lost, describing each one of them tenderly and in detail. Lee could not follow the conversation, but he could tell that Jacob had piqued the old Indian's interest. He would have liked to interrupt his friend and ask him what he was talking about, but he sensed it wouldn't be a good idea.

Jake told Ku-Sox about the tribes he had fought and other Indians he had befriended. It turned out they had friends in common and shared some of the same enemies. Jacob informed Ku-Sox that the Great War in the east dragged on. Thousands of soldiers on each side died. Ku-Sox had never heard of a fight that lasted so long but seemed happy to hear the news. He hoped they would all slaughter one another, but didn't suppose he'd be that lucky. The Soldiers would be back, just as soon as they stopped killing each other.

Ku-Sox went out to take a piss and Jacob asked his translator, White Hawk, how he happened to be in a Pawnee village. White Hawk told the story of how he was captured and taken as a slave. When Jake relayed the story, Lee was shocked.

"I didn't know Indians kept slaves," Lee said.

"Not all, but these do, I rekon."

Lee looked at White Hawk, taking note of him for the first time. There was sadness there, but defiance too.

The conversation dragged on for another couple hours. The two White men were then led to a vacant patch of floor in a corner of the lodge and given buffalo skins to sleep on. Away from the fire, it was dark and cold. Lee pulled the skin over his shoulders and stared out at the dark forms of men, women and children sleeping all around him. His mind was spinning with all he'd seen and heard.

The next morning, they woke to the bustle of village life. Going unnoticed, they took up wooden bowls and ate with the others. White Hawk joined them.

"Where are you headed?" White Hawk asked Jacob.

"Fort Laramie, for starters," Jacob answered.

"If you see my people, tell them where I am and what has happened. It is Marchambeau's band."

"I heard of him," Jake replied

"They be camped along the Yellowstone, come summer."

"I'll tell em, if we see them."

"Tell my wife I will try to find a way back. She hates it when I am away too long. She will be angry."

"Leastways you got a good excuse," Jacob said in English.

White Hawk nodded, though the meaning escaped him.

When Lee and Jacob were packed up and had retrieved their mule they asked to see Ku-Sox again. The Chief stepped out of the lodge, bringing White Hawk with him. Two Mother was already yelling at White Hawk to come over and carry her tools out to the fields for the day's work, but he ignored her.

"I thank you again for your hospitality. All I meet will hear about the great Pawnee chief, Ku-Sox." Jacob said in Absaroka, waiting while White Hawk translated.

"Don't tell too many," Ku-Sox smiled. "We'll be feeding every loafer on the plains."

Jacob nodded and was about to leave when Lee stepped forward.

"I don't know what your custom is, and I apologize if I make offense," Lee began. "But this here mule is a mighty fine animal. Does the work of two horses."

Ku-Sox glanced at the mule impassively.

"Truth is, we don't have much need of him, traveling light like we do."

Jacob gave Lee a stern look, wondering where this was going.

"What is it you suggest?" Ku-Sox asked.

"I was thinking we'd trade him for your little buddy, here," Lee said, indicating White Hawk.

If Ku-Sox was surprised he didn't let on. He looked from the mule to White Hawk and then back to Lee.

"A mule is not worth as much as a full grown man," Ku-Sox said.

"This is an uncommonly forceful mule," Lee said.

It was a cumbersome conversation, since Jacob had to translate Lee to White Hawk who then translated to Ku-Sox. But if the Chief was irritated, he didn't show it.

"I have no use for a mule." Ku-Sox said. "But I would trade him for that rifle." He gestured to the Spencer Lee carried in his right hand.

Lee realized, too late, that he should have kept the rifle hidden, but there was nothing that could be done about it now.

"This rifle is special to me. I cannot trade it," Lee said.

Jacob grew uneasy. There was nothing preventing the chief from taking the rifle, the mule and their scalps if he chose to. He was struggling to think of a way to salvage the situation when, suddenly, Ku-Sox said. "Fine. I'll take the mule."

White Hawk knew the Pawnee had no need for the mule and that the trade was Ku-Sox's way of granting him his freedom. White Hawk looked at the chief and gave a barely perceptible nod of thanks. Ku-Sox signaled a boy to lead the mule away and Lee hurriedly untied the packs while Jacob turned to White Hawk.

"Go fetch your gear," he said.

"There is nothing. I am ready now."

Lee handed White Hawk the packs, bowed his head to Ku-Sox and the three of them started down the path to the river.

Two Mother, who'd been waiting impatiently, saw White Hawk walking away and rushed forward.

"Where are you going?" She snorted. "You've got work to do."

"White Hawk spat. "You are the most vile woman to ever walk the earth,"

White Hawk spoke with such hatred that Two Mother stumbled backward in shock.

"I pray that our paths may cross again. I will split your fat head in two and feed your brains to a pig."

Two Mother's jaw dropped in astonishment. Ku-Sox laughed heartily.

Lee hurried down the trail. He knew he'd get an ear full from the Old Man, but Jacob caught him anyway. He could walk fast when he needed to.

"What were you thinking, boy?" he asked. "You traded away our mule."

"What are you complaining about? He's carrying the packs."

White Hawk was struggling under the weight of the packs. Jacob snorted.

"How long you think a little feller like that's gonna hold up?"

"I'll help him."

"You almost bargained your life away once Ku-Sox got a load of that rifle."

"Yeah, didn't figure on that," Lee agreed.

"We run into Injuns out here, you better let me do the talking."

"Alright," Lee answered. "But it didn't seem right just leaving him there."

"Injuns do things different. You can't go putting your rules on em."

"Just didn't seem right," Lee said.

"He'll probably run off first chance he gets. If he don't cut your throat first."

Hardin County, Tennessee

The war wasn't turning out the way he'd hoped. Other young officers he'd come south with had already been promoted to Captain, and they were all inferior men. Fredrick March considered himself an outstanding officer. There wasn't a single black mark on his record, and he'd already seen action in five different battles. He was sure one of his superior officers had taken up against him. To make matters worse, his company was now being given only secondary roles in the fighting, making it even more difficult for him to distinguish himself. Time was running out. The war would end and, with it, his chance to advance, to use his prestige as a war hero to escape the life of a clerk in a small town mercantile.

Part of the problem was the poor caliber of recruit they assigned him. They were, to a man, stupid, lazy and inept; a motley group of micks, half-breeds and ner'do wells. The more he tried to whip them into shape the more they backslid into insolence and sloth. He knew he was not well liked and he didn't care. Men needed discipline. He'd love nothing better than to charge the whole lot of them into a confederate artillery barrage; the only problem was that he'd have to lead them. But this morning he'd received a summons to report to Command. Perhaps they were finally ready to recognize his talent and give him the commission he deserved or, at least, an assignment that would allow him to prove himself. The Union army was massed for one of the biggest offensives of the war. Thousands of troops were being brought south for a campaign that, scuttlebutt had it, would end the war. The Command tent was on a hill overlooking the river. He reported to the adjutant and was brought before Colonel Smith, a weathered old officer with bushy eyebrows and a thick beard. Smith had seen men die. He'd seen men rise to glory, and he had seen men whose only thought was to survive.

"Lieutenant Fredrick March, reporting as ordered," he said, standing at attention.

"At ease, Lieutenant," the Colonel said, without looking up.

The Colonel searched through a pile of papers on the campaign desk in front of him and handed one to the Lieutenant.

"You've been ordered to the rear," he said. "Pack your gear; you've been posted out West."

"But Colonel, what about the battle? I've been waiting for months to. . ."

"Listen," Smith cut him off. "Men are going to die by the thousands in the next few days. Consider yourself lucky."

March took the orders, saluted and walked out of the tent. He knew these orders might save his life but, at the moment, he didn't care. He glanced down at his orders.

Fort Benton? Where the hell is Fort Benton? he mumbled to himself.

Chapter VIII

THE CHASE

They made us many promises, more than I can remember, but they never kept but one; they promised to take our land, and they did.

Red Cloud

Nebraska Territory

White Hawk didn't run away. That first night they camped along the river and White Hawk sat beside them, ate his food quietly and didn't say a word. Jake's comment about their throats being slit didn't sit well with Lee. Up until yesterday, he'd never seen any real Indians, and now he had to worry about being killed in his sleep.

They woke up in the morning still alive. White Hawk helped with what chores there were without being asked. Jacob would share a word or two with him, but it didn't amount to any kind of conversation as far as Lee could tell. They fell into an easy pattern, starting out in the morning just after sunrise, walking west by northwest, following the general flow of the Platte towards the mountains. White Hawk let it be known that he didn't take to walking and that they needed horses. Jacob cursed him with words the Indian couldn't understand, eliciting a quiet chuckle from Lee. Where the Indian expected Jake to come up with a horse in the middle of the open prairie Lee couldn't imagine. Spring had arrived in all its glory and the grass was knee high. Mornings were still cool, but the days were hot and there was no shelter from the sun. Come evening, one or another of them would range off in search of game. White Hawk made himself a bow and formed a few arrows. Lee was fascinated by the simple elegance of the weapon and the skill with which White Hawk formed the arrowheads and secured them to the shaft. The Absaroka found a dead hawk in the grass and harvested the tail and wing feathers, securing them with strips of rawhide. A competition arose to see who could bring in the plumpest victuals. White Hawk could stalk game patiently and quietly, but a gun was a gun. White Hawk wouldn't have minded having a rifle, but he didn't think it likely the White men would give him one. Most evenings, the Indian was able to bring in something, even if it was only a hen or a prairie dog. Jacob wasn't going to be out provisioned by a Red man. You could hear him blasting away somewhere near to hand, despite his warnings to Lee about the noise. Lee, for his part, heeded the old man's warning and tried not to fire the Spencer unless he found game big enough to warrant it. Not only did the sound of the big gun carry for miles across the open plain, but it blasted a big chunk out of any small critter. More importantly, he didn't know when he'd get another chance to buy cartridges.

The next afternoon Lee spotted clouds on the horizon, which was strange since it was an otherwise clear day. At first, he assumed it was a storm blowing in and told Jacob and White Hawk as much. Then he noticed that the clouds were closer than he first thought and supposed it was a dust storm. Jacob and White Hawk looked at each other and headed to the top of a hill to gain a better view. Lee came up beside them and stared out over the prairie. Even from a distance, they were impressive. The animals were more than thousand yards off, but he could feel the vibration from the sheer weight of them.

"Buffalo?" he asked.

White Hawk made the sign for buffalo. Here, at last, was the herd his people had searched for, that his friends had died for, finally found, but too late for any of them.

"We can jump em down in the valley there," Jacob said, pointing with his rifle.

It took them an hour to reach the draw. The three hunters looked down from the crest of the hill, watching as the lead animals filed through. The line went on forever, painting a black swath across the prairie. They were huge, bigger than any cow Lee had ever seen, their shaggy coats matted with dust. They seemed to rip up whole bushels of grass as they grazed, using their massive necks to tear it free, chewing slowly, ceaselessly. Calves, even the newly born, walked closely by their mother's side. Once the lead bulls were a few hundred yards past their position, Jacob raised his long rifle to fire, but White Hawk pushed the muzzle down. He put the side of his hand to his mouth to signal quiet and slowly lifted the bow from his shoulder. White Hawk signed for them to follow. Jake shook his head.

This should be entertaining, he thought.

White Hawk and Lee walked down the hill toward the herd, crouching in the tall grass. They crawled to within twenty yards of the great beasts and then White Hawk rose very slowly onto one knee, notched an arrow and raised his bow. The point buried itself to mid shaft below the shoulder of a young bull. Almost before the animal had taken a step White Hawk had another arrow in flight. The bull toppled to its knees and fell over. None of the other buffalo moved; they continued grazing as if nothing had happened.

Lee was amazed. White Hawk had killed the bull without making a sound or alerting any of the other buffalo. A cow walked up to the fallen animal and sniffed, then moved off a few yards to continue grazing. Lee walked over. It was lying on its side, near death now, but it sensed his presence and swung its massive head. Lee barely managed to jump out of the way.

"Careful," Jacob said, walking up. "Hard to kill these beasts with those little darts."

White Hawk walked to the buffalo and began to sing. Whether it was of thanks or praise Lee was unsure. Then they went to work. They rolled the bull onto its back and gutted it, the still warm entrails spilling to the grass. Lee watched as White Hawk skinned the buffalo, making careful cuts around the legs and neck. He signed Lee to grab the edge of the hide where it had been parted at the neck and the two of them peeled it back. It took all their strength to do it. Lee was surprised by how large it was. Laid out on the ground, it was as big as a small room.

White Hawk took a knife blade in two hands and showed Lee what to do. Using it as a scraper, he cleaned a portion of the inside of the hide, scraping off the thick layer of blood and the strands of connective tissue that stuck to it.

As Lee went to work on the hide, White Hawk turned back to the carcass. He freed the bladder and drained it on the prairie. It would make a good water bag. They couldn't carry all the meat back to camp, but White Hawk cut away the choicest pieces, the tongue, the rump and the flanks. By the time he was finished his arms were red with blood and grease. Lee wasn't looking too dapper himself; he looked like he'd fallen through a meat grinder. They loaded the meat back onto the hide and rolled it up, tied the two ends and hefted it to their shoulders.

It was like a giant sausage made of fur, Lee thought

they set up camp a thousand yards north of the kill and got a fire going. There was still a lot of work left to do. Lee cut a few sapling poles and they fashioned a rack, covered it with the tarpaulin and shoveled hot coals onto the ground beneath it. Onto this they laid some freshly cut grass. White Hawk sliced meat from the stash and stretched it over the rack to smoke.

"I was hoping we'd find em," Jacob said. "I was getting tired of sleeping on bare ground."

Jacob cut some of the meat, skewered it with a sharp stick and began roasting it over the fire. The smell set Lee's stomach rumbling. There was more meat than they could eat and they would gorge themselves. The night was clear and cold and the red moon rose nearly full in the east. Coyotes were yipping and yapping. They'd most likely found the kill and were eating their full. They'd be at it all night, most likely.

Sometimes all it took was a little food to make you feel right about things. The meat would do them good; rabbit and prairie dog were alright but too lean to put muscle on a man. You needed a steak dripping with fat so thick it coated your face.

It was late by the time they had eaten their fill and all the work was done. Lee took up the water bag and said he'd hump it to the river for water. His stomach was too bloated for sleep and he was still covered with blood and grease. The Platte was a mile south, but Lee could see its silvery reflection as he crested a hill. He carried the water bag in one hand and his Spencer in the other, walking contentedly through the thick grass. Too often, out here, there was only worry and trouble on your mind. Either you were tired of walking or your mind was set on where you'd stop. Or you were thinking about whether you'd find food, or you were worried about being spotted by injuns. It wasn't a debilitating fear, just a persistent gnawing that prevented a man from enjoying himself, like a deerfly that buzzed around that couldn't be swooshed or swatted. But tonight, he was free of it. They had meat aplenty, nowhere to go and the memory of the hunt was fresh in his mind. He'd hold onto that for a while.

Back at camp, Jacob and White Hawk laid their blankets down beside the fire. Jacob pulled out his pipe and took his time filling it. He picked up a twig from the dirt, held it to the fire and lit his pipe. He pulled in the first sweet breaths, filling his mouth with the hot smoke and exhaling it slowly into the clear night sky. He looked over at White Hawk, who was staring out over the Prairie with a thoughtful look on his face.

"Long time?" Jacob asked him in his own language. White Hawk looked back.

"Long time," he agreed.

"You're free to go, anytime," Jacob told him.

White Hawk looked confused.

"Then why did you trade for me?" he asked.

"Wish I could say t'were my idea. Truth is, it were Lee's. Didn't like the idea of it, I s'pose. But we got no need of slaves. First light, take some of the meat and head out."

The Indian was quiet for a while. Jacob couldn't tell what he was thinking.

"I better stay and help you to the fort," White Hawk said. "Two White men like you will never make it alone."

The Platte was a mile wide, slow moving and sparkling in the moonlight. Lee looked for some rocks to set upon. He laid his rifle where he could get it in a hurry, took off his boots and pulled his shirt off over his head. He walked into the river up to his calves and dipped his shirt into the water, rubbing the sleeves together, watching the water change color as the blood and dirt washed away. The water was cold, much colder than he thought it would be. In no time, his feet were numb. Once his shirt was thoroughly washed he stripped off his trousers and did the same, wrung them out and laid them over the rocks to dry, then leaned over, cupped his hands together and splashed water up over his face and hair. He scrubbed his face; felt the beginnings of a beard there. About time, he thought.

Lee rubbed his hands clean till his fingers ached with the cold, then set about filling the water bag. He sat on the bank and tried to still his shivering. He looked at all that water flowing by, wondering why it didn't just melt into the ground the way rain did, wondering how it managed to find its way to the Mississippi and then all the way to the sea.

After a while, he gathered up his wet clothes, pulled his boots back on and lifted the rifle onto his shoulder. He started up the hill in his underwear, feeling clean and thinking it was worth the long walk. By the time he got back to camp the moon was high. He hung the water bag, piled more wood on the fire and crawled in under the blanket. He was sound asleep before he had time to settle into a dream.

They walked for another week, seeing no one at all. Jacob figured they were approaching Wyoming territory. One afternoon White Hawk was leading the way when he stooped to the ground to examine something. Lee knelt beside him and saw the tracks in the fresh mud. There were plenty of them, but Lee wasn't a good enough tracker to say how many. In a few minutes Jacob caught up.

"Whadya got, there?" he asked.

White Hawk pointed to the tracks, indicated the direction they were heading.

"Injuns," Jacob said out loud.

"Lakota," White Hawk said. "One day."

"How many do you think?"

Jacob studied the tracks and looked to White Hawk, who flashed his open palms twice.

"Twenty," Jacob confirmed

"What are you thinking we should do?" Lee asked.

"Not much we can do, cept keep our eyes open," Jacob said.

Things were different now. They made slower time now that they had to avoid the high ground and skulk around. There was no more ranging apart; it was too risky, and fires were out of the question. Lee was getting tired of chewing on smoked buffalo meat, but he was grateful to have it. There were more tracks, but no sightings. On the evening of the third day, they made camp along a small creek, a trickle of water flowed down the cut bank with no trees for shelter. A cold wind blew from the north and Jacob figured a storm was coming. They slept without a fire to warm them. Just before sunrise Lee was startled awake by the soft sound of a horse's hooves in the sand and, opening his eyes, he saw an Indian moving toward him. Lee jumped up and grabbed his rifle, and then realized it was White Hawk leading three horses. He shook Jacob awake.

"Jesus Christ," Jacob cursed.

"Where'd he get the horses?" Lee asked.

"Shoulda figured," Jacob said. "His people are blood enemies of the Lakota."

"Stolen?"

Jake was none too happy with White Hawk.

"Better pack up quick. We gotta skedaddle. That's the last time I do an Injun a good turn. We shoulda left him with the Pawnee."

They threw their gear onto the horses and Jacob led them up out of the creek bed away from the rising sun. For the next half hour Jake cursed White Hawk for all he was worth, but the Indian made no apologies. He swore right back and gave as good as he got. To Lee, it seemed stupid. Stealing the horses might bring the Lakota down on them and they'd been making out just fine on foot, but it was too late to do anything about it now.

The first sign that they were being chased came later that morning when they crossed a stretch of open prairie and saw a plume of dust a mile behind them, rising into the sky. This was open country without a tree or even a bush to grace it. There was no place to stop and no place to hide. They kept ahead of the riders without over-tiring the ponies and the afternoon wore steadily on. The sun set but they dared not stop. Jacob was hoping the Lakota would not want to range too far out of their territory and would turn back, but he wanted to put some distance between them just in case. They came to a small creek. They watered the horses and grazed them for a while, then rode down the center of the stream for a few hundred yards to avoid laying track. There was enough of a moon to travel by, but once the moon set they had to stop; it was too dangerous riding across rocky ground without being able to see a damn thing. Jake and Lee slept while White Hawk kept watch. He was supposed to wake Lee in a couple of hours but when Lee woke just before sunrise White Hawk was still on watch and Jacob sound asleep. The Indian signed that they'd better get going. It was midday before they were on ground high enough to see their backtrail. The Lakota were still coming. They didn't appear to have gained any ground; or lost any either.

"How long you reckon they'll keep at it?" Lee asked.

"Hard to tell. Way I figure, we can keep running till they get tired of chasing us or we can lay ambush and discourage them."

"Think it'll work?"

"Running's a sure thing. Fighting's a roll of the dice," Jacob replied.

"We might find help?" Lee said.

"Fort Laramie's less'n a week away. Might be a patrol out. But I wouldn't count on it."

They ate the last of the dried meat later that afternoon. Their other provisions were long gone. Hunger might take its toll, but they couldn't take the time to hunt. White Hawk would occasionally pull up a tuber from the earth, take a few bites and then toss it to Lee. He forced himself to eat, though they were uniformly awful. Another sunset and dark clouds rose up on the horizon. Lee hoped there'd be rain to quench his thirst and hide their tracks. They rode long into the night. They'd been riding since daybreak with hardly a break and the horses were worn out despite every small rest they could afford to give them. After midnight, they rode into a grove of cottonwoods that wove through a dry ravine. A rocky escarpment rose high above them. It was the best cover they'd seen in days. They staked the horses to graze and laid themselves down to get some shuteye. They were sound asleep almost immediately.

It was still dark when Lee felt the rain on his face. He rolled over and pulled the blanket over his shoulder. He heard a little snort from one of the horses. He was ready to ignore it and go back to sleep when he heard the faint click of one rock scraping another. He sat up. It was very dark beneath the trees, but his eyes made out the shape of the tree trunks and branches arching overhead and the motion of the horses slightly stirring. He reached out and shook Jacob, then looked over to White Hawk's rug, but the Indian wasn't there. Without waiting to hear why he'd been woken, Jacob rolled up his gear and moved towards the horses.

"You go ahead," Lee said. "I'll head up to the rocks and cover you."

"No, you go," Jacob said, you ain't never done this."

"Oh, yes I have," Lee answered.

Jacob took a quick look and understood what he meant. He swung up onto his horse and Lee handed him the reins to the other two horses.

"I'll wait just beyond the rocks. Give em hell. Then bolt," Jake said, kicking the horses into motion.

Lee had only taken a few steps when the first arrow pierced the air above his head. He couldn't see a thing and wasn't sure where it had come from. He ran, using the cover of the trees. The ground was slippery from the rain and it was too dark to pick out a path. They had been too tired to reconnoiter the camp, but Lee remembered the escarpment and felt the ground rising under his feet. Another arrow struck the tree beside him and two quick shots rang out. A cry of pursuit went up; the Lakota were spreading out and chasing him. Lee scrambled up the slope, slipping between boulders. If he met with a dead end he'd be trapped. He heard the Indians moving through the trees and he crouched behind a rock and listened, trying to figure out which way they were coming. He didn't move a muscle, waiting, listening. He swung his rifle up and took aim, looking for a target. He caught a glimpse of something moving below him and fired; heard a muffled cry. Swinging his rifle back to the trees, he searched for the next target the way he'd been taught, but his pursuers had vanished.

They were moving silently now, not giving away their position, but Lee knew they were there. He left the cover of the trees and moved quietly up the hill; more shots ricocheted off the rocks beside him. He ducked behind a boulder and turned, targeting, waiting. A Lakota had taken cover behind a tree fifty yards below him. Part of his leg was exposed, just the smallest part of the knee. Lee took aim and fired. The knee blew apart and the Indian tumbled into the open, screaming. Lee didn't follow up; he was already looking for the next target. Another Lakota slid behind the rocks. There was no shot, so he ignored it. He kept moving. A bullet kicked the dust in front of him.

Lee stared into the darkness. He detected movement to his left. He swung onto it, surprised any of them had gotten up the hill so fast. His shot caught the Lakota in the chest and Lee stumbled back against the rocks. Another sound caught his attention opposite. The Indian had his bow raised and Lee knew he wouldn't have time to bring his rifle to bear. Suddenly the sound of an arrow split the air and Lee saw it catch the Lakota in the throat. Before Lee could react, White Hawk jumped down next to him, grabbed him by the arm and pulled him up the hill. They ran to the top and peeled off to the west.

Jacob was waiting ahead on a game trail that led down from the summit. He was turned on his pony, looking back their way. White Hawk got there first and jumped onto his pony in a single fluid leap; a moment later Lee lifted himself up and grabbed the reins. Without a word they kicked their mounts to a dead run down the slope. Lee looked back but couldn't see anything and then they were into the hills again and didn't have a sight line. The rain came heavy now and would cover their tracks, or at least make tracking them slower and less certain. Jacob cut north and kept the line for a few hours. They'd have to rest the horses, but not yet.

They kept hard at it. The sky lightened but there was no sign of the sun. The rain continued to fall, and the temperature dropped. They rode, searching out rocky terrain where their trail wouldn't stick and changing direction at random. Every chance they got they looked back, but there was no sign of their pursuers. Either they had lost the trail or been discouraged by the fight. The Lakota were far from home and being led even further away. The rain kept up all day and the creek beds were starting to run. Lee felt sure they could relax a little, but Jacob pushed them forward, searching for a camp they could defend. At nightfall Lee shot a young doe, dressed her out and lifted her onto his horse. An hour later they found another grove of stunted trees, made camp and started a fire. Lee hadn't had anything to eat in days, but now that the chase was over his mind wasn't on food. He was angry. He ate in silence, brooding and aloof. Jacob had seen him like this before.. After they had eaten, Lee looked up at White Hawk.

"Tell him something for me," he said to Jacob.

"What?"

"Tell him I owe him for saving my hide back there, but it was his own damn thievery brought it on. He ever does anything like that again, it'll be him needs the saving."

Jacob translated, being careful to find the right words. White Hawk shrugged. Neither man's opinion made the slightest bit of difference to him.

Fort Laramie, Wyoming Territory

Lieutenant Colonel Avery Billings Cain had his hands full. The tribes were on the move. The Blackfoot were killing miners and harassing trappers to the north, the Lakota were stealing horses and whatever else they could get their hands on to the northeast, the Shoshone and Arapaho were raiding to the south, and the Cheyenne were harassing emigrants coming west. The war had left the western outposts short-handed and the Indians, their resources squeezed and buffalo getting harder to find, were becoming more belligerent. His biggest fear was that they would band together for a concerted campaign against him. If that happened, they wouldn't stand much of a chance. His troopers were raw and untrained. His best strategy, he reasoned, was to make calculated shows of strength to maintain an image of power. To bluff, in other words.

But it was the Kiowa who concerned him right now. Their story was typical. In the last hundred years they had been pushed out of Canada by the Lakota, pushed out of Montana by the Blackfoot and then pushed out of Wyoming by the Cheyenne. They were still a formidable tribe, but they were running out of places to go. They roamed a large area east of the Rockies that included parts of southern Wyoming, Colorado and Oklahoma, raiding over great distances. You never knew where they'd show up or what mischief they'd get into. Without a military presence in the area, they were making a stand. They couldn't be pushed much further south without running afoul of the Comanche, the most powerful and brutal of southern tribes. Miners moving into Colorado were being fired on and there were reports that a Kiowa band had settled along Lodge Pole Creek to the south.

Cain organized a Cavalry detachment to be commanded by his best field officer, Captain Hayward Scott. He armed them with the best of their somewhat antiquated munitions and staffed it with his most experienced troopers. He ordered them to find the Kiowa village and get them to agree, under show of force, to move out of Cheyenne territory and promise to stop harassing White miners and emigrants. Cain had instructed Captain Scott to avoid fighting, if possible, but act decisively if necessary.

The patrol had been gone two weeks and no word had been received. Cain was beginning to suspect Scott had met with more trouble than he could handle. The Kiowa were clever fighters, not prone to direct engagements but masters of ambush and attrition. He decided to send a small contingent south first thing in the morning to find out what happened.

As it turned out, that wasn't necessary. The column was spotted heading north late that afternoon and Captain Scott rode into the fort with what was left of his brigade. There had been casualties, and the men were battle scarred and worn out. The Colonel arranged for the sick to be cared for and the troopers fed, then he ordered Captain Scott back to the command post.

The Captain was a Westerner, a tough old veteran who'd seen his share of action. He was thin and wiry with a bushy black moustache and tired brown eyes. He was covered in dust and there was blood on his blouse and pant legs. Cain pointed to a chair and told Scott to sit, and then he went to the cupboard behind his desk, pulled out a bottle of Bourbon and poured the Captain a glass.

"Thank you, Colonel," he said.

"I was about to send the scouts out after you," Cain said.

"Sorry, sir. We ran into some trouble."

"What happened?"

Scott took a sip of his whiskey and sat back in his chair.

"We found em. Settled into a little valley along the creek. Bigger bunch than we figured, over a hunert."

"Lodge Pole?" Cain asked.

"Yes, sir. Rode in without trouble. Chief by the name of Pierre."

"Strange name for an Indian?"

"French, I reckon. We smoked the pipe. Seemed like it was going alright. They complained about the miners and the Cheyenne. Said they wouldn't move onto a reservation. Said White hunters had run the buffalo off. They weren't happy, but at least we were talking. Didn't get anywhere that first night, so we agreed to come back the next day an' try again. We moved off and set up camp a few miles downstream. I posted a guard but didn't really spect no double dealing. That night was quiet. Next morning, I took half the troop with me into the village. They jumped us in the narrows. Came at us with maybe fifty, sixty bucks. We took some hits right off, but luckily, we were close enough to camp that the men heard the shooting and came to help. We turned back the ambush and they lit out, hoping we'd chase em, I rekon."

Cain exhaled slowly. "Did you get many of them?"

"Can't say. Not many."

"Then what happened?"

"I sent some of the men back to camp with the dead and wounded and reorganized the company. Then headed straight for the village. They were preparing to head out when we rode in. There were some braves put up a fight, but it was mainly women and children and some old men. My men were riled up, some of the women and old folks were kilt afore I got a handle on it."

"How many?" he asked.

"Colonel, things were happening fast."

"I understand."

"We went through the village. Took all the guns we found, burnt the lodges. Then rounded up the horses that were left and took them too. I knew the war party was near. If they hit us again we'd be in a hard place. So, we broke camp and headed back here."

"What were your casualties?"

"We lost eight men at the creek and another ten wounded. But that wasn't all, Colonel." Cain nodded for him to continue.

"They dogged us all the way back. Ten, twenty at a time. Shootin from behind trees or rocks. We went out after them most times but could never catch em. I sent out scouts to stop the ambushes and we lost some of them, too. You should have seen what was done to them, Colonel. Wasn't an easy sight."

"I'm sorry, Hayward. I should have sent a bigger contingent."

"No way you coulda knowed, Colonel. We lost ten men coming back, another twenty wounded."

"When was your last contact?"

"Oh, they quit us a few days south a here. Haven't seen em since."

"You get some rest, Captain. Take a couple of days and write up the report. See that your men are cared for."

"I'd like to go out after em, Colonel. We should put together a bigger force and make em pay. Can't leave em thinking they can get away with it."

"I'll think about it, Captain. But we're short-handed as it is. And we've got a lot of territory to cover."

"There's one more thing, sir. A white woman, bout thirty years old, I rekon. Found her when we were going through the village."

"Is she alright?"

"Yes, sir. Thing is, she was hiding. Didn't want us to find her. Doesn't speak a word of English. Fought like a she-bear when we grabbed her."

"She wasn't being held against her will."

"No, sir. Musta been taken years ago. All Injun, now. I wasn't sure what to do, she being White an all. So, I took her with us. Hasn't said a word since, won't eat neither."

"You did the right thing, Captain. Where is she now?"

"Had em put her in one of the store-rooms. One that locks. She'll bolt if she gets the chance."

"I see. Well, she's my responsibility now, you go get some rest."

The two men shook hands and the Colonel walked Scott out to the steps.

At supper, Cain told his daughter about their new guest. Elizabeth wanted to go see her at once, but the Colonel would not allow it, at least not until he had a chance to assess the situation. The next morning, he walked down to the storeroom where she was held. It was a small room, eight feet by ten. When he first stepped through the doorway he couldn't see a thing. His eyes had to adjust to the dim light. There were no windows; the woman had been kept in total darkness and he was not happy about that. At least they had brought her a cot and some blankets, but he could see that the cot had not been used. She had spread the blankets on the dirt floor and sat with her back against the wall, watching him.

"Hello," he said.

There was no indication that she understood him. Her face remained impassive, there was no relief, no entreaty, not even fear or hatred in her expression. One thing was certain. She was White, with strawberry blonde hair, though it was dirty and wildly unkempt. Her eyes were blue, her skin browned by the sun. He was standing there trying to decide what to do when Elizabeth came into the room.

"Papa," she said, trying to adjust to the darkness. "You can't keep her in here. There are no windows."

"I am just finding that out. I thought I told you to stay out of this?" he said.

But, by this time, his daughter had made out the dark figure of the woman on the floor and, before he could stop her, Elizabeth had gone to her and taken her hand. The woman gave Elizabeth the briefest of glances, and then looked down at the floor without saying a word.

"We'll put her in one of the guest cottages," Elizabeth said.

"I'll get somebody to clean her up, find her some clothes," The Colonel said.

"Don't bother," Elizabeth said angrily, "I'll take care of it."

Elizabeth helped her wash up and found a smock for her to wear. She seemed to welcome the chance to wash the dirt away but resisted the clothing. Cleaned up, she might have been the wife or sister of any of them. Eventually she allowed Elizabeth to dress her, but without lifting a hand to help. It was like dressing a corpse, Elizabeth thought. Elizabeth had brought a hair brush and tried to use it, but the brush snarled immediately, and the woman covered her head with her hands and refused to allow it. Elizabeth looked into the young woman's eyes and would never forget the look she saw there. As wild as she might appear, you had only to look into her eyes to see that the woman was not crazy, only desperate to go home.

The Colonel sent inquiries to the war department asking about women who were reported missing on the frontier, but it would be weeks before he could expect a response. The woman continued to refuse food. She hadn't eaten a thing since the day she was captured. Elizabeth took it upon herself to care for her. She spent as much time with her as she could spare. She talked to her and read her books, hoping that the sound of the English language would refresh memories long forgotten and that the words would come to mean something to her once again. The woman seemed comfortable with Elizabeth's presence, and there were small glimpses of appreciation, but she never ventured a word.

A week passed and a trapper came through the fort who spoke some Kiowa. As soon as the trapper started to speak, the captive sat up and became quite animated. Her name was Autumn Grass, she told him, and she was not White. She was Kiowa, she insisted, and she wanted to go back to her husband and children. She had two young children who needed her. The soldiers had no right to keep her.

The Colonel, through the translator, told her that she was not Kiowa. She was White; she could not go back. She had family somewhere back east that had probably been looking for her all these years.

"My family is here," she yelled.

She looked at Elizabeth, and then lapsed back into passive silence.

She was weakening. It'd been more than two weeks since she had eaten anything. One afternoon, Elizabeth was trying to convince her to eat, again to no avail, when the Colonel stopped in to check on her condition.

"No luck?" he asked, not without compassion.

"Papa. We're going to have to let her go."

"I can't do that, Elizabeth. We've had no luck locating her family, but I have heard from the army. We are not to allow White captives to rejoin their captors, no matter how comfortable they have become."

"That's ridiculous. She's an Indian now."

"Maybe we'll hear something in the next few weeks," he said.

"What would it matter," Elizabeth said angrily. "She doesn't care if she has family in Baltimore or New York."

"I can't send her back to a bunch of savages."

"She was probably taken when she was a little girl. She's a wife and mother, now. A bunch of men back east can't be expected to understand that."

"Nevertheless, there's nothing I can do."

"Of course, there is. You can do what's right."

"I have orders. I can't disregard them."

"Then you can watch her die," Elizabeth said with tears in her eyes.

Cain took another look at the young woman. She was watching him with an expression that gave no hint of what she was thinking. Cain turned and left the room.

Weeks passed. Autumn Grass grew steadily weaker. Her body thinned and the color drained from her face. When she was alone, she sang, hour after hour in a faint, trembling voice. No one could understand the words and the melody was sad and haunting, but it was clear that there was meaning and importunity to the song. It made Elizabeth cry and it affected all who were close enough to hear it. Elizabeth argued with her father, but this time he could not relent. His responsibility as commander trumped his desire to indulge his daughter, but there were times when he wondered if it superseded his duty to God.

Chapter IX

FORT LARAMIE

What do we want with this vast, worthless area, this region of savages and wild beasts, of shifting sands and whirlwinds of dust, of cactus and prairie dogs? To what use could we ever hope to put these great deserts, or those endless mountain ranges, impenetrable and covered to their very base with eternal snow?

Daniel Webster

Fort Laramie, Wyoming Territory

They crossed the North Platte and followed the deeply rutted path to the Fort. The place was a bustling oasis of activity on the empty prairie. Soldiers, civilians and Indians wandered about, intent upon the day's business. New buildings were under construction and brick chimneys churned smoke into the air. Lee's grip tightened on the reins as a group of riders in Cavalry blue passed by, but they paid him no mind. The trip, which had started out so leisurely, had taken some hard turns. For Jacob, it was a big relief to have finally made it. He headed straight for the Post Trader. It was a large cabin built of logs and split shingles. They tied their horses and entered the store. They hadn't taken more than three steps when a booming voice rang out.

"Jacob McCune! You old ghost."

Seth Carrington had been a trapper, but he came down out of the mountains with Bill Sublette and found that he liked sleeping out of the rain with a steady supply of whiskey and hot food near at hand. His wild ball of gray hair grew into his wild thatch of gray beard and he stood like some great gray grizzly bear behind the high wooden counter. He was a big man, tall and husky. The shelves behind him were full, row upon row, with merchandise for sale or trade. It was, for the most part, the only place between Kansas and the coast where such things could be purchased. Jacob walked up to the counter and extended his hand.

"Was wondrin if you was still here?" Jacob said. "Been a poke."

"I thought sure you was scalped by now. Or froze solid."

"No. Ain't neither," Jacob grinned.

"What you been up to?"

"Same as always, trapping, trading," Jacob pulled Lee forward.

"Lee, this here's Seth Carrington, he's the Sutler here. "Son of a bitch gotta be two hundred years old."

"Naw, I only look like it." Seth said, reaching out to shake Lee's hand.

"Please to meet you," Lee said.

"Me and him just strolled in from Kansas." Jacob said.

"Well, it sure is good to see ya, you old fernicator," he said. "What're you boys doing out here?"

"Passin through. I'd surely like to tell you all about it, but I'm a mite dry," Jacob said, nodding towards the bar in the next room.

"Go on in. I'll be right along," Seth said.

Jacob believed an afternoon spent drinking whiskey with old friends was never time wasted. Seth introduced Jacob all around, saying how he was one of the old timers, one of the original mountain men who came west when there were still plenty of beaver left to trap. Jacob was not one to shy away from attention or refuse a drink, especially if somebody else was buying. Lee stayed back. He enjoyed listening to the stories. He knew the old timers liked to retell every story they'd ever heard, casting themselves in the most interesting light. Made for better telling, Lee supposed. When they staggered out a few hours later the sun was already low on the horizon.

"Where do ya spose White Hawk got to?" Jake asked.

"He was having a look around."

"Keep an eye out. That son of a bitch can find trouble faster'n a pig can find shit."

They untied the horses and walked toward the river. There was a whole community of sorts outside the fort. There were White men like themselves, just passing through. And there were emigrants stopping for provisions before pushing on to the coast. Mostly there were Indians, hangers-on who had set up lodges on the north end of the clearing. Night was coming on and cooking fires were being lit. The Indians cooked whatever food they could get their hands on. They weren't composed of a particular tribe but were a refugee sampling of the dispossessed who begged for food and drink and performed menial tasks for the soldiers. Jacob paid them no mind.

They found White Hawk under the shade of a large cottonwood; sound asleep with his head propped on a saddle bag. His horse was grazing on the grass that grew on the riverbank. Lee wondered if he had found some liquor, but he woke right up when Jake nudged him with the tip of his foot. White Hawk rose to his feet, picked up his bag and walked over to collect his horse. When he got back, he looked at the two White men with suspicion, moved close and smelled the whiskey on their breath, shaking his head. Lee couldn't tell if he disapproved or was simply envious.

They headed for the south end of the clearing. Lee noticed an old Indian watching them. Suddenly the old man rose from the stump he was sitting on and came towards them. Lee supposed he was looking for a handout, but the old man called out in a steady voice. They waited for him to hobble over and the old man walked right up to White Hawk and put his hand on the younger man's chest. Lee could see that he wasn't drunk or looking for a handout, just old and poor. Then White Hawk recognized the fellow and seemed excited to see him. White Hawk asked him a few questions and Lee could tell from the look on his face that the answers did not contain happy news. By the time their conversation was over White Hawk's eyes were cast down in sorrow and Jacob led their friend away.

"Who was that?" Lee asked. But Jake didn't answer right away.

There was a meadow by the river where a small tent city had sprung up. Jacob sat White Hawk down on a stump and pulled Lee aside to help him forage for poles to make a shelter. While they were working White Hawk got up and walked away. Jacob made no move to stop him.

"What happened?" Lee asked.

"The old man was from White Hawk's tribe, the band he was fixin to head back to. They were jumped a few months ago and near all of em kilt, White Hawk's squaw and daughter among em."

"Good Lord," Lee whispered.

"Hard for a man to get over a thing like that," Jacob agreed.

Jacob and Lee tied the saplings together and stretched the tarpaulin tightly across it. Lee started stacking a few rocks to make a fire ring but quickly lost interest, spread his buffalo skin and blanket on the grass and passed out.

It wasn't raining in the morning when he woke up, but there was a mist so heavy it might as well have been. Lee staggered to his feet and got the fire going. There was no sign of White Hawk. They had bought coffee at the Post and Lee fumbled though the sack looking for it. He found the coffee pot and walked down to the river to fill it, making such a racket that Jacob started to stir.

"Can't you keep quiet," he moaned.

"It's morning. Time to wake up." Lee responded.

"Why. We ain't going nowheres. Might sleep all day. Hell, I might sleep a couple a days."

"White Hawk ain't back."

"Not surprised," Jake said, pulling the blanket around him. "Might a lit out. Or be off getting drunk. I would, if'n I were him."

The camp had come alive around them; people doing morning chores, cooking breakfast and packing their wagons to continue on their way. It was a pretty enough spot with the cottonwood trees casting broad limbs across the bank. The Laramie River circled around the fort and, at this time of year, was running fast. A line of mountains rose in the distance, their slopes covered with pine. Jacob finally gave up and slowly lifted himself to his feet, walking unsteadily to the river. Kneeling on one knee, he cupped his hands and splashed water onto his face, soaking his head and beard. That'd do for a bath. He walked back to the fire to warm his hands.

"Feels strange being with folks again," he said.

Lee poured him a cup of coffee and then poured one for himself; it was so strong that Jacob tossed in a palm full of sugar to cut the bitter. They'd bought a few provisions at the Post and Lee pulled them out. He positioned a cast iron fry pan over the fire, cut a few strips of bacon, laid them in the pan and watched them sizzle. There was no smell like it.

"How bout you?" Lee asked, suddenly serious.

"What you mean?" Jacob asked.

"Where you heading next?"

"Don't rightly know," Jacob answered with a quizzical look. "Don't got nowhere I needs to be. I just wanted to see the mountains again."

"There they are," Lee said, pointing west.

"Them ain't mountains. We're close, but you ain't seen em yet."

"Just want to see the mountains?"

" Why? You got some notion?"

"Well. I'm thinking on trying to make a little money."

"Go, on. I won't laugh."

"Heard there was work north. Up the Bozeman. Haulin, or maybe some mining."

"This pilgrim ain't doing no mining. And I don't recommend it for no man. Miserable work and a fool's errand."

"Maybe get our own spread."

Jacob was sorely tempted. It'd be so easy to ridicule the boy that Jake had to bite back the words. But he had promised not to laugh. Sometimes young men just had to give voice to such foolishness.

"Ranchin, eh?"

"Why not? We know the work. Sort of."

"Where bouts?"

"Don't know," Lee said, taking a mouthful of food.

"I rekon you got an idea," Jacob laughed.

"Alright then, Montana. Heard it's fit for grazing. We could homestead out a parcel."

"Ain't too partial to your hair," Jacob smiled.

"Well," Lee said with sudden finality. "I guess we'll be parting ways."

"Now don't go getting all uppity. I got it in mind to see Montana, myself."

Once they finished eating, they spent an hour setting up a proper camp, driving the poles in firmly and stretching the tarpaulin out with stakes and rope. They found a tree from which to hang the food and walked the horses out into the field to graze. Someone had set up a large tub on the riverbank and was selling hot baths, so Lee pulled two bits out of his bag and had himself one. He'd never liked baths back home, but this was different. A bath wasn't so bad when you really needed one. The soap had so much lye in it that his skin tingled, but it got the dirt off. Afterward, Lee took a small piece of it and scrubbed his clothes. It'd be nice to get a haircut, he thought.

Just before noon the two of them decided to walk back up to the fort. Now that he was clean and fed Jacob was feeling sociable again, calling greetings to friends, new and old. He was a man people took to.

"How long you think we'll stay here?" Lee asked as they walked.

"Not long. Be nice if we could pick up a coupla saddles so we can ride like White men."

"Ain't smart to stay too long," Lee said.

Jacob looked at him and nodded slowly. Two Indians ran up to them, their hands out, talking fast and trying to reach into their pockets.

"Who are these people?" Lee asked, fending them off.

"Lowest of the low, beggars and thieves looking for a handout, willin to rent out their squaw for a mug of whiskey. No self respectin Injun would live within twenty miles of a fort."

The mist had mostly lifted and the sun began to come out. A gentle breeze blew down from the mountains. As they walked onto the parade ground they noticed a caisson with two black horses hauling a raw pine casket up the hill to the burial ground. There was a small cortege of officers and a few women walking slowly behind it.

"Look at that," Lee said. "Seems like too nice a day to be burying someone."

"Yea. Or to be dead," Jake replied.

The Post Store was crowded, as usual, soldiers and settlers coming and going, buying everything from candy to axle grease. Seth was busy with customers but waved as they came in. They passed the time with some emigrants, asking if anybody had been up the Bozeman and what news could be had. When the crowd thinned out Seth waved them over.

"Settled in?" he asked.

"Yep, regular town down there by the river," Jacob answered.

"There's digs here at the Fort," Seth said, "Want em?"

"We're just fine. Don't like sleeping inside, less it's snowing or raining."

"Figured as much," Seth said.

"Listen friend," Jake said. "We're in the market for a couple of saddles. Nothing fancy. Just some old leather."

"None here. But talk to Burns down the stable. They sell the old one's now and again."

They made their way down to the stables and waited patiently till the Sergeant had the time to talk. Sergeant Burns was burly and rough, a fireplug on two bowed legs, and he went about his work with a scowl on his face.

"Hiya, Sarge," Jacob called. "Why don't ya take a break and come over for a spell."

"I got too much to do to be jawing with the likes of you," he said, continuing with his work.

"I'm a friend of Seth's. He said you're the man I should talk to. Name's Jake McCune."

"I heard of you," Burns said. "Can't remember why, exactly."

"I'm right famous, these parts. Ain't I boy?" he asked Lee

"You say so," Lee responded.

That got a smile from Burns, who finally stopped what he was doing and walked over to the fence.

"Seth said you might have a couple of saddles for sale?"

"We ain't in the business a selling saddles, Mister."

"Thought you might have some old ones. Gotta coupla horses, but I'm too old to be ridin like a redskin."

"Weren't you through here a coupla years ago. All shot up."

"Yessir, but I weren't shot up. T'was a Cheyenne arrow. Right in the shoulder. Doc pulled it out. Still have the arrowhead."

"Yeah, I remember. Hold on."

Burns walked back to the storeroom. They could hear him rustling around, cursing and throwing things. Lee looked over at Jake, but the old man had taken to whistling a tune and wasn't paying attention. In a minute the Sergeant came out carrying two old rigs.

"Rekon we won't be using these. Pretty much worn out, though." He said, dropping em onto the dirt.

"How much?"

"You can have em. Saves us the trouble a haulin them away."

"I owe you one, friend." Jacob said.

They carried the saddles back across the parade ground, thinking they'd buy saddle soap to work into the cracked old leather. Besides, it was one o'clock in the afternoon.

"Time for a drink," Jacob said.

They made their way to the counter and had a whiskey poured. There was a bent backed half breed by the name of Sam Jones standing at the bar. They got to talking and he told McCune that he'd run wagons up the Bozeman the better part of the previous year, but he wouldn't do it anymore. He refused to make the trip without an army escort. Too dangerous. He'd slipped through a few times on luck and a dime, but figured he'd used up his fair share. There were just too many Indians, and they'd grown bold and blood thirsty. Lee listened and browsed around the store, trying his best not to be noticed. He was starting to get jumpy with so many soldiers around.

A group of officers entered the store and walked up to the counter. One of them was a tall Lieutenant Colonel.

"Good afternoon, Mr. Carrington," The Colonel said.

"Howdy, Colonel," he said. "Mighty spiffed up for a week-day."

"That Kiowa woman finally passed," The Colonel said. "Starved herself to death."

"Heard tell," Seth said. "Damn shame."

"Never seen such a thing. My daughter's hardly speaking to me."

"No one claimed the woman?"

"No. Sometimes the families don't want them back. Figure it's shameful to have gone injun like that. Bad business, all around."

"Colonel. There's someone's I'd like you to meet," Seth said. "This here's Jacob McCune. Best hunter, scout and trapper left in these parts. Know'd him bout forever. Been all over these mountains from Schatewa to Santa Fe.

The Colonel shook Jacob's hand warmly.

"Avery Billings Cain," he said. "It is a pleasure to meet you, Mr. McCune."

"Likewise," Jacob answered.

"Is this your boy?" Cain asked, turning to Lee.

"Naw, ain't got no younguns I know of," Jacob said. "This here's Lee."

The Colonel reached out his hand. "Pleased," he said, again.

Lee shook the Colonel's hand nervously. Cain smiled; he was used to shy young men.

"Have a last name, Lee?" he asked in a friendly manner.

"Why yes, sir." Lee hesitated. "Grant. Lee Grant."

"Interesting name," the Colonel commented.

"Got both sides covered," Seth laughed.

"Where you coming from, Mr. McCune?" The Colonel asked.

"Might as well call me Jake. We're up the Platte these two months from Kansas. Had a little run in with the Sioux just east of here."

"What sort of run in?" Cain asked, concerned.

"Chased us a ways. T'was a close thing."

Jacob left out the part about them stealing their horses right out from under them. He figured the Colonel wouldn't take to travelers stirring up the tribes.

"How many?" Cain asked.

"Twenty, I rekon. Less'n a few by the time we got away, thanks to Lee here. Best damn shot I seen anywhere. Better'n me even. And I ain't never said that afore."

Lee winced, wishing Jake could keep his mouth shut.

The Colonel frowned. He'd been working hard to keep the peace with the Sioux; but allowed he didn't know the circumstance.

"They're on the move," the Colonel said. "You're not the first who've been hit coming across. I'd say you're damn lucky to have made it, just the two of you."

"Have an Injun of our own traveling with us. Absaroka. But, yea, we're happy to be here with most of our hair."

"The Blackfoot are even worse," the Colonel continued. "But we just don't have the man-power to protect the trails just now."

"Was wondering bout that," Jake said. We're thinking of headin up the Bozeman."

"Can't recommend it. At least not by yourselves."

The Colonel handed Seth a list of supplies. Seth read the list, nodded and turned to start filling it.

"How long you here?" the Colonel asked.

"Not more'n a week."

"So, you were a hunter, eh? Ever hunt grizzly?" The Colonel asked.

"I hunted everything that roams these mountains," He replied, getting a little too caught up in his own notoriety.

"I've always wanted to hunt Grizzly. Maybe we could put together a little expedition. We could use a man with your experience. If it's convenient, that is?"

"I ain't real busy," Jacob answered.

After talking a bit more and picking up his groceries, the Colonel left, telling Jacob he'd have Seth arrange things. Lee decided to head back to camp and check on the horses, but Jacob spent a few more hours at the bar, gathering information, as he called it. He sauntered back to camp later that afternoon.

"Evening Mr. Grant," he called out.

"T'were all I could think of." Lee said.

"Coulda been worse. You could a said you was Tecumseh Lincoln or such."

"We better not dawdle. I'm bound to slip up sooner or later."

"Colonel seems nice enough," Jacob said. "We might need a favor or two afore we're through."

Laramie Mountains, Wyoming Territory

It was still dark when Jacob and Lee finished tying their bags onto the horses. No one in the little camp by the river was up yet. They rode to the Commandant's quarters. The Colonel's adjutant and half a dozen enlisted men were waiting out front. The Colonel's horse, a fine chestnut gelding, was being led by one of the men. The fort was quiet at this hour of the morning.

Lee turned as the front door opened and Cain stepped outside. A moment later, a girl about Lee's age followed him onto the porch. In the dim light of the open doorway Lee could see her long dark hair and the full shape of her.

"Who's that?" Lee whispered to the enlisted man beside him.

"That's the Colonel's daughter. She's something, eh?"

She was that, and Lee couldn't keep his eyes off her. Cain said his goodbyes, kissed her on the forehead and then walked over to the men.

"Morning gentlemen."

"Good morning, sir," his adjutant replied. He was a tall thin man from Pennsylvania named Adam Fowl. Like the Colonel, he'd been wounded in the war, not twice but three times. He walked with a limp from a rebel ball that shattered his leg and he'd been lucky not to lose it. Only a crowded ward and the confusion of the battle front had caused the surgeons to neglect him long enough to keep the appendage. He was offered his release, but he had nowhere to go and no prospects, so a friend of the family pulled strings and he was sent West with the rest of the rejects and volunteers.

"You check provisions?"

"Personally, sir."

"Mr. McCune, Mr. Grant. You have everything you need?" the Colonel asked.

"If I ain't got it, rekon I'll just do without," Jacob replied.

"Alright then, let's get started."

The Laramie Mountains rose up out of the plains west of the Fort and, as the sun climbed, they could see their outline clearly. They might not be as impressive as the climax peaks further west, but they were a welcome sight to Jacob after months on the plains. The morning was bright and sunny and the traveling easy enough. Jacob and the Colonel struck up a conversation. Cain had always wanted to hunt Grizzly and was delighted when he heard that a large bear had been spotted in the mountains nearby. Lee hung back with the enlisted men, avoiding questions and keeping to himself.

By afternoon they reached the foothills and continued north until they found a spot to set up camp. While the others unloaded supplies and staked the tents, Jake took Lee and rode off to scout the area, looking for some sign of the bear. By nightfall they were back. They had picked up a trail. One of the enlisted men led them to a tent.

"Nice having someone do the work for you," Jacob said to Lee.

Lee agreed it wasn't half bad. There was somebody to cook the food, make the coffee, and even do the dishes. All Jacob had to do was entertain the Colonel with his tales and track the Griz. They ate a good meal, smoked a cigar, drank a glass of bourbon and, when they were tired, they went off to sleep.

The next morning the Colonel left three of the enlisted men at camp and the rest of them mounted up and followed McCune into the mountains. To Jacob's way of thinking, it was still too many. It was hard to be stealthy with a bunch of greenhorns trampling through the brush. Jacob led them to the spot where he'd picked up the trail the day before and they tied up the horses. They'd track the bear on foot. Lee pulled his Spencer rifle out of the deerskin scabbard White Hawk had fashioned for him and the Colonel noticed it right away.

"Nice rifle. I've heard about them but haven't actually seen one. Mind if I take a look?"

"Sure," Lee said, handing it to him.

Cain worked the lever and sighted down the barrel. Lee stood impassively, trying to conceal his nervousness.

"Mind If I ask where a young man like you would get such a fine piece? They're hard to come by."

"I won it," Lee replied.

"Won it?" The Colonel asked.

"In a shooting contest. It was first prize."

"Humm. You must be good," The Colonel said, handing back the weapon.

"Just lucky, I guess."

Lee was sweating and hoped the Colonel didn't notice. He was grateful Jake had schooled him in the tale. Who knows what he might have said if he didn't have an answer already made up.

It was only a game trail, and it led steeply uphill through thick trees and underbrush. The ground was dry and rocky and didn't take much of a track. It sure wasn't the kind of place you wanted to surprise a Grizzly. The tracking was slow with so many men to hold back. Jake would lose the trail, and then pick it back up. It took some guess work and back tracking but, after a couple of hours, the track grew more distinct and the sign fresher. There were scrapes on the Aspen and scat on the forest floor. They made their way over rocky ground toward a stand of fir, of small diameter and growing closely together. It was hard to see more than thirty yards ahead. Jacob wasn't too happy about that but there was nothing to be done about it, so he proceeded slowly, listening for any sign that the bear might be ahead of them. He strained his eyes, staring into the trees, and hushed the troop so he could listen. After another hundred yards he signaled for them to stop. He listened and then crouched down, trying to see what was up ahead.

Adrenaline was pumping now; everyone could feel it. Lee felt his heart pumping the way it did before a battle, and he tried to calm his mind the way he'd been trained. Jacob inched forward, avoiding twigs and loose rocks, trying to be as quiet as possible. Cain and the others followed. They were looking through the trees up a steep slope and they were upwind. The situation was less than ideal. Jacob thought about trying to circle around, but it would take too long. Then they spotted him.

He was feeding on a carcass, and not a fresh kill from the look of it. The faint odor of decay hung in the air. The grizzly was so intent on the meat that he hadn't sniffed them out yet, but that would change soon. He pulled the Colonel up beside him. The bear was seventy yards up the slope, turned broadside to them, his snout buried in the carcass. They could hear deep grunts as his teeth sought purchase on the rotting flesh. The Colonel looked for a position that would provide a shot, but the trees and the uneven ground made it difficult. Suddenly the bear stood on his rear legs and looked around. Something had alerted him to their presence and now he was sniffing them out. The grizzly lifted his nose into the air, turned and took a step forward. He was big, almost nine feet tall and over five hundred pounds. Looking up at him from below made him look even more enormous. He dropped to all fours again and made deep huffing sounds. They sounded like a warning, and Lee was inclined to heed it.

"Get ready, Colonel," Jacob said. "Make it a good one."

"I don't have a clear shot," the Colonel whispered, lifting the Hawken to his shoulder and sighting up the hill.

The grizzly took another step toward them, still only curious at this point. Lee tightened his grip on his rifle. He could hear the enlisted men moving behind him. They'd been told to freeze, but they were backing slowly down the hill. Suddenly the bear stood on his hind legs and roared; Lee was shocked at the power and volume of the roar. Without any further warning, the grizzly dropped and charged straight down the hill toward them.

He was huge, utterly unstoppable. How was it possible for an animal that big to move so fast? Jacob put his hand to Cain's shoulder. The Colonel took aim, waited till his hands stopped shaking and pulled the trigger. Time moved fast and slow at the same time. The smoke cleared. The grizzly was still charging toward them, if he was hit there was no indication of it. Cain reached for the other rifle that Jacob thrust into his hand, but the bear was closing fast. The Colonel fumbled for the trigger and fired again, losing his footing to the recoil and falling to the ground. Lee looked over at Jacob who, for the first time, seemed worried. He had given his rifle to the Colonel and was now unarmed.

Jake grabbed the Colonel by the collar and hauled him roughly to his feet, turning to find a place to flee. Lee hesitated, quickly realizing there was no one else left to shoot and the grizzly was just yards away. In one fluid motion he swung his rifle up and fired. The round hit with an audible thud and the bear went down in a heap, almost at their feet.

"Damn," the Colonel muttered.

Lee levered another cartridge, stepped around the tree and approached, looking for signs of life.

"Put one through his heart, just to be sure," Jacob called out.

Lee fired, but the grizzly was already dead. Jacob moved forward and pushed the bear with his moccasin.

"Sweet Jesus!" Cain exclaimed. "How many times do you have to shoot one of these beasts before they go down."

Jacob leaned over and rolled the huge animal onto his side. There was a single bullet hole in the center of his forehead.

"Just once," he said. "If'n you hit him in the right spot."

The Colonel directed the enlisted men to help with the skinning. He was not happy. He'd been put into the line of fire and been found deficient. He stood to one side, smoking a cigar and watching the men work. Nobody said a word and the atmosphere was tense. Jacob was directing, telling the men to be careful not to cut through the hide. Cain would want the bear skin as a trophy, even with the large hole in its forehead.

"Bear makes good eatin," Jacob said, trying to lighten things up. "Ever et bear, Colonel?" he asked.

Cain shook his head, indisposed to speak. It took an hour to skin the bear and cut choice pieces of meat from the carcass, then a couple more to hump it back to the horses. The horses weren't keen to the smell of bear, but they settled down soon enough. Back at camp Lee and Jacob unpacked the hide and went to work, scraping it clean, salting it and staking it out to dry. Cain opened a camp chair and sat under a tree, smoking and reading a book. Lee wiped his hands on an old rag and looked over at the Colonel. After a while he walked over.

"Excuse me, Colonel," he said. "Mind if I take a look at that rifle of yours?"

Cain looked up, puzzled. "Why?"

"Something weren't right."

The Colonel stood up and walked over to his tent, reached in and drew out the Hawken. Lee examined it carefully, sighting down the bore.

"Mind if I load it?"

"Go right ahead," Cain said, handing him the sack. The Hawken was a muzzle loader, usually a reliable weapon. Lee loaded the powder, drove the ball down the bore and used the ramrod to pack it. By this time, Jacob and a few of the others had walked over to see what was going on.

"Can somebody set something on those rocks over there?" Lee asked.

The Lieutenant grabbed an empty tobacco box and walked about eighty yards down range, setting it on the rocks. Lee lay down, rested the barrel on a log, took aim and fired. The box didn't move. He reloaded, aimed again and fired. The shot echoed through the trees but the box remained untouched.

"What is it, Lee?" the Colonel asked.

"Barrels not true. Been bent, I spect."

"I should have sighted it in before we went out. Damned foolish of me."

"I can fix it for you, if you'd like. Just need the use of your shop when we get back."

"I'd be much obliged," the Colonel said.

Cain was in a much better mood at dinner. They roasted slabs of bear meat over the fire and cooked up fry bread, slathering it with the butter and honey the soldiers brought. It was a luxury the civilians didn't usually enjoy at camp.

The blacksmith shop at Fort Laramie was in one of the original adobe buildings down by the river. Mud was falling from its wall in chunks and the whole structure leaned downhill. The Adjutant escorted Lee to the shop and introduced him to Karl, a big Swede who worked the shop for the army, making money on the side fixing broken wagon wheels and shoeing horses for the emigrants passing through. It was a busy time of year for him and the big man wasn't happy about having to turn over the use of his shop to a youngster. Karl's face was as red as the iron he melted in his forge, and his unkempt beard was singed short and blackened in places. Lee looked over the tools; they were rusty and unoiled and the floor was cluttered with old horseshoes and wagon parts. It was nothing like his father's smithery. Lee apologized to the Blacksmith and cleaned off one of the work-tables. Despite himself, Karl was curious.

"You know what you're doing, Lad?" he asked.

"Yep," Lee answered.

"Where'd you learn how?"

"Picked it up, here and there."

"Oh yea, where bouts?"

"You don't have to watch me. Don't you got work to do?"

"Sure, I got work. But I best keep my eye on you."

Lee ignored the older man and bent to his task. He disassembled the Colonel's rifle, spreading the parts out on a cloth. He took the stock and sanded it till all the scratches and imperfections were gone, then took a cloth and a little linseed oil and worked it into the walnut until it glistened in the firelight. He would need to repeat the process a couple more times, but the improvement was noticeable. Karl stood looking over his shoulder.

"You have any bee's wax?" Lee asked.

"What for?" he asked.

"To polish the wood."

"No," he replied, scratching his beard. "None to speak of."

"Think you can get some?"

"Maybe," he said.

Lee lifted a piece of the firing mechanism and examined it in the light. Using a cloth dipped in solvent, he scrubbed the soot and powder residue away. He repeated the process with the other parts. He used a small file and reworked the metal surfaces, removing any scratches and imperfections and then, with a small pad that was part of his own gear, he polished the surfaces till they shined. By the time all the metal was cleaned and polished the sun had gone down.

"That's bout all I can do for now. I'll be back tomorrow. Nobody will touch this?"

"Nah," Karl said. "I'll lock the place up."

Lee nodded, though it was clear anyone could walk through the holes in the walls if he really wanted to.

Lee was up early the next day, walked up to the fort and made his way to the smithery. Karl was already there stoking the forge. Lee helped him load in as much wood as it would hold. He busied himself while the coals were building, all the time loading in more logs. Karl bitched at him for wasting wood but made no move to stop him. The pine and cottonwood they burned here didn't produce as hot a fire as the oak he burned back home, but it would have to do. It brought back good memories, stoking the fire and fanning it to an intense heat.

Lee laid the octagonal gun barrel down on the table surface and rolled it. He could tell by the way it wobbled where the warp lay. Using thick leather gloves, he buried the gun-barrel in the hot coals, turning it till it glowed red. He used metal tongs to pull it from the forge and laid it on the block, wielding a heavy iron mallet to pound it straight, then dipped it in water to cool and rolled it on the table again. He had to be careful not to affect the diameter of the bore anywhere along its length. It had to be hot enough to bend, yet still retain its shape. Lee repeated the process five more times until he was satisfied that the barrel was perfectly straight. He took one of the fifty caliber balls and dropped it through the barrel. It fell all the way through without binding. Then he went to work sanding and polishing the barrel, adjusting the sights and vigorously cleaning the bore. It took hours of hard physical work but, by the time he was done, the sun was setting and the rifle looked better than new. It was a thing of beauty, walnut and steel polished to perfection. The mechanism was smooth and the trigger required just the right amount of steady pressure to release. Karl had been watching him the whole time; if he had work to do, he seemed in no hurry to do it.

"Nice work, Lad." Karl said, smacking him on the back. Lee smiled happily.

"I forgot how much fun this is," Lee responded.

Lee packed up his gear as the Blacksmith watched.

"It's a gift you've got," Karl said.

"Thanks," Lee answered. He nodded at the rifle lying on the table. "Will you see that the Colonel gets that?"

"Don't you want to give it to him yourself?" Karl asked.

Lee shook his head, nodded his goodbye and headed back across the parade ground to their camp.

A short while later Karl knocked on the door of the Colonel's quarters. He was shown into the Colonel's study. The Blacksmith handed him the rifle.

"My God, I hardly recognize it," the Colonel said.

"That boy's an artist, I'll tell you," Karl said.

Cain rubbed his fingers along the stock, lifted the gun to his shoulder.

"Let's test it, shall we?"

They walked around to the side of the house and out into the yard. While Cain loaded the weapon, Karl walked out into the field and placed an empty bottle on the fencepost a hundred yards out. Cain took aim, pulled the trigger and a cloud of smoke belched from the gun. The bottle shattered into a hundred pieces.

The next morning, Jacob and Lee were sitting on their stumps drinking a cup of coffee when a corporal walked down the hill from the fort. A ripple of fear washed over Lee as the young man walked over to the fire. Jacob stood up in greeting.

"McCune?" the Corporal inquired.

"That's right," Jacob answered.

The Corporal handed McCune a slip of paper folded in half. Jacob opened it, glanced at it briefly but not knowing how to read, he handed it off to Lee.

"It's a dinner invitation," Lee said, horrified. "For the both of us."

"Don't say?"

"May I have the pleasure of your response?" the Corporal asked.

"Let's see," Jacob said, scratching his beard. "We got any previous engagements?"

"I sure hope so," Lee answered.

"We're much obliged. Tell the Colonel we'll be there."

"But we don't got any proper clothes," Lee protested.

The Corporal looked at their worn and greasy clothes and shook his head.

"I'll tell the Colonel you'll be there," he said, turning to go.

When the Corporal was gone, Lee turned to Jacob angrily.

"Why'd you say yes?"

"Couldn't rightly refuse without rousin suspicions," Jacob answered.

"Sure, you could, just send word you're feeling poorly."

"Stop fretting. It'll be good to set at a fine table and eat food that don't have dirt and ash stuck to it. Sides, you'll get another look at that purty daughter of his."

Instead of making him feel better, that only made matters worse. He'd be expected to talk to her and he couldn't, for the life of him, imagine what he'd have to say. He considered packing up his gear and heading out, but that'd be a cowardly thing to do. Damn, he swore to himself. I'm going to have to wash my clothes again.

The Commandant's quarters were in a two story wood frame building centered on the parade ground. It was the finest structure at the fort. The clapboard was neatly whitewashed, the windows had lace curtains and there were paintings and home-made quilts hung on the walls. The pine plank floor gleamed from constant polishing and the woodwork, while simple, reminded Lee of the fancy houses in St. Louis he used to admire. Lee and Jacob were shown into the parlor by an enlisted man in full dress uniform. Mrs. Audin, a portly woman married to one of the officers, came over and introduced herself.

"Good evening, Gentlemen. I've heard so much about the two of you. I'm delighted that you could come and join us."

"Don't see many good looking women folk like you in our line of work," Jacob said. "Wouldn't a missed it."

"Oh, Mr. McCune," she said, loving every word.

Lee had combed his curly blond hair and slicked it down as best he could. His boots didn't shine, but he'd cleaned most of the mud off them. He stood a good head taller than Jacob and towered over Mrs. Audin. His fair skin was burnt copper by the sun and his grey eyes were alive and piercing. He was a handsome young man; even Mrs. Audin looked twice.

Despite the fact that the fort stood on the very edge of the frontier, the furniture in the small house was of a quality Lee had seldom seen. The dining table was polished mahogany and set with beautiful, and Lee feared delicate, China. The carpets were deep red and richly embroidered. The flickering light from the glass candelabras cast a warm glow on the party. The Colonel was in fine spirits and seated his guests around him while the enlisted man and a young Indian girl served dinner. Captain Audin and his wife sat at the opposite end of the table. Cain introduced Ambrose Wheeler, a railroad man who was making an exploratory trip through the territory. The Colonel's daughter, Elizabeth, sat next to him. Her dress was sky blue and the prettiest thing Lee had ever seen. Her long dark hair flowed over her shoulders and framed her soft ivory skin. She wore a necklace of small white pearls that had belonged to her mother and they rested on the bare skin of her neck. It was clear that she was enjoying the excitement. Jacob, as usual, was the life of the party.

"What you doing up these parts, Wheeler?" he asked.

"The railroad's going to start back in once the war is over. I'm trying to identify promising spur lines where folks are likely to settle."

"Where you looking?"

"They say gold was discovered north of here."

"You don't want no railroad up there," Jacob said.

"And why is that?"

"Injuns'll run ram-shod over the whole bunch of you. And winter lasts half the year."

"Is that right?" Wheeler asked

"Sides," Jacob continued. "You'll bring in nothing but farmers and shopkeepers. Gonna spoil the whole damn country.

"I hardly think the railroad is going to avoid commerce simply because you don't want any company."

"Wouldn't pect em to. But you'd do better off down in Colorado. Nice and pretty, winter's not so long and the injuns are a mite more civilized."

"I appreciate the advice, Mr. McCune.

"Don't mention it."

"Lee," the Colonel interrupted. "I wanted to thank you for the fine job you did on the Hawken. I was quite impressed."

"You're welcome, sir. I enjoyed doing it."

"The Colonel showed me your work," Wheeler said. "Where'd you learn to do that?"

"I worked for a gun smith a while back. Took to it well enough."

"Why didn't you stick with it?" Wheeler asked. "It's a good trade."

"Got an itch to come west, then I ran into Mr. McCune here and we lit out."

"Where are you from, young man? Where are your folks?" Mrs. Audin asked.

"My folks are gone, Mamm. Just me now."

"I'm so sorry."

"It's been a while now."

"Where'd you say you were from?"

"Indiana. . . originally," he stammered.

"We had us a hell of a trip west," Jacob interrupted, trying to change the subject.

"I'm from Indiana," Wheeler said. "What part?"

Lee hesitated again, looking at Jacob. "Don't rightly know. My Pa moved around. We left when I was still pretty young."

"Surprised you didn't get drafted," Cain said, still in a friendly tone. Lee noticed Elizabeth looking at him, smiling, as though she knew how uncomfortable he was.

"I was gone long before the war started. Then I met up with Mr. McCune, here."

"Took him up into the mountains, trapping for a spell."

"That must have been exciting," Elizabeth said.

"My daughter loves the West," Cain said. "She'd have made quite a mountain man herself."

Luckily, dinner was served and Jacob steered the conversation to other subjects. He talked non-stop about his travels and his years in the mountains. Lee was still feeling anxious and awkward. He hadn't wanted to come. It had been a bad idea and he was angry with Jacob for talking him into it. But he had to admit that the food was good and the company friendly enough. After dinner, the Colonel moved the men into his study for a smoke, but Elizabeth suggested she show Lee the garden, her small swatch of paradise blooming in the arid soil. He was relieved to get away from the questions and good intentions.

A warm wind blew across the prairie and the moon illuminated the wild- flowers lining the path. It was a beautiful night and Elizabeth walked close beside him, so close he could smell her, fresh and natural, not like the girls in Belville. He was jumpy. And irritated at himself for being so.

"You did all this by yourself?" Lee asked

"Reminds me of home," Elizabeth nodded.

"Where's that?"

"Massachusetts."

"You miss it?"

"No. Not really. I like it here."

Suddenly, Lee had nothing to say, though he was content to walk along with her in silence.

"You looked a little uncomfortable in there," Elizabeth said. "Thought you might like some air,"

"Thanks," he said. "I don't take to cigars much."

"What do you take to?" she asked.

She had a way of looking at him, as though she'd known him all his life. Part of him didn't like it, but part of him did. And she didn't look away when he supposed she would, so he didn't know if he should look or turn, talk or wait for her to say something. It was unsettling and exciting at the same time. He finally stopped trying to figure it out and just kept walking.

"Oh, I don't know," he said. "I like to see new things. Wandering about, seeing the country, learning about new places and how people live. I like seeing how things work. I like putting things together. Kinda like taking em apart too, truth be told. Folks here are mighty nice."

Elizabeth stopped, turning to face him with that smile again. Her long black hair fanned out behind her, catching the moonlight, and she reached out to take his arm so that they were walking side by side.

"Papa wanted to ship me off to a boarding school, but I wouldn't hear of it. I put up quite a fuss."

"This ain't no place for a young girl," Lee said.

"Oh, Lee," she said, disappointment in her voice. "Of course, it is."

"I'm sorry."

"And anyway, I'm not a girl. I'm seventeen years old. Mama was already married by my age. I can take care of myself."

"No doubt," Lee laughed, enjoying the flush of anger he saw rise in her cheeks.

A wooden bench sat at the edge of the garden on the top of the hill overlooking the river. Lee asked if she would like to sit.

"Papa likes you. He says you saved his life."

"I don't know about that. It all happened so fast."

"Well, thank you, anyway," she said, her hand touching his shoulder, letting it rest there for a moment. She could sense his embarrassment but wanted him to know how grateful she was.

"What else?" she asked, changing the subject.

He sat quietly, unable to think beyond the feel of her bare arm against his and the smell of her perfume spinning his head.

"What?" he asked.

"Is there anything else you dream about?" she asked.

Lee leaned down and plucked a blade of grass and twirled it between his fingers.

"When you're moving about," he began. "You got plenty of time to daydream, but mostly all you think about is where you're heading, what's over the next hill, where you're gonna sleep and what you're gonna be able to scrounge up for supper. But you see lots of pretty country and you get to wondering what it'd be like to settle down. Might be nice to have a place of my own. A big spread, nestled in some little valley where I could work hard for myself and wouldn't have to worry about where my next meal was coming from. Does that make sense?"

"Yes. It does. Any idea where this valley might be?" Elizabeth asked.

"No. But I figure with all the wandering we're doing I'm bound to stumble onto it eventually"

"You better be careful. Pa says that men take to wandering sometimes and never do settle. Get to like the moving around and don't take to responsibility. Lots of men like that in the army."

"I guess," Lee said. "But I rekon it'd grow old afore too long."

"I suppose it would."

"I like to read about far off places. But I don't really expect to see them."

"You like to read?" Elizabeth asked, surprised.

"Sure. I don't read too good, but I can muscle through most things. Don't come across many books out here, though."

"You're just full of surprises, Mr. Grant."

Lee looked at her with a big stupid smile on his face and shrugged.

Too quickly, it was time to return to the house and Lee had to extricate himself from her arm. Elizabeth held on a few moments too long, enjoying his discomfiture. And then they were back inside and Elizabeth went over to speak to the others. Later in the evening the Colonel walked his guests to the door and out onto the front porch. He reached out and shook Lee's hand.

"You know, Lee. We could use a gunsmith with your abilities here at the fort. I'm sure Mr. McCune would miss your company, but it's a steady job with good wages, and it's a lot safer than wandering through Indian country right now."

Jacob looked at Lee. Lee looked the Colonel in the eye.

"Thank you, sir. I appreciate the offer. But I'm not ready to settle just yet."

"Well, think about it. Hate to lose a bright young man like yourself."

"Thank you. And thanks for dinner. Best I've had in a long while."

As they walked back to the camp, Jacob broke out laughing.

"What the hell you laughing about, you crazy old coot."

"World is looking mighty good to you, bout now. Ain't it?" Jake asked.

"What're you talking about?"

"You been bit hard. Don't blame you none, that Lizzie's a looker."

Lee tried to ignore him, but Jacob kept right on chuckling.

"She take a shine to you? You steal a kiss out there in the moonlight?"

"You've lost your mind."

"I'd a tried. Gotta be bold. There's a whole garrison stationed here and ain't but one pretty girl."

"We just talked. Civilized conversation. Nothing you'd know bout."

"I'll tell you, Boy. White women's too much trouble. Lots of sitting around and talking and headin home with a hard one and nothing to show for it. And likely shot dead or run outta town for the trouble. Just find yourself a fat little squaw and close your eyes. Pretend it's your Lizzie," Jacob laughed.

"You old Goat!" Lee said. "You'd jump a jack rabbit if you were fast enough to catch one."

"Don't knock it, Boy. Leastwise till ya tried it."

Chapter X

Gold

Immigration, which even the war has not stopped, will land upon our shores with hundreds of thousands more per year from overcrowded Europe.

I intend to point them to the gold and silver that waits for them in the West

Abraham Lincoln

Fort Laramie, Wyoming Territory

They repaired the new saddles as best they could and soaped them until the leather was as supple as it was ever going to be. Lee figured it was time to go. There was only one thing that could keep him at the fort, and he was smart enough to know that would only get him in trouble. Jacob, for his part, was reluctant to leave, but he understood why Lee needed to go. There was always the chance that somebody might recognize him. They said their goodbyes to the Colonel, but Lee couldn't get himself to call on Elizabeth for a proper goodbye. He meant to, but never quite got up the gut.

On the way out they stopped by the Indian encampment and Jacob went to look for White Hawk. They hadn't seen hide nor hair of him since the day they first arrived. He found him passed out, dead drunk, in the shade of a tree. Jacob shook hard but White Hawk could not be roused. Frustrated, Jake grabbed him and dragged him to his horse. This finally woke him, and he kicked and screamed and made such a ruckus that Jacob finally knocked him out cold with a hard punch to the jaw, threw him up onto the horse and tied him down. A few Indians began to gather and Lee thought there might be trouble, but Jacob took off before they could react. It's a hell of a way to start a trip, Lee thought.

They were a mile from the fort when White Hawk came to. Jacob untied him with a stern warning that he'd hit him again if he caused any more trouble. White Hawk swore below his breath. He looked like he'd aged ten years and was even thinner than when they had pulled into the fort. The three of them rode for a few hours along the North Platte, enjoying late spring along the Rocky Mountain front. They were following a trail ridden for centuries by the Shoshone and Arapaho but lately it was the Lakota who controlled it, robbing and killing travelers heading up to the mining camps in Montana. The Colonel had warned Lee to be careful; the army was no longer a presence in the area. They were on their own.

After two days they turned away from the Platte and followed the eastern foothills of the Big Horn Mountains. There was plenty of water and good grass and deer were plentiful in the bottomlands along the creeks. It felt good to be heading north. Jake said he'd always had luck heading north. But on the fourth day out they had to detour up into the mountains to avoid a band of Sioux camped along the Powder River and Lee knew it was a good thing they hadn't been spotted. With the tribes as militant as they were, they could expect no mercy if they were caught. This made for slow going. They rode up past the Big Horn River, finally crossing into Montana Territory along the Bozeman Pass into the Yellowstone River valley.

Jacob knew the country well. Every mile meant another story, an Indian fight or bear kill, or a winter's camp with a string of rich plews. The land was more beautiful than any Lee had seen before. Fast moving rivers flowed down out of the mountains, cutting serpentine swathes through the thick green grass. Wildflowers covered the hillsides with purple, gold and crimson. Broad stands of timber rose along the foothills. The rolling grasslands stretched as far as the eye could see until they dissolved into a jagged line of snowcapped mountains on the horizon. Lee was so busy looking around that he had trouble keeping his attention on the trail. Jacob was not surprised by his young partner's reaction. He told White Hawk to ride ahead and keep his eyes open.

"Told you it were purty," Jacob said.

"You were right," Lee agreed.

Black Hills, Montana Territory

Virginia City was a hardscrabble mining town where a little gold made a big difference. It took them three weeks to get there from Fort Laramie, skirting war parties most of the way. It was one of the few times Jacob was happy there were only three of them; it made it easier to stay hidden and slip unnoticed through the country. As they rode into town, Lee found it hard to imagine that so many men had made it into the Black Hills without losing their hair. This was land that still belonged to the Bannocks and the Blackfoot. A year ago, it was open country, empty as a beggar's bowl, nothing but green fields and a slow-moving creek. Now there was a main street with shops and saloons, though most consisted of nothing more than a rough framed wall with a lean-to roof of stretched canvas. They were doing a brisk business, nonetheless.

The hillsides along both sides of the stream were dotted with tents and the smoke from camp-fires settled along the valley floor like morning fog. There were men working the creek up and down stream and the pungent smell of raw sewage hung in the air. They quickly got the lay of the land. Jacob bought a shot of whiskey at a saloon consisting of nothing more than a wood plank laid across two sawhorses. There was whiskey and only whiskey and it was poured from a brown jug into a tin cup. White Hawk tried to saddle up to the bar but got such a look from Jake that the usually fearless Indian stepped away. They decided to set camp outside of town where they could find fresh water and a have little privacy. The next day, they nailed together four walls using a crude framework of scavenged lumber, stretching their tarpaulin tightly across it with a lodge-pole lifting it in the center so it'd shed water. Lee made low cots out of saplings and spread the blankets on top. It was pretty comfortable, except when it was too hot or too cold, which was most of the time. Of course, White Hawk refused to enter. He slept outside on the ground in front of the fire, unless it was raining. Only then would he come inside, grumbling under his breath about the smell.

Lee was excited about the possibilities. All the talk was of men who had panned a fortune out of the gulch. It seemed so easy; he was about to be rich. He considered it a thing already accomplished. After a couple of days Lee met a miner who was willing to sell him a claim to fifty yards along Alder Creek for one hundred dollars. Lee considered it a bargain.

"I don't care if it costs ten cents. I ain't panning for gold," Jacob announced. "I spent years getting my boots wet and my fingers froze trapping beaver, and I sure as hell won't do it for dirt."

Lee had the money he'd saved from his winter's work at the Double Eagle, and he assumed Jake would go in halves with him. After all, they were partners, weren't they?

"Well, if you won't pan, at least lend me the money," Lee asked.

"I don't got that much money. I had expenses."

"Yeah, whores and whiskey. How much you got left?"

"Thirty something. And I need to keep something in reserve for freshments. Till you strike it rich," Jacob insisted.

Lee went back with what money he had and dickered, refusing to let the man walk away, though several times he tried. Lee badgered him till the deal was done. He knew he'd made a good bargain, even though it left him without a penny in his pocket and they still needed a shovel and a couple of pans to work the claim. Lee and White Hawk rode up into the mountains and shot a bull elk to sell for meat. It fetched a good price. Like most boom towns, the cost of basic necessities in Virginia City was highly inflated. Things like bread and eggs cost ten times what they did in St. Louis, and dry goods such as clothes and tools were either impossible to find or exorbitantly expensive.

Lee woke up early the next morning and shook White Hawk out of his slumber. White Hawk would have ignored the summons but he was curious to see what all this business was about. They walked to the claim in the dim light of morning and laid their tools against the bank. Lee had only a general idea what placer mining was all about. He'd spent part of yesterday afternoon watching the other miners and asked plenty of questions but, till today, he hadn't actually tried it himself. The creek was still muddy from recent rain and the water was cold. Lee told White Hawk to watch, stepped into the creek up to his ankles and scooped up a pan full of gravel. He swooshed it around in the water till the bigger rocks were washed away, then continued till there was nothing left in the pan. White Hawk thought the boy had completely lost his mind.

Lee dug in again, sluiced through another pan and had the same result. He tried to wave White Hawk into the water, but the Absaroka shook his head and sat down on the bank, watching with a bored expression. After an hour, Lee's feet were numb and his back ached, but when he sifted through the next pan a few grains glittered in the sunlight. Lee shouted and carried them over to White Hawk. There was gold! And he had found it.

White Hawk knew the White men were crazy for the worthless yellow metal, but he had never seen the sickness manifest itself in person. He had heard that they would readily kill each other for just the smallest amounts of it. Judging by Lee's reaction, he could see that it was true.

When he was younger, White Hawk had found gold in the stream beds near his village. It made a pretty pebble but you couldn't eat it and it was too soft to make a good knife. Lee opened the small jar he'd brought along, deposited the gold and stashed it in his pack.

"We're gonna be rich," he told White Hawk.

"Bullshit," White Hawk said. Jacob had been teaching him English.

Annoyed by White Hawk's lack of enthusiasm, Lee leaned over and lifted the Indian right off the ground. White Hawk didn't weigh much, but it was like lifting aan arm-full of sidewinders. He kicked and squirmed and would have bit Lee's ear off if he could have reached it. Lee carried him a few steps into the stream and dropped him in the water.

"Crazy fool," White Hawk said in his own language.

"Rich!" Lee said again, cupping his hands together to signify plenty, and then dipping them into the water to splash White Hawk in the face. He walked back to shore and threw White Hawk a pan.

White Hawk caught the pan and reluctantly dug it into the gravel, sluicing away rock the way Lee had. He went through his first pan with no results. He liked the young White boy, but he often acted crazy.

"Bullshit," he said again.

By the end of the day Lee's little jar held a few grains of gold. They made their way back to camp, cold, wet and tired but Lee, at least, had a bounce in his step. He couldn't wait to tell Jacob that they'd found gold. True, it wasn't much to show for a long day of backbreaking work, but it was a start. Jacob had a fire going and was cooking a couple of rabbits he'd trapped with a wire.

"Back from the mines," he greeted.

"Bullshit," White Hawk repeated.

"I agree completely," Jacob said, puffing on his pipe.

"Won't think so once I start bringing in more of this" Lee said, holding the jar up.

"I'll be damned," he said. "You got some."

"We're getting the hang of it," Lee said. "It'll go faster if you lend a hand."

"That ain't gonna happen. But you keep at it. Hard work's its own reward."

"Then maybe you can take this into town tomorrow, see what it comes to." Lee said, handing him the jar.

"Be happy to," Jacob said.

The next day Lee was up early and dragged White Hawk back down to the claim. Lee searched for likely places. He overturned rocks, hoping to uncover a nugget that'd been lying there since the ice age. A ton of gravel made its way into his pan and a ton was washed away. They found gold, but it amounted to less than he'd hoped for, less than they'd found the day before. By the time they dragged themselves back to camp it was getting dark. They'd worked more than twelve hours in the creek; though White Hawk was prone to unscheduled breaks and an afternoon nap. Lee didn't really mind. It was nice having company. And White Hawk was learning new words and loved using them, though many were unspeakable.

When they got back, Jacob was nowhere to be seen. There was no fire and no food. White Hawk quickly built a fire while Lee pulled some dried beans and jerky out of the pack. It was well past dark when they heard a horse coming up the trail and the sound of Jacob whistling a tune. Lee could tell he had a good head on.

"Bout time. Old Man," Lee said. "We was hoping you'd have supper on by the time we got back."

"I ain't your squaw," he said, flopping down next to the fire.

"Did you get the gold assayed?" Lee said.

"Sure did. Come to forty dollars," Jacob said.

"Where's the money?"

Jacob pulled out a leather sack and dumped a handful a coins into Lee's outstretched hand. Lee counted the money.

"There's only twenty two dollars here," he said.

"I was in town all god damn day. You know what they want for a whiskey round here?"

"Jesus, we ain't gonna get nowhere if you go drinkin all the profits."

"Why you in such a rush? You been burning it from both ends ever since we got here," Jacob said.

"No, I ain't."

Jacob said something in Absaroka to White Hawk and the Indian nodded his head and laughed.

"That ain't fair," Lee complained.

"Bullshit," White Hawk replied.

By 1863, Henry Plummer had had enough of the gold business. He'd gone to California in the big rush of forty-nine and had managed to strike it rich, only to run afoul of the law not once, but three times. The first time, he was sentenced to ten years in prison for shooting and killing a jealous husband. Only a last-minute pardon by the governor got him off. He certainly had winning ways with the ladies, though it usually caused him grief. And he was good with a gun, which proved handy when husbands and sheriffs came poking around. Two more men soon lay dead by his hand and Plummer figured it was time to give up the gold business and head back to the coast of Maine from which he hailed.

But fate has fickle ways. He was making his way across the Rockies, trying to reach Fort Benton, where he planned to catch a steamer down the Missouri. News reached him that gold had been discovered in Montana. Men flooded in. Some from the already panned out fields in California, some from the east and many from the war-ravaged remains of the Confederacy. The irony could not escape a man like Plummer. It was like fishing all day without a nibble only to have a twenty pound trout jump into your boat as you rowed home.

The town of Virginia City had risen from nothing to become one of the biggest towns west of the Mississippi. To Plummer, it was a dream come true. Gold was being hauled out of the rivers by greenhorns and bumpkins and there were no authorities to put a damper on his activities. He quickly staked a few claims, found men to work them and began planning his empire. Mining itself was too much work and there were better ways to use his talents. He bought into a hotel and a saloon and offered his services to the miners and shopkeepers, who elected him sheriff. It was a rough and dangerous town, isolated from the rest of the country by mountains, snow and hostile Indians. Even reaping the benefits of this new-found wealth meant shipping the gold two hundred and fifty miles up to Fort Benton for transport down the Missouri to St. Louis. Plummer was in charge of organizing the armed transport and it was a perilous business; not only were the Bannock and Blackfoot Indians likely to attack anyone crossing their territory but outlaws rode the trail looking to highjack the shipments. After a couple of the couriers were killed, it became increasingly difficult to fill the job. There were better opportunities. After all, there was gold in the rivers, and no one was shooting at you.

It was two o'clock in the afternoon when Jacob rode into town. His usual time. The Golden Goose, a new hotel and saloon, had sprung up almost overnight. Now the prospectors had someplace they could spend their money. And Plummer made sure they had a little musical accompaniment and a painted lady or two to help them. But at this hour of the afternoon the town was quiet; most of the men were still out working their claims. Jake figured he could get a drink and have the ladies all to himself for at least an hour or so, but when he stepped out of the bright sunlight into the saloon he saw all three of the ladies seated at a card table laughing and talking to a tall, good looking gentleman with dark hair, deep set eyes and a sternly chiseled jaw. Jacob, never one to shrink away from sociability, walked right over.

"It's nice to see the town ain't completely gone over to sweat and toil," he said. "I'm Jake McCune. And if these gals r' botherin you, I can run one or two of em off."

The stranger laughed and kicked out a chair out for Jacob to sit on.

"They are bothersome," he said, extending his hand. "The name's Henry Plummer."

"I heard of you. You're what passes for the law in these parts," Jake said. "Damn shame. Once the law takes root all the color drains from a town."

"I whole-heartedly agree," Plummer said. "Girls, get Mr. McCune here a drink.

"I hope you ain't aiming to shut this place down," Jake said. "It just opened."

"God, no. I own it."

"Good," Jake nodded. "Saloon's an important socializer for a town. Kinda a like a church."

"Great minds think alike, Mr. McCune. I take it you don't cotton to panning for gold?"

"That's young men's work. And a fool's to boot. Money ain't worth having if'n ya got to work that hard to get it."

"Then what brings you to these parts."

"Use to trap beaver in these mountains. Hunted every peak and valley between here and Santa Fe. Now I'm just enjoying the days. Something will turn up."

A bottle of whiskey appeared and glasses were poured. Jake flirted with the ladies. Plummer kept his hands moving, usually somewhere they didn't belong. After a while, miners began to drift in for a drink, and then a few of the shopkeepers and tradesmen.

Plummer made a point of saying hello to everyone he knew and introduced himself to those he didn't.

"Hard work or not. A lot of gold's been dug out of the creeks hereabouts," Plummer said.

"I ain't agin it on principle," Jacob said. "Just ain't for me."

"Well, maybe I got something that might prove more to your liking."

"What would that be?"

"You might have heard we lost our last transport to Fort Benton."

"And the one afore that."

"That's right. Maybe a man like you'd have better luck."

"Sounds like suicide, to me," Jacob said.

"We were a little too loose with the information last time. Nobody's gonna know about the next one. Not when it's going or who's taking it. And there'll be plenty of guns along this time. That's where you come in."

"I don't know. I'd hate to deprive these ladies of my company."

"It's just a week. And it pays a hundred dollars."

"Jesus," Jacob swore.

"I thought that'd peak your interest."

While Jacob was drinking in the saloon, Lee was down in the creek working his claim. The work was back breaking and monotonous, but at least it was his own. Ever since he'd told Elizabeth about his dream of having his own ranch, he'd grown impatient to make it happen. Mining gold was a means to that end, a way of building his fortune. And he was prepared to build it one grain at a time, if he had to. The work went easier if he was daydreaming about the ranch, what it would look like and how he'd work it; no detail was too small to ponder.

Lee learned all he needed to know about panning for gold. He diagramed his claim and set about systematically working every inch of it, marking his progress so he never panned the same patch twice. Some days he got next to nothing, but on other days he was lucky. He stashed away every grain, every ounce, and kept on digging. Every pan brought him a little closer to his dream. And he stopped passing it on to Jacob for safekeeping.

He got to know the other miners, his neighbors along Alder Creek. It was hard not to. You could shout downstream or up to the next claim to pass the time of day. White Hawk hadn't grown any more industrious as the weeks passed, but he came out every day. He'd watch for a while, sleep, and then walk over to one of the other claims. The prospectors took to him right off. They enjoyed hearing him cuss and taught him new filth, which White Hawk would parrot with great acuity and enthusiasm. His vocabulary was the foulest in the territory, which tickled the miners no end. White Hawk didn't mind the little gulch, even if it was filled with White men. He thought it comical how they'd stand in the water all day for a few grains of sand. But he didn't really trust them. He figured he needed to keep his eye on the boy. Lee was a hard worker, but not especially bright, he thought.

What the prospectors were not happy about were the thefts and lawlessness that was spreading through the Black Hills. A few of the miners had turned up dead, their gold missing and not a clue left behind. Then the shipments to Fort Benton were robbed and everybody was on edge. The miners were a rough bunch. They'd break their backs to help a friend, but working a claim was a paranoid business. The thought of losing all they'd worked for at the point of some outlaw's gun spurred them to action. They banded together to form a vigilance committee to look after their interests. For a while, it kept claim jumping and fights to a minimum. Lee was proud when they asked him to join; it was a measure of the respect in which he was held, despite that fact that he was the youngest among them.

Moses McCain was a man with no luck. He worked a piece of creek just west of town but despite long days and a bent back he hadn't pulled more than a few dollars' worth of gold out in weeks. They caught him moving boundary stakes one night when he thought everyone was asleep. There was no trial or debate. He was strung up on the spot from one of the big alders that grew along the creek. The Sheriff came by when McCain was already swinging, took one look at him hanging from the tree and walked back to the Golden Goose for a drink.

When Lee and White Hawk walked down from their camp the next morning, Moses was still swinging in the breeze. Lee heard the whole story before he was halfway to his claim. White Hawk looked up at the body. The man had crapped and pissed himself and the smell was ripe.

Chapter XI

JUSTICE

No hanging judge is worse than a mob demanding justice.

Roy Bean

Black Hills, Montana Territory

The cold woke him up. Lee was shivering and pulled the buffalo robe tighter around him. A coat of frost lay atop the grass. He forced himself out of bed and got the coffee going, preparing for another day's work at the claim. Jacob stumbled out of bed, pulled a blanket around his shoulders and came over to the fire to warm up.

"I'm too old for chill like this," he said.

"I'll say," Lee agreed. "It's June, for goodness sake.

"Weather's changeable, up north."

"When's the snow begin to fall in these mountains?" Lee asked.

"Could be this afternoon.

"No. I mean for real."

"I've seen it. But usually, it's October afore it falls steady."

"I hope it holds off," Lee said.

White Hawk sat facing them. "Big Snow, this winter," he said. His English was improving every day.

158

"How can you tell?" Lee asked.

White Hawk shrugged. "Big snow," he repeated.

"Got myself a job." Jacob announced.

"Job?"

"That's right. Struck up a quaintaince with the Sheriff. Gent name a Plummer, up from California."

"What kinda job?"

"Riding shotgun on the gold shipment to Fort Benton."

"I hope you're joshing. Last two shipments got highjacked. All the guards were killed."

"I knows it. But this time we'll have plenty of fire. Sides, it pays a hunert dollars."

"That's something. But since when do you care a hoot about money?"

"Oh, I like money well enuf. Just don't like working so hard to get it."

"Seems risky."

"That's why it pays a hunert dollars."

A week later Plummer sent word that Jacob was to come by the hotel. When he arrived, Plummer told him the shipment was going out that night and that they were to rendezvous by the thunder struck cottonwood east of town at midnight. Jacob packed his saddle bag and cleaned his rifle. At midnight he rode down the hill and spotted Plummer waiting with three other men. Plummer introduced everybody.

"Let's keep this short. This here's Martin," he said, nodding towards a burly man with a dark beard and the worn buckskins of a plains hand. "He's in charge. That's Bobby settin next to him, and this here's Joe Willins.

"Howdy," Jacob nodded, taking them in and measuring them up.

"This here's Jake," Plummer continued. "He's been all through these mountains."

The men nodded. None of the men knew each other, and the looks that passed between them were measured and wary. Each wondered if the other was someone he could trust. But there was no telling just by the way a man looked. They had no choice but to trust in the Sherriff and hope that he'd chosen well.

"Try to avoid folks. Don't stop to pass the time a day. If you see someone coming, get off the trail and lay low till they pass."

"Got it," Martin said.

"Don't drift. I don't gotta tell you what happened to the others."

Martin nodded. He looked over at the men riding with him to make sure they got the message. Jake stared back at him. He thought this Martin looked capable. He had a steady look to him. The others, he wasn't so sure about. Bobby was just a boy, not much older than Lee, eager enough but a mite green. Joe Willins sat his horse like a scarecrow. He couldn't weigh more than a sack of grain and seemed a bit jumpy. It wasn't the formidable posse he thought it would be. Jake supposed he should have checked into things more thoroughly, but it was too late to do anything about it now. Martin had an eight-gauge slid into his scabbard, Jake had his rifle and the others were sporting six guns.

The Sheriff headed back toward town and the men started away. It was a dark night with a heavy cloud cover hanging low over the hills. It was difficult to follow the trail, especially when it wove through the trees and they could see no further than the man in front of them. Jacob supposed that was a good thing; they wouldn't be easily spotted. The trail was so narrow they had to ride single file with Martin out front, trying to scout the trail ahead and keep an eye out for trouble. He was worried. He didn't know the men he was riding with and didn't fancy men he didn't know riding at his back. But he couldn't trust them to pick out the trail either. Once they got into more open country he could relax. Till then he'd have to trust stealth and the darkness to protect them. Two hours later they began to descend a line of rocky switchbacks that wound down out of the timber. To one side was a sheer drop of more than a hundred feet. The footing was treacherous and the horses balky.

The first blast caught Martin in the chest and he was blown off his horse, falling over the cliff onto the rocks below. The others barely had time to draw their guns before bullets were flying around them. They were caught in a cross-fire and could see nothing but muzzle flash and smoke. Joe was hit twice but was still firing his pistol blindly toward the trees. Jacob heard the bullets whizzing by and leaned into his pony's neck for cover. He knew it was only a matter of time till he was hit. He tried to turn his horse around but quickly realized there wasn't room on the narrow trail. He had just swung his rifle toward a muzzle flash when his pony was hit. The horse's legs buckled and Jacob was pitched forward, tumbling blindly down the trail. His rifle flew out of his hand and he hit the ground hard and rolled forward. He was trying to stop himself when everything went black.

Fort Laramie, Wyoming Territory

When Elizabeth found out that Lee had left without saying goodbye she was surprised. She was surprised that he hadn't taken the time. She was surprised that he didn't want to see her one last time. But she was mostly surprised that she cared so much. There had never been any boys in her life. Sure, there had been plenty of young men who came to call back home in Massachusetts, and there were plenty still who looked at her with that covetousness she'd come to recognize, but there were none she'd ever taken any interest in. She hadn't even realized that she was interested, until he left.

They had only seen each other a couple of times. Lee was shy and bold at the same time. There weren't many people Elizabeth could talk to out here on the frontier. Maybe that was all it came to. But she didn't think so. He was handsome, she had to admit. And there was something about his eyes.

Ever since the Kiowa woman had died, Elizabeth felt a little lost. Nothing else had brought home to her the random cruelty of life on the frontier. Elizabeth hadn't really known her, and they weren't able to communicate in words, but she had been with her in those last weeks as she willed herself to die. There was no other way to describe it. She accepted, even welcomed, her own death in a way Elizabeth could not grasp. Her father had finally received a report a few weeks after she'd been buried.

Her name was Clara Adkins. Clara. It seemed like such a plain and simple name. She'd been captured by the Comanche when she was eight years old and her parents had been killed. The Adkins had staked out a little farm along the Arkansas in 'forty three'. It was dangerous territory and they had no business being there. After she was taken, there had been an uproar. It was a story repeated up and down the frontier. The Comanche usually killed children too small to travel or be useful, but they kept some and raised them as their own. Others they sold to the half breed Vaqueros who traded with them. Clara had been sold north. Who knew how many times she'd been sold and resold till she found a home with the Kiowa, who did not hold her as a slave but embraced her as a daughter, a wife and a mother. When Captain Scott took her in the raid, she'd been married for many years to a Kiowa warrior named Dark Sky, who loved her despite her tainted blood. She had a strong young boy of eight who was already too big to sleep with his mother and a little girl. Willow was five years old and had straight black hair like her father but had her mother's light blue eyes. All the old women said she would be a great beauty when she came of age and Clara loved her with all her heart. Once she was captured, and it became clear that they wouldn't let her go, the thought of never seeing her children again was too painful to endure. No one back east had been looking for her. No one but the Kiowa loved her.

Elizabeth kept busy. There was always plenty to do at the Fort. Every day new travelers arrived, and they all had their own troubles and stories to tell. Her father was a busy man. Many times, Elizabeth would be called upon to greet the emigrants and pass messages back to the Colonel. They were families, for the most part, folks just looking to make a new start, to find a place where life might be a little better. Life in the West wouldn't be easy for them; Elizabeth had learned enough to be certain of that. But she hoped they'd find part of what they were looking for.

Some were saying that the war would soon be over. The South was rapidly running out of the resources it needed to survive. Elizabeth wasn't sure how this would affect their lives. People would be moving. The railroad line between the coasts would be starting up again. There was so much land that they couldn't possibly fill it all up, but things were bound to be different.

Living on the frontier had forced her to grow up. She could not simply bury her nose in a book or busy herself in the garden. Men died from simple things out here, women too. A horse could step in a prairie dog hole and throw its rider. You could stumble across a rattlesnake. Even a small splinter could turn septic and poison your blood. This was no place for the squeamish. There were cures to be studied, torn flesh to be sewn and broken limbs to be set. There were babies to be born and the dead to be buried. It was frightening, this life. But it was exciting too.

She got to thinking, sometimes, about what Lee had said; about how he wanted a place of his own, a place he could build up with his own hands, where he could be of use to his neighbors and play a part in the goings on. She'd never thought of such things before. In his simple way, he had been quite eloquent. She might want those things too, someday, if the right man came along. It was strange, thinking she'd be quit of her father and would live with another man. What would that be like? She knew of men who beat their wives and drank themselves senseless. But she had better sense than to choose a man like that, didn't she? How could you really know a man's heart? Maybe you couldn't, but she would know what was important. And then she thought about Lee heading out without even saying goodbye and she wasn't so sure.

Black Hills, Montana Territory

When he came to it was still dark, but he lifted himself onto one elbow and saw the dawn rising on the eastern horizon. Jacob tried to remember where he was and what had happened. The pounding in his head was so intense that he figured his skull was split. He brought his hand up to check. There was a deep gash along the side of his head and blood had flowed down his neck and soaked his shirt. He tried to push himself up, but his leg collapsed beneath him. Broken, he thought.

He reached down to see if he could feel the break, managed to get to one knee and pushed himself up by grabbing the rocks. His leg wasn't broken, but he'd wrenched his knee and his ankle was so sprained he could feel the swell against the side of his boot. His horse lay a few yards away, twisted and rigid in death. The bodies of the other riders were sprawled along the trail. Bobby had been shot at least three times and his eyes were cast up in surprise. Joe Mullins lay crushed under the massive weight of his horse and Martin lay sprawled on the rocks below, his legs and neck unnaturally askew. There was nothing Jake could do for Joe; it would take three men to roll the dead horse off him; and with his injured leg going after Martin was out of the question. But he pulled Bobby off the trail and settled the body as best he could, covering the boy's face with his jacket. He pulled a canteen out of Joe's saddle bag and took a drink, then poured a little of it onto the gash at his skull, wincing with the pain. He gathered himself a bit and decided he better look for his rifle. He found it in the bushes beside the trail. It was banged up but serviceable, and he reached into his pocket to make sure he still had powder and balls. Then he stood there for a moment wondering what to do.

It was brazened, a highjack so close to town. He knew the only reason he was still alive was that they took him for dead. He found a dead limb and wrapped his jacket around the top to make a crutch, then tested his weight against it. The sun had fully risen by the time Jacob started the long walk back to town and every step he took hurt like hell.

It was past noon by the time he made it back. A few tradesmen saw him stumbling into town and rushed over to help. He asked to be taken to the Sheriff and someone said they'd seen him in the saloon. When they came in through the doors Plummer turned, took one look at Jacob and told the men to sit him in a chair.

"What the hell happened?" Plummer asked.

"Hit us," Jake said.

"Where are the others?"

"Slaughtered."

"Did you see who it was?"

"No, it were pitch dark. We were in close timber. Perfect bushwack."

"How'd you get away?"

"My horse got kilt and I hit the ground hard." He turned to show them the side of his head. "Musta taken me for dead."

Plummer stood over the old man and looked down at him. His expression conveyed neither surprise nor anger, only the look of a man working things out.

Lee was working the claim when one of the miners came down and told him McCune was in jail. Lee was ready for just about anything with Jake, but this was surprising. Lee threw down his tools and headed up the hill.

The jail was nothing more than two rooms, a back room without windows for the prisoners and a small office with a single window and the only door. Refinements like iron bars would have to come later. When Lee arrived, there were already fifteen to twenty people confronting the Sheriff. Tempers were raw. Sheriff Plummer stood out on the stoop trying to calm everybody down. Lee knew most of the miners by sight and pushed his way forward.

"Is it true you've arrested Jake McCune?" he asked.

"That's right. What's it to you?" Plummer said with a menacing look.

"We're partners. Been travelin together."

"Partners?"

"Why was he arrested?"

"The gold shipment got highjacked. I suspect he's involved."

"That's ridiculous. He was hired to protect it."

"That's right, along with three others. McCune's the only one left alive."

When the crowd heard this, they began to shout at once, surging forward. Plummer stopped them with a scowl and one hand on his pistol.

"Sheriff. Jake's may be a scoundrel and a drunkard but he ain't no thief."

"What's your name, boy?" Plummer asked, staring him down.

"Grant. I got a stake along the creek."

"And where were you last night?" Plummer asked.

"Ah, come on Sheriff. The boy's alright," One of the miners shouted out.

"Turn McCune over to us," Another called.

"I ain't turning nobody over," Plummer barked.

"Can I see him?" Lee asked.

"No," Plummer said coolly.

"What are you planning to do with him?" Lee asked.

"Right now, I'm just trying to figure this out. Maybe after a night or two in jail he'll want to talk. If not, I s'pose I'll try to find a judge so he can be tried and hung legal."

"You can't do that. He's innocent and you know it."

Plummer's look was so threatening that Lee took pause. The Sheriff's hand had never left his holster. Lee knew the man had a reputation as an unhesitant killer. Lee was a good shot with a rifle, but he was no gunfighter. He had never faced a man down and, even if he did and managed to survive, there was still the mob.

"I'm holding you responsible," Lee said, not backing down. "Don't do nothing hasty. I'm gonna find us a lawyer."

"I don't know where you'd find a lawyer round here, but you better hurry."

"You're the Sheriff, not the judge" Lee said.

"Round here, might amount to the same thing," Plummer said and went inside, closing the door behind him.

As soon as the Sheriff left, the miners crowded around Lee.

"How well you know McCune?" Flint McCullough asked.

"He wouldn't do something like this."

"It's a lot of gold"

"He doesn't care about money, cept to have some in his pocket for a drink now and then."

"You could buy a lot of whiskey with that much gold."

"We worked hard for that money. If he stole it, we want a chance to squeeze out of him where it's hid.

"It's not him, I tell you. And the more time you waste with him the less you'll have to catch the real thieves."

"Seems kinda suspicious. Him being the only one left alive," another said.

"That's right. Can't never really trust nobody," said McCullough. "Not with gold."

When Lee got back to his camp he told White Hawk the whole story. It was testing the limits of his communication skills, but White Hawk got the gist. Their friend was in trouble and it would take some doing to figure a way out. Lee had no idea if there was a judge or lawyer anywhere in the territory and wasn't sure it would do any good even if he found one. The Vigilance Committee seldom waited for such things, and the Sheriff didn't seem inclined to stand in their way. One thing was for certain; Lee wouldn't stand idle while they lynched his friend. He'd gone along when they arrested his father, thinking his own show of loyalty would give testimony to his father's innocence. His Pa died in a cold Union prison. He wouldn't let that happen again. He went into the shack and pulled his Spencer from its scabbard.

It was well past midnight when Plummer left the saloon. He had both his pistols loaded and wore a dark coat and a black hat. The street was deserted and only the dying embers of campfires glowed dimly down along the creek. He walked around back and saddled his horse, swung up into the saddle and rode slowly out of town down the western road. A few hundred yards out, he stopped and turned, checking to see if anyone was following him. He had every reason to believe he was alone, but he wasn't taking any chances.

White Hawk had been waiting in the brush behind the hotel since dark. His face and body were blackened with charcoal and mud. Men had walked right by and not suspected a thing. A good horse thief could lie motionless for hours, and White Hawk was one of the best. Even on foot White Hawk had no trouble keeping up with the Sheriff, who kept his horse at a steady but quiet walk. A half hour out of town Plummer turned off the road and rode into the hills. There was no tree cover, but White Hawk kept low and was all but invisible in the tall grass.

The Sheriff eased his horse down into a grove of cottonwoods crowding the banks of a slow-moving stream. He rode for another twenty minutes and then stopped and tied his horse to a low hanging limb, pulled his rifle and continued walking along the creek bed. White Hawk followed silently. He could see the glow of a fire up ahead but, now that Plummer was on foot, he had to drop back to remain unseen. Suddenly he heard loud voices and he hurried forward. Two men were seated around the fire and Plummer had his rifle drawn on them. One of them tried to say something but Plummer shouted him down. He was angry about something, and White Hawk could hear the fear in the other men's voices. He ducked behind the trees, trying to get closer, hoping he might understand a few words of what was said, but while he was moving into position two shots rang out. By the time he found a vantage point, he saw that the two men were dead. Plummer calmly walked over to their saddle bags and pulled out a canvas sack, opening it to check the contents. He untied the men's horses and whipped them up into the hills, then turned and walked back to where he'd tied his horse. He loaded the sack into his saddle bag and headed back the way he had come. White Hawk waited till the Sheriff was well ahead and then turned and followed him back.

Plummer rode up to the jail, woke the watchman who had fallen asleep in his chair, and sent him home. White Hawk climbed up into the branches of a willow that grew next to the building and watched through the small window as the Sheriff slid the desk out of the way and pried up a plank of pine flooring that was fitted loosely beneath it. He deposited the sack under the floor, replaced the plank and pushed the desk back into position. Plummer then took off his boots and coat and lay out on the cot.

Lee was shaken out of a sound sleep. An Indian in jet black war paint stood over his bed. It took only a few seconds to realize that it was only White Hawk, but much longer to still his racing heart.

"Jesus. You scared the tar outta me. Why you all blacked up."

"Sheriff steal gold," White Hawk said.

"What?" Lee asked. "Are you sure?"

"I follow. Meet two men. Kill."

"Fight?"

"No fight. Just kill," White Hawk said.

White Hawk tried to tell Lee about how he'd followed Plummer back to the jail. The telling wasn't easy. There were nuances beyond his ability to communicate, but eventually Lee got the story. White Hawk went to clean himself up while Lee tried to figure out what to do. Plummer was not a man to be trifled with; whatever accusation Lee made had better stick. As the hours till dawn ticked away, he formed a plan. At first light he threw on his clothes, pulled on his boots, grabbed the Spencer and walked into town.

Most of the miners were already down at the creek setting up their equipment. Lee avoided the main street and instead followed the creek bed toward town, stopping at every claim along the way and asking whoever was there to follow him. Given the events of the previous day, they were all too willing to hear what he had to say. By the time he'd gotten abreast of the jail there were nearly fifty men gathered around.

"What's up?" one of them asked. "You got news?"

"I do," Lee answered.

"What'd you find out?"

"White Hawk found out what happened to our gold."

The men gathered closer, so they could hear. "Where is it?"

"Plummer's got it. He left town in the middle of the night for a rendezvous. Met up with two of them road agents. Plummer shot em both in cold blood, took the gold and hid it. White Hawk saw the whole thing, says he knows where it is."

"Where?" they asked.

"Stashed in the jailhouse."

"That son of a bitch!"

"Question is, what do we do?" Lee asked.

"There's no question," Flint McCullough said. "We go and get it."

Those who didn't already have them went back and got their side arms. Those who didn't have guns grabbed a shovel or pick. Within minutes they were heading up the hill towards the jail. It was still early. Only a few of the shops were open. The jail sat on the north side of town above the creek and the Sheriff's horse was still tied to the rail out front. Without hesitating the miners stormed up to the steps and rushed in through the door. Plummer had been sound asleep, but he bolted right up when the miners burst in.

"What's going on?" Plummer asked, with a quick sidelong glance to his rifle, still lying on his desk on the other side of the room.

McCullough moved over to the desk and grabbed the rifle. Plummer stood and confronted the mob. Lee and White Hawk had pushed into the room, which was rapidly filling up with men; more spilled into the street outside.

"Where's the Gold?" one of the miners asked.

Plummer hesitated, he knew the mood was ugly and he needed time to turn things his way. He calmly sat back down on the cot and pulled on his boots, as though he was in no particular hurry.

"Good news," he said. "I recovered the Gold. Shot the men who stole it, too."

"Where is it?" McCullough asked.

"Safe," Plummer said, rising to his feet and tucking in his shirt. "It's evidence, now. It'll get returned in due course."

"Evidence, my ass," one of the miners said. "We want it now."

"You get the hell out of my jail," Plummer said, losing his temper. "I'll have you all arrested."

One of the miners pulled White Hawk up to the front. Plummer was a big man and looked down at the Indian with bitter contempt, but White Hawk stood his ground without a hint of fear or intimidation.

"Where is it?" McCullough asked the Indian.

White Hawk pointed to the spot under the desk. The miners started to push the heavy desk out of the way, but Plummer knocked one of them down with a forearm to the chest and tried to block their way. The miners grabbed him and pinned his arms behind his back. They pushed the desk aside and found the loose board.

Reaching down into the hole, they pulled out the canvas sack.

"Wait a minute." Plummer shouted. "I told you I had it, God damnit."

"How'd you know where to find them?" McCullough asked.

"Yeah, and how come you shot em, instead of bringing em in?" another asked.

"They were going for their guns." Plummer spat out.

The miners opened the bag. The gold was there, in separate sacks marked with their owner's names just as it had been packed. Joshua Garrity looked deeper into the space below the floorboards.

"Look at this," he shouted, pulling another large sack out of the cavity."

He handed it to McCullough, who opened the sack and pulled out more bags of gold.

"It's the gold from the last shipment. The one you said was highjacked."

The Sheriff pushed forward but someone clubbed him across the jaw with the butt of a rifle. Plummer started to go down but two men held him up. They carried him out into the street and down to the big cottonwood that grew next to the bakery. Plummer's hands were tied behind his back. They threw a rope over a high branch. Plummer was still groggy from the hit but was coming to as they tied a crude noose and lowered it around his neck.

Lee watched. His feelings were mixed. He hated Plummer and knew he would have killed Jake without blinking an eye. But the mob was unstoppable. A half dozen miners grabbed the end of the rope and pulled Plummer into the air. The noose tightened and the Sheriff's mouth opened wide as he struggled for breath. The rope was tied off to the tree trunk and the miners gathered round to watch. After all the hollering and cursing, the mob had gone silent. All that could be heard was the sound of the Sheriff gasping for beath. After a few minutes his struggling ceased.

Once the hanging was over, Lee made his way back to the jail. He found the key to the back room and unlocked the door. Jacob was sitting on a cot in his sweat stained long johns. The only light in the room was cast by pinprick beams of sunlight shining through cracks in the wooden walls.

"You alright?" Lee asked.

Jake got up and stretched. "Just dandy. What the hell was going on out there? How's a feller s'pose ta sleep?"

Lee helped Jacob gather his things. He had a hell of a lump on his head and his knee and ankle were swollen, but these were ills that would heal. As they walked out into the light of day, Jake saw Plummer swinging from the tree. Nobody made a move to cut him down. McCullough was removing the sacks from the bag and reading out the names as, one by one, their property was returned to them. Lee's name was called and he shouted out. A bag was tossed to him.

"Let's get you home," Lee said to Jacob.

"Good idea," Jake said. "This town is rough as cobb."

Chapter XII

RENEGADE

For a short time, we lived quietly, but this could not last. White Men had found gold in the mountains around the land of winding water.

Chief Joseph

Marias River, Blackfoot Territory

Three weeks after the White Eagles raided the Absaroka camp, Mountain Sun made his way back to his father's village on the banks of the Marias River. He was in a bad mood, but he wasn't sure exactly why. The truth was, he did not understand his own feelings about the battle. One minute, he would convince himself that they were right to have killed their enemies and that he should be proud. He was a warrior. This is what he had dreamed of since he was a boy. But then he would remember the faces of the old women and children. He tried not to think about it, but the images stayed with him.

Blue Jacket rode beside him. He was the other member of the White Eagle Society who hailed from Broken Claw's band. Mountain Sun knew Blue Jacket well, had known him since childhood. He was short and thick with a head full of black hair that he tied behind his head with an eagle feather. He wore an old union army tunic that he'd decorated with beads and paint. He looked very fierce on horseback, but Mountain Sun knew him to be a pleasant man with a wife and two young children. It was a long ride back to the Marias. Blue Jacket tried to engage Mountain Sun in conversation, but the young man was not in the mood to talk. After a while Blue Jacket left him alone.

They rode over a high ridge and dropped into the valley. Their band was camped along the river. It was a pretty site. The lodges were arranged on the golden summer grass and the blue river wound northward, sparkling in the sunshine against a backdrop of high peaks. They could see the horses grazing in the field across the river and the women working along the bank. When they got closer the dogs barked out a warning and Blue Jacket's children ran to greet him. He pulled them up onto his horse, one in each arm, and hugged them to him. Mountain Sun rode on to his father's lodge.

His mother was on her knees working a buffalo hide that was staked out on the ground. She was known for how well she could tan and soften the tough hides. It was hard physical work that had made her old before her time. She could not remember when her fingers, elbows and shoulders did not ache, but she took pride in her work. Scattered around the village, other hides were being worked. Meat was drying on racks and pemmican was being pounded in stone vessels. His mother moved to him as he approached. Mountain Sun endured her examination and, once she saw that he was uninjured, she finally relaxed. His father, Broken Claw, came out of the lodge and welcomed him home.

"It is good to have you back. Are you well?" his father asked.

"Yes. I'm fine." Mountain Sun answered.

"Was the raid successful?"

"Yes."

"That's good news. Was anyone injured?"

"Nothing serious. It was a small village, mainly women, old men and boys too young to fight. We should have just left them alone."

"That's how it is, sometimes."

Mountain Sun shrugged. "I suppose."

"Come on," his mother said, "Let's eat."

The rest of the summer was uneventful. The band stayed on the river and no contact was made with other tribes or with the White men. Mountain Sun's status, however, had changed. He was treated like a man now, invited to join in discussions with the other men and voice his opinion. Most often, he found that he had no opinion to offer. He was content to sit and listen.

He began to spend more and more time away. He'd head up into the mountains, often for a week at a time, and would return with his pack horse loaded with meat. His reputation as a hunter grew, but the trips were just an excuse to get away by himself. There was an anger growing in him that he could not explain or understand. It was like lighting fire to the prairie to flush game, easy enough to start, very difficult to control.

Without seeking it out, other young men in the band began to look to him for leadership. He had always been a little bigger and stronger than most, and he carried himself with a quiet authority they admired. They hovered around him and asked if they could accompany him on his hunts. Even though he preferred being alone, he sometimes took one or two of them along.

In the last days of summer, a rider came to the village. He was a messenger, sent by the White Eagles to summon Blue Jacket and Mountain Sun to another raid. They'd ride against the Cree, their traditional enemies. Mountain Sun had come to the conclusion that he wanted nothing to do with the Society, not because he was afraid to fight but because he refused to do so at somebody else's whim and saw no honor in killing where there was no threat. He told the messenger he was not going. When pressed for a reason he shrugged his shoulders. Blue Jacket and the messenger were stunned. To their knowledge, no one had ever refused to come when called. Blue Jacket took up the matter with Broken Claw.

"What is it you want me to do?" Broken Claw asked.

"You need to talk to the boy. It will be a black mark on him if he backs out now."

"He must make his own decisions."

Broken Claw didn't ask his son why he had refused to go, but he knew there would be consequences. Part of him wanted to force his son to go, but another part was proud that Mountain Sun was that rare brand of man who could think for himself and stand up for what he believed, even if there were consequences. And before long, it seemed that there were. When he got back from the raid, Blue Jacket took his family and left. A few weeks later, another of the band's most valued warriors packed up his squaw and his children, saying that he was concerned for the future of the band. The vitality of any band was a delicate thing. It was a question of manpower, a balance between having too few and too many. Losing two good families was cause for concern. Losing more might be catastrophic.

Mountain Sun understood he was the cause of the problem and he couldn't stand the thought that he had brought this difficulty upon his father. One cold and rainy morning he announced, in front of the whole village, that he was leaving. He wished them well, telling them he would gladly give his own life for any of them but that he did not want anyone to suffer on his account. Most wished him well, but they were secretly relieved. He embraced his mother, who could not hold back her tears.

"I'm sorry, father," Mountain Sun said. "To have caused you so much trouble."

"You are the only one of my son's left alive," his father told him, looking him in the eyes. "I will always be happy that you are my son."

Mountain Sun collected his horse and packed his few possessions and without further discussion he rode off into the mist. He made his way toward the mountains and climbed into the foothills. He felt sad to be leaving his father and mother, but he was also happy to be off on his own. He meant to prove that he was not a coward. He would perfect his skills as a hunter and he would be like the great chiefs of legend, who went off on their own and trained their body and mind until they were like a piece of hard steel against which others would break their lances. He would fight whoever came before him. But it would be of his choosing, not someone else's.

That night he camped by the bank of a creek along the eastern slope. The rain had stopped, and the clouds had blown away, but the temperature had dropped and it was very cold. Even so, stars lit up the sky so brightly that Mountain Sun took it to be an omen of good fortune. He was deep into the foothills and felt secure enough to keep a fire banked against the chill. Suddenly, he heard horses coming up the trail. He threw more wood onto the fire so that the riders would not be able to see against the glare, then he grabbed his rifle and slipped into the trees, letting the darkness envelope him. Two riders wound their way into view. Mountain Sun knew they had seen the fire, but they continued to come, slowly, without weapons drawn. When they got to his camp Mountain Sun watched as they swung down off their horses and turned.

"Low Eagle. Crooked Scar," he said, stepping out from behind a tree. They were his friends from the village. Mountain Sun had known them his whole life.

"Mountain Sun," Low Eagle said. "We've been trying to catch you all day."

"Why?" Mountain Sun asked. "What's happened?"

"Nothing's happened." Crooked Scar said, throwing his sack down and seating himself by the fire. "We've come to join you."

"That's right," Low Eagle said. "You got anything to eat?"

The next morning Mountain Sun awoke with the dawn and watched as the sun rose over the hills. He was not sure how he felt about his friends joining him in his exile but could think of no reason why they shouldn't. Low Eagle was his own age, a little thicker in the middle than most Blackfoot but surprisingly quick on his feet and good with a rifle and bow. His hair was thick and he was inordinately proud of it, wearing it loose and flowing about his head and face even though it meant he was continually brushing it out of his eyes. He could be pensive, almost philosophical one moment, then silly and irreverent the next. You never knew if he was serious about something or only joking.

Crooked Scar was a year younger, and he followed Low Eagle everywhere. He was well known for his bravery. Even as a child, he would accept any dare. Knowing this, the other boys were always quick to come up with one. He had a long scar across his chest from the time they dared him to release a young wolverine from a trapper's snare. He was badly clawed in the encounter. On another occasion, he'd broken a leg in a fall from a horse, racing for a bet, and would forever walk with a slight limp. He was sarcastic by nature and had been in many fights when someone took one of his jokes the wrong way. His friends encouraged him to keep his mouth shut, but it was not in his nature. Mountain Sun shrugged and decided to let things run their course. Who was he to tell them what to do?

"What are we going to do now?" Low Eagle asked.

"What would you like to do?" Mountain Sun asked.

"I don't know. I thought you had a plan."

"My plan is to do whatever I want. Whenever I want.

"Oh great," Crooked Scar moaned. "There's no plan."

"I'd like to eat something." Low Eagle said.

"Alright," Mountain Sun said. "We'll start with that. But is there anywhere you've always wanted to go. Anything you've always wanted to see."

"I've heard there's a place where the three rivers meet. I don't know if it's true. But it's supposed to be south."

"I've heard that too," Crooked Scar said.

"Alright. Let's go," Mountain Sun said. It did not really make any difference to him. It was just a direction.

For the next few months, they roamed the plains and mountains, hunting where they wanted to hunt, resting when they wanted to rest, never bothering to worry about the approaching winter. It was the first time they'd been out on their own. It was difficult, at first, but the taste of freedom was intoxicating. They drew strength from the hard life and became so toughened that they scarcely missed the comforts of home. They stalked game so patiently and silently that they began to hunt with the lance, instead of the bow or rifles they also carried. They followed a great bear for a whole day, moving within yards of it without being seen or scented.

Sometimes they came across a band of Blackfoot and would enjoy the company of their own people for a few days. It was nice to share a meal and talk. Low Eagle and Crooked Scar would want to stay even longer. Mountain Sun didn't rush them, but if he wanted to leave, he left. His friends could catch up with him later. Occasionally, they happened across a hunting party. Often the older warriors would treat Mountain Sun and his friends with condescension; after all, they were hardly more than boys. Mountain Sun, who was usually polite and respectful, was quick to take offense and would be insolent and insulting in response. He was eager to fight, to prove himself. If he were pushed, he'd launch himself at his opponent with unrestrained ferocity, caring little for his own safety. He was often injured, sometimes seriously, but had always held his own. Low Eagle and Crooked Scar grew wary of strangers, knowing the slightest provocation would cause another fight.

At one such village they picked up a new companion, a brave of twenty summers named Horn Song, who was on the eve of marriage to a squaw not known for her beauty or temperament. He'd been talked into the union and was having second thoughts. Horn Song's family was poor and she was the only squaw he could afford; he was only too eager to run away and join the bachelors. And now that he had escaped, he was determined to romance every squaw on the eastern divide. It was a bold plan, except that he was not a handsome man. His face bore the deep marks of a childhood pox, and one of his front teeth was chipped. He was clever enough, but the gap in his teeth caused him to hiss and whistle and sometimes even spit when he was talking, especially when he was excited.

The following week they came across a young Gros Ventre named Little Dog. He had set off to avenge the murder of his brother by a party of Cree and had been tracking them for weeks, but the Cree had retreated back across the Missouri. He was now far from home and was lucky to have been found by Blackfoot, with whom the Gros Ventre were allied. His horse had broken its leg in a tumble down an embankment and Little Dog had camped by the carcass and subsisted on the flesh. He wore a beautiful buckskin shirt embroidered with turquoise traded from the southern tribes. He was a friendly and intelligent man with a calm and patient manner, prepared to sit where he was until a worthwhile plan came to mind. He knew something would come along. Mountain Sun took to the fellow right away. He offered him a horse and enough food to get back to his people. Little Dog was so moved by this generosity, and by the spirit of adventure these young brothers embraced, that he decided to stay with them awhile.

The days grew shorter and the snow began to fall. They were unconcerned, trusting fate and their skills to provide. They were not surprised when a small herd of buffalo presented itself. They gave thanks to the buffalo for their sacrifice and two were slaughtered. Rather than trying to find a sheltered valley, as his people usually did in winter, they continued to roam. They traveled south and stole horses from the Shoshone. They were chased by the White man's cavalry but were never in any real danger of being caught. They stole the best horses they came across and no one dared to stop them.

It was near the solstice when the days were at their shortest and bitter winds blew across the plains. They moved north, crossing the

Teton River, hoping to find shelter in the cuts along Birch Creek. It was a good place to hunt. Deer and elk came down out of the highlands and foraged for grass exposed by the wind. It was getting late in the day and Crooked Scar complained about the cold and suggested they stop and put up the lodge. There was plenty of fallen timber nearby with which to make a fire. The others kidded him that he didn't have enough meat on his bones to keep himself warm.

The five of them worked their way up out of a creek bed to skirt a section of trail flooded by beavers. The wind whistled loudly as they climbed onto the ridge and, suddenly, less than fifty yards in front of them, was another group of Indians. Both groups, caught unaware, grabbed their rifles but, before any shots were fired, it became clear to them that this was another group of Blackfoot.

Both groups dismounted. It was the custom to share a meal or smoke a pipe together on occasions such as this. If fate led their paths to cross, then it would be bad luck and extremely rude not to honor the meeting. There were only four of them at present, but their leader had killed a deer a mile back and would be joining them shortly. Low Eagle was happy to hear that somebody was bringing meat, and even happier to hear there'd be a fire to cook it over.

It was growing dark. Mountain Sun and his band did not usually erect their lodge if they were stopping for only one night, but the temperature was dropping and a storm blowing in, so it seemed worth the trouble. The lodge was up and a pile of wood had been gathered when a rider approached the camp, the body of a freshly killed doe slung over his horse's back. Mountain Sun stood when he heard the sound. He froze when he saw that it was Omak, the leader of the White Eagle Society. Omak swung down from his horse, a magnificent lilac roan of more than sixteen hands. He was already being introduced to Mountain Sun's friends, who were clearly in awe of the huge warrior. Even without his eagle robe and headdress, Omak was an intimidating sight.

Mountain Sun was only a few feet from Omak and looking him straight in the eye when he realized that the big man did not recognize him. But something about the way Mountain Sun was staring at him gave him pause.

"Do I know you?" Omak asked, taking a step closer.

Mountain Sun was big for a Blackfoot, six feet tall and a hundred and ninety pounds, but Omak dwarfed him. He was six inches taller and fifty pounds heavier, his arms knotted with muscle and his chest thick and broad.

"I am Mountain Sun, son of Broken Claw."

Omak smiled. "The coward. I was hoping our paths would cross."

Anger shone in Mountain Sun's eyes. Omak pulled his knife. Everyone took a step back. Mountain Sun's first instinct was to give in to his rage and throw himself at the older man, but he knew that would be suicide. Omak was taller and heavier and, by all accounts, a great fighter. Mountain Sun pulled his own knife and circled, testing his footing on the snow and loose gravel. With his first feint he jumped forward, never really intending to get within range of the larger man's blade, hoping only to draw him off balance so he could strike in earnest. But Omak didn't react; Mountain Sun would have to do better if he intended to draw him out. A minute passed without engagement.

"Come on, Coward. Are you waiting for me to die of old age?"

"No, I have something else in mind," Mountain Sun replied.

"Then hurry, it's getting dark and I'm hungry."

He had barely finished the words when Mountain Sun sprang forward but, instead of engaging him head on, he dove. Omak's knife split the air but Mountain Sun was rolling past him, slicing his sharpened blade along the side of his opponent's thigh. By the time Omak turned, Mountain Sun was already on his feet. A deep cut bled down Omak's leg, but he did not so much as glance at it. He lunged at Mountain Sun and only luck and the reflexes of youth pulled him clear of the slashing blade. Omak was fast, incredibly fast for such a giant. At first, Mountain Sun thought the attack was over; but the warrior didn't let up. He swung and jabbed and Mountain Sun was forced to jump backward and roll away, never completely gaining his balance, always an inch away from death. The tip of Omak's blade cut him again and again, but never beyond the depth of flesh. Omak slashed again and Mountain Sun ducked. He avoided the knife, but Omak's foot caught him hard in the ribs. Mountain Sun felt like he'd been kicked by a horse and rolled away, trying to suck air into his lungs. And still Omak came. He kicked again, barely missing Mountain Sun's head. Omak's knife arched overhead but Mountain Sun rolled partway down the hill and slid behind a tree to buy himself time. When Omak reached him, Mountain Sun scurried on his hands and feet back up the hill again. He could hear the laughter of Omak's companions.

Getting to his feet, Mountain Sun waited for the big man to climb up to him. There was an almost undetectable slowing in his step. Omak's sustained attack had winded him and he seemed content, for a moment, to stalk the younger man, cutting off his lines of retreat and preventing any more of this running around.

"I've got you now," Mountain Sun said, taunting him.

Omak spat, a flush of anger rising in his cheeks.

Mountain Sun jerked right and, when Omak reacted, reversed direction and cut across the big man's forearm. Omak instinctively grabbed at the wound and Mountain Sun jumped forward and drove the tip his blade into the man's huge bicep. Omak swung with his knife hand, slashing at Mountain Sun's throat, but the younger man was a half inch out of reach and already countering, sliding in past the attack, slicing at the rib cage and circling behind him again. Omak now had four deep cuts, all bleeding freely, but none debilitating enough to stop the fight.

Omak realized that Mountain Sun was too quick to take with a knife, so he stashed the blade in his belt and picked up a three-foot pole that lay nearby. It was as thick around as his leg, but he wielded it as though it were a sapling. If he were hit, Mountain Sun realized, the fight would be over. He fell back on the defensive, rolling away from the thunderous blows. Time after time he barely managed to avoid being crushed by the club, never managing to get close enough to use his knife. But by now both of Omak's hands were slippery with his own blood and the effort of wielding the limb was taking its toll. Suddenly Mountain Sun slipped on the wet snow and went down on one knee. Omak lifted the great club over his head and brought it down with all his strength. Only at the very last second did Mountain Sun roll to his side to avoid being crushed. But Omak had swung with such violence that the club flew out of his hands and, before he could stop his momentum, he stumbled toward the rising youngster. Mountain Sun's knife was still in hand as Omak fell toward him and Mountain Sun stepped in and slashed across the big man's throat. Mountain Sun heard the rush of hot air expelled from his lungs and felt a surge of blood pour over his hand. He supported the huge man's weight for a second and then stepped aside, letting Omak fall to the ground, grasping his throat, trying to keep his life's blood from draining onto the snow.

There was a stunned silence. Only the hiss of blood gargled breath broke the evening gloom. Nobody ran forward to help; it was clear the wound was fatal. After a moment, the whistling stopped and he was dead, a widening pool of blood spreading beneath him. Both groups remained motionless and then, at last, Low Eagle ran over to Mountain Sun and waved Horn Song to come help. Mountain Sun was covered in blood, but much of it was his enemy's. When they tried to lift him, Mountain Sun winced; ribs had been broken. They carried him to the lodge, laid him on a skin and cleaned the blood away.

"I thought you were a dead man," Horn Song said, shaking his head.

"So did I," Mountain Sun replied.

The men of both bands agreed that Omak should be prepared for burial. It took four of them to lift him onto a horse. They rode up the trail and tied a platform in the crook of a tree. They settled the body and sang the songs that would ease his passage to the next world. It was completely dark by the time they made their way back to camp.

They hurriedly built a fire and ate a silent meal. Omak's band was still in shock that he'd been killed, and at the hands of a Piegan hardly more than a boy. Mountain Sun's friends were no less surprised. They held a healthy respect for Mountain Sun but, until now, considered him as much a friend as a leader. That had changed. They had witnessed something almost miraculous, and they were proud to have woven their fate to his.

In the morning, Horn Song let it be known that they'd be staying for a few more days. The storm had blown in and Mountain Sun was in no shape to travel. All the braves from both groups crowded into the lodge to see Mountain Sun and discuss what to do next.

"I am sorry that I was forced to kill your friend," Mountain Sun said.

One of the band, a man named Nine Feathers, stepped forward.

"He was a bully. He beat his squaw and children and anybody else who got in his way. But he was a mighty warrior. We didn't think he could be beaten."

"Anybody can be beaten," Mountain Sun said.

Both groups nodded their heads solemnly.

"When you return to your village," Mountain Sun said. "Tell them that I alone did this; that we fought without tricks. Omak fought bravely and died a good death. I am not part of any band and have turned my back on my family. I alone am responsible."

"We will tell them. But it will not matter to the White Eagle Society. They will mark you now."

"Let them," Mountain Sun said.

When Omak's band left to return home later that morning, Nine Feathers and Black Tree asked to stay behind and join the band. Before accepting them, Mountain Sun had a long talk with each of them. He wanted to be sure they weren't hot-heads or sycophants. If he could not see them as friends, then he would rather not be responsible for them. Nine Feathers was witty and confident without being arrogant. Mountain Sun liked him and asked him to stay. But he told Black Tree that there was no place for him among them. Black Tree was angry and his response insulting, only verifying Mountain Sun's impression of him. But one more enemy at this point hardly mattered.

When Black Tree and his companions packed their gear and rode off, none dared reach for the reins of Omak's horse, the magnificent lilac roan.

Chapter XIII

THE SEARCHERS

Since I lost my horse in the service of the law, I helped myself to the Sheriff's.

Jacob McCune

Montana Territory

Jacob wasn't of a mind to linger. Lee would have liked to pocket a little more money before they left, but he had to agree that mining for gold was a fool's errand. Winter was coming, and it wouldn't be long before snow closed the passes. As soon as he found a greenhorn willing to buy his claim, he signed it over and even made a few bucks in the bargain. It wasn't the best time of year to be heading out, but they'd made up their minds to go. It was better than being stuck in Alder Gulch till Spring.

Jacob had passed many a winter in the Rocky Mountains, and it was his contention that they were less brutal west of the Divide. There was good country to the north and the Nez Perce and Flathead were less bloodthirsty than the Blackfoot. They rode out on a bright autumn morning. The mountain sides were streaked with the yellow and gold of aspen and larch and the last hint of green had gone out of the meadows, replaced by an ocean of golden grass that stretched to the horizon. White clouds, backlit by the flat light of autumn, floated in a brilliant blue sky. It was good hunting weather. The deer and elk were coming into rut and, most days, they were able to bag fresh meat.

For the first week they traveled north up the Blacktail. The rivers were low and crossing was easy. Jacob thought there might still be beaver this far north, and Lee was looking for a place with grass so thick no herd could overgraze it, and so pretty he'd never want to leave. White Hawk was just happy to be away from all the White men, clear of all the dirt and foul smells. By the time they reached the Clark Fork, the first snow began to fall.

It was rugged country, well treed and with big rivers flowing down out of the mountains. He figured they had another three or maybe four weeks before they had to find a sheltered valley to hunker down in. For a week they rode, traveling at a comfortable pace. White Hawk put together a lodge using some of the hides they'd collected and strapped it to the spare horse. When it was snowing or raining, they slept late, in no hurry to crawl out from under their blankets. They weren't driven to put miles behind them; each day's ride offered new country, country they had never seen. If they spotted any sign of Indians, they went out of their way to avoid them, but the land was mostly empty, and they hadn't seen a White man since they'd left the Gulch.

They followed the Clark Fork, taking side trips into the Garnet Mountains or hunting the cane breaks along the Bitterroot. White Hawk continued to work on his English and made progress, though Lee suspected his speech would be forever colored by the obscene. As the days grew shorter, they reached a river flowing into the Clark Fork from the north. Jacob figured it flowed out of the big lake he'd heard about. Low clouds, dark with moisture, blew in from the north and the temperature began to drop. White Hawk knew that once the snow began to fall it would fall for days on end and he told Jacob they should push on. When they woke the next morning, a foot of fresh powder lay on the ground. More flakes, light as the wind, continued to fall. They packed up the lodge and continued. The snow was so dry and light the horses were able to push through it easily but, over the course of the day, the wind began to howl and the gentle dusting turned into the blizzard they knew was coming. Jacob was all for stopping, but White Hawk pointed to seagulls flying low on the western horizon. Lee hadn't seen a gull in years but the Absraoka attached a lot of significance to the sighting. They followed the river north for another two hours as daylight drained from the sky. White Hawk was in the lead, pushing his little pony though the deepening drifts. Jacob spurred his horse forward.

"First cover, we stop," Jacob said.

White Hawk nodded his head and pointed. As though on cue, the clouds parted and a shaft of light fell low across the horizon, illuminating the largest body of water any of them had ever seen. It stretched beyond the haze and along its eastern shore the mountains rose steeply, their peaks lost in the clouds.

"Is that the ocean?" Lee asked.

"No, just a damn big lake," Jacob said.

FLATHEAD LAKE, Montana Territory

They worked their way along the natural damn at the foot of the lake and traveled up the eastern shore till they found a timbered tract rising above the bay. Jacob liked the look of it. A stream tumbled down from the mountains that could provide fresh water near to hand. The hill provided a good vantage point to spot anyone approaching from the south or by boat across the lake and the trees offered a buffer from the wind and snow. It was a good spot to ride out the winter. A lake this big was unlikely to freeze and he had heard that the Flathead were peaceable. They put up the lodge, collected wood for a fire and spent the first night warmly ensconced.

The next morning the storm abated, though the sky was still heavy with clouds and snow fell in fits and starts. They set out to get the camp in order. A wide meadow stretched along the flats beside the outlet, and the grass was still lush. Lee skirted the wetland and waited till a doe emerged from the trees. He took her with one shot, dressed her out and carried the meat back to camp. It was the first fresh meat they'd had in a few days.

Jacob and White Hawk scouted the hills and shore for a couple of miles to the north. It was difficult to grasp the size of the lake. Jacob tried to explain to White Hawk what an ocean was, but he wasn't inclined to believe it. Jake told him about boats so big they could hold a hundred men and fish so large they could swallow a man whole. White Hawk was indignant that the old man thought he'd ever believe such nonsense. That evening they built a fire out in the open and burnt the logs down to coals. They roasted the venison and ate their fill. After they were finished eating Jake pulled out a bottle of whiskey he had stashed away to toast their new home.

They spent a few more days exploring. There seemed to be plenty of game. A few weeks later, when the snow began to accumulate on the steep hills along the shore, they came across a bull moose and two cows grazing in the shallows.

"What the hell is that?" Lee asked.

"Them are moose," Jake answered.

"Damn they're big."

"And cantankerous, too."

"Look at them antlers. Must weigh more 'an a hundred pounds. What kind of creature can tote a rack like that all day long?"

"One full of muscle. Them bulls is strong. Take aim at one of the cows."

Lee rested his shoulder against the tree and took aim. It was a strange looking creature, without the grace of a deer or the majesty of an elk. He pulled the trigger and she went down in the shallow water without taking a step. The other cow ran off into the forest, but the bull turned and faced them, trying to figure out where the threat came from. The huge animal charged out of the water and straight up the hill. Lee and Jacob ducked behind a tree. The bull stopped twenty yards in front of them, lowered his head and snorted, swinging his rack from side to side and stomping the ground. Lee waited for him to move off, but he seemed disinclined to go. Lee had a clear shot, and he thought he might have to take it, but he was more interested for the time being in watching the animal.

"He's something, ain't he?" Jacob whispered.

"Sure is. Reckon we'll have to shoot him?" Lee asked.

"Put one at his feet."

Lee brought the barrel up. The loud crack of the gun and the explosion of dirt sent the big animal moving off into the trees. The two men walked into the shallows and dragged the cow to shore. Jake figured she weighed nearly seven hundred pounds. Jacob brought out his skinning knife and began to sharpen it on his whet stone.

"Could go back for one of the horses. But I reckon it'd be quicker just to cut her up here."

"I'll do it. You go get a horse, so we can pack the meat back to camp."

"You ain't never butchered a moose."

"Just a big deer."

"I spose. Try and get the hide off in one piece."

Jacob finished sharpening the knife and handed it to Lee, and then the two of them turned the moose so he could get at her. Jacob took up his rifle and headed back to camp. In a few minutes he had rounded the corner and was out of sight. Lee stood for a moment looking out over the lake. Dark clouds were moving in from the southwest. The water fell in and out of shadow and the wind whistled gently through the aspen along the hillside. Lee looked down at the bull and wondered where he should start. It struck him as wondrous that he was up here in Montana, living on this colossal lake where no White man had likely been before. He took off his coat and threw it over a stump, then sunk the sharp knife into the soft belly of the cow.

Within a few weeks they had the camp well laid. They had wood enough and a fair amount of meat smoked and seasoned. Even White Hawk had to admit it was a good camp. One morning, without so much as a word, he got up, walked down to the water and went to work.

"What's he doing?" Lee asked

"He's making a bullboat," Jacob replied.

"What's a bullboat?"

"It's a round canoe made from a single stretched hide."

"Where's he going?"

"Damned if I know."

Lee helped where he could, carrying saplings back to camp and braiding green vines to make rope. White Hawk took the most flexible saplings and bent them into a hoop, tying them closed with a rawhide lash. Then he took other saplings and bent them in opposite directions until the ribs of a shallow bowl were formed. At first, it was rather flimsy, but by the time he had all the ribs cross lashed to each other it was surprisingly strong. Finally, he took the hide out and stretched it tightly across the frame, tying it off along the rim. It was as tight as a drum. Lee and White Hawk carried it down to the water and dropped it in. It floated as lightly as a lily pad. Lee spent a day whittling paddles out of a pine limb under the critical supervision of the Indian. Once it was all finished, Lee turned to White Hawk.

"What do we do now?" he asked.

White Hawk pointed up the lake. "Go." he said. "Look."

That night, when Jacob came back from a hunt, Lee gave him the news.

"We're taking the boat up the lake," he said. "Gonna explore some."

"Have fun."

"You're coming too," Lee said.

"Like hell I am. Ain't setting foot in that thing."

"It's seaworthy. We tested it thorough."

Jacob walked away shaking his head.

The next morning, they woke to a blue sky and bright sun. They carried the boat to shore and loaded the gear.

"Come on Jacob, we'll stay close to shore," Lee said.

"I'll stay on shore, right here."

"You can't swim?"

"Don't think so."

"You'd know if you could swim."

"Never tried it."

"If anything happens, I'll haul you out. The lake's still as a bathtub"

"Is now. But fer how long?"

Eventually they shamed him into it. Lee and White Hawk paddled the boat and it bobbed along pleasantly. They headed across the lake and up the western shore. Jacob sat in the middle gripping with knuckles bled white. It was hard to steer, at first, but once they learned to work together, they could direct the craft wherever they wanted. It sure beat breaking trail through the deep snow along the shore.

An hour into the trip they came around a bend into a wide bay and spotted an Indian village. Snow covered hills rose gently above it. It was a large village and smoke lifted gently from the cooking fires into the clear winter sky. They began paddling to shore and, as they grew closer, a crowd of Indians walked down to greet them. A few of them pulled the boat up onto the beach and gathered close around them. Lee could detect no hostility on their faces, only curiosity, but White Hawk kept his hand on his paddle, just in case. Lee heard a commotion and looked up the hill. A priest was making his way down to the beach.

He was a small man with long brown hair and a welcoming smile. Lee recognized the long flowing robes of a Jesuit.

"Accueil!" the Jesuit said, extending his hand. "Qu'une surprise heureuse."

"How's to, Padre." Jacob offered. "French ain't too good. Speak any Angliase?"

"Yes, yes. A little. Welcome. What are your names?"

"I'm Jacob," he said, "and this here's White Hawk."

Lee stepped forward and offered his hand. "I'm Lee. Pleased to meet you."

"Father Adelarde," he replied, taking Lee by the arm and leading him up the hill.

"These Flatheads?" Jake asked as they walked.

"Oui," the priest said. "My flock."

"You mean they's Christian?" Jake asked, surprised.

"Oui, Roman Catholic," Adelarde shrugged.

"How long have you been here?" Lee asked.

"Nearly ten years."

"Didn't think there was no White men in these parts," Jacob said.

They walked to the heart of the village and the priest showed them the little church he'd built at the top of the hill, a log building with a pitched roof and a wooden cross. It was small, but Father Adelarde was very proud of it. The Flathead were engaged in any number of enterprises, drying fish, sewing garments and weaving cane to make the baskets they used to carry grain. Adelarde stopped at the largest structure in the village, a type of log cabin made from lodge-pole pine. The pitched roof was thatched and a ribbon of smoke rose from a hole in the center. As they approached, a tall Indian in buckskin pants and a large red woolen coat emerged. His big smile exposed a mouth full of crooked teeth and his hair was cut short in western style, though unevenly and to poor effect. Father Adelarde introduced him.

"Gentlemen. Let me introduce Francois Two Stick. He is the chief of these Flatheads," The Priest said, quickly translating for the chief.

Two Stick invited them inside and made them comfortable. He called for one of his daughters to bring tea. The pipe was brought out and they smoked together, drank the tea and introduced themselves. This far north, the sun went down early at this time of year and it was already getting dark. Two Stick ordered a feast prepared.

"Where you from, Padre?" Jacob asked.

"Quebec," Adelarde said. "But I have been out West for a long, long time."

"You don't ever go home?" Lee asked.

"No. This is home, now," the little priest said, with a sad look on his face.

Pere Adelarde was a font of information on the tribes of the western divide and lower Canada. Two Stick, himself, had lived in this valley all his life and remembered the time, before the White men came, when his people crossed over the mountains to fight the Blackfoot and hunt buffalo on the plains.

"Why don't they no more?" Jacob asked the Priest.

"Aren't enough of them, anymore. And the Blackfoot are too strong."

The Priest explained that the area was remote, and they didn't see as many Whites as the tribes further south. The northern mountains presented too formidable a barrier and the snows were deep and long lasting.

The women brought platters of food: wild rice, venison, dried fruit and a hard, dry bread. As many men and women as could fit pushed themselves into the building and gathered close. The White men were quite an attraction. As soon as their bowls were empty, they would be refilled, and Lee ate three helpings before he finally had the nerve to say enough. The children weren't shy. They crawled closer and closer until three of them were in Lee's lap, playing with his hair, scraping the rough growth of his week-old beard, reaching into his pockets and vying for his attention. Neither Two Stick nor any of the other Indians tried to chase them away. White Hawk busied himself with his food and made no attempt to join in the conversation. Lee wasn't sure if his indifference was real or just a subtle show of snobbery. But once he was finished eating and his plate was taken away, White Hawk began to look around. There were many young maidens squeezed into the lodge, and a few of them seemed fascinated by the stern and handsome Absaroka. A smile was not an expression that sat easily on White Hawk's face, but Lee thought he saw one directed at one of the young women nearby.

By the time the feast was completed it was too dark to return to their camp in the boat. They thanked Francois Two Stick for his hospitality and followed Adelarde out into the night. The priest set them up in a corner of his own lodge. It was one of the smallest in the settlement, and as humble a dwelling as Lee had ever seen: small, cold and dark with none of the comforts a White man might be expected to demand. Once again, Lee was impressed by the sacrifices the priest had made, to be exiled from his own people and his own country for all these years, living a life of service to savages who'd accepted him as one of their own.

Adelarde was eager for news of the world, though Jacob and Lee didn't have much. They told him that the war was winding down in the east, and that gold had been discovered in the territory. The priest was not happy to hear this and asked if any of the miners were likely to come this far north, but Jacob wouldn't speculate on where the avarice of men might lead them. Father Adelarde told them of the movements of the northern tribes and the British traders who sometimes passed through. The priest tried to convince them to move their camp to the village for the winter, though Jacob was resistant to the idea.

"Why not?" Lee asked. "Don't seem like such a bad idea."

"Injuns have different ways," Jake explained. "If you're a guest they make allowances. But living close, yor apt to slip up. Who knows what'll cause offense."

"Fine by me," Lee said. "But it ain't like you to be unsociable."

"I spent most my life alone," Jacob replied.

"Not lately."

"We ain't far. We'll visit often enuf."

As the night grew colder, they wrapped themselves in the few skins and blankets the priest had in his procession. Adelarde talked about how the injun way was dying. He lamented the fact that the Flathead numbers were in decline and he didn't hold out much hope for their survival. But he was determined to do whatever he could to help them, to prepare them for an encounter with white settlers if they ever did make it over the mountains in sizable numbers. Lee suspected they would, but he was thankful that he was getting this opportunity to see their way of life before it was too late.

The next morning, they packed up their gear, presented Two Stick and the priest with the gift of wool socks, for which Adelarde was especially grateful, and then climbed back into their bull boat and paddled home. As they looked out over the snow-covered hills west of the lake, Lee turned to Jacob.

"This would be good cattle country," Lee said.

"Would be that."

"Well, whadda you think?" he asked.

"What would you do with em?" Jake replied.

"What do you mean?"

"No railroad. No army to sell to. No townsfolk. You'd have to get them across the mountains to sell them."

"I suppose you're right," Lee said.

"A corse I'm right," the old man said, holding tightly to the rim of the boat.

The winter was long but uneventful. Fierce storms raged over the valley. Francois Two Stick claimed it was the most snow he'd ever seen and White Hawk reminded them that he had predicted this. As Jacob suspected, the big lake did not freeze, except in the shallow bays along the shore. When they got restless and bored, they packed their bullboat and visited the Flathead. Father Adelarde was always grateful for their company, and Lee was impressed by how well the Flathead weathered the hard winter. Jacob used the time to good effect, finally letting all his bumps, scrapes, aches and pains heal. White Hawk made a few solo excursions into the village, saying he was in need of a woman, but whether he was successful they could not tell. Father Adelarde seemed to have eyes in the back of his head, though Jacob sincerely hoped that the Flathead had not completely embraced the notion of mortal sin.

Chapter XIV

Crown of the Continent

The Mountains ran from north to south, as far as the eye could see. They were snow-capped and seemed impenetrable, which was just how Jacob liked it.

Lee Grant

Blackfoot River, Montana Territory

It was well into March and the snow kept falling. Another week passed and then the rain came. When the rain stopped, it snowed again. Lee was restless; he was tired of the small lodge and tired of being tied to one place, but Jacob said there'd be too much snow in the mountains to make it across. The days wore slowly by. There'd be a week of warm weather and the snow would melt, and then the rain would come again. The streams flowing into the lake overran their banks and the wetlands flooded, but the peaks were still white with snow. Lee began to wonder if they'd ever be able to leave.

Finally, by April, grass began to sprout in the open patches between the drifts. They made one last trip to the Flathead village to say goodbye to Francois Two Stick and Father Adelarde. The priest was sorry to see them go; they were a connection to a world he dearly missed. They packed their gear carefully; spreading the food and supplies evenly in case they were separated. The night before they were to leave, Lee walked down to the lake. The stars were out in all their glory and the Milky Way painted a glowing swath over the mountain tops. Lee wondered if he would ever make his way back here again. In a land so large and dangerous, you could never be sure.

Jacob wanted to follow a valley he'd discovered that ran southeast along the foot of the mountains. He'd heard there was an easy pass across the divide; a pass once used by Lewis and Clark. It was said to follow a river that flowed down out of the mountains into the Clark Fork. There would still be snow at the higher elevations, maybe a lot of snow, and they'd need some luck if they were going to make it onto the plains before summer.

The morning dawned cloudless and cold and a thick fog clung to the low ground. They had explored the first miles of this trail many times over the course of the winter, but they soon passed the furthest point of their previous wanderings. The valley weaved between the hills to the west and the high mountains to the east. Between the snow and the mud, travel was slow and their winter legs burned with the effort. The streams plummeting from the high ground were running full and the crossings took time. They sometimes detoured a mile or more downstream till they found a place where the horses could cross. They put in a long hard day and, by late afternoon, they were tuckered out and didn't have many miles to show for it. From the meadow where they camped that night, they could still see the big lake glistening in the sunset.

After two weeks of hard travel, they emerged from a cleft torn between two peaks into a broad valley. A fast-running river flowed down from the east. Jacob supposed it was the Blackfoot, the river Lewis and Clark followed across the Divide. They hoped the traveling would be easier up the wide valley, but if there was a trail they couldn't find it. They had been struggling ever since they left the Flathead and hadn't even started over the high pass. They were coming into more traveled country and, after the peaceful winter, had fallen out of the habit of vigilance. White Hawk took to scouting ahead. War parties were on the move at this time of year and there were only the three of them. They would have to skirt trouble if they could. They climbed up into the mountains. The icy peaks on each side rose thousands of feet. If they couldn't find a good trail they'd backtrack down the valley and find another way.

Lee tried to estimate how far they traveled each day, but Jacob inevitably concluded that his figures were too optimistic. Fifteen miles through the mountains was a good day and the only thing you could say for it was that it made you forget the cold and sleep soundly that night. A lot of time was spent finding forage for the horses, who were already thin from the winter's grazing. Food was another problem. There'd been plenty of game in the lower valley, but as they rode into the high country there was little to be found. They hunted whenever they saw fresh tracks, but they weren't having much luck. They still had dried meat and the wild rice the Flathead had given them, but they had to conserve their supplies. They didn't know how long the crossing would take. It had been days since they'd been able to make a dry camp and, at the elevations they were headed, the snow would be even deeper. Lee couldn't feel his feet. He'd heard that if your feet froze your toes would fall off. He checked them every night, just to make sure they were still there. Luckily, despite the snow, there was still enough downed timber to make a fire.

"Jacob. I think I been frost bit. I gonna lose my toes?" Lee asked.

Lee lifted his foot into the old man's lap and Jacob shook his head.

"They're alright. Just keep em dry as best you can."

"How can you tell they ain't bit?"

"They get ugly. Turn black as stones. Don't fret it too much. I lost a few toes. Won't kill ye."

The valley narrowed as it gained elevation. The sight of the mountains rising sharply to each side gave pause. Lee had never seen anything so rugged and impenetrable. Even White Hawk, who'd grown up in the shadow of the shining mountains, had never been this high. The sun didn't rise until late in the morning and dropped behind the mountain before it had any chance of warming the frozen land. They saw the occasional track of a snowshoe hare or a fox that had tracked it. They would have been mighty glad to come across either one but were having no luck. Night after night they made their lean camp, tying their tarpaulins to the branches of a tree, too tired to make a proper shelter. Jacob rationed the food, but it didn't make much of a dent in their hunger. Nobody was sure how much further they'd have to travel, and Jacob knew plenty of stories about men who had starved trying to cross the mountains.

As they approached the summit, a bitter wind blew down from the pass, making travel slower and even more miserable. It was damned annoying. Jacob wondered why Lee had been in such a hurry to leave their cozy perch by the lake. They could have waited till the snow melted and it wouldn't have made a damned bit of difference.

After a few more days they reached the spring from which the river sourced and crossed the Divide. Jacob bragged on his guiding skills and Lee got a kick out of the notion that he was standing upon the razor thin demarcation of vast and powerful watersheds; streams and rivulets flowing either east or west, working their way to the Pacific Ocean or winding down to the mighty Mississippi he knew so well.

The trail down from the pass worked its way east. The snow began to give way to patches of grass. For a few days they made good time. White Hawk took a shot at a goose and missed. They found a sheltered spot in the lee of the rocks to make camp and Lee dreamt of suppers fat with meat and bread and gravy. The next morning, they worked their way down and the land began to open. Another day's travel brought them into a thickly timbered slope. They no longer had the river to guide them and the terrain broke into several valleys, all running east or northeast. Jacob didn't know the best route onto the plains, but it wasn't the first time he'd been in that predicament. He'd follow his nose, like he always did.

Slowly the mountains gave way to open patches of green grass with evergreens and aspen along the foothills. Late in the afternoon they came to a broad meadow that rolled on gently for a mile or more.

They had been traveling since sunup and were dead tired. They set the horses to graze and made camp. Steep cliffs walled off the south side of the valley and a broad stand of aspen, just coming into leaf, spread out across the slope. White Hawk tied his horse up as soon as they made camp and walked off into the trees. He came back a half hour later with a turkey. Jacob could have kissed him, but he managed to restrain himself. The Indian sat down on a log and plucked the feathers. It wasn't work he liked, but there were no squaws around to do it. Lee collected wood for a fire and, by the time he had it going, White Hawk had the bird denuded. Jacob rigged up a spit and, for the first time since they started out there was a smile on his face.

Wolf Creek, Montana Territory

Mountain Sun always preferred wandering the high canyons. There was plenty of game, fewer soldiers to avoid, and it enabled him to ride onto the plains at will, knowing the mountains were there to hide him. He was content to roam without a plan, knowing that each drainage was unique, that each tree and rock held a secret, and that the spirit of his ancestors rode with him. But he sensed his men were growing restless. For some of them, it was not enough to wander aimlessly. They wanted a chance to prove themselves. This was one of the reasons Mountain Sun had not wanted to be part of a band. He didn't want to raid simply to satisfy the blood lust of others. That was why he had turned from the White Eagles. But there were other times when even he grew restless. He couldn't reconcile these contrasting desires. Perhaps this was his fate.

When the afternoon sun dropped below the western mountains they were riding a narrow trail that wound through aspen. He had an uneasy feeling. He couldn't see through the backlit shadows of the forest and was riding blind. A bear could be dozing in the underbrush, or an enemy could be hiding in the trees waiting for them to come into range. He had just decided to turn back when something caught his eye. He reined in the roan and stared through the trees. A mile away, where the rocks gave way to a meadow, he detected movement. Low Eagle rode up beside him.

"What's the matter?" Low Eagle asked.

"There," Mountain Sun gestured across the meadow.

Low Eagle squinted into the sun. There were horses grazing, and the smoke of a small fire rose gently on the breeze. Mountain Sun signaled the men behind him and turned his horse, heading down the trail to look for better cover. He quietly led his men to within two hundred yards of the camp. Boulders at the edge of the meadow provided cover and they'd become expert at approaching without detection. Mountain Sun counted four horses and resolved to steal them. He called his men around him. It would not be easy. The White men were out in the open; they had made no attempt to hide their camp. The Blackfoot would have to cross open ground to get to them, but they would wait until it was almost dark. Mountain Sun knew they wouldn't get away without being seen but he would split his forces. While a couple of them grabbed the horses, the rest would lay down fire to cover their escape. Crooked Scar and Nine Feathers crept on all fours and crouched within yards of the grazing horses. Mountain Sun took Low Eagle and circled south, instructing the remaining three to wait in the trees until the shooting started. He told everyone to stay low on their ponies. He knew from experience that most White men could shoot.

As dusk fell, the meadow grew deathly quiet. Mountain Sun could hear the White men talking, the sound carrying clearly in the still air. He noticed that there was an Indian with them. The three of them sat around the fire eating a bird. They tore at it ravenously, as though they hadn't eaten in days. They were so focused on the food that they were oblivious to everything else. Mountain Sun hoped their vision would be dulled by staring into the flames.

Jacob brewed coffee while Lee and White Hawk held onto their tin plates, leaning close to the fire to fight the evening's chill. Crooked

Scar and Nine Feathers crept toward the horses. Crooked Scar had a gentle way with animals and ice in his veins. Horses could sense his calmness. He moved slowly. The animals moved a few steps away but displayed no skittishness. He reached the first horse and stroked its neck. If the Whites were to turn and look, he'd be clearly visible, but they were focused on their food. Crooked Scar cut the first hobble and handed Nine Feathers the rein. He cut the next without trouble but, when he approached the Black, the horse reared, raising the alarm. Without hesitation Mountain Sun charged forward with the other Blackfoot right behind him.

Lee was the first to see the Indians bearing down. Jacob saw the look on his face and turned. An arrow flew by so closely that he heard its whistle. White Hawk ran for his weapons, but Lee was forced to crouch for cover as a bullet slammed into the rocks beside him.

Lee looked for his rifle and saw it leaning against a log ten yards away. He cursed himself for his carelessness and started for it. The next arrow cut a neat furrow in his pant leg. Lee saw blood but didn't have time to check how badly he'd been hit. He made another run for his rifle, but a shot kicked up the dirt at his feet and he rolled beneath a log.

"Find some cover," Jacob yelled, heading for the rocks.

White Hawk retrieved his rifle and crouched behind a small bush that offered little protection. The Blackfoot had spread out and kept them pinned down. Jacob scrambled into the rocks and ducked as shots splintered the stone beside him. White Hawk saw Lee trying to get his rifle and called over to him.

"Go, I cover."

A round slammed into the log and Lee ran. The Blackfoot had single shot muskets, but they were spacing their fire so that the White men were kept pinned. Crooked Scar swung onto one of the stolen horses and Nine Feathers handed him the reins of another. He immediately kicked the horse into a run down the valley. A moment later Red Sky rode in, grabbed the reins from Nine Feathers and followed Crooked Scar to safety. There was only one horse left. Nine Feathers jumped onto the broad back of Plummer's Black and grabbed a handful of mane, but the big horse tossed his head and fought, unwilling to run. Nine Feathers kicked and the horse backed and then reared, throwing Nine Feathers to the ground. Jacob, watching from the rocks, shot at the Blackfoot but missed, kicking up dirt inches from the Indian's head. Nine Feathers ran for cover.

Mountain Sun saw that his men had gotten away with three of the horses and that Nine Feathers was clear. He was about to whistle his men back when Little Dog emerged from the cover of the trees and charged the White Men. Mountain Sun saw that the tall White boy was facing away, watching Nine Feathers run for cover, and had raised his rifle to make a shot. Little Dog was almost on him, rifle tight against his hip. He had a clear shot. White Hawk saw him coming at the last second. He had just fired his rifle and was trying to reload, but realized he wouldn't have time. He dropped the rifle and stepped in front of Lee, drawing a knife from his belt. The shot took him in the chest.

Lee turned. He thought, at first, that White Hawk had stumbled. He reached out with one hand to hold him up and only then noticed the blood, but he didn't have time to do anything about it. In two more steps, Little Dog had leaped over the log and was on him, swinging his rifle like a club and catching Lee squarely on the side of his head. Lee fought for consciousness. Little Dog swung again, hitting Lee on the shoulder and knocking him to the ground. Little Dog raised the rifle, preparing to drive the butt end into Lee's skull. Jacob's shot hit him in the gut, tearing a hole clear though and blowing him back. Jacob hurriedly reloaded his rifle while Lee tried to clear his head and find his gun.

Mountain Sun saw Little Dog go down. He was angry that his friend had charged into the open. Everything had been going according to plan. They could have easily gotten away. Mountain Sun lifted his rifle and shot at the White boy but missed, and then Lee had found his rifle and was shooting back. Even though he had good cover, the White boy was peppering the rocks beside his head. Mountain Sun turned and ran for cover.

Lee raised his rifle for a last shot as a round splintered the granite beside him, shards of stone as sharp as razors cut into his face. Low Eagle had fired from behind the trees to cover Mountain Sun's escape. Jacob jumped down and turned Lee over, thinking he'd been shot. His face was a bloody mess, but the wounds were superficial.

It was over as quickly as it started. Lee and Jacob lay crouched in behind cover for another few minutes until they heard the pounding of hooves fading down the valley. Jacob looked over at Lee.

"How is it?" Lee asked.

"Looks worse than it is. Face wounds bleed overmuch."

White Hawk lay on his back a few feet away, his eyes wide open, the knife still clutched in his hand. Blood covered the front of his tunic and soaked into the ground. Lee walked over and knelt beside him.

"I reckon he saved your life," Jacob said.

"So did you."

"There was no yellow in the man," Jake said, looking down at White Hawk.

"No. None."

"Poor son of a bitch had a streak of bad luck he just couldn't shake," Lee said.

"Least he's past that, now."

Lee heard a moan and saw the Blackfoot lying a few feet away. A wave of hatred rose in him. Jake saw the fire come into his eyes. Lee looked down at the Indian. He was still alive, his chest slowly rising and falling as he fought for breath, his eyes watching. He was bathed in blood, and the hole Jake's buffalo gun made in his belly was big enough to put your fist through. Lee looked down at him and their eyes locked, and not once did either man's gaze drift.

"You murdering bastard," Lee swore. He had seen men die and he'd been a part of the killing, but he had never been vengeful before now.

"He ain't gonna last much longer," Jake said, kneeling beside him.

Little Dog shifted his gaze towards the old timer. Jake held his knife out in front of him. Little Dog tried to move away; his eyes locked on the knife.

"Should scalp him, I spose. It's what he woulda done to us."

"Scalp him?" Lee asked.

"We'll wait till he passes, a corse," Jake added.

"We ain't gonna scalp him."

"Why not?"

"Just leave him be," Lee said, the anger leaving as quickly as it had come.

"He was brave," Jacob said. "Charging us like that. Hell, he ain't no older than you are."

Lee realized he was right. Lee saw Little Dog wince and realized it'd be a kindness to kill him, but he didn't have it in him. Jacob reached down and pried the knife out of the Indian's fingers. It had an iron blade with a bone handle, cheap goods the trading companies handed out by the dozen. It was worthless, and Jacob tossed it aside. When Lee looked down again the boy had stopped breathing and his eyes were closed. Jacob took Lee by the arm and walked back to the fire.

"Let's clean up them cuts," he said, dipping a cloth into the water.

"They got our horses, "Lee said, trying to wiggle away.

"All 'cept one. That sheriff rode a testy critter."

Jake washed the blood off Lee's face and scalp. None of the cuts were too wide or deep, but the rag was red with blood by the time he finished. He helped Lee to his feet and looked down at the two dead Indians, shaking his head.

"We got too comfortable, living with them god fearing Injuns. These Blackfoot's a different breed."

Mountain Sun and the rest of his band scattered. Those who were not on horseback ran down to the trees where they had tied their ponies. The others rode east to the rendezvous. Mountain Sun thought about Little Dog. He had been one of the few in the band he could talk to. He'd liked him since the day they'd first met, sitting there beside his dead horse and looking like there was nowhere else that he would rather be. Mountain Sun was still angry with him for taking such a stupid risk and charging the White men. It was the type of foolish display that some thought would make their reputation. The White men had good guns that could fire without reloading; those kinds of tactics wouldn't work anymore. Little Dog had thrown his life away.

At least they had gotten the horses, most of them anyway. He should have gone after the big horse himself. Blackfoot ponies were small and easy to handle. Nine Feathers had never ridden a horse that big and powerful and it bucked him easily. He was lucky he got away with his life. It was already dark in the trees as they rode down the trail. Mountain Sun knew there'd be some that would want to go back and kill the two White men. They were free to do whatever they wanted, but Mountain Sun saw no reason to go back. They'd gotten what they wanted, and the White men would be vigilant now. They would find a good camp, sing for their fallen brother and decide what to do next.

Chapter XV

RED CREEK

All over the land are vast and handsome pastures, with good grass for cattle, and it strikes me the soil would be very fertile were the country inhabited and improved by reasonable people.

Alvar N. C. de Vaca

Montana Territory

They would have to wait until morning to do anything with the bodies. Jacob thought about bears. There was a lot of blood and grizzlies were drawn to it. They laid the bodies side by side and covered them with a blanket, then pushed a few logs into a circle and piled brush up around the sides. Lee doused the fire and Jacob went to collect his horse. The Black was still skittish from the incident but allowed the old man to lead him close to camp, where Jacob tied him with a short rope. They would stand watch all night; in case the Blackfoot made another run at them. Lee volunteered for first watch; he couldn't have slept even if he wanted to. It was cold. A fire would be nice, but out of the question. As he sat there with his back against a log, Lee heard that the night was full of rustlings that he had never taken notice of before. He was as jumpy as an alley cat and didn't wake Jacob till dawn.

"Why didn't you roust me?"

"I figured I couldn't sleep anyway."

Both were relieved that the night had passed without more trouble. Jacob pulled the blanket off the bodies. They'd gone rigid in death, their skin blue and the disposition of their limbs grotesque.

"Rekon we should say something for White Hawk," Jacob said.

"What's usual, for them?"

"These horse Indians have plenty of ritual. Sing and dance and make quite a ruckus. But I don't know none of it."

"We can't just leave him."

"They like to be put up off the ground. Lash a couple of limbs to a tree and perch em up high, close to the Spirits."

Jake untied the Black and walked him over. Lee laid White Hawk across the saddle.

"Damn, he don't weigh much at all," Lee said.

"Let's go."

"Wait. What'll do we do with the other one?"

"Leave him be. Critters'll make short work of him."

"I don't know," Lee said. "Don't seem right."

Lee reached down and lifted Little Dog. He was heavier, but not by much. He laid him next to White Hawk. The Black shied, but Jacob held him firmly.

"Get some rope," he said.

They walked a quarter mile to a stand of broad limbed trees and Lee collected branches thick enough to support the weight, and then climbed up into a tree. He tied the branches to the limbs while Jacob lit his pipe and held the horse. Jake would miss the little fellow, but he couldn't help thinking it wasn't such a bad morning, since it wasn't him that was dead. Once Lee had the platform secure, he called to Jake.

"Bring em on over."

Jacob walked the horse under the tree and lifted White Hawk high enough for Lee to grab him. Lee pulled him onto the platform and took a minute to settle his arms and legs. The Indian's long hair was stiff with frost and blood, but Lee did his best to straighten it. He looked down at his friend, but he didn't recognize him. Not like this.

Lee climbed back to the edge of the platform and Jacob lifted Little Dog up to him. Lee hauled him up and dragged him beside White Hawk and performed the same chore, though without as much care. He took one last look at the two Indians and then climbed back down and stood next to Jacob.

"I hope they don't mind laying side by side like that."

"They ain't in no position to complain."

"You want to say something?"

Jake took a slow draw on his pipe and looked up at the platform, then blew a long stream of smoke in their direction.

"Lord. You might consider making an exception and letting this boy in. He was a heathen. But a good man."

Lee nodded his head and started back toward camp.

"What're we gonna do now?" he asked. "They got our horses."

"They got your horse. I reckon you'll have to hoof it."

They went through the gear and made some hard decisions. With only one horse between them, the sensible thing would be to use him to pack the gear, but Jacob wasn't about to walk. They tossed everything they could do without, made a travois out of lodge poles and Lee convinced Jacob to pull it behind the Black. It was mid-morning before they headed down the valley, still alert for trouble. Jacob figured the Blackfoot were miles away by now, but it didn't pay to be fast and loose about it. They didn't make many miles with Lee walking and the Black dragging a load.

"I reckon we better detour," Jacob said. "Hate to be too predictable. They might have another go at us."

"What're you thinking?"

"Let's cut north, up one of these valleys."

They found a good camp that night and took the time to provide cover and work out the firing lines. Then spent a cold and sober night without the heat of a fire to warm them. The next morning, they woke to fat white clouds floating in a pastel blue sky, the rising sun working its way in and out of shadow. They soon found a creek flowing northeast and followed it down into a valley. The soil was rich in iron, lining the bank and making the water, from certain angles, take on the color of rust. The hillsides were heavy with aspen and fir and the valley thick in grass. They were descending into the foothills now and it seemed that they could see all the way down to the plains down below. As they made their way down the valley widened, at places more than a mile across. The valley floor was almost level, dropping just enough to allow the slow- moving stream to serpentine through the grass. Other creeks tumbled down from the high country to join it. As he peered into the water Lee could see fat trout darting in and out of shadow. The whole basin was an uninterrupted sheet of sweet mountain grass so thick it could hold a man's weight, giving way to rising slopes of thickly timbered hills. Lee slowed down to look around. Jacob had ridden ahead without noticing.

Lee called out. "Hold on a minute."

The old man was smoking his pipe, lost in his own thoughts. He reined in the Black and turned in the saddle.

"What's the matter?"

"This is it."

"What're you talking about?"

"This valley."

Jacob gave him a questioning glance and then looked around, taking in the broad sweep of the valley. He slowly nodded.

"Yea. It's as fine as any."

"Going to take some work."

"If you got the energy. I got the knowhow."

"That's what I was afraid of," Lee said.

They spent the afternoon exploring. There were no signs the creek was prone to flooding and the valley ran south to north, cutting off the worst of the winds blowing in off the plains. It was lush. Mountain Bluebell and Silver Lupine cast brush strokes of color against the deep green of the meadow. The Beargrass was just coming into bloom on the shaded hillsides, their white puffs visible clear across the valley.

Jacob checked for sign that Indians frequented the valley but found none. This was their hunting ground and they could be anywhere, but it was far enough off the main route through the pass to make it an impractical detour. Lee looked to the west. The tall peaks of the Great Divide could still be seen, the snowpack aglow in the late afternoon sunlight. He walked down to the meadow and felt the ground. It was firm and relatively dry. Lee turned to Jacob.

"What do you think?" he asked.

Jacob scratched his beard. It didn't matter much to him; he was a wanderer. But there was no arguing with another man's vision. He gave a nod.

"It'll do, I suppose," Lee announced nonchalantly. He tried to sound disinterested, but his heart beat with excitement.

Abraham Lincoln signed the Homestead Act in 1862. It allowed for one hundred sixty acres for every man who filed for land in the territories and stayed to work it. That meant one hundred and sixty acres for Lee and another one hundred and sixty acres for Jacob, plots adjacent to each other and worked as one. Jacob and Lee walked it off. On the south side of the valley, the stream curved around a rock ridge, forming a natural boundary. They figured if they claimed all the land for a thousand yards downstream by the whole width of the valley that would constitute the three hundred twenty acres. The hillsides were so steep and rocky they figured nobody would claim them.

"What about the rest of the valley?" Lee asked. "Can't we claim it?"

"Getting land greedy already? You just got here."

"You know what I mean."

"We stake what we can and act like the rest of it is ours," Jacob said. "Possession is nine tenths, don't they say? First chance you get, lay claim to the rest or buy it up. Till then, if somebody comes in too close you gotta be prepared to run em off.

"Sounds awful convenient."

"Sides," Jacob said. "Ain't nobody but you fool enough to live out here."

"I'm sure old Abe wasn't thinking 'bout Montana when he scribed those numbers. A hunert acres ain't nothing up here. Who'd want to live that close to his neighbor?"

On the opposite end of the meadow, below the rock ridge, a raised bench of land extended above the creek. It commanded a fine view northeast down the valley and northwest to the snow-clad peaks. It'd be a fine place for a cabin. It was close to timber and a small spring rose nearby. Lee decided they'd make camp there. He unpacked the supplies and took stock of what they had. The afternoon was drifting into evening and the sun was filtering through the pines on the western slope. He untied the lodge poles and laid them on the grass. He began to clear a large circle in the grass and found the shed antlers of a bull elk lying half-buried, a massive rack from a huge animal. Lee held them up.

"There are Elk, at least. Damn big ones, from the looks."

Lee put up the shelter. It wasn't as taut or as pretty as when White Hawk did it, but it'd keep the rain off. Lee climbed up onto the bench and crossed his arms, watching the beams of golden sunlight fade to shadow as the sun dropped below the mountains. It was hard to imagine that his search was over, but he knew that he couldn't have picked a better spot. The elevation was low enough that they wouldn't get the heavy snow-pack of the mountains, but still high enough to get some relief from the heat of the plains down below. The hills provided enough shelter that the biting winds would not be as brutal as they were down on the open plains. There was plenty of timber, water and grass and a stream that flowed year-round. He pulled a piece of paper out of the saddle bag and made a crude map, drawing in all the principal features, marking the springs and creeks and prominent trees and making careful notes. There was no need to wander any further. Now was the time to plan, make good decisions and build.

They settled into their new home in the valley. Jacob spent his time hunting. He'd explore with Lee if the mood fit him but, more often than not, he was content to watch the young man scurry about, busy with his plans and prospects. Everyday Lee wandered further afield, exploring the surrounding area. One morning he told Jacob that he wanted to go a little farther afield.

"You want to come?" he asked.

"My back's been poorly."

"Then you won't mind if I take the Black."

"No, spose not."

"I might stay out a night."

"You be careful with that horse," Jacob warned.

"I will be."

"He's the only one we got," he snorted. Jacob could be touchy about his horse.

As the trail descended, Lee rode through hillsides covered in timber. He spent most of the morning riding the lower drainage of the main creek and then came out of the trees onto a vista stretching over the low hills to the plains below. The Missouri river was clearly visible in the distance, a silver ribbon of light flickering in the mid-day sun. A mile further on he came to another watershed branching off to the west, back up into the mountains and he decided to explore it. The canyon rose steeply and a stream dropped in short falls from one pool to another, but a game trail wove between the rocks and Lee was able to ride into the high country beyond. He rode most of the day, alert to the sights and sounds around him. He flushed plenty of game, mainly deer and elk, and saw sign of a large bear that had raked its razor-sharp claws across the thick bark of a tree. Farther up, the trees began to thin and he came to a large lake, a glacial blue in the sunlight, lying at the foot of rough peaks littered with scree.

Lee followed the shore until he came to a wide marsh at the inlet. Two bull moose moved off as he approached. Lee was amazed at how quickly they could run through the trees. This valley was different from his. But, in its own way, it was just as beautiful, and it seemed to extend deeper into the high country than he first thought. He rode past the lake, picked up the trail again and continued to ride. Late in the afternoon, the trail leveled off into a narrow valley a few hundred yards across but stretching west farther than he could see in the fading light. There was plenty of sign. Bear scat lay drying along the game trail and the tracks of deer were imprinted in the mud. Lee decided he'd try to shoot a small deer and spend a night by the lake. He swung down off the Black and tied him carefully to a limb, then followed the trail as it rose through the trees. A hundred yards on, the fir gave way to a grove of ancient and gnarled aspen, their trunks weathered a deeply mottled brown. The stirring of their leaves rustled softly and, if he were a man who took to such notions, he'd have sworn the grove held a power of sorts. He walked forward quietly. He heard the flow of rushing water growing steadily louder and the trail rose in steps to an outlet stream dropping from a lake somewhere above.

Suddenly, he heard a sound and he froze. He slipped forward, keeping within the cover of the trees. Thirty yards ahead, the aspen gave way to a small meadow and beyond that lay another long alpine lake, its water turquoise blue and as smooth as glass. Two yearling bucks were grazing on the fresh spring grass. Lee was just about to step forward for a better shot when an Indian emerged from the cover of the trees not twenty yards in front of him.

Mountain Sun hid in the aspen, watching as the deer emerged from the forest and slowly made their way across the meadow. He forced himself to remain patient. He'd ridden into the mountains that morning. Alone. His friends were used to his habit of disappearing. He'd be gone for a day or a week, not allowing anyone to come along. Sometimes his band would stay put. At other times, they would move on to a new camp and he'd catch up. Mountain Sun had been to this valley before. He had found it when he first began his wandering, and it was one of his favorite places. The hunting was good and he'd never encountered anyone before. He was relaxed and focused on his prey. Too relaxed. He lifted his bow. An arrow dangled loosely from his fingers. He notched the arrow, raised his arm and pulled the bowstring back in one fluid motion, but the bucks must have seen the movement and suddenly jumped. He loosened the arrow and saw it fly high over their backs into the field beyond.

Lee had his rifle up. The Indian's broad back was turned to him and Lee knew that he'd been stalking the deer from the cover of the trees. Lee suddenly realized that he had seen the man before. He was one of the Blackfoot that had attacked their camp, one of the Indians who killed White Hawk. It was only luck that Lee had spotted him first. Lee wondered if the rest of his band was nearby. Lee watched as the arrow sailed wide and the deer bolted for the trees. The Indian was completely unaware of Lee's presence. Lee had the Spencer leveled at the man's back and his finger began to bear down. At the last instant, he swung his rifle away and pulled the trigger. A belch of smoke filled the air, but Lee saw the slug catch the buck below the shoulder, dropping him in a step.

The deafening explosion took Mountain Sun by surprise and he dropped his bow. He had just time enough to see the buck fall and swung around to see who had made the shot. A White man was right behind him, his rifle raised, gun smoke still lifting into the air. The man started forward and Mountain Sun stumbled backward. His hand went to his belt, but it was too late. Mountain Sun waited for the shot but the man brushed right by him and walked into the meadow. Mountain Sun bent, picked up his bow and pulled an arrow from his quiver. The White man never looked back and kept walking toward the fallen buck. He tossed his sack down in the grass, laid his rifle across it and pulled a knife from his belt.

Mountain Sun thought he must be dreaming, but something about this White man seemed familiar, then he realized that it was one of the White men, the younger one, whose horses they'd stolen. Mountain Sun did not understand why he was still alive.

Lee turned and looked back, waving him over. Without waiting, he pushed the buck onto its back and sank the knife into its lower abdomen, cutting up along the belly. Mountain Sun moved forward as though in a trance, mindful of a trick, but also aware that his life had been this man's to take. What other trick mattered? Lee's knife stalled when he reached the chest cavity and, instinctively, Mountain Sun grabbed the buck's legs and pulled them clear so Lee could make the cut. Without a word, they worked together until the animal was cleaned and gutted.

An unspoken decision was made. Neither spoke the other's language. No attempt at verbal communication was made, but by example and sign they communicated. They were the same age and alone in this neutral place. Nobody was here to tell them how they should behave, and their curiosity and mutual respect lent an unexpected measure of collegiality to their actions. They carried the carcass to a spot just inside the tree line overlooking the lake, as pretty a camp as they were likely to find. Both men retrieved their horses and brought them to the meadow, the Lilac Roan and the Big Black nudging each other in similar curiosity. The sun set and a soft twilight settled over the valley. Lee collected firewood and built a fire while Mountain Sun cut strips off the backstrap and skewered them on sharpened sticks. They watched each other, but mostly out of curiosity rather than distrust. Lee had a small pot and brewed coffee. The tin cup was hot and Mountain Sun took it from Lee's hand and sipped. It was nice and warm but the taste was bitter and unpleasant, but he drank it to avoid giving offense.

There were questions Lee wanted to ask but he hadn't a clue how to go about it, so they sat in silence, sipping their coffee, watching as the shadows spread slowly across the still surface of the lake, broken only by the spreading ripples of trout rising to feed. Mountain Sun handed Lee a skewer and Lee reached into his bag and took a pinch of salt, then handed it to Mountain Sun. They ate in silence, and then went down to the lake to wash the grease from their fingers. Only the faintest flush of amber backlit the mountains. Mountain Sun pointed to hundreds of small grey bats slicing through the air on the opposite shore. Lee watched for a moment, and then piled more wood on the fire. Neither had a pipe or the makings of a smoke, so they sat staring at the fire as men have done for thousands of years. Lee took a stick and sketched a rudimentary outline of North America and the course of the Mississippi across it. He pointed to himself and then to the place where he imagined St Louis would be. Mountain Sun nodded. He didn't recognize the drawing as a representation of the continent they lived on and only supposed it was some talisman important to the White man. Lee handed the stick to Mountain Sun, who took it and scratched out his own map, drawing the valley and then the peaks of the mountains marching north, the semicircular line of the Missouri river and the broad plains to the east.

"Pika'ni," he said simply.

"Lee," he answered, assuming he'd been told the Blackfoot's name.

As the night passed, a conversation took place. Words for an object were learned: the moon rising in the clear night sky, the fire before them, coffee, horse, tree, water. Lee showed him how the Spencer worked and handed him a cartridge. Mountain Sun was fascinated. Lee chambered a round and handed the rifle to Mountain Sun, who took aim at an aspen seventy yards down range. The blast echoed across the basin and they could hear the thunk of lead hitting wood. Mountain Sun clearly liked the Spencer and Lee hoped he wasn't expected to make a gift of it, because he wasn't about to go that far. They "talked" into the night and, when the conversation exhausted itself, they spread out their blankets, laid down in front of the fire and fell asleep.

The next morning, they rose at first light. Lee had a few biscuits in his saddle bag and handed one to Mountain Sun, but he could tell from his new friend's troubled countenance that he was forcing it down. Lee made the Blackfoot take the hide and the rest of the meat and gave him the bag of salt and the little bit of coffee he had left. Mountain Sun reached into his bag and pulled out the eagle claw and feather he'd been given by Omak after his initiation. Lee guessed it was a thing of value and was reluctant to accept it, but he knew better than to refuse. They rode down the valley and Lee admired the effortless horsemanship of the young warrior, who hardly held the reins and somehow willed the magnificent horse forward without command. By late morning, they'd reached the end of the valley and Lee bade him farewell and watched as he rode toward the foothills. It was late afternoon before Lee got back to the homestead. For the last few miles, he went over in his head how he was going to shape the telling of the tale.

The days were growing longer. Each day, Lee spent a little more time at his chores. He laid out the plan for the ranch, orienting the cabin and arguing over whether or not a well should be dug. Lee was for it, Jacob against. They marked out the site for a barn, a corral and working pens. He made a list of tools they needed. Some they could make for themselves, others would have to be purchased, little by little, as they could afford them. They had some cash money, but they would need most of it to purchase a herd if they were ever going to get started.

Lee wasn't sure where the cattle would come from, but it was too early to worry about that, anyway. They would need to head in to Fort Benton in a few weeks to homestead their parcel and buy supplies, and it would be a long walk, with only one horse between them.

Lee planned the cabin, calculating the number of logs they'd need and their lengths. He spent a few days in the forest marking lodge poles and figuring the distance he'd have to drag them. Jake was helpful one minute and would backslide the next. Despite himself, the old man was gaining enthusiasm for the project. They worked long days and by sundown were tuckered out. Sleep was not a problem.

One morning, a week after Lee returned from his hunt, he woke early and stepped out of the lodge. There wasn't a cloud in the sky and the Waxwing and Warbler filled the air with sweet music. Lee stretched and looked down the hill across the meadow. Three horses were grazing in the meadow.

"Jacob," Lee called. "You better get out here."

"Don't you be pushin me, boy. I'll take a switch to your hide."

"Come on. You gotta see this."

Jake stepped out and Lee pointed across the meadow to the horses. Lee had his boots on and was already walking down the hill. Jake pulled his own boots on over his long underwear and followed. After a hundred yards, they could see that these were the horses that had been stolen in the raid.

"I ain't never heard of such a thing," Jacob muttered. "You musta made quite an impression on that fellow."

Fort Benton, Montana Territory

Fort Benton was founded by the American Fur company. Its position on the Missouri River, at the foothills of the Rockies, made it an ideal spot for trappers and Indians looking to sell their furs. The most famous of the Mountain Men had passed through and traded their plews to the Company men for the provisions they'd need to get them through another year. But as the days of the fur trade faded into history, so too did the economic vitality of the Fort. As the Western migration increased with the opening of the Oregon Trail, the army was called upon to protect the routes from the predations of the horse tribes. In due course, the government bought the fort and operated it as a garrison.

The ride down from the homestead was easy enough, a gentle grade through rolling hills, well-watered and free of obstacles. Lee knew that would be important if they had to drive cattle along the route. It was still cool on the prairie and the hills were green. They approached the fort across a level plain in clear sight of the blockhouses. The walls were fourteen feet high, very solid and built of adobe brick formed right here on the banks of the Missouri. They passed through the timbered gate and rode onto the quadrangle; surprised by the amount of commerce and activity going on. Indians of different tribes were allowed through the gate, a few at a time, to sell hides at the trading post. Boat captains, passengers, soldiers, traders, and gold seekers all went about their business. The fort was rustic, the buildings crudely constructed, the windows mostly without glass or other refinements. The quadrangle was mired in mud and it stuck to everything: boots, horses and wagon wheels.

Jacob asked a trooper where they might find the Commandant and they were directed to his office. A fresh-faced adjutant Lee's own age opened the door and stiffly asked them their business. Jacob hated uppity adjutants and told him they needed to speak to the boss. His tone did not brook argument and they were shown into his office. As soon as the door opened, Colonel Avery Billings Cain looked up from his papers and broke into a grin.

"I knew I hadn't seen the last of you two," he said, coming around from behind his desk to warmly shake their hands.

"You must have riled somebody back in Washington to get posted up here," Jacob said.

Billings laughed. "Supposed to be a promotion. You know how the military works. First Commandant of a new garrison."

"How long you been here?"

"Three months. Now that the war's over they're shuffling things around."

"The war's over?" Lee asked.

"You boys have been out of touch."

"We weren't never in touch," Jacob said.

The Colonel turned his attention to Lee. "And look at you. Aren't you the old hand. Haven't been able to shake this old cuss, yet?"

"Not yet, sir.

"What have you boys been up to?"

"Been busy," Jacob answered. "Worked Virginia City for a while, then some wandering, and a little hunting."

"Tried your hand at digging for gold, I suppose?"

"No, not for me, I'm too old for that," Jacob said. "But Lee here gave it a shot."

"No luck?"

"Some, Lee said. "Not much."

"What brings you to Fort Benton," he asked.

"Youngster's got a notion," Jacob answered, nodding towards Lee. Cain turned.

"Well," Lee began. "We found a nice little valley in the hills a few days west of here. We're thinking of starting in on the ranch business. Want to homestead it. One for each."

"Long as it's not Indian land, we can handle that," Billings said, smiling. "It's about time you boys settled down. Was a time or two I wondered if you hadn't already lost your scalp."

"Was a time or two we almost did."

"That right? What happened?"

Lee told him about the Blackfoot raid, and how they lost their horses.

"It's been tense," the Colonel agreed. "Things will be quiet for a while and then something sparks. Maybe a band of young bucks out looking to make a name for themselves. Or some miner will wander somewhere he shouldn't be and will get himself killed."

"Blackfoot?" Jacob asked.

"Mostly. Proud people. They're spread out across the upper plains into Canada and are still strong.

"That's what we're finding out," Jacob agreed.

"We're not sure how many are out there," the Colonel added.

"Colonel, sir. How is Miss Elizabeth?" Lee asked.

"Just fine, Lee. Just fine. She's been wondering what's become of you two."

"She's here?" Lee asked.

"Yes. She's here," Cain laughed. "You stop in and see her before you go."

"Yes, sir. We'll do that."

"I'd like to spend more time and visit, but I'm up to here with work. Williams here will direct you to the clerk." He turned to his adjutant. "Have the clerk bring the papers directly to me for signing. I don't want any mix up with the filings."

"Yes, sir," the adjutant replied.

"You boys come by and see me before you head back."

"Surely will," Jacob said.

The clerk's office was small, without windows and with only a single stout door. Its walls were lined with ledgers. A large iron safe occupied one corner of the room. Williams introduced them to the clerk. He was thin and bald with skin so white and pasty that it was difficult to believe he ever saw the sun. He had been in the war and was taken to nervous fits, but he was content, now, to sit in his dark little room all day, copying maps and keeping accounts. It suited him just fine. He took the paper from the adjutant and looked through his files, then unrolled a map of their section of the Montana territory.

"Where's your piece?" he asked.

Lee looked at the map, but it took him a while to get oriented. He found the pass they'd traversed and then the creek that flowed off to the northeast, but the map was not entirely accurate. Lee pointed out the inaccuracies to the clerk, who was reluctant to make changes on the say so of a man younger than he was. Lee told him how they wanted the sections drawn up, giving him as accurate a description of the landmarks and distances as he could from the notes they had taken walking it off. The clerk made note of the parcels in his book, wrote up the homesteading deeds and handed them to the adjutant, who left to obtain the Colonel's signature. The clerk explained that they needed to work the land for five years to gain title. Once they held title, they had the right to purchase adjacent acreage from the government at going rates. The adjutant returned in a few minutes with the signed deeds, handed them to Jacob and wished them luck. They walked out into the late afternoon sunlight, a proud pair of Montana ranchers.

It was cause for celebration and it had been a good long while since Jake had had a good glass of whiskey. Lee went to the trader's store and began bargaining for the tools and supplies they'd need. Everything was expensive and Lee was tight with the money, driving such a hard bargain that the trader almost threw him out of the store.

The next morning, they packed up the horses, trying to keep the loads level and secure. Lee was dragging his heels. Earlier that morning he had hopped out of his bedroll and walked down to the river to wash up. Jacob smiled. He knew what was on the young man's mind, though fun like this didn't present itself too often.

"Hurry up, boy. I'm dying to get back and start in on all that work,"

Lee looked at him as though he were crazy.

"Alright," Lee said.

"Got a long ride. If we start now we might. . ."

"Well, actually," Lee interrupted. "I was thinking about stopping in to say hello to Miss Elizabeth."

"Who?"

"You know who," Lee snapped. "Told the Colonel I would."

"Hummm. Maybe I'll go with you."

"Why don't you go get yourself a drink," Lee said, irritated.

"It's pretty early, yet?"

"That's never stopped you before."

"Suit yourself," Jacob said in disgust. "You know where to find me."

"Not too many," Lee called as Jacob moved away. "We've got a long ride."

Lee stood there a minute, frozen. But he turned and walked toward the Commandant's quarters, one leg ahead of the other, willed by a force stronger than his nerve. He knocked, fighting the sudden urge to turn away and run. But when Elizabeth opened the door, he was struck speechless. He'd supposed a servant would answer.

"Lee," she said. "I thought you'd slipped away without saying goodbye, again."

She was even prettier than he remembered. Her long black hair fell past her shoulders and her bright green eyes were unrelenting. She smiled broadly and seemed genuinely happy to see him.

"I wouldn't do that."

"You did once before."

"Oh, Yeah. Sorry bout that."

"Where's Mr. McCune? Isn't he here with you?"

"In the store. Sends his respects."

She led him into a simple parlor, smaller and rougher than the quarters they had at Laramie, but Elizabeth had made it her own, making it look cozy, even elegant, by frontier standards. Lee noticed a tall officer in full uniform in the center of the room, watching him intently. He had curly brown hair and a moustache trimmed neatly above his lip. He held himself in military posture, back straight, but his movements were languid and minimal.

"Lee. I'd like to introduce you to Captain March. He's second in command here and a friend of my father's."

"And of yours too, I hope," the Captain said to Elizabeth, reaching out to shake Lee's hand.

"Jason. This is Lee. We met him and his friend Mr. McCune at Fort Laramie. He saved Papa's life."

"Is that so?" March asked.

"Just a little excitement on a hunting trip," Lee said.

"I'm sure you're being too modest. What brings you to the territory?"

"Just trying to find my way, same as everybody else," Lee replied, uncomfortably.

"Well, I've got to report for duty. It was nice meeting you." He said, and then he turned to Elizabeth. "I'll see you soon, I hope."

Lieutenant March picked his hat up from the table, tucked it beneath his arm and headed for the door, but not before giving Lee a long and questioning look. Lee stared back, knowing already that he did not like or trust the man, and not only because he'd been calling on

Elizabeth. After she showed March to the door, Elizabeth returned and took Lee's arm, putting him quickly at ease again. She led him to the sofa and made him sit, then she sat beside him, so close he could smell the perfume she wore, so close it made him nervous and excited and speechless all over again.

"I was a little upset with you. Papa said you were coming yesterday."

"I had some business."

"That's alright, I suppose," she said, with just a hint of a pout.

"Is that your beau?" Lee asked. Elizabeth looked at him disapprovingly.

"I beg your pardon?"

"Just asking?"

"A girl gets a lot of attention out here. All these men."

Lee sat in silence for a moment, not trusting himself to say anything. Elizabeth watched him, in his rough buckskin pants and moccasins, his hair longer than the last time she'd seen him, falling in such disarray that it was all she could do to prevent herself from brushing it out of his eyes. He was more handsome than she remembered.

"Been a while since I seen you. You look. . ." Lee hesitated, and then forced himself to turn to her. "Nice."

Elizabeth almost laughed, but something warned her against it.

"Thank you. You've changed as well. You look older. More sure of yourself."

"We've had ourselves some adventures."

"Imagine running into each other again. Way out here."

"I was surprised to see your Pa."

"Yes. I had to put up quite a fight this time. Seems they consider Montana too dangerous for women."

"It's coming around. Towns are springing up. Even have a theater down in Virginia City."

"Well, there's nothing like that around here."

"It's still pretty raw."

"What are you doing here at Fort Benton?" she asked.

"Jacob and I are laying claim to some land. Going to start in ranching."

"Oh, that's wonderful. Near here?"

"A little valley just into the foothills."

"Oh, she said, looking disappointed. "What about here? All this land just waiting to be settled. Wouldn't you rather be near the Fort?"

Lee was surprised by her reaction. He imagined she'd be impressed, even happy for him.

"You should see it, Elizabeth. It's like nothing you've ever seen before. The grass goes on forever. And the hills are covered with wildflowers. I don't know their names, but you should see them. A stream comes out of the mountains and everywhere you look there's something pretty to see. It's paradise, or as close as I'm likely to get."

Elizabeth watched his eyes as he spoke, and she could feel his excitement. All his shyness and awkwardness were gone, replaced by his vision of what he was going to do, what he was going to create.

"I wish I could see it."

"Oh, you will. It's not too far. Once we have a cabin built you can come for a visit with your father. The hunting's good. He can have himself another shot at a grizzly. Think you might like that?"

"I'd love it. But I don't know how long we'll be here."

"You're leaving?"

Elizabeth laughed gently. "Not yet. But posting change."

"Just promise me that if you have to leave you'll get word to me first," he said.

Without being conscious of it, he leaned forward and took her hand. Elizabeth looked up at him, content to let him keep it.

"The clerk here has a map of our place. Get word to me somehow and I'll come see you."

"Alright."

"You promise?" he asked, suddenly aware that he was holding her hand and then dropping it instantly.

"I promise, Mr. Grant."

"Well. I better get going before I have to carry Jacob out of there. But I'll be back, now and again, for supplies and such."

By the time Lee got back to the horses, Jacob was waiting.

"And how is Miss Elizabeth?" he asked.

"Fine. She sends best wishes."

"I didn't spect you back so soon. Mighty quick."

"I was there awhile!"

"You got to take your time. Woo a lady slow like."

"I'll try to remember," Lee said, swinging up onto his horse.

It was only then that Lee noticed another old timer standing next to Jake, watching them, and listening to their conversation.

"This here's Chance Wilson," Jake said. "Looking for work. Figured we could use a hand."

Chance wasn't exactly old, but he'd seen his day. Lee wondered how much work was left in him. Lee envisioned himself saddled with a posse full of geezers who drank too much and were too worn out to put in a full day's work. Chance had a long grey beard and bushy grey eyebrows, a painfully thin frame, bowed legs and teeth so darkened by tobacco they were almost black.

"Please to meet you. But I don't know that we can afford a hand right now."

"Oh, I work cheap. I been mining these few years and, to tell the truth, I'm sick of it. Like to find a more healthful profession. Mr. McCune here's been telling me about your ranch. Seems like just the thing."

"We don't even have a cabin. Yet."

"That's alright. Been building most my life. I know how to swing a hammer. I don't look like much, but I'm strong as a smithy."

Chapter XVI

A CABIN IN THE WOODS

I hadn't lived in a regular house since I left home as a young buck. Got so I didn't feel comfortable with walls closin in on me. But Lee wanted a proper ranch house with all the trimmings and his spine was stiffening. I wern't having the same luck talking him outta things. When we started in on it, just seemed like too damn much work. But once in the thick of it, even I had to admit there was a certain pleasure to be taken in the task.

Jacob McCune

I do not want to settle down in the houses you would build for us. I love to roam over the wild prairie. There I am free and happy. When we sit down, we grow pale and die.

White Bear (Kiowa chief)

Red Creek Ranch, Montana Territory

That first day they spent organizing their tools, sharpening the saws and axes and building a sawyer's rack on which they could suspend a log and slice it into planks. Chance was as good as his word. He knew how to put things together. Jacob argued for a small cabin, a single room. But Lee had his own ideas. He took a line and staked out the footprint: a main room, two sleeping rooms, and a detached kitchen that connected to the main house by way of a covered walk. He studied the way the wind blew, mainly from the east up off the plains, and sited the kitchen on the far northwest corner so that if a fire started it would not blow towards the house.

Lee's plan called for a large hearth, big enough for logs to burn all night. There would be a covered porch running the length of the house, overlooking the valley. They would be able to sit out in the morning and drink their coffee; or relax in the evening and still be able to look out over the herd. Lee spent a morning laying out the perimeter and the rest of the day arguing over the details with Jacob and Chance. Jacob said it was too much too soon, but Lee was stubborn. There were a few points he was forced to concede, especially if Chance said they were impractical, but by day's end they had a plan.

Early the next morning they started clearing the site, digging out the sod and leveling the lot. They dug a simple foundation one foot wide and three feet deep. There was more rock than dirt in the soil and it was back breaking. Chance went at it with a pick and shovel and Lee was impressed. He worked hour after hour and, despite his age, seemed never to tire. It took two days to dig the foundation, and then Lee carried buckets of water to the trench and flooded it, pounding it down with the flat end of a heavy log. Despite the thick gloves, his hands were soon badly blistered, but he knew they'd callus up soon enough.

Chance made a wheelbarrow. It was cut from the first sawn planks they milled and had a solid wooden wheel, but it worked just fine. They began hauling flat rocks up from the creek. Lee laid them in the trench, filling in around them with gravel and mud. It took more than a week but, when the foundation was finally finished it was as solid as a slab of granite.

Jacob scouted the hills. He was looking for logs, fallen or standing dead. They'd be drier and lighter than green timber. The standing dead he chopped down, making a note of where they were and what size, so they could be collected later. All the logs had to be trimmed and topped, and it was hard and sweaty work. Mosquitos and biting flies were stirred up by the disturbance and Jacob had welts over his face and neck, for which he readily blamed Lee. Even dry, the logs were heavy, and a path had to be cleared. Chance rigged up some tow ropes and they harnessed the horses and dragged the logs to the site. Before long, the clearing was covered in logs.

To work on a log, they had to lever it onto the rack. The logs were unwieldy and the purchase poor. One slip and a leg could be easily broken. The first few logs were muscled into place but, after a while, they learned to coordinate their efforts. Once they had the log on the rack, Chance would peel the bark with a draw knife. Lee knew a little about building, but Chance had far more experience. Lee was content to watch and learn, asking questions now and again, but mainly doing what he was told.

The logs for the base row were carefully shaped so that the top and bottom edges were flat and the taper removed. These were laid atop the rock foundation and packed with sand and clay. At the corners, the logs were laid perpendicular to each other and a straight rule and knife transferred the curvature of the first log onto the second. Chance used a saw to cut to the depth of the line and then an axe and chisel to form a half circular notch. Most logs had a natural bow and wouldn't lay flat, so Lee straightened them with an adze. It was satisfying, locking the clean white logs together with nothing but the joinery to secure them. The first few were rough, but the fitting got better as they went. The butt end of each log extended past the corner and Lee used a sharp hatchet to chamfer the ends.

The long end of the cabin measured thirty-five feet, too long for a single log, so each row required two logs joined with a half lap so perfect it looked like a single piece. Chance bore holes through the center of the lap and pounded wood dowels to secure the joint. Wooden dowels were whittled around the fire at night, all three of them competing to see who could make the straightest most consistent peg. Lee took it upon himself to make sure the tools were kept sharp and oiled. It was something his father had drilled into him and something he took pride in. If a handle snapped, they made a new one out of stump wood and lost little time in doing it.

By June the days were long and the sun seemed reluctant to set. Jacob set aside a patch of ground for a garden, dug up the grass and planted the seeds he'd brought from the fort. He planted potatoes, onions, peas, turnips and cabbage. He wasn't about to water it by hand so he dug a channel and rigged a sluice so he could water the whole kit and caboodle at one time. It wasn't long before he was waging a protracted battle with the rabbits and birds. When he wasn't farming or working on the cabin, he took care of the meat. He preferred hunting to manual labor, anyway, especially if he got to take Lee's rifle. Lee and Chance would be working on the cabin and hear a shot echo across the valley. An hour or so later Jacob would pack in the meat. They laid in a supply of beans, rice, flour, coffee and sugar from Fort Benton. After a day of hard work, they were usually mighty hungry.

As the walls rose, they talked about doors and windows. Lee wanted the windows to be big, but Jacob argued the whole thing would come tumbling down if too many holes were cut into the walls. Lee suspected Jacob was just being ornery, as he was wont to be. The other problem was that the nearest glass was a thousand miles away. Chance suggested they keep them small for the time being. They could be cut larger in the future. Chance suspected that the price and scarcity of glass combined with the harsh winter winds would make future changes unlikely. They cut the openings and Jacob's pride was satisfied. There was no glass, and likely wouldn't be for a while. But what a difference a square hole made, even a small one, if it framed a view of the meadow and trees with snow-capped mountains in the background.

Chance selected special logs for the gable ends and roof trusses, and the cleanest and largest of all for the ridge beam. The ridge ran a little longer than the length of the main room and gabled down to each corner. It was an impressive pile of lumber when it was all laid out on the ground. It took another three weeks to frame the roof. Lee hadn't thought about how they were going to keep the water and snow out but, luckily, Chance had. There was a stand of Cedar a mile to the west. Chance cut a log, sectioned it into smaller pieces, dragged them to the site and made up a clamp to hold the blanks. With a little practice, Lee was chopping off long tapered shingles. As soon as he had a fair-sized bunch, he climbed onto the roof and nailed them down.

While Lee worked on the roof, the old men started in on the fireplace. The fact that it was so damn big still sat poorly with Jacob, who considered it prideful. Lee and Chance hauled up a pile of rocks and as much clay as they could dig from the stream bed. They mixed the clay and mud with dried grass, and it worked well enough if they were careful about fitting the stones. As the rock sides grew higher, they cut out the logs above it until the mantle was a good six feet off the ground. For the mantle cap, they found a flat slab of slate five feet long and a foot thick and rested it on the rock columns. It took all of them and a horse to lift it; but was a thing of beauty once they wrestled it into place. Jacob marked the occasion with a day off and slept until nine the next morning. Lee hardly blamed him; he was tired himself.

There were two doors and six windows. Lee and Chance lifted a pine log onto the sawyer's rack and cut two-inch thick planks. Chance used a block plane to flatten them, mating the edges perfectly. Cross braces were cut and the doors were pegged and nailed together. He cut thinner planks to jamb the openings and pegged them down. Chance had been working on wooden hinges each night by the campfire. He mounted them to the door, hung them on the frame and stood back to give it a try. The door swung open and closed easily. Even a fifty caliber Henry wouldn't pierce it. Chance shaped a sturdy latch for everyday use and a lock bar on the inside to secure it for trouble.

The cabin had been drying and settling in the hot sun for weeks and the logs were ready to be chinked. Lee collected dried grass and mixed it in the barrow with clay, then pounded it in place using a wooden chisel and mallet. This would have to be repeated as the logs dried, but it would keep the cold wind from blowing through come winter.

The main cabin was completed by August. A prettier structure none of them had ever seen. But there was still plenty of work to do.

The inside was still untouched and there was the kitchen, barn and the porch to build; big projects, but nothing on which their life would depend. They'd build the furniture come winter when they were shut in and needed something to occupy their time.

The windows were still open to the elements. Sometime before winter they would need to seal them with oiled paper; they couldn't expect any real glass until spring at the earliest. But for the time being it was nice to look out unencumbered. Chance sawed the planks for the porch and Lee set aside small logs for the posts, but digging holes in the rocky ground was difficult. They needed to be sunk deeply if the porch was to be covered, and there was no point in building a porch in Montana if it didn't keep the sun off in the summer and the rain and snow off all the other times. The platform afforded a clear view down to the creek and the valley below and Jacob was already talking about the rocking chair he wanted Chance to fashion for him, so he could sit out in the evening and smoke his pipe.

Fall came early, as sometimes happens in Montana. The mountains were alive with color, aspens turning gold and crimson and whole slopes of Tamarack lighting up the hills in streaks of amber. The nights were growing cold, and the men finally dismantled their lodge and moved into the cabin. It was strange to have four walls around them, but the big fireplace threw plenty of heat and made the place feel cozy from the very first night.

By September, the elk were beginning to come into rut and Lee could hear them bugling on the hillsides. There were deer in the lower meadow and ducks and geese were beginning to move south. The garden was just about played out and Jake knew it was time to lay in some meat for the winter.

In October, the first snow began to fall. The days grew short and the nights cold, but the cabin was snug and the roof nearly leak-free. They built up the wood pile and wandered afield to hunt. They could build a barn come spring and a proper work room; maybe even a blacksmith shop with a forge that his papa would be proud of. Lately, in the quiet times when he was riding the ranch or when he was lying in bed at night, Lee thought about him, finding it hard to believe that he was gone forever. Or about his Ma, missing her and wondering how she fared and if he would ever see her again.

Chapter XVII

CHRISTMAS

Frontier life could be cruel, but Christmas was a time of joy for many of the settlers. Often faced with loneliness and despair, the holiday gave an opportunity for companionship. Many families were fortunate enough to have neighbors, a town, or a military fort nearby where Christmas was often celebrated with feasting and dancing. At such events, the women of the area would prepare a meal in the early evening and after it was finished the dance would begin. This ball would last until the next morning when breakfast would be served. Afterwards, people would stay a few more hours, the women and men engaging in idle talk and the children playing before heading home, tired but happy.

John K Davis

Red Creek, Montana Territory

By December, the meadow was an undulating blanket of the purest white snow, with the creek cutting a blue ribbon across it. Mornings, it was easy to stay in bed and dream. It is said that the Lord made winter so Men might rest. There was still plenty of work to do, but without stock to care for, life was about as restful as it was ever going to be. But Lee was too full of beans to lie abed. There was too much to think about, all the things he was going to do, all the things he was going to build, and about Elizabeth, with her soft skin and warm clean smell.

Lee tried to keep track of the days, but quickly lost track. But he knew Christmas was coming, give or take a week. None of them had much in the way of religion; but being out here convinced you that there was something bigger than yourself, something to wonder at. One evening, as they sat down to supper, Lee announced that he was riding into Fort Benton.

"It's the dead of winter," Jacob said.

"Snow's not deep yet," Lee said.

"No need to risk it. We got what we need. We can sit till spring."

"There's things we can use. Another couple weeks and I might not get through," Lee argued.

"I ain't going with you," Jacob said.

"Don't expect you to," Lee said.

"I'll go," Chance volunteered.

"No. I'll go alone."

"Bring me some whiskey?" Chance asked.

"Sure," Lee agreed.

"It's that damn female, ain't it?" Jacob asked.

"Corse it is," Chance laughed.

"You gonna come back hitched or dead," Jacob barked. "And I don't know which is worse."

The next morning dawned clear and cold. Lee swung up onto his horse and buttoned his coat up to his chin. Jacob watched him breaking trail through the snow. He wasn't really afraid of the boy getting there in one piece. Lee could take care of himself. It was once he got there Jake was worried about. A woman could make a sensible man reckless, like one of those bull elk in the throes of the rut.

Lee took his time. The footing was uncertain, and he didn't fancy being afoot in this weather. It was a lonely feeling to be riding down out of the mountains, the wind blowing the snow across the trail, covering every rock and tree. But it was hauntingly beautiful. He could easily believe he was the only person for a thousand miles around. Not only was there no sign of men, Red or White, there were no living creatures to be seen. The buffalo had most likely wandered south or were huddled in some low sheltered canyon, and the deer and elk would have found somewhere to winter by now.

The next afternoon Lee rode through the gate and straight to the Colonel's office. Colonel Billings gave him a warm welcome and gave orders for Lee's horse to be fed and stabled.

"Is everything alright?" the Colonel asked. "You look frozen solid."

"It cuts through you, that's for certain," Lee said. "Everything's fine. Just thought I'd come down for a few things."

"Well, your timing's good."

"Why's that?" Lee asked.

"It's Christmas Eve. Don't you boys have an almanac up there."

"No, sir. We don't. I thought it was a week off yet."

"Well, everyone around these parts thinks it's today."

"I'm sure they're right. Lost track, is all."

"How are things out at the ranch?" The Colonel asked.

"Real good. Main house is about done, but there's still lots of work left."

"I'll bet. Any more trouble with the Blackfoot?"

"Haven't seen any," Lee replied. "We've been lucky, I guess."

"You be careful. You're on your own, out there."

"We are that, but we'll be alright."

"So, what's your plan?" Billings asked.

"Come spring, I'm heading south to buy some stock, if I can find them at a price."

"Soon as you're ready, you drive some of them here and the army will buy them from you. We've got a lot of mouths to feed."

"That's mighty kind of you," Lee said.

"Good business, that's all," the Colonel said, reaching out to shake on it.

"Elizabeth will be glad to see you. There's a party tonight."

"Party?"

"Christmas celebration," the Colonel said. "People are coming from all over the territory. We'll set you up in the NCO's quarters. Go clean up and get some rest. You'll be up late."

Lee went to the Post store and bought the supplies he needed. Everybody was excited about the upcoming festivities. Folks had been baking pies and other sweets for a week now and the men in the store were talking about all the food and drink they planned to consume. Lee packed his saddle bags full of the beans, coffee, flour, sugar and rice that would get them through until spring. And wrapped two bottles of whiskey in heavy paper for Jacob and Chance. It would be their Christmas presents, he supposed. He made his way to the NCO quarters, a cold windowless room ripe with the stink of unwashed men. A corporal pointed him to an empty bunk, clearly unhappy that a civilian was being thrown in with them. Lee tossed his saddle bags to the floor. It had been too cold to get much sleep last night in his rough camp and he'd started out before first light. He was dog tired but had no intention of sleeping during the day. That was for when you were sick or dying. And he was having second thoughts about being here. He hadn't planned on going to a party; couldn't even remember the last time he'd been to one. Since he didn't know what else to do, he laid down on the bunk, crossed his hands behind his head and stared up at the rough wooden planks on the ceiling.

He woke a few hours later in darkness, disoriented and unsure of where he was or how he had gotten there. He shook himself awake and made his way to the door. It would be nice if he could rustle up a bath.

He found a candle on the table and lit it. There was a washbasin and a bucket of water. Lee held it up to the light. It was clean, or near enough. He took a bar of soap and scrubbed. The water was very cold and he was plenty dirty. There was no mirror, so he had no idea if he had scrubbed himself clean. He had a change of clothes in his saddlebag, but they were as wrinkled and frayed as everything else he owned.

He cleaned his boots as best he could and even used a little of the bootblack he found on the table. His boots would shine, leastwise where they weren't scuffed. A sergeant came in from his shift and told him the party would start in about an hour. He was a big man with a thick black beard and piercing brown eyes and he reminded Lee of all the sergeants he'd run up against in the war, tough and humorless men whose job was to keep the recruits in line and moving forward. Lee walked outside for some fresh air.

The mess hall was decorated with brightly colored cloth and ribbons. Candles burned brightly along the walls and a Christmas tree had been brought in and gaily decorated with paper ornaments and ribbon. It was as bright and festive a setting as Lee had ever seen, especially in contrast to the somber aspect of the rest of the fort. At the other end of the room, five musicians beat a lively jig. They were soldiers thrown together for the occasion and had been practicing all week, but what they lacked in talent they made up in enthusiasm.

The room was crowded. The enlisted men wore their cleanest uniforms and the officers had their collars starched and their brass buttons polished. The civilians were dressed in everything from buckskins to silk shirts. Unfortunately, there were only a few women, soldier's wives, a few married civilians and Elizabeth, the only unattached woman in the room. A crowd of men swarmed around her. Lee wandered around for more than an hour and had been unable to get her attention. He watched from a distance as she was spun roughly across the dance floor by a tall private with all the grace of a wounded buffalo, but she was smiling and gave every indication that she was having a wonderful time.

It took his breath away to see her again. Her ankle length red velvet dress was trimmed in white satin. Even beneath all that fabric, he could see the full curves of her figure. She had tied her hair with a length of red ribbon and wore white silk gloves that came to the middle of her forearms. Her cheeks were flushed from the heat of the dance and she smiled sweetly to the private when the song was over. She was even more beautiful than Lee remembered.

All the wives were dutifully taking turns dancing with the enlisted men. Rank held no sway on the dance floor; it was every man for himself. The music was lively. It made you want to dance, even if you didn't know how, and most of the young men didn't. Toes were stepped on and shins kicked. The women winced and managed to smile but, despite the pain, they were enjoying the attention. Punch was served. It had a little rum in it, but not too much. It was designed to quench the thirst and lighten the spirits, not deaden them. Lee settled against the wall with the other bachelors and watched. They were nice enough, his age and younger, all wishing, no doubt, that they had a belle as pretty as Elizabeth.

Lieutenant March had to wait, just like everybody else. He sulked around the edge of the floor without talking to anybody. When it was finally his turn he approached Elizabeth, bowing quite elegantly and reached out his hand. He was impressive in his dress uniform. His slim physique favored the long finely tailored coat he wore, brass buttons glistening in the candlelight, his hair curling up over his forehead and his collar starched and unsoiled. Lee noticed that he was the only officer in the room who wore his saber, which he dutifully unbuckled and handed to a private to hold.

Elizabeth greeted him with a warm smile, but she had done no less with every other soldier. The Lieutenant was an accomplished dancer and led Elizabeth gracefully around the room. Lee realized, with regret, that he'd fare poorly by comparison. Lee couldn't hear what was said but Elizabeth laughed gaily, and March moved an inch closer. But when the song was over, even he had to relinquish Elizabeth to the next in line, and his irritation was plainly visible. Elizabeth appeared not to notice as she was swept away again with hardly a moment to catch her breath.

Lee made his way across the room. Cakes and cookies were laid out on a large table along the wall. They were deliciously sweet, and he was determined to sample every one of them. The Colonel noticed him and waved him over. Lee popped a cream filled pastry into his mouth and made his way over.

"Merry Christmas," the Colonel said. "Having a good time?"

"Yes, sir. Thanks for inviting me. Ain't heard music like this in a while."

"They're not bad. It's too bad Jacob didn't make the trip."

"He'll be put out, that's for sure."

"Maybe next year," the Colonel said. He introduced Lee to the man standing beside him.

"Lee, this is Lieutenant Tom Almanor."

Almanor shook his hand. He was a head shorter than Lee, with eyes quick to move from one place to another. His handshake was weak and clammy.

"Have you danced with Elizabeth?" the Colonel asked.

"No, Sir. There's quite a line," Lee answered.

"You're going to have to be more assertive if you plan to wade into that fray, young man."

"That's alright. I'm not much of a dancer."

"Don't seem to be stopping those boys," Almanor noted, nodding toward the wild display of flailing arms and elbows that passed for dancing among the recruits. "You couldn't do much worse."

"Oh, I don't know about that," Lee said. "I've got mighty big feet. Both of them lefts." They laughed again. The Colonel liked this youngster with his big smile and easy confidence. He'd make a good officer, he thought.

Lieutenant March stood watching from the other side of the room, resenting the boy's familiarity with the Colonel and the way he insinuated himself into the fabric of the Fort. He didn't like the attention he paid Elizabeth and most especially despised it when Elizabeth jabbered on about him. March felt superior to her other suitors at the fort. They were his subordinates. But Lee was a civilian, independent and out of his control. He made his way across the room.

"Ah, Jason," The Colonel greeted him. "You remember Mr. Grant?"

"Yes, of course," March said, nodding stiffly. "What brings you back to the Fort this time of year?"

"We needed a few supplies. Figured to stock up before the snow got too deep."

"You're alone, then? Had an old gent riding with you, as I recall?"

"Jake's back at the ranch?"

"Ranch?" March asked. "And where might that be?"

"A few days ride. North of the Blackfoot"

"A long way to come for supplies," March commented.

"Had some business to discuss with the Colonel while I was here."

March wanted to ask what that business was but didn't quite dare, especially since Cain made no effort to volunteer the information.

"How long have you been out west, Mr. Grant?" March asked.

"About two years, now."

"Must have been in the war, I suppose. Confederate?"

"No, Sir. I wasn't in the war, neither side."

"How did a Missouri boy like you avoid serving, I wonder?" Almanor asked.

"Who said I'm from Missouri?" Lee asked.

"The accent. Clear enough if you've heard it."

"No, sir. I'm from Indiana. But we moved around. Never got settled."

"What did your father do?" March asked. "That kept him moving around?"

"Excuse me. I think I'll take the Colonel's advice and try my hand at a dance," Lee said, nodding at the officers and heading away.

Lee didn't much like this Lieutenant and felt sure he meant him ill. Lee saw him talking with the Colonel, still glancing his way. There would be no backing down from the likes of him, Lee knew. He'd seen his kind, too. In the war, and on the trail west. Men who thought they were better than everybody else. Men who sought advantage, whether fair or foul.

The tune suddenly ended and he found himself a few feet from Elizabeth. She had her back to him and was bowing to her last partner. A few quick steps and he cut in and took her hand.

"Lee," she said, surprised.

"Hey now, friend," a young Corporal said, tapping him hard on the soldier.

Lee ignored him, looking into Elizabeth's eyes.

"Would you mind, Michael?" she said sweetly. "He's an old friend. Just one dance and then it's your turn."

The Corporal took a step back, "I suppose so," he said, but the resentment still simmered in his eyes.

"I'm sorry," Lee said with mischief in his smile. "The line was too long."

"No, I'm glad you did. I was tired of being pawed."

"Don't count your blessings. I ain't much of a dancer."

"Papa told me you'd arrived. I'm so happy you made it."

"Just luck. Didn't even know it was Christmas."

"Well, Merry Christmas, Mr. Grant." she smiled.

"To you too, I guess."

It would have been nice if the next song was slow and easy, but it was another rousing jig. That was all the band knew. Lee followed Elizabeth's lead, but he was no better than the rest of the young men and almost knocked her down.

"You're a wonderful dancer," she said.

"I'm not," he replied. "But I wish I was."

"Did you get something to eat?" she asked.

"I did. Haven't had sweets in quite a spell."

"They won't even let me stop to eat," she said, stepping lightly over his misplaced boot without missing a beat.

"I'll toss you some as you dance by," he said.

She smiled, and then swirled away as the dance steps indicated. Away she went, and then back again, her small hand clutching his.

"You look beautiful," he said. She smiled, reached up and brushed the hair out of his eyes, the way she'd always wanted to.

"I wish we had more time to just sit and talk," he said.

"Maybe tomorrow," she said. "I want to hear about your ranch."

Lee knew his time was almost over. Elizabeth was looking at him, a strange look, as if she were searching for something in the depths of his eyes. Before he knew what he was doing, he pulled her towards him, wrapped his arms around her and kissed her on lips still half open in surprise. She lifted her hand to his chest to push him away. It happened so fast. He relaxed his hold of her. Her face was flushed and she looked angry.

"Lee!" she said, looking at him and then away.

Lee heard clapping. Some of the enlisted men had seen the kiss and were hooting it up. Lee didn't know what to do, so he turned around and walked away. He brushed by Lieutenant March, who had glanced up at the clapping but didn't seem to know what it was about. Lee threw open the door and went outside, silently cursing himself. Elizabeth was angry and the Colonel would probably have him arrested.

He walked out onto the quadrangle. The fort was deserted except for a few guards waiting for their turn to be relieved so they could join the party. It was a cold dark night and he walked quickly across the yard to his quarters, took off his boots and lay down on the bunk. The music reached him clearly. He wondered who she was dancing with now. A part of him wanted to go back to the party but he stayed put, looking up into the darkness. He was the type of man to whom things didn't come easily, but he usually got what he wanted by sheer persistence and grit. But he wasn't sure that strategy worked with women. Elizabeth seemed so rare and unattainable a prize that he wasn't sure he was up to the challenge. How often could he make the trip into Fort Benton, especially now that Jason March was openly hostile towards him?

The next morning, Christmas morning, Lee was up early. He made his way to the stable and packed and saddled his horse. A light snow was falling and the visibility was poor, but at least some of the chill had gone out of the air. He rode west, toward the mountains he couldn't even see, but his horse knew the way home. Lee was content to sit back and let his mind wander.

Elizabeth slept late. The party had lasted into the morning and she was exhausted but happy. She'd had a wonderful time. Life was monotonous on the frontier and the party had been a welcome break. Her thoughts kept returning to the memory of Lee and the feel of his lips on hers. She smiled. He was bold, wasn't he? By the time she got dressed and took care of her morning chores it was almost noon. She stepped outside into the quadrangle and looked up at the grey sky and lightly falling snow. She thought about all the things that had happened yesterday. She had to admit she liked being the center of so much attention. She reached the NCO's quarters and asked a sergeant if Mr. Grant was still sleeping.

"No, Miss Elizabeth. He took off hours ago. On his way home, I spect."

Chapter XVIII
URSUS HORRIBILIS

Those who have packed far up into grizzly country know that the presence of even one grizzly on the land elevates the mountains, deepens the canyons, chills the winds, brightens the stars, darkens the forest, and quickens the pulse of all who enter it.

John Murray

Their valley was different in winter. It moved to a different rhythm, but it moved, nonetheless. Winter was long and hard, but the plants, the trees and the animals all adapted in their own ways. The cabin was as warm and snug as they could make it. Lee had to fill the cracks in the chinking twice over the course of the season, picking at the frozen clay on the riverbank and melting it over a roaring fire to soften it enough to pound it into the seams. Chance said once the logs were dried out, they wouldn't need to do it as often. But it would take a year, maybe two. Jacob showed Lee how to make a pair of snowshoes and Lee worked at it till he got it right. After a while, shoeing through the drifts was as natural as walking on solid ground. Lee explored the valley upstream and down, hunting and just trying to fight off cabin fever. Game was scarce, but he could usually rustle up a rabbit or a wild turkey. There were critters that left their marks in the fresh powder and there were the predators that preyed on them. The fox moved effortlessly across the fields of snow and it was rare to spot one. Lee would have liked to trap one for the beauty of its golden-brown fur and thick rich tail, but it was almost as good to watch one dive into a snowbank in search of the buried prey its keen nose detected. Wolves were more plentiful, and more dangerous. They were skilled hunters, and Lee sometimes came across their kills, grizzly scenes of bone, guts and blood strewn across the snow. Their howls, muffled by the falling snow, made the hair on the back of his neck stand up.

The days were short, and Lee tried not to be caught outside after dark. Oftentimes, he hiked home in the frail light of a winter's evening and saw the broad snow swept valley rising to meet the evergreens beyond. The cabin was situated at the top of a rise. The warm glow shining through the windows, and the wisp of smoke rising from the chimney, were welcome sights. Some evenings, he sat on the porch and watched the light seep from the valley. The cold bit hard, but he'd wrap himself in a buffalo robe and watch the snowflakes float gently to earth.

They kept themselves busy. There was furniture to build and Chance cut planks for a table and joined them to four sturdy legs. They made benches and bedsteads and carved a set of wooden plates and spoons. It took up so much of their time that Lee wondered what they'd do next winter to keep themselves occupied. Lee tried to stem his natural impatience, to take his time and enjoy every chore he undertook, not just for the object itself, but because the work itself was its own reward. It was something that the older men seemed to already understand.

When the worst of winter was over, and the snow started to melt, Lee prepared to head out. He packed his gear and kept an eye on the weather. He'd ride out onto the plains and head south, making his way into Idaho and maybe even Utah, looking for cattle to buy. It was a perilous undertaking. He was alone, and spring was a dangerous time to travel. The tribes would be out hunting after the long winter and he'd need to stay alert. Before he left, he went over a list of improvements he wanted Jake and Chance to start in on. They needed a barn and pens built before he brought in a herd. Chance listened carefully, but Jacob just looked at him with a weary expression that did not inspire confidence. They were easing into spring and Jake didn't see any reason to rush. Lee rode out with a big smile and a wave of his hand. Jake and Chance looked at the list. Every day, they'd raise a log or two and then quit, content with the day's progress. Without Lee to crack the whip, the pace was considerably more relaxed.

A few weeks later, Jacob discovered that one of the horses was missing. He followed the trail down the valley and found tracks. Indians. But at least it was a small band or they might have gotten them all. The loss of one horse was bad enough, but Jake knew they were likely to keep coming back till they had the rest. He made his way back to the cabin and took stock of things. They would have to graze the remaining horses within sight of the cabin. And he'd have to bring them into the half-completed barn at night, wishing now he'd been a little more diligent in its construction. This was why he hated settling down in one place. You made nothing but a target of yourself. They were low on meat and he needed to hunt, but it was risky going out alone when there were injuns about and one of them had to stay behind and watch the horses. It was way too much responsibility for a man accustomed to roaming as he pleased.

Fort Benton, Montana Territory

Jason March knocked on the Colonel's door. Cain was sitting at his desk going over requisition forms. Boats would be coming up the Missouri soon. And just in time. No army can function on an empty stomach. That should be the first thing they taught at West Point.

"Good afternoon, sir." March said, coming to attention, then relaxing at a nod from the Colonel.

"What can I do for you?" The Colonel asked.

"I received a letter that might interest you. I have a friend back in the war department. I took it upon myself to make some inquiries. Seems there was a German family in St. Louis before the war. The father was a gunsmith, and he had a son who was apprenticed to him."

Cain looked up, "Go on."

"The father was imprisoned for Southern sympathies, or some such, and the son was conscripted into the Sniper Corp. Hell of a marksman, from what they say, but he was reported missing after the battle of Rock Ridge. No trace was ever found. They think he might have deserted.

"Why are you telling me this?"

"There's been a federal warrant out for him ever since."

"And?"

"That Mr. Grant that comes around matches his description. I remember you telling me what a fine job he did on your rifle, and what a good shot he was."

"Do you have a photograph?" The Colonel asked.

"No, sir. None ever taken. But I'd like to arrest Grant and send him back to be identified."

"Do you have any proof he's the same man?"

March hesitated. "He matches the description."

"Lee claims he's not from Missouri."

"He's lying," March interrupted.

"Listen, Lieutenant. A man has rights, even here on the frontier."

"Yes, Sir. But we can't just let it go."

"We have no authority to hold somebody and ship them fifteen hundred miles on the basis of some far-fetched theory. I suggest you drop the whole thing."

"I can't do that, Colonel. I'm quite certain I'm correct."

"That is not a request. It's an order. You have a job to do. Is that understood?"

March glared at the Colonel. "Yes, sir."

As March left the room, an uneasy feeling came over the Colonel. March was a schemer, but the Colonel understood that it could be true. The West was full of men, Union and Confederate, who were trying to start over. In his view, most deserved a second chance.

Red Creek Ranch, Montana Territory

Jacob hated being pinned down in one place, and he was tired of worrying. It wasn't manly, to his way of thinking. Worrying if your horse would be stolen, worrying that your cabin would be torched or worrying that some young un without a lick of sense would make it back to the valley with his scalp intact. He'd had enough. He took up his rifle and told Chance to stay put and keep his eyes open. He was going to do some hunting before ranch life sucked the gut right out of him.

The snow was gone from the valley, but here in the trees patches still lingered. Jake followed a game trail that wound up into the high ground. The forest was dense, fir and tamarack above with aspen on the lower slope. There was plenty of sign that deer and elk used these trails to work their way down into the meadow and the creek beyond. He had gone less than a mile when he heard movement up ahead. He stopped. Whatever it was, it hadn't caught the scent of him yet. He moved forward, straining to see through the brush. More movement. It was big, probably a bull elk, dangerous in close quarters. And it took a good shot to drop one. He saw the bushes shake and stepped off the trail, alert to his footing, moving from rock to rock, avoiding the sticks and twigs that might crack away his presence.

Suddenly, rising in front of him, was the biggest damn grizzly bear he'd ever seen. It rose on its hind legs and roared, spittle flying from its mouth. Jake froze, trying to melt into the landscape. The bear took a step forward, nose high, trying to catch the scent of him. Jacob lifted his rifle, an inch at a time, slowly, ever so slowly, but the grizzly caught the movement; with a deep roar and a violent shake of his head, he charged.

Jacob swung the rifle up and fired; a great cloud of smoke blinded him for a fraction of a second. Before it cleared the bear hit him. The rifle flew from his hands and Jake was knocked back. The bear rose up again, towering over him, and he knew he was a dead man.

Jacob flipped over onto his stomach and tried to scramble away, but the grizzly pounced, slamming Jake's face into the dirt. His spine felt like it had been snapped in two and the air was knocked out of him. The bear tried to flip him over, but Jake fought to stay face down, clutching at rocks and branches. He felt the rake of claws ripping across his shoulders and down his back and then hot breath as its teeth clamped down on his head. The Griz couldn't find purchase against the bone and came away with only a mouthful of hair and scalp. Jake howled in pain, crawling away, grabbing at saplings to pull himself forward. The bear bit down on his buttocks and lifted him off the ground, shaking him like a rag doll and dropping him again. Jake kept moving and almost managed to get to his feet when suddenly he was knocked sideways. He felt a stabbing pain in his side and his arm went limp. He landed in thick brush and started burrowing like a mole, branches and thorns tearing at his face and hands.

The bear stood and shuffled after him, ripping up a large clump of brush with one effortless swipe. Jacob burrowed faster, so deeply that he was afraid he'd run out of brush. The bear grunted and roared, making another swipe at the brush, but not as intently as before. Jacob hunkered low and made himself small. He couldn't see the grizzly, but he could hear him. He chomped, swung his torso from side to side and sniffed the air. Jacob was sure his shot had hit, but it hadn't slowed the bear one bit. After a few minutes, the Grizzly turned and rambled back the way he had come.

Jacob didn't move. A minute, an hour, he couldn't have said. He began to feel the pain. His ribs were cracked, and he knew his arm was broken. He was awash in blood. He felt the back of his head. Something hung there, loose and bloody. It took him a moment to realize that it was his hair and the flesh of his scalp. Pain washed over him, and he fought to stay conscious. He tried to find a way out of the bushes. It was a surreal world in which he found himself, a green burrow overspread, but it had saved his life. In his rush to get away he'd dug into the thorny brush with superhuman zeal and at considerable cost to his face and hands. Now, when he tried to crawl free, he paid the price. Whenever a branch scrapped across the open wounds he howled in agony. He wormed along and, with a little wiggling and an excruciating pain, pulled himself out. He'd lost his gun. But he could come back for it. If he lived.

Chance was bringing the horses in when he saw Jacob stumble into the meadow. He had been gone since morning, but Chance never considered going after him. He was no tracker. He could tell by the way Jacob stumbled that he was hurt and hurt badly. Chance ran to help and was shocked by what he saw. His friend had lost a lot of blood, and his face was bone white. His shirt and pants were soaked in blood; dirt, blood and leaves covered him from head to heels. He draped Jacob's arm over his shoulder and the old man cursed soundly.

"Be careful, god damnit," Jacob spat.

"What the hell happened to you?"

"Griz," he whispered.

Pondera Creek, Montana Territory

The hunters had gotten lazy. They usually made a point of staying well south of the Missouri river, even if it meant they had to cart their hides an extra hundred miles to ship them by boat to St Louis. But the buffalo were getting harder to find. There were four of them, a shooter, two skinners and a driver running a light rig with two mules. The shooter, Bill Mack, had been wandering the plains for years, but only in the last few had he gotten into the buffalo hide business. And business had been good. He recruited two strapping farm boys from Iowa and taught them how to strip a carcass. They could pull the skin off a buffalo in a matter of minutes. The wagon they found along the old Oregon Trail, broken down and abandoned. It took them a couple of days to mend but it was always one hard jolt away from collapse. Mack hired a driver, bought two mules and headed west. They traveled up the Bozeman in late June, lucky enough to avoid the tribes out hunting the plains. They also avoided Fort Benton, learning it was better to steer clear of the military. Most commanders didn't like buffalo hunters moving through their territory.

They had been following the same herd for a week. They'd picked up their trail north of the Musselshell and shot thirty that first day. It took them a day of skinning, and then they loaded the cart and followed the herd north. The next day another twenty were killed. This was the fifth time they had culled the herd and the wagon was nearly full. Hides spilled over the buckboards and Mack figured this would be their last kill before they headed to the Missouri to offload. If he was lucky, he'd take another thirty hides. If he couldn't pack them on the wagon, he'd cache the hides on the prairie and come back for them later.

They left the cart a quarter mile back and moved in on the herd on foot, setting up a perfect kill zone from the top of a hill, downwind and covered by a clump of prairie sage. The buffalo were spread out in a shallow draw, hundreds of them slowly grazing toward the creek. Mack propped up the wooden perch he used to steady his model 1851 Sharps rifle and dropped the first bull. The large caliber bullet pierced its heart, and the buffalo fell without taking a step. The other animals moved off a few feet and continued grazing. He reloaded and was about to take another shot when something fell against his legs. He yelled at the boys to stop fooling around and saw a splash of blood fall across the sage. He turned and saw that one of the lads was hit in the chest and was grasping at the shaft of an arrow. The other boy was running off down the hill.

The Indians were almost on him and he turned and fired. The lead pony went down, launching its rider through the air. Then Mack was hit in the shoulder and dropped the Sharps. He'd taken a step toward it when another arrow caught him in the ribs. His driver and the farm boy took arrows in the back and the buffalo began to run off. Everything was moving slowly now. He reached out for his rifle, unable to catch his breath or get his feet under him. Then one of the Indians jumped off his charging pony and landed on him, grabbing him by the hair and jerking his head up. He felt a sharp pain and was blinded by the flow of blood pouring into his eyes.

A few days later, the column led by Second Lieutenant Almanor left Fort Benton to patrol the upper stretches of the Teton. The second day out they looked across the hills and saw buzzards circling in the distance. The Lieutenant diverted north to check it out and found dozens of buffalo carcasses rotting on the grass. None of the meat had been harvested. Skinners had moved into the area.

Almanor knew the Colonel hated buffalo hunters; there were standing orders to drive them out of the territory. Almanor didn't see why. They were only trying to make a living, just like everybody else. But orders were orders. One of his scouts found wagon tracks in the soft dirt leading northeast, so the Lieutenant resolved to follow them. Later that afternoon, another column of buzzards was spotted. The big birds were jousting with coyotes for the remains of a kill. As Almanor approached, he saw it wasn't buffalo they were feasting on.

Four dead white men lay stretched across the hill. The first was a big lad no more than eighteen years old. He'd been scalped and his body mutilated, his ears sawn off and his genitals hacked away. A few yards away, a buzzard pecked at them, swung them up into his gullet and hopped away. Almanor looked over at the other bodies. They had suffered similar indignities. He felt his stomach rise and had to turn away. Sergeant Howard rode up the hill toward him.

"Lieutenant. We found a wagon back aways."

"Any more bodies?"

"No, sir. Wagon was empty. They took all the hides. Took the horses and mules, too."

"Alright, Sergeant. Have the men dig some holes. Get these poor bastards in the dirt."

Red Creek Ranch, Montana Territory

Jacob lost a boatload of blood, his arm was broken, his ribs were cracked and his back had been ripped open from shoulder to hip. The white bone of his skull was clearly visible, and the loose flap of skin and hair hung by a thread. Chance carried him onto the porch and managed to get the door open. He hardly knew where to start and was afraid it would be for nought. He fetched a pail of water and started cleaning him up. With every touch, Jacob clenched in pain. Chance knew animal wounds needed to be cleaned and cleaned thoroughly. Once gangrene set in you were as good as dead. Chance brought over the whiskey and Jacob took a long pull. Chance dipped a cloth into the pail and tried to clean the torn flesh across his back.

"Don't poke at it," Jacob winced. "Wash it out good!"

"Looks bad, Jake,"

"Pour some whiskey on it," Jacob said.

Chance lifted the bottle, took a drink, and poured the whiskey over the wounds. Jake's body shook, but the tough old trapper didn't make a sound. When Chance looked up again, he knew why. Jacob had passed out.

Chance washed the cuts until the water ran clear. Better get him sewn up while he's still out, Chance thought, getting up to search for his needle and thread. All he had was the thick needle and the coarse thread he used for stitching leather. It wouldn't be pretty.

There were three separate tears down Jacob's back, one of them deeper and longer than the others. Chance took his time, trying to be as delicate as possible, but it was hard to get a good grip on the bloody skin. It took a good long time to sew it up and Chance's hand was shaking by the time he finished. Chance fetched the razor and cut away the matted hair from the back of Jake's head. The grizzly's teeth had punctured the skin but, luckily, had only slid along the skull instead of piercing it. A dollar sized flap of scalp dangled by a strap of skin, exposing the bone beneath. Chance tried to pat it back into position but decided it would never heal that way. He sewed it back as best he could, cleaning the wound with water and whiskey and wrapping his cleanest bandage around it.

He gently rolled Jake over and cleaned the cuts on his face and chest. Most had been made by the thorns he crawled through and looked worse than they were. There wasn't much he could do about the ribs. They would have to knit themselves together in their own good time. He felt along Jacob's arm until he found the break and used all his strength to pull the bones back into line. He was grateful that Jake had passed out; knowing the pain would be close to unbearable. He wrapped the arm, tightly enough to keep the bones from slipping out of line, but loose enough to allow the blood to flow. Or at least he hoped so. He was no doctor.

He made Jake as comfortable as possible, stripping off his muddy buckskins, cutting the rest of his shirt away and propping his head on a pillow. He started a fire in the hearth and kept it going through the night. The next morning, Jacob was still unconscious. Chance checked the wounds. The flesh around the stitching was red and swollen. Chance felt the old man's cheek and it was warm to the touch. Jacob was fighting for his life. Chance lifted his friend's head and tried to force water down his throat, but he was too far gone to swallow. Chance was not much on praying but, if there was ever a time, this would be it. He couldn't remember any prayers, but he mumbled some words of his own design and sat silently for a while, trying to make up in piety what he lacked in recital.

For three days Jacob fought, never waking. Chance fought the fever as best he could, but it burned and burned, and Chance felt helpless against it. Toward evening of the third day, Jacob opened his eyes. He was too weak to speak and didn't know where he was or what had happened. Chance got him to drink some water. He hadn't left his side except to check on the horses; but was beginning to feel hopeful that Jacob would pull through.

Weeks passed. Jacob's condition continued to improve, though he wasn't able to get out of bed for almost a month. Chance knew how vulnerable they were. One by one, the horses were stolen, except for Jake's Black, and he was spared only because Chance moved him into the spare bedroom at night. If the Indians decided they wanted more than horses, they'd be done for. Chance was a terrible shot. Jacob told him to load all the rifles and keep them close. But their luck held. Jacob's strength slowly returned, and he was able to get out of bed and sit outside, at first for just a little while, and then for longer and longer periods. Chance's stitches left a jagged scar and Jacob cursed him, saying it'd scare the ladies away, but he was grateful, and Chance knew it.

Supplies were running low. They were almost out of food and neither of them had been able to hunt. Chance caught an occasional trout, but he wasn't very good at that, either. One evening, a deer wandered out onto the meadow at sunset and Chance took a shot at him and Missed. Jacob cursed him loudly.

Each day he grew a little stronger. Before long he was able to do a little work and started to build back some of the muscle he'd lost. Never fat, he was now rail thin. As soon as he could walk, Jacob went out to hunt again. The fresh meat went a long way in building back his strength. And he kept a gun nearby, even if he wasn't hunting. Between the Indians and the Grizzly bears, he felt better having his rifle handy. He wondered what happened to that old grizzly bear. He didn't suppose he'd killed him, though he was pretty sure he'd winged the son of a bitch. Chance asked Jacob if he was afraid to go back into the bush since his run in with the bear. Jacob thought about it and surprised himself when he realized he wasn't. Sometimes you hunt, sometimes you're hunted. It was natural enough.

One afternoon, they were working on the large double doors for the barn when Jacob saw something that made him step up onto one of the rails of the fence and look down into the valley.

"Well, I'll be damned," he said.

"What is it?" Chance asked.

"Beeves."

It took an hour for them to climb to the meadow. Jacob and Chance walked up to the porch and watched as the cattle were herded up the valley and fanned out over the pasture. There were about fifty head, Jacob guessed. Lee had picked up a couple of riders who were helping him drive the herd and Jacob was happy to see them wrangling a few horses, as well. Once the cattle made their way down to the creek, the cowboys separated the horses and worked them up towards the house. Jacob and Chance opened the gate to the new corral and the riders maneuvered the horses their way. With a cloud of dust and a pounding of hooves, the horses ran into the corral and Chance pushed the gate closed behind them.

Lee rode up and flashed the big self-satisfied smile that had always made Jacob laugh. He jumped down and gave Chance and Jacob a warm handshake.

"Mighty good to see you boys. Was a bit apprehensive till I spotted you."

"We was starting to wonder about you, too," Chance said.

Lee took a good look at Jacob and the half-healed scars.

"What the hell happened?" he asked.

"Had a little run in with a Griz," Jacob said, impassively.

"Pert near lost him," Chance added.

Lee let this sink in and slowly shook his head.

"Ripped him wide open," Chance said. "You should see his back. Show em yor head, Jake."

"Oh, it weren't so bad," Jacob put in. "But they do grow their Grizz sizeable hereabouts."

"You alright?" Lee asked.

"Mostly," Jacob said. "Ribs'r still a bit sore"

Two cowboys rode over and dismounted, tying their horses to the fence.

"These boys helped me bring the herd up." Lee said as the two men walked over.

"This is Joe Cantson," Lee said, introducing a dark-skinned man with a deeply lined face. He wore a faded serape and a hat that, at one time, was probably white.

"Howdy," he said, shaking their hands.

"Pleased," Jacob returned.

"This other feller is Meers Bolm."

Meers was the same age as Lee, more or less, but his light brown hair and wispy moustache made him look younger.

"Go head and put your horses in the barn," Chance said, "I'll go start us some supper. You boys must be hungry."

"Very much," Meers said, with a bit of an accent.

"Sorry I took so long," Lee said, walking toward the cabin. "Couldn't find no stock. Nothing at Fort Bridger. Had to go all the way into Utah. Mormons. Glad to be shook of em. They drive a tough bargain."

"Seems like you did well enough," Chance said.

"Have any trouble bringin em up?" Jacob asked.

"Lost a couple in the Jefferson. River's still pretty swollen. By and by we took it slow and kept em together. Took time, was all."

Chance went off to put together a meal. The others went inside and made themselves comfortable while Jacob got down a bottle and poured everyone a glass. They toasted Red Creek's first herd.

"May they multiply and be fruitful," Meers said.

"Amen to that," Lee added.

"You boys staying long?" Jacob asked the hands.

"No, sir," Joe replied. "Just a day or two, if that's alright with you. Thought we'd head down to Virginia City and try our luck."

"Virginia City." Jacob said. "I had enuf of there."

"Why's that?" Joe asked.

"Long story," Jake replied.

"The barn looks good," Lee said, "You got some work done, at least"

"Did the best we could. Didn't have enuf muscle to put a roof on. Maybe we could talk these boys into giving us a hand before they head out," Jacob said.

"I'm afraid the payroll's used up," Lee said.

"I rekon," Jacob said.

Joe moved on to Virginia City to try his luck in the gold fields, but Bolm asked if he could stay on through summer. He liked the valley and wanted to try his hand at ranching. He told Lee not to worry about paying him till some of the stock was sold. Lee was reluctant to take on a man without being able to pay him but, when he saw the extent of Jacob's injuries and realized how much work was left to do, he accepted the offer. Meers was born in Holland, but he'd heard the call of adventure at a young age. He served as a cabin boy on a schooner bound for the New World and jumped ship to see the Wild West. He was tall and had a boyish charm that radiated from his bright blue eyes. His face was perpetually sun burnt and his lips painfully cracked. His English wasn't great, but he worked hard and rode confidently, though without the grace with which he carried himself on land. Lee had met him in a saloon down in Idaho. Lee's German and Meers' Dutch were not close enough for them to converse fluently, but it worked well enough for them to keep their meaning private when they had a mind to. Meers had a plan to work his way out to the west coast. But it wasn't unusual for him to change directions if something better came along.

Every morning Jacob rode out to check the stock and move them on to new pasture, as needed. Lee, Meers and Chance worked on the barn and fences. The roof was raised and the beams fitted and pegged. Shingles were cut and nailed into place. Summer was coming; the days were growing longer and the wild-flowers lit up the hillsides. There were no more depredations of the stock except for one cow that was half eaten by a grizzly. It was Jacob who found the carcass and he shook his head and grinned.

"Better him than me," he said to himself.

Chapter IXX

REPRISAL

I looked about me once again, and suddenly the dancing horses without number changed into animals of every kind and into all the fowls that are, and these fled back to the four quarters of the world from whence the horses came, and vanished.

Black Elk

Fort Benton, Montana Territory

The Colonel's office was too small for all the men crowded around the table. Lieutenant Almanor, still ripe and dusty from the trail, reported straight to the Colonel. He didn't dare delay bringing the news. He stood in front of a map and pointed out to the Colonel the route the buffalo hunters had traveled up into Montana and the spot where their bodies were discovered. The company's two sergeants crowded around. Sergeant Howard had been on the patrol and Sergeant Sean Kelly stood beside him. They knew the territory and weren't surprised by what happened to the buffalo hunters.

"How did they slip by us?" the Colonel asked.

"The Buffalo hunters don't have no use for the army, less they're in a fix," Kelly said.

"I had no reports of hunters in the area."

"Never should have been that far north," Sergeant Howard volunteered. "That's Blackfoot territory."

"You think they knew that?" March asked.

"I think so," Almanor replied. "Probably thought they'd get in and out without getting spotted."

"Not likely, leaving a trail of dead buffalo behind them," Sergeant Kelly said.

"You say the wagon was empty?" the Colonel asked.

"No hides, no mules. Nothing but bodies," Almanor said.

"Who did it?" the Colonel asked.

"Blackfoot, I suppose. It's their territory."

Cain looked at the map and shook his head. The Blackfoot nation outnumbered his garrison a hundred to one. He had neither the men nor materiel to mount a campaign against them.

"Doesn't matter," March said. "We can't let this go. Next time it'll be miners. Or settlers with women and children."

"I know. But we are in no position to launch an extended campaign against the Blackfoot. We're short-handed, with inexperienced troops and a five hundred mile frontier to secure. Those hunters shouldn't have been there. I'm not saying they had it coming. But they were certainly aware of the risk."

"Maybe so. But you can't just look away," March insisted. "If you don't show a strong hand after something like this, we might as well head back down the river."

"What do you think?" Cain asked Seargeant Howard.

"He's right, Colonel."

March walked over to the map and ran his finger along it.

"There are rumors that a renegade band of Blackfeet are roaming up and down the front." March said. "They're raiding mining camps and stealing horses as far south as the Powder. This is just the kind of trouble young bucks would get into."

"You think it was them?" Cain asked the Lieutenant.

March shrugged. "Does it really matter?"

"What else do we have?" Cain asked Lieutenant Almanor.

"Nothing but tracks heading northwest."

"May I have permission to take a Cavalry detachment and go after them?" Lieutenant March asked.

Cain shook his head. "Risky."

"We'll travel light, hit them hard and come straight back, before the rest of the bands get any inkling of what we're about and have time to mount any resistance."

The Colonel considered his options. He knew one of the biggest mistakes in warfare was letting the enemy lure you into battle, especially on their own terrain. But sometimes, inaction was just as dangerous.

"Alright," the Colonel said. "Take some men and a scout and track them down. But get the Indians responsible for this. I don't want things getting out of control."

"I understand."

"And bring the leaders back here for trial, if you can. That'll show them we mean business."

Eagle Creek, Montana Territory

Lt. March took his hat off and brushed the hair away from his eyes, kicking his horse into a trot until he was abreast of Almanor. They had turned north of the river and were following the furrowed drainage of a creek bed. Thirty mounted troopers were strung out in a line behind him. Sergeant Sean Kelly rode beside the Lieutenants. He was almost forty, too old to be riding the Plains. And Lieutenant March was a mite too eager for his taste, but so were most of these young lieutenants. Kelly's long brown hair was already running to grey, but he didn't fancy losing it just so some up and coming lieutenant could make captain.

March had brought along a scout, a French trapper named Jean Ouilet. He was familiar with the country and spoke the Blackfoot language. Oiulet wore his hair pulled back from his face and tied with a leather strap. He wore faded buckskins and kept a Bowie knife strapped to his belt. He claimed to know most of the Piegan camps along the northern front. But he had mixed feelings about the Blackfoot. He'd been trading with them for more than a decade but had never been completely accepted into their society. They tolerated him only because of the trade goods he brought. He was a necessary evil, a convenient intermediary. Ouilet had taken a Salish squaw as his wife. He'd loved her, in his own way, and she had followed him around the northwest, bearing more than her share of the burdens. But she had drowned last year when the canoe they were paddling down the Snake River had capsized. Since then, he seemed to lose interest in trapping and started scouting for the army.

March looked out over the land spread before him. Cain is an imbecile to think we'll ever find out who is responsible for the killings, March said to himself. The Blackfoot roamed all over this country and any of them would have killed the White hunters given half a chance. By that reasoning, it didn't much matter who he brought in. The important thing was that the message be sent and the lesson learned. Later that morning, Ouilet picked up the trail of unshod horses heading north, and he rode off to scout it out. The rest of the troop followed behind. The Lieutenant knew the men were skittish. Even with their advantage in fire power, they were in the heart of enemy territory and badly outnumbered. If luck wasn't with them, none of them would be making the trip back. He didn't have to warn them to stay alert.

Late in the day, Ouilet rode back to tell the Lieutenant that he'd found the village. March took Almanor and the scout to take a look. They climbed to a safe vantage point above the Indian camp. There were at least twenty lodges. Judging by the way they went about their business March knew his presence had not been detected. He ordered the troops brought forward. March considered backing off to go in at first light but was disinclined to do so. They would run the risk of being discovered and they were vulnerable out in the open. He broke the men into three columns and gave the order to advance. They crested the hill at a gallop and swept down on the village.

They were fifty yards into the descent when they were spotted. The women ran for cover with young children in tow and the warriors ran for their ponies. It occurred to March that, if he wanted to avoid bloodshed, he should have made his presence known and requested a parley; but that really wasn't his intention. He wanted the advantage a surprise attack could give him; the time for words was past. A few braves found their ponies and charged out to meet them. They were quickly gunned down. Almanor took the left flank, Sergeant Howard took the right and March charged up the center. One and two at a time, Blackfoot warriors rode out and were shot down. In a matter of minutes, the soldiers were in the village. The troopers were shooting at anything that moved, and the Blackfoot quickly realized they were surrounded. The women pushed their families behind them for protection while they tried to surrender, but the soldiers were pulsed for action and did not, at first, heed their officers' commands. Half the villagers were shot before March got his men under control.

A great wail went up from the women who were left alive, many of them clutching their dead children to their breasts in despair. March ordered the troopers to separate the surviving men. Most of the braves were wounded and, if their women refused to leave them, they were beaten away with fists and rifle butts. The braves had their hands tied behind their back and were lifted into the wagon. The troopers went through the lodges, confiscating any rifles they found. Less than an hour had passed when Sergeant Howard rode over to March.

"Everything's secure, sir."

"How many did we lose?"

"Two killed. Evans was thrown from his horse and broke his neck. Blystolt was shot in the charge. A couple others were wounded, none too seriously."

March ordered Sergeant Kelly to form a detachment to follow him into the field north of the village. He looked out over the meadow where the Blackfeet horses moved about restlessly. They'd been spooked by the shooting but were picketed and unable to run away. They represented the wealth of the tribe and meant more to them than money or precious minerals. Kelly ordered the troop forward and March gave the order to open fire. The first line of horses went down with the loud braying of panicked animals. The other horses reared, trying to get away. But with their feet tied, they tripped over the fallen animals. The troopers continued firing until the field was covered in bloody, writhing horseflesh. The troopers grimaced as they pumped round after round into the herd. Cavalry men have a great affection for horses and killing them was not something they enjoyed. The Indians they'd just shot conjured no such regrets.

When it was all over March ordered his men to reload and fall in. The Indian women sat together in shock, crying over their dead and still uncertain of their fate. But once the troopers were assembled, they rode back the way they had come. They were a more than a quarter mile away before the wails of the women could no longer be heard.

Red Creek Ranch, Montana Territory

With four men at the ranch there was plenty of muscle on hand to do the heavy work. Jacob took charge of watching the herd. He had the experience of working the Double Eagle behind him and he liked being out in the open, alone with his thoughts. Despite his rough demeanor, he had a gentle way with animals. He hadn't been asked to perform this chore but, with his bones still healing, it made the most sense. If he suspected there was a mountain lion or wolves in the vicinity, he'd fetch Lee and they'd camp down near the creek. It was cool and pleasant in the open air, with only the gentle music of the herd to listen to and a night sky brilliant with stars to look upon.

Chance took young Meers under his wing. The Dutchman was quick to learn, and the old man liked having someone to talk to. Before long, the barn was finished, and they went to work on the pens and workshop. Lee helped with the work but, when they could spare him, he took it upon himself to break the horses, though he was far from expert at it. He spent a few hours with them every day. Before long, they grew comfortable with him and the sound of his voice. He'd lead them, one by one, out to fresh pasture and, if he had time, would sit with them for a while. There was a paint that was gentle enough and she would trot over to Lee whenever he entered the yard. Lee figured she'd be a good horse to start with. He led her into the corral and let her have a good sniff at the blanket. When she was comfortable with that, he laid it across her back. She shook her head and jumped away but, after a few more tries, she let it be. He went through the same process with the saddle, but she didn't want any part of it. He knew it took patience, and he knew he was not a patient man.

It wasn't long before Jacob and Chance took an elbow at the rail. The older men looked at each other, knowing this was something they had to see. It took a while, but the mare finally allowed Lee to lay the saddle across her back and, after a few tries, Lee got it cinched down. He led her around the corral, talking to her the whole time in a soft voice. Once the mare got used to the saddle Lee lifted his boot into the stirrup and leaned his weight against it, holding on to the pommel but not climbing up into the saddle. The mare took off, but Lee managed to hold on until she brushed him off against the fence. He got ahold of the reins again, stroking her until she calmed down. His heart was pounding, and his pride was hurt, but he forced himself to take his time, rubbing her neck and soothing her with the sound of his voice. What the hell, he thought, swinging up into the saddle and holding on for all he was worth.

He was thrown almost immediately and landed heavily on his back. Jake and Chance thought that was the funniest thing they'd ever seen. Lee got up and brushed himself off and had to endure Jacob's advice. He listened, though he knew the old man was far from a great rider himself. It was Chance who finally stepped in. He took a more indirect approach. Lee approached it like it was simply a matter of muscle, but Chance explained to him that you never climbed onto a horse until you were sure it would carry you. It was a healthier approach, though lacking entertainment value, to Jacob's way of thinking.

Chance led the mare into a chute and held her while Lee got back into the saddle. He sat there, without moving, until the paint had gotten used to him, all the time stroking her neck and talking in a gentle voice. At some point, without much being made of it, Chance led her out into the corral. She followed Chance around the corral without protest and, after a minute he handed Lee the lead and he was riding alone, sitting tall in the saddle with a smile on his face.

The weeks passed quickly. There was plenty to do and nothing but work to break up the days. Every night, Lee went to sleep thinking about what he'd accomplish tomorrow. At day's end, he could look back, knowing he had something to show for his efforts. Jacob might need to let loose every now and again, but Lee was made of steadier stuff; duller stuff, Jake might say. The building was coming along, and the fences, gates and chutes were proceeding apace. The cattle had settled in and were fattening up. A few calves had already been born and more were on the way. It was money in the bank and Lee loved calculating the profit. He didn't know much about breeding cattle, but the bulls seemed to know what they were doing, and you could learn a lot by observation.

Chapter XX

THE GOODS

The only source of knowledge is experience.

Albert Einstein

Fort Benton, Montana Territory

It was early September and the rivers were low. Most of the crossings were easy. Driving twenty head over gentle terrain was not a particularly onerous chore, especially if you were in no particular hurry. Lee, Jacob and Meers could handle the beeves easily enough and still keep their eyes open. They ran the cattle up onto a patch of prairie a quarter mile south of the fort and let them graze. Lee figured he'd set up camp and then go see the Colonel, but they weren't a half hour into the chore when Lee saw soldiers ride out of the gate headed their way. Lee's stomach sank when he saw that it was Lieutenant March. Lee and Jacob dropped what they were doing and awaited his arrival.

"Howdy," Jacob said, friendly as could be.

March didn't bother to dismount. "What's going on?" he asked.

"We're delivering stock," Lee said, stepping forward.

"To whom?" he asked.

"Colonel said he'd buy as soon as I could bring em in," Lee said.

"We're not in need of beef at present."

"Maybe you better go ask the Colonel."

"I don't need to ask."

"Then I'll ask him myself."

"I'm in charge of provisioning," March said, raising his voice. "And we don't need your goddamn cattle. If you don't get them moving right away, I'll have my men shoot them from the blockhouses."

"These are private property," Lee said, his temper flaring.

"They're on army land. You have fifteen minutes." March said, reining his horse around and heading back to the fort.

"I told you not to get on his bad side," Jacob said.

"That's the only side he's got," Lee replied.

"Who was that?" Meers asked.

"That's the Lieutenant. Lee's sweet on the Colonel's daughter and March has his sights set on her. They been in a pissin match ever since."

"Oh, grand! What do we do now?"

"Let's move em off a ways," Jacob said. "Till we figure something out."

An hour later, the stock was resituated further south at a spot not visible from the fort. Jacob was worried about the boy's temper when it came to March. And rightly so. It galled Lee to have to obey. Selling the cattle was beside the point. As soon as the stock had settled down, Lee turned his horse and took off for the fort without saying a word. Jacob had it in mind to go by himself and was just about to suggest it, but when he looked up all he saw was a cloud of dust and Lee beating it back to the fort.

When he got to the gate, Lee was expecting trouble, but they waved him through. He rode right up to the Commandant's office. The guard asked his name and told him to wait. Lee wondered what type of reception he'd receive but was so mad he didn't care. One way or another, he'd have his say. The door to the inner office opened and Cain stepped out.

"I got a bone to pick with you," The Colonel said with a serious expression.

Lee was puzzled. The words were threatening, but a grin worked its way onto the Colonel's face.

"Why's that?" Lee asked.

"What's this about a kiss?"

"It didn't mean nothing. It was Christmas."

The Colonel laughed. "I'm just teasing you."

"Was Elizabeth mad?" Lee asked.

"I don't know. You'll have to ask her."

"Don't know what's proper around ladies, I guess."

"It's a complicated subject."

Lee stood there somberly, and when he didn't say anything, Cain asked.

"Thought we'd see you long before now. How have you been?"

"I've been better, sir."

"What's the matter?" the Colonel asked. "Is Jacob alright?"

"Oh, he's alright. Had a run in with a grizzly bear a few months back. But he's mostly healed up. But that's not the problem."

Cain led the young man into his office and shut the door behind them. Lee told him about the confrontation with Lieutenant March.

"You know, Lee. I shouldn't be saying this, but March has a mean streak in him. He's a fine officer, but he's not a man you want set against you. Course, in your case, it seems a little late for that."

"I'm not afraid of Lieutenant March," Lee said. "But, out of respect, I wanted to let you know what happened. If you don't need the stock, we'll drive em back."

"Absolutely not. We always need fresh meat. And you and I made a deal. March let his personal antipathy interfere with his duty and I'm going to let him know about it. But I'll try to keep you out of it, to whatever extent that's possible. You go back to your camp and I'll send some men down to drive the cattle into the stock yard. You can pick up your money from the quartermaster."

"Thank you, sir."

"It's only right," Cain said, shaking Lee's hand and leading him to the door. "You and Jacob come to dinner this evening. Elizabeth would love to see you."

"Are you sure, Colonel? We wouldn't want to impose."

"We want to hear all about this ranch. And don't worry. I think it might be prudent not to invite the Lieutenant."

As soon as Lee was gone, Cain sent for Lieutenant March. The animosity between the two young men was troubling and would lead to no good. The Colonel needed to get to the bottom of it. As angry as he was, he was unsure how hard to come down on his second in command. March was a brooding man and any insult to his character was bound to fester. There was a sharp knock on the door and the Lieutenant entered.

"Colonel," he said, coming to attention. "You wanted to see me."

"At ease, Lieutenant. I heard you took it upon yourself to order Grant and McCune to remove their stock from the pasture."

"That's right, Sir. I hadn't been informed that we requisitioned any of their cattle. They were ready to drive them right into the quadrangle."

"You should have checked with me." the Colonel said sternly.

"I'm the requisition officer, March replied, coolly.

"You know I am acquainted with the two of them. As a matter of fact, I made a previous arrangement with Grant."

"You should have made me aware of it."

"Don't be insolent," Cain said, angrily. "You surely bear the man ill will, or you would have consulted me as a matter of course."

"I didn't feel it was worth troubling you over."

"Send some men down there and drive those cattle into our pens. And I don't want any more trouble between the two of you."

"I know the boy saved your life. I can understand that you're beholden to him. But I have more information."

"What's that?" the Colonel asked.

"The sniper who deserted during the battle of Rock Ridge was about the same age as Grant. And his record states he was the same height and weight. Both had blonde hair."

"Circumstantial."

"But the most incriminating fact is that those irregulars were trained and equipped with Spencer repeating rifles. Same model Grant carries. If you give the order, he'll have to let me take a look at that gun. I've written to the war department to get the serial numbers of all the rifles assigned to their company. They might even be able to tell us the specific number issued to Stemler. That's his real name, by the way. The boy's a thief and a deserter."

"I've been in the army long enough to know a good man when I meet one. If you ever aspire to command, it's something you'll need to learn."

"Colonel, you're ignoring the facts. It's your duty to look into this."

"Don't tell me what my duty is. You're pursuing a personal vendetta."

"Very well. But I must respectfully inform you that I am going to write to the war department and report the matter. And I'll be forced to mention that you have consistently refused to look into it."

"You go right ahead, Lieutenant. Just make sure you have somebody bring those cattle in."

"Yes, sir." March saluted, turned and walked quickly from the room.

After Lee left the fort, he rode straight back to camp. Jacob and Meers were sitting with their back against a log looking out over the stock.

"Didn't throw you in the stockade, I see," Jacob said.

"I got it settled. You were right, I guess. The Lieutenant ain't my biggest admirer."

"How'd it pan out?"

"Colonel's gonna take the stock."

"That's good news," Meers said.

"And you and I are invited for dinner," Lee said to Jacob. "Sorry, Meers."

"That's alright," he said. "Though I'd like to get a look at this lass before we're through."

Lee and Jake cleaned themselves up. Lee had brought a clean shirt with him, just in case and, when it was time, they rode back to the fort. Jacob stopped and picked a bunch of wildflowers on the way. When they got to the Colonel's quarters, they tied the horses, climbed up the steps and knocked at the door. Just before it opened, Jake shoved the flowers into Lee's hand.

"Lee, Jacob," Elizabeth said, coming out onto the porch and giving Lee a hug and Jake a kiss on his bearded cheek. She looked down at the flowers and Lee sheepishly held them out.

"Thank you. That's so sweet," she said, taking them from his hand and leading the men into the house.

Elizabeth had tied her hair with a red ribbon and was wearing a plain white dress that clung tightly at the waist but flared gracefully to the floor. Her arms were bare below the elbows and she smelled far sweeter than the flowers.

"It's been so long," she said. "I expected to see you long before now. Where have you two been?"

"I had a run in with a bear," Jake said proudly, showing her the gnarled scar on the back of his head."

"Oh, my. No one told me."

"Ain't hardly front-page news."

"Were you badly hurt?" she asked, leading him into the parlor and making him sit on the sofa beside her.

"I weren't dead. That's the best that can be said."

Lee continued to stand, holding his hat in his hand, but she quickly motioned him to a chair.

"And what about you? I seem to recall you saying you'd come and visit."

"I was down in Utah, trying to buy stock. Took longer than I thought. Then we had a pile of work to do. Before I knew it, summer was gone."

"So, you're a rancher, now?" she smiled.

"I told you I would be," Lee said.

"Something smells good," Cain said, as he stepped into the room, shaking hands with his guests and kissing his daughter lightly on the cheek.

"Damn, Jacob," he said. "You look like you could use a good meal. You're thin as a rail. I heard we almost lost you?"

"Griz jumped me. Almost et me."

Elizabeth had been cooking all afternoon. She sat everyone down at the table and served them herself. Despite warning the men not to expect too much, it was the best meal they'd had since the last time they'd been here. Cain informed them that the cattle were being brought in and apologized for the trouble. Both the Colonel and his daughter had a thousand questions and Jacob hadn't heard any flatland news in all the months lately passed. Cain told them the transcontinental railroad was getting started again. In a year or two, you'd be able to ride it all the way from New York to San Francisco. Jacob thought that was a frightening thought and wasn't shy about saying so. The Colonel told them about the trouble with the Blackfoot and about the buffalo hunters who'd been killed. He was surprised when he learned that they hadn't had any Indian trouble out at the ranch. When dinner was over the Colonel asked the men if they'd like to take a cigar and a glass of brandy out on the porch, but Elizabeth had other ideas.

"It's such a beautiful evening. I was hoping I could convince Mr. Grant to take a short ride with me before dark."

"I don't know, Elizabeth. I don't like the idea of your being outside the walls this late in the day."

"Oh, Papa. It won't be dark for another hour. We won't go far."

Cain looked to Lee, who let it be known through a glance that it he didn't want to be the one to say no to Elizabeth.

"Alright. Though I can't imagine that Lee would prefer your company to ours. How bout you, Mr. McCune? You a brandy man?"

"Colonel, I ain't had nothing but water for two months. I was afeard I'd have to go rootin for it myself."

Elizabeth ran upstairs to change, and the men walked out to the porch. As the Colonel and Jacob lit their cigars, Lee leaned against the post and waited for Elizabeth. When she came out again his jaw dropped. Trousers. He'd never seen a woman wearing pants before, had never even heard of such a thing. He couldn't have been more surprised if she'd come out buck naked. The Colonel laughed out loud.

"Don't look at me. I've had that discussion."

Without waiting for more commentary, Elizabeth swept forward, took Lee by the arm and led him away. He untied his horse, and they walked across the quadrangle. Elizabeth asked one of the grooms to get her horse ready and he led the pure white pony with black socks out of the stable and handed her the reins.

"That's a beautiful animal," Lee said

"Thank you. Isn't he grand?"

"What's his name?" Lee asked.

"Boots," She smiled.

This was the horse Blue Wolf had given her back in Wyoming and she had come to love him. Elizabeth stoked the thick muscles on the side of his neck and the horse leaned in against her. Then she grabbed the pommel, lifted her boot into the stirrup and swung up into the saddle more gracefully than any cowboy. Lee shook his head and did the same.

"Where to?" he asked.

In addition to the denim slacks that she had sewn herself, Elizabeth wore the same cavalry boots she'd carted from Laramie. The only touch of femininity she allowed herself was a light cotton blouse that she wore tucked into her pants. They turned their horses and rode towards the gates. Everyone who saw them stopped and watched.

"You like shaking things up, don't you?" Lee asked.

"Sometimes," she smiled.

"Well, you look good on a horse," he said.

"Thank you," she replied. "So do you."

They rode through the gate onto the sloping bank leading down to the river. The sun had already dipped behind the mountains and the clouds were blushing pink with the sunset. Elizabeth's skin was flush with the warm glow and her smile lent testimony to her love of being on horseback.

"I've been meaning to apologize," Lee said.

"For what?"

"That kiss. It was mighty presumptuous. Don't know what come over me."

"What kiss?" Elizabeth asked.

"You know, at Christmas."

"I don't know what you're talking about, Mr. Grant."

Lee knew he was being fooled with, but what he couldn't figure out was why. He thought about pursuing the subject. But if she wanted to pretend it never happened, then that was alright."

"How are things?" Lee asked. "I mean, with you."

"We've settled in alright. The Blackfoot have Papa worried. They have some of them locked in the stockade, poor fellows. I feel sorry for them. They look so miserable."

"I've come to know a few."

Elizabeth seemed surprised. She half turned in the saddle.

"What are they like?" she asked.

"Same as us. Proud and independent. But not savages, not the way they're made out."

"They frighten me,"

"They should. They're deadly fighters. But we frighten them, too."

Elizabeth nodded, knowing all this was true.

"Tell me about the ranch," she said

"I think we got the prettiest piece of land in Montana."

Elizabeth nudged her horse a little closer and they turned up the trail that ran beside the river. Where the water ran fast, silver patterns, like fluttering coins, flashed across the surface; in the still pools, the deepening pink of sunset lit the water aflame.

"Tell me about it," Elizabeth said.

"It's not way up in the mountains. The prairie rises into the foothills gradual like, but our valley is so green and ringed by pine and aspen, that it looks like a mountain meadow. You can see the high peaks from the cabin, snow-capped year-round. And there's a fair-sized creek that runs though, slow moving and deep, kinda wiggles its way across the valley. The bank is lined with thick moss and, on hot summer days, I take my shoes off and dip my feet. Water's nice and cool.

"Sounds wonderful."

"There's all kind of critters," Lee continued, warming to his subject. "Deer and elk, even a few moose. You ever seen a moose?"

"No. I haven't."

"Damn odd looking creatures. Tall and ungainly. At night, you can hear coyotes yipping or the howl of a wolf pack further off. It's a sound you'll never forget. Wolves can tear up a cow real fast. We've got to keep a watch. But it's a great place to raise horses. We're trying to build the remuda. We got ten now. And, first chance I'm able, I'll buy some brood mares."

Lee glanced over, not wanting to bore her, but he could see he had her attention.

"When you and the Colonel come visit, I'll take you riding. We'll go up into the high country, one lake prettier than the next, one right after another, like pearls on a necklace. That's where I met Mountain Sun."

"Who?"

"Blackfoot warrior. Fierce looking fellow."

Lee told her the story of how the horses had been stolen and they discovered the valley. Then how he had met the young Indian and they had become friends."

"That's incredible," Elizabeth said. "It's like something out of Cooper."

"Yeah. Things like that don't happen too often."

They'd ridden almost a mile and the trail began to rise against the narrows that banked the river. There was still light in the sky, but it was fading fast. Lee looked over to Elizabeth.

"We better turn around. I don't want your father worrying about you."

"Alright. But I wish we could keep on riding. I want to see some of the things that you've seen."

They swung the horses around and headed back towards the fort. The evening star shone brightly, framed in the narrow Vee of a mountain pass. Elizabeth glanced over and saw Lee looking at her, but his face was hard to read. Then, he slowly reached out and took her hand in his. It was an innocent gesture, but for two young people with little experience and deep emotions, it was infinitely exciting. They rode together in silence, neither daring to risk losing this feeling to the blunt instrument of speech. But then the path narrowed, and their hands pulled apart.

"I'm sorry I haven't come by since Christmas," Lee said. "I wanted too."

"It sounds like you've been busy."

"The worst of it's over. I'll be by more often."

"I hope so," Elizabeth said.

Jacob and the Colonel were still sitting on the porch when they rode in. The cigars we're long gone, but the brandy wasn't.

"Have a nice ride?" The Colonel called.

"Yes," Elizabeth replied. "The sunset was beautiful."

Elizabeth glanced over at Lee, who couldn't think of anything to say, and looked down at the ground.

"I'm bringing Boots back to the stable. See you in a minute," she said.

"I'll give her a hand, I rekon," Lee said, leading his horse away.

Jacob and Cain looked at each other, and the look had the makings of a long conversation.

"He's a good lad," The Colonel said.

"Yup," Jacob agreed.

"Listen, McCune," Cain began. "If I ever send word out your way, you get that boy away from here."

Jacob looked over at the Colonel, but he was looking away. It was clear he wasn't going to say any more.

"I will," Jacob replied.

Chapter XXI

UNFAITHFUL SERVANT

To take it like a grain of salt, is all I can do, It's no one's fault.

Robbie Robertson

Red Creek Ranch, Montana Territory

It was a dark afternoon. A light rain was falling, and a cold wind blew down from the north. Lee was in the workshop hammering an iron latch for the gate when he heard Chance call. Lee grabbed his rifle and walked outside. An Indian was riding across the meadow. Lee recognized the horse first. Jacob was out back fiddling with the garden. For all his cursing about the darn sod busters ruining the country, he'd developed quite a green thumb and spent time each day weeding, trimming and watering the plants. Now that the weather was turning cool again, he'd be harvesting the last of the vegetables. Lee asked Chance to fetch him.

Mountain Sun held up his hand in welcome and Lee did the same. He'd been wondering when their paths would cross again. Mountain Sun swung down off the horse as Jacob rounded the corner. He stopped short and took in the scene, then walked up beside Lee, who made the simple introduction.

"Jake," he said, gesturing to the old man.

The Indian nodded, and then tapped his own chest. "Mountain Sun."

Jacob spoke some Blackfoot. Not well, but enough to communicate a few things. It was just a matter of remembering how to start.

"Is this the one brought us back our horses?" Jake asked.

"Yeah," Lee said. "Invite him in."

Jake turned back to the Blackfoot. "We have food and water."

They walked up the steps to the porch and Lee went in first. Mountain Sun hesitated at the doorway, bent his head and looked inside. He had never been inside a wooden house, and he strained to see in the darkened interior. Finally, he stepped through the doorway. If he was nervous or afraid, he hid it well. As his eyes adjusted, he looked around. He was impressed by these lodges the White men built. They looked strong and warm, but were too stationary to suit his taste, anchored to the land like a tree or a boulder. Jacob motioned him over to the table with its two long benches on each side.

"Tell him I'm glad to see him again," Lee said.

Jacob fumbled for the words; but managed to express his meaning.

Mountain Sun looked at him. "You have made many changes in this valley since I last saw it."

"Yes. We aim to live here," Lee said.

Jacob translated and Mountain Sun nodded slightly.

"But you are welcome any time. To hunt or to visit."

Mountain Sun nodded, but thought to himself, how like a White man, to give me permission to come onto land my people have hunted for generations.

Chance brought meat and bread to the table. Mountain Sun took a piece, smelled it, and placed a small bite in his mouth. They ate in silence for a few minutes, but when it began to close in around them Jacob looked up.

"What brings you to our valley, Friend?" he asked.

"I wanted to see if my White brother had managed to hold onto his hair."

Lee tapped the top of his head and the unkempt hair that was always in need of trimming.

"So far," he smiled.

"I've told our people that you are a friend. But you never know who will listen."

"We haven't had any trouble in a while," Jacob said. "We owe that to you?"

Mountain Sun shrugged; maybe it was true, maybe not.

"There is another matter," Mountain Sun said, more seriously.

"What is it?" Jacob asked.

"The Long Knives," Mountain Sun began. "There was a village north of here. A peaceful village. The White men from the fort attacked. They killed most of the men and many women and children."

"We heard about it," Jacob said. "You had family there?"

"No. I knew many from that village, but it was not my father's band. I do not understand. Why would the Long Knives kill women and children?

"White hunters were killed. They were trying to punish those responsible."

Mountain Sun nodded. "These hunters were killing buffalo. They were on Blackfoot land."

"That's no reason to kill them," Jacob said.

Mountain Sun shrugged. "I don't know who killed them. One buffalo I can understand, but what they were doing. . ."

"Both sides need to come to an understanding," Lee said. "Before more are killed."

Mountain Sun spoke to Jacob, but he looked towards Lee.

"I have explained to my brother, but I am not sure he understood. I do not live among my father's people. I ride alone, with warriors who think as I do. We go where we please and we choose our own enemies. But now the Long Knives have taken Blackfoot men and locked them up."

"I know," Jacob nodded.

"They must be allowed to return to their homes."

"We have no influence over the Chief at the fort," Jacob explained.

"Perhaps you can warn them."

"We can try. But I doubt they will listen."

"Then more will die," Mountain Sun said, calmly.

"The White chief will sit in judgment over them? To decide what will happen to them."

"These men did nothing."

"I hope they'll be set free, once an agreement is reached."

"How can there be an agreement? Our people are scattered. And the clans will not meet again until the summer. But they would never agree to allow White hunters to slaughter the buffalo. They do not even harvest the meat; they leave it to rot on the prairie."

His face conveyed the contempt he felt toward such men. Lee did not doubt what would happen if Mountain Sun and his men ran across them.

"I understand." Jacob said.

Mountain Sun was quiet for a moment, wondering whether he should express his thoughts. He sensed that these men had good hearts and might listen.

"There have been many councils, but all agree that this village should not have been attacked and our men locked up like animals. If they are not released, we will have to ride against the Long Knives. Even with all their guns and their strong wall, they will be killed."

Lee thought for a moment and then spoke slowly.

"The Chief at the fort is a good man. I know him. I can't believe he would order the killing of women and children. There must be some other explanation."

"The women are dead. The children are dead," Mountain Sun said.

"Let me talk to the Colonel. I will try to get your friends released."

Mountain Sun nodded, acknowledging the offer.

"I am traveling north to visit my father and mother. They will be camped along the Heron. I will talk to the war chiefs and tell them we have a friend and try to get them to wait. I don't know what they'll decide to do."

"You can only try," Lee said.

Lee tried to get Mountain Sun to stay longer, but the Blackfoot was suddenly uneasy and wanted to head back. They walked out the door and Mountain Sun took the reins and swung effortlessly onto the Lilac Roan's broad back. Lee extended his hand, and Mountain Sun grasped it firmly.

"Good luck, Brother. I hope you are successful," he said.

"So do I."

Fort Benton, Montana Territory

Lee wanted to leave right away. Jacob didn't like the idea of getting mixed up with the army, and he particularly didn't want Lee spending any more time at the fort than was absolutely necessary, but once the boy set his mind on something there was no talking him out of it. Lee cleaned the Spencer, packed a few things and asked Meers if he would come along. They left the next morning. Lee rode Jake's Black, which he had unofficially appropriated as his own. They made the fort in two days and were allowed to pass through the gate. They rode up to the commandant's office and tied their horses.

"What're you going to say?" Meers asked him.

"I don't know. I guess I'll just lay it out for him."

"Now, don't lose your temper."

"I won't. Not with the Colonel."

"Want me to go in with you?"

"No. Why don't you go have a drink. I'll come get you later."

"Alright. Good luck," Meers said, walking away.

Lee walked up to the Commandant's door and told the adjutant on duty that he needed to see the Colonel but was told that the Cain had made a trip down to Fort Laramie. Lee thanked him and walked back outside. He considered talking to Lieutenant March but quickly decided against it, but at least he could see Elizabeth and try to get some information from her. He walked his mount across the quadrangle and approached the Colonel's quarters. There was a soldier stationed by the door, looking bored and restless.

"Afternoon," Lee said as he approached. "Is Ms. Elizabeth in?"

"Who wants her?" he asked, looking Lee up and down.

"I'm a friend. An old friend."

"What's your name?"

"Lee Grant."

"Oh, I remember you," the trooper grinned. "From the Christmas party."

"That's right," Lee shrugged.

"She's around back, having lunch. I'll go tell her you're here."

"That's alright. I'll surprise her," Lee said, walking away.

"I guess that's alright. Seeing how she knows you and all."

There was a small yard behind the house that Elizabeth had planted with flowers and vines; not as large or lush as the garden in Laramie but an oasis of charm and color compared to the monotone grayness of the rest of Fort Benton. Lee walked around back. There was a small picnic table set up on the grass where Elizabeth and her father sometimes dined on hot summer evenings. But, at the moment, Elizabeth was having lunch with Lieutenant March.

March had been pestering her for a month. Until now, she had always begged off. Jason was polite and cultured, even handsome, but there was something about him that Elizabeth did not like, not the least of which was his antipathy toward Lee. She had her back turned to the gate but March saw Lee turn the corner and walk toward them. March reached out and took Elizabeth's hand in his. She was surprised by the gesture, so surprised that she did not immediately pull away. And then, in a moment, Lee was standing over them, had taken in the scene. She could tell from his expression that he was not pleased.

"Elizabeth," he said. Not quite a greeting, but almost a question.

Elizabeth was so surprised that she didn't know what to say.

"Mr. Grant," March said with an insouciant smile. "What brings you out of the woods?"

"I came to see the Colonel," Lee said without expression.

Elizabeth tried to gently pull her hand away, but March held onto it firmly.

"He's not here," Elizabeth said. "He won't be back for a few days, at least."

"You're in charge?" Lee asked Lieutenant March.

"That's right."

"Please sit down and join us," Elizabeth offered nervously. "We were just having lunch."

Lee looked down at the table, and the hands being held. Elizabeth finally managed to free her hand from the Lieutenant's grasp, but she was flustered and wore her guilt plainly.

"Never mind," Lee said, abruptly turning and walking away.

"Lee," Elizabeth called to him, but he didn't turn around and continued towards the gate.

"I'll go talk to him," March said, rising to his feet.

Elizabeth was so distraught that tears came to her eyes, but she was angry too. She was angry at Jason for taking liberties; and even angrier at Lee for not allowing her to explain.

Lee was almost to his horse by the time March caught up with him. He signaled the trooper guarding the residence to come to his side and confronted his rival.

"That was awfully rude. Don't they teach you manners back in Missouri?" he asked.

"Mind your own business, March. I've got nothing to say to you."

"What did you want to talk to the Colonel about?"

"I hear you have some Blackfoot locked up?"

"That's right. What business is it of yours?"

"I also heard that the army attacked a Blackfoot village north of here?"

"I led the column myself."

"Figures," Lee said.

"They were hostiles. Killed four White hunters just a week earlier."

"They had nothing to do with it."

"How would you know that?" March asked.

"There were women and children."

"Things get out of control in the heat of battle. Men get carried away. You remember that, don't you?"

"You don't know what you're talking about?" Lee said, the blood rushing to his face.

"How do you know so much about this, anyway?" March asked.

"I have a Blackfoot friend. Told me the whole story. Says the tribe's mighty upset about it. I came to warn the Colonel that if the captives aren't released, he'll have a war on his hands."

"Who is this Blackfoot? Is he a chief?"

"No. Just rides with other young bucks like himself, but he has no reason to lie. He says they'll fight if the army rides into their territory again. Or if the men you're holding aren't released."

"I'm not releasing them. They'll most likely be hung."

"Why? What evidence have you got against them?"

"Where's this friend of yours now?"

Lee hesitated. He shouldn't have even started talking to March. Nothing Lee could say would sway him. His arguments would fall on deaf ears and his information used to ill effect.

"I don't know," Lee said.

"I think you do know. And that you're withholding information and aiding the enemy in time of war."

"War? We're not at war with these people."

"Of course, we are, Stemler?" March snorted.

Lee froze at the mention of his name. He forced himself to remain calm, though he could not prevent himself from staring at the Lieutenant with such a look of controlled rage that March shook his head in mock pity.

"You're pathetic," he sneered.

"I'll be back in a few days to see the Colonel," Lee said, taking the reins in his hands and getting ready to swing up onto the Black."

"You're not going anywhere," March said, drawing his side arm and signaling the trooper to cover him. More soldiers were called, and Lee's hands were tied behind his back.

"Lock him up," March ordered.

Chapter XXII

INTO THE BREACH

I thought trouble was behind me, though it won't never be and I was foolish to think it. I got to thinking I was wrong to let Lee go off alone. I told him he should steer clear of it. That the Blackfoot and the Army both would blame him should trouble come, and surely it would.

Jacob McCune

I would be willing, yes glad, to see a battle every day during my life.

George Armstrong Custer

Fort Benton, Montana Territory

Meers had been at the bar for hours and he knew he had to slow down or run the risk of making a fool out of himself. He'd already drained over half a bottle of the woodsy brown cat gut they sold as whiskey and his ability to communicate was rapidly deteriorating. This was alarming, since the soldiers and rivermen at the counter had a hard enough time understanding him when he was sober. They were friendly enough, but there was a mean streak in many of these frontier types and Meers didn't want to let his guard down.

It was nearly dark when he stumbled outside to get some fresh air. He looked across the yard where Lee had tied his horse, but it was gone. He didn't suppose Lee would head out without telling him, but the fort wasn't so large that he'd need a horse to travel anywhere within it. Meers was at a loss, so he sat down on the edge of the step and waited. It wasn't long before a group of troopers wandered by in search of a drink. They were most likely coming off duty and Meers figured they might have an inkling of where his friend had gotten off to.

"Excuse me gents," he called, rising to his feet unsteadily.

The private closest to him was a rail thin wisp of a man with bright red hair and close-set eyes. Meers reached out and put a hand on his shoulder.

"You boys see the man I rode in with?" Meers asked.

"I ain't never seen you before, Mister."

"Sure. But this is a big lad. My height, but thicker. Rides a big black horse?"

"No, ain't seen nobody like that,"

Another enlisted man stepped up beside him. His face and hands were dirty and bits of straw clung to his clothes. Meers caught a whiff of him, even from a distance.

"I was working in the stables when they brought in a horse like that. He said Lieutenant March locked up a civilian who had the nerve to sass Miss Cain. Had him thrown in the stockade and put a guard on him."

"Oh, my," Meers said. "When was this?"

"Couple hours ago, I rekon."

"That'd be him, I imagine. You lads know where I might find the Colonel?"

"Colonel's gone. Down to Laramie."

"Many thanks," Meers said, sitting down on the step again.

The soldier gave the Dutchman a suspicious look, but they were more interested in quenching their thirst than figuring out what he was about. Meers wasn't sure what he should do. He knew of the antipathy between Lee and the Lieutenant, but he didn't imagine it would get Lee thrown in the stockade. Meers thought about the Colonel. He was an ally, as Meers understood it. But the Colonel was gone. That left Lieutenant March in charge. Lee had landed in shit, Meers concluded.

They'd be locking the gate for the night and, if they found out he was riding with Lee, he'd probably be locked up as well. He figured he'd better get word to Jacob. He untied his horse and climbed into the saddle, riding out from the fort just as the sergeant at arms gave the order to secure the gate.

March knew he didn't have a lot of time. The Colonel was due back any day now and any hope he had of subjugating the Blackfoot and destroying the renegades would be quashed. He had Stemler locked up in the stockade. He was certain he would lead him to the renegades if the right pressure were applied. But once Cain returned, Lee would be released and he himself would have hell to pay. Luckily Elizabeth hadn't caught wind of anything. He meant to keep it that way.

The Lieutenant gave orders not to discuss the prisoner with anyone under pain of the lash and then set about organizing the campaign. He would take every available horse soldier and leave only the infantry behind to man the fort. He needed to cover a lot of ground as quickly as he could. March met with his sergeants and Lieutenant Almanor and told them his plan, telling them to prepare to move out at first light. They'd have fifty mounted cavalry and enough food and ammunition to remain in the field for two weeks. He'd take the Blackfoot prisoners, under the guise of returning them to their people. Of course, he had no intention of doing this, but they might prove to be valuable hostages.

At five in the morning the men assembled in the quadrangle. While Lieutenant Almanor checked the baggage and equipment, Sergeants Kelly and Howard inspected the men and horses. March spent the time brooding over how much was riding on the expedition. Finally, he had sole command of a military expedition without his bumbling superiors at hand to prevent him from earning the victory that had long eluded him. A light drizzle fell on the darkened yard; dawn would be slow in manifesting itself. The Blackfoot prisoners were brought out with their hands tied. They were helped onto horses and Ouilet explained to them that they were being returned to their tribe. The scout explained that they would remain tied till the time came to release them. Their hands were lashed to their bridles and a long rope connected one to the other so that they could not give in to the impulse to make a run for it.

Just before they were ready to ride, Lee was brought out. He took in the scene and could guess what was going on. He noticed the butt end of his Spencer protruding from March's scabbard. Lee's hands were tied and his horse was brought forward.

"How am I supposed to ride like this?" he asked.

"You'll manage."

"I'm still a prisoner?"

"Yes," March said calmly.

"What's the charge?" Lee asked.

"Treason."

Lee didn't speak. He looked at the assembled troopers and the line of Blackfoot prisoners.

"Where are we going?" he asked.

"You have volunteered to assist us in a punitive expedition against a hostile tribe. You're going to lead us to your friends."

"Like hell I will."

"We'll find them one way or another. It'll go poorly for you if you don't cooperate."

"I don't give a damn," Lee said.

"And it'll go even worse for them," March said, nodding toward the Indians.

"You son of a bitch," Lee said.

March spurred his horse forward and kicked Lee in the chest, knocking him off his horse. Lee landed hard on the flat of his back, knocking the wind out of him. The troopers kept their rifles trained on him and there was nothing he could do. He picked himself up off the ground and stood, unflinching. He walked over to the Black, grabbed the pommel and pulled himself up into the saddle.

The line reported ready, and March gave the order to move out. The Cavalry swung toward the gate, riding right by the Commandant's quarters. There were no lights on and the house was quiet. Elizabeth, tossing in her bed upstairs, heard the sounds of horses, but the damp earth muffled the noise and she stirred, only to fall back to sleep.

Red Creek Ranch, Montana Territory

Jacob had been in a bad mood all day. It wasn't unusual for something to irritate him, but this was more than run of the mill orneriness. Chance quickly found a chore that needed doing, as far away as possible. It had been three days since Lee left for the fort. He was not expected back yet, but Jacob had been mulling over his decision to let Lee go alone and had come to regret it. The lad could usually take care of himself, but he could be hot if he got his dander up. Jacob finally gave up and decided that he wouldn't get any peace until he found out what was happening, so he went looking for Chance.

"Chance, God-damnit. Get on out here," he said.

"What's a matter?" Chance asked.

"I'm heading out."

"Where to?"

"Fort Benton. I need to find out what's happening with Lee and these god damn Injuns."

"Want me to go with you?"

"Naw. Just keep an eye out and drive the herd up closer to the cabin till I get back."

"Alright. You figure something's amiss?"

"Yeah. I figure all hell's broke loose. But I'm hoping I'm wrong."

Jacob was five miles down valley when he saw the rider. He hoped it was Lee, but he spurred his horse into the trees in case it was somebody less friendly. When the rider drew closer, however, Jake could tell it was Meers Bolm. The fact that he was alone did nothing to lighten his mood.

"Where's Lee?" Jake asked as soon as Meers reined his horse to a stop.

"Trouble," Meers answered. "Lee got into a spat with Lieutenant March and got thrown in the stockade. I'm not sure what the charge is, but I figured I better get back to let you know."

"What about the Colonel? Didn't Lee see the Colonel?"

"Colonel's away. March is in charge."

"Oh Lord!" Jacob said, shaking his head.

"What're you going to do?"

"I rekon I'll head in and try to sort this out."

"I'll go with you."

"No. Your horse is played out. And I don't suppose there's much you could do, anyway. Head back up to the ranch and keep an eye on things. I'll be back as soon as I can."

"I don't feel right about letting you go in alone," Meers said.

"I ain't no welp," Jake said, getting riled again. "And I been up and down these mountains more times than I can remember with nobody but myself for company. Just head on home and take care of that horse."

"Yes, sir," he said. "But you be careful."

"I aim to be, son. I aim to be."

As Jacob spurred his horse down the trail, he thought about all the ways Lee could have brought trouble down on himself. You didn't need to be a fanciful man to imagine plenty. If they'd figured out who he was and where he came from, Lee was done for. The Colonel would do what he could, but Jake imagined it wouldn't be enough. The world was a big empty place, but the past had a way of sniffing you out.

Heron Creek, Montana Territory

It had been two years since Mountain Sun had left his father's lodge, but it seemed like a lifetime ago. In that time, he'd wandered the whole range of the Piegan Blackfoot and even further south into Wyoming and Idaho. He and his band had traveled into Canada and lived among the Bloods and Northern Blackfeet. He moved about the country, seeing new lands and meeting new people. Even amongst a people who prided themselves on their freedom of movement, he was considered a rolling stone. As his reputation grew, young men approached him and asked to join his band. He took these requests seriously, but only a few were accepted. It was not his intention to be a war chief. He had never tried to organize his own band; he simply went where he wanted to go and let some of his friends come along. He wanted to know that he could count on the men around him, that he could trust them with his life. He had no interest in organizing a large force and no desire to cajole men into doing things his way. His freedom was too important to him. He would have preferred to travel unnoticed, but somehow all the Blackfoot now knew of him and he was widely feared. When word of his fight with Omak got out, even the White Eagles left him alone.

A few of his friends had dropped out to settle down along the way, usually when some handsome young squaw had caught their eye. They departed as friends with a bond that would carry into the future. New men took their place, eager to show their bravery.

Mountain Sun had not intentionally avoided his father's village, though perhaps, on some level, he had. He thought of his family often and had wanted to see them, but he did not wish his status to endanger them. Since that danger seemed to have diminished, he thought it might be a good time to return, if only for a short time. He was also worried about the Long Knives and the danger they posed. He meant to convince his father, Broken Claw, to move north, possibly even across the English line. Mountain Sun intended to make good on his threat to organize against the Whites if Lee wasn't successful in his bid to get the prisoners freed.

His father's band was camped along the creek north of the Heron. They rode in on a bright morning and the whole band turned out to greet them. His mother cried when she saw him and held on for so long it embarrassed him. His men looked the other way, so he would not lose face. His father showed more dignity, but Mountain Sun could tell that he was happy to see him. It was testimony to his father's strength that he maintained his composure in front of men he did not know.

His father's band had only recently returned from the buffalo hunt and they had taken enough meat and hides to last them the winter. The women were working the skins and drying meat while the good weather lasted. Mountain Son asked his father's permission to set up their lodges beside the creek and, having received it, instructed his men to set upon the task. No sooner had the words left his mouth than his mother grabbed his hand and led him away, opening the flap of their lodge and making him comfortable on the buffalo skin couch. She started preparing him food, as though he had not eaten in the two years since she'd last seen him. Broken Claw sat down opposite him.

"It is good to have you home. I had not realized how good."

"It is nearly two years," Mountain Sun said.

"Wherever I go, the people tell me stories about you. I've been able to follow your travels."

"We have seen much."

"How did you come by all these men? How well do you know them?"

"They are all good men. I would trust any with my life."

"Some of the stories I've heard were troubling."

"Then they are not true. We have done nothing that you would not approve of," Mountain Sun said.

Broken Claw was relieved. "You have always had a good heart."

Mountain Sun smiled.

"Why now?" Broken Claw asked. "Why have you come back at this time?"

"You heard about the White hunters who were killed?"

"Yes. Bad medicine. But they should not have been hunting on our land."

"I agree. But now the Lehoe band has been wiped out."

"I know. Some of the survivors have taken refuge with us."

Mountain Sun nodded. "Some of the men were taken prisoner. They are being held at the fort."

"I was not sure if they were still alive."

"They may yet be killed. But I have sent word to the fort that the prisoners must be freed or there will be war."

Broken Claw's head sank and the breath went out of him. There had been much talk of this among the clans, but the older men counseled against such an ultimatum. He had never imagined that it would come at the decree of his son, though he did not doubt that he meant it.

"I have come to ask you to move out of the area." Mountain Sun said. "Cross the Milk River and don't come back until this is over."

"This is our home," Broken Claw said, looking his son in the eye.

"Find a new home," Mountain Sun said with more force than he intended. "We are Piegan. Free to go wherever we wish."

"I will think about it."

Mountain Sun lowered his voice. "I know that you and my mother would have liked me to remain with the band. Have children of my own. I would like these things for myself. But I do not believe that we can expect justice from the White man unless we can demand it from the point of our lance."

"I suppose you are right," Broken Claw replied.

"I'm sorry that it has worked out this way," Mountain Sun said, sadly.

"Maybe you are not as smart as I thought," Broken Claw said. Mountain Sun looked up.

"You are young and strong. You will not be so forever. You are fighting for what you believe in? Then you don't need to ask my blessing. If you have decided to fight, then fight. What could be better than dying a brave death with your brothers around you? What do you want? To grow old, watch your muscles turn to fat, wake up with pain in your fingers and aches in your back and knees, till you can't make it through the night without having to go outside to make water, and even then it hurts. There is nothing wrong with living a long life, if that's what the Great Spirit has chosen for you, but it is not the only path."

Mountain Sun smiled at what his father was saying.

"It hurts when you piss?" he asked.

Upper Missouri River, Piegan Territory

Lieutenant March did not pressure Lee to reveal where the enemy was hiding. Not the first day. In fact, he didn't speak to him at all. He planned on giving him a little rope before he tightened the noose. But he ordered the French trapper, Ouilet, to ride with the young man and get whatever information he could in the course of conversation. The column passed the buffalo carcasses the White hunters had shot. Despite the fact that they were only two weeks slaughtered, the bones were picked nearly clean, only the bulbous head remained fur laden and intact. It was a bizarre image, the eyeless stare from an oversized head hung from a skeletal frame. Lee was shocked by how many of them littered the prairie and he could understand how this would raise the ire of the Blackfoot. He himself was a hunter and had come to take pleasure from the chase, but he had never hunted solely for sport or without need of meat.

They passed more carcasses as they continued north and Lee wondered if they would come upon the remains of the slain White hunters, though he supposed the Army had taken the time to scratch them out a shallow grave.

Toward evening, they made camp along the river and set up tents, staked out the horses and set a formidable guard. March wasn't taking any chances. Lee was tied up and a trooper was assigned to guard him. March gave the order that no fires were to be lit and the men ate the cold rations and grumbled. Once the camp had settled down, March made his way over to Grant. The Lieutenant wore a long woolen campaign coat with the collar turned up and drew from a willow root pipe he dangled loosely in his fingers. A trooper brought him a folding stool and he sat down in front of Lee.

"A military campaign is an impressive thing to witness. Don't you think?"

March's manner was friendly and his voice unthreatening; he spoke as though he were addressing an old friend.

"The start of a campaign is always orderly. Morale is high. Everybody is optimistic about success. You must have seen this?"

"No," Lee mumbled.

"But it's later on that the true worth of a leader is tested. How do the ranks hold up to fire? What happens to morale after the casualties start to mount up? Are the men willing to die for you, like they were for old Robert E. Lee? Comes down to discipline, don't you think. Discipline and organization."

"It comes down to character," Lee said.

March knocked burnt tobacco against the heel of his boot and blew air through the stem before sliding the pipe into his pocket.

"They say these Indian campaigns are different," March continued. "But I don't think so. The enemy's less civilized. There are no rules of engagement or exchange of prisoners, but war is still war. Overwhelming force is the only sure means to victory, that and the willingness to use it. McClellan had the forces to win in sixty- three, but he didn't have the guts to use them. How many times did he have the rebels in his grasp and then let them slip away because he wasn't bold enough to finish the job?"

"Is there a point to this history lesson?" Lee asked.

"Yes, actually there is." March said. "I'm doing these Indians a favor. By eliminating these militant elements, the rest of the Piegans can go back to living peacefully. If we allow this friend of yours to continue, more bands will join him and the army will have no choice than to take more concerted action. The Indians can't possibly succeed. We have battle hardened troops freed up from the war, artillery, rifles and an almost limitless supply of ammunition. My god, all we'd have to do is kill off the buffalo and they'd starve to death."

"I saw the evidence of that," Lee said.

"Your problem is, you don't know which side you're on. Or you're on nobody's side but your own. That why you ran away last time? Or was it simple cowardice?"

"Why are you telling me all this?"

"Because I'm going to make it simple for you. Sometimes the few have to suffer for the greater good. You're going to tell me where the renegades are camped."

"Go to hell." Lee said.

"You're going to tell me, because if you don't, I will shoot one of the captives every morning until you do. Oh, it'll be legal. As legal as it needs to be."

"You're out of your mind," Lee said.

"No. It's quite rational. You can think about it tonight. But if you don't come to your senses by morning, one of them dies."

"What makes you think I care?" Lee asked.

"Oh, I think you care. But whether you do or not, once they're all dead, It'll be your turn."

Fort Benton, Montana Territory.

Jacob McCune cursed himself for letting Lee take the Black. He'd made the ride as fast as his horse would carry him, but it wasn't as quick or as comfortable as it would have been on his Black. When he finally crossed the river and rode through the gate into the fort, days had been lost and he was bone tired. He went straight to the Commandant's office. Elizabeth stood next to her father and was so distraught that she barely acknowledged his presence. Cain walked over and reached out his hand.

"Jacob," he said. "I'm glad to see you."

"Wouldn't have come, cept I'm expecting trouble."

"Well, we've got it. I just got back a few hours ago; I was down at Fort Laramie these last weeks."

"Where's Lee?"

"Seems he got into it with Lieutenant March while I was away. He was placed under arrest and March set out after a band of renegade Blackfoot he claims is responsible for the murder of three hunters who were killed just north of here. Took Lee with him."

"Couldn't you talk sense to him?" Jacob asked Elizabeth.

"I didn't know about it. They left in the middle of the night. Lee came in as mad as a hornet, and the next thing I knew everybody was gone."

"March had to know I wouldn't condone it. That's why he left before I got back. He's been causing plenty of trouble lately. Made accusations about Lee deserting from the Sniper Corp."

If Jacob was surprised by the mention of Lee's past, he managed to conceal it.

"What are you going to do?" Jacob asked.

"I've been trying to figure that out. March took the whole cavalry detachment. All I have left is infantrymen. We'd never catch them."

"No, we gotta move faster than that."

"Worst yet, we've only got a dozen horses and some have been on the trail with me all the way from Wyoming. They need to be fed and rested."

"We can't wait," Jacob said.

"I agree. We'll outfit as many men as we've got horses to carry. Once we catch up, I can assume command of the company."

"There's one more thing," Jacob said. "Lee made a friend of one of the Blackfoot. A young Brave. He came to warn us that the bands were all riled up about the village that was shot up and the prisoners who you've got locked up here at the fort."

"March took the prisoners with him."

"What for, I rekon?"

"Well, if I know the Lieutenant, it wasn't to set them free. But if what you say is correct who knows how many Blackfoot will be waiting out there."

"We better fetch them back," Jacob said. "Quick."

"I want to come along," Elizabeth said.

"Absolutely not." Cain said, and this time she knew he'd brook no argument.

"Then take my horse," she said.

Cain called Lieutenant Nate Willis and his only remaining non-com, Sergeant Sam Midden, into the office. Willis had been on the trail with him to Laramie and was just as tired as he was. He was a man of medium build with sharp wits and admirable loyalty who the Colonel thought had a bright future in the army. Being posted to Fort Benton, however, was unquestionably a detour on that path. Midden had been left in charge of the fort when March's column rode out. He was insolent to the point of insubordination, to March's way of thinking, and his attitude infected the ranks. March had intentionally left him behind because he had a habit of speaking his mind, but the Sergeant had more miles under his belt than anyone else at the fort and his advice was usually sound.

The Colonel introduced them to Jacob and told them to round up every available horse. They were to select the best riders and marksmen for the mounts. Willis would have to remain behind at the fort. It could not be left without a responsible officer in command. But Midden was instructed to pack his gear and start selecting the men and horses. When they had left the room Cain turned to McCune.

"I'm sorry Jacob, but we've been on the trail since sun-up. I'm going to need a few hours' sleep."

"Me, too. Won't help nobody if we're falling off our horses."

"First light, then" Cain said.

Chapter XXIII

PREPARING TO DIE

What is life? It is the flash of a firefly in the night. It is the breath of a buffalo in the wintertime. It is the little shadow which runs across the grass and loses itself in the sunset.

Crowfoot (Blackfoot orator)

Fort Benton, Montana Territory

They were able to rustle up fourteen riders. Some were part of the Cavalry escort that accompanied Cain back from Fort Laramie. A few were veteran infantrymen, proven fighters who might come in handy. With Jacob, Sergeant Midden and the Colonel, they needed every available horse left at the fort. They had no scouts at their disposal, but Jacob McCune could read trail as well as most. Each man took as much food and ammunition as he could carry, but there'd be no mules or packhorses. They had to travel fast and would be pushing the horses as hard as they dared. If anybody's mount came up lame he'd have a long walk back to the fort.

Elizabeth hugged her father as he said goodbye and there were tears in her eyes. Jacob stood respectfully off to the side but, before he got a chance to follow the Colonel away, Elizabeth threw her arms around him and hugged him tightly.

"You bring Lee back," she said. "And my father too."

"I will," he said, pulling away. "Don't fret."

315

The patrol rode through the gate and headed northwest at a trot. Cain wasn't sure how far ahead Lieutenant March had gotten. He hoped the man had the good sense to proceed cautiously. March was leading a large party and had prisoners to contend with. Cain hoped that would slow them down some. They knew where March had crossed the river, but it had rained since they left and Jake hadn't picked up the trail yet. He would need to find it soon if they were to have any chance but, even if he did, it might still be too late.

Upper Missouri River, Blackfoot Territory

Lee couldn't sleep. He was angry with himself for allowing March to get the upper hand and kept thinking of all the things he should have done. He went over his choices but, no matter how many times he worked his way through it, he could not come up with a plan that had much chance of success. He knew that Mountain Sun and the Blackfoot would be camped along the Huron. Those were the last words his friend had said before riding away from the ranch. But Lee wasn't going to tell that to Lieutenant March, even if it cost the lives of the hostages, even if it meant his own life. He needed to buy time. With any luck March would search the prairie for a week or two without finding Mountain Sun or any other Blackfoot. Then he'd have no choice but to head back to the fort. If March was serious about his threat to execute the prisoners there was nothing Lee could do, but it was hard to imagine that he'd go through with it. Despite what he said, it was murder, plain and simple.

Lee knew that the country was wide open with the prairie stretching unbroken in all directions. But the French scout that March had brought along seemed to know his business. Lee had seen what a good tracker could accomplish. Sometimes it seemed like magic.

Lee brought his knees up to his chest and tried to stay warm. He had been dumped in the grass without even a horse blanket to cover himself with. He'd been given nothing to eat since they headed out and his stomach growled. It didn't surprise him. The Lieutenant had his mind set on staying in the field till they found the renegades. He wasn't about to waste the small amount of food they could carry on Lee or the Blackfoot prisoners. Lee didn't care; he had no interest in eating or sleeping until he found a way out of this. If he could escape, he could ride ahead and warn Mountain Sun, or head back to the fort and tell the Colonel, though he wasn't even sure if he was back from Wyoming yet. Lee stretched out on the ground and tried to push the rope down over his wrists, but the bonds were too tight and the rope wouldn't budge.

At sunrise, good to his word, March walked over to the patch of damp grass where they had dumped Lee. Sergeant Howard, Jean Ouilet and a detachment of troopers followed, one of them with a length of thick hemp rope in his hands. Lee stood stiffly and looked March in the eye.

"You hungry?" March asked.

"I'm alright," Lee answered.

"Have you come to your senses?"

"Just what are you going to do when you find the Blackfoot? Will you give me a chance to talk to them, to get them to surrender?"

"Of course."

"Why should I believe you? The last village was massacred."

"Nonsense. There was no massacre. There were casualties, that's all."

March slowly unfolded a map and held it open. Ouilet leaner closer and looked over his shoulder.

"Your choice," he said, looking Lee in the eye.

"I told you I don't know. What makes you think I would?"

"Just a hunch. Don't matter, much. One way or the other, we'll find them."

"Then why do you need me?"

"You're under arrest for a capital crime. I'm not letting you out of my sight. Besides, you might prove useful before this is over."

March turned to Sergeant Howard. "Bring one of them out."

There was a lone cottonwood growing in the bottom of a dry ravine a few yards east of the camp. It was twisted, stark and weathered. March and the others walked towards it and Sergeant Howard and two of his men freed one of the Blackfoot from his bonds. As soon as the Indians realized what was happening, they started to shout and move forward, but they were tied securely and the ropes staked to the ground. If any of them got too far, one of the guards knocked him down with the butt end of a rifle. The soldiers dragged the Blackfoot to the tree; he fought hard against his captives, but his arms were tied behind his back and he was dragged by the hair across the dirt. One of the enlisted men threw the rope over a low limb and tossed the end to a rider who tied it off against the pommel of his horse.

Sergeant Howard stepped forward and tried to lift the noose over the prisoner's neck but he continued to fight and scream, throwing his head from side to side, kicking and biting at the soldiers, preventing them from getting close enough to tie him off. Finally, after a minute of this, the Sergeant took out his sidearm and brought it down on the Indian's head with enough force to render him unconscious. Two soldiers held him up while another lifted the noose over his neck. Howard signaled the horsemen to move forward, and the Blackfoot rose up off the ground, bobbing with the shifting movements of the horse, until his head snapped unnaturally to one side and he went limp. Lee watched from his spot on the grass fifty yards away. The young Indian was silhouetted by the blinding light of the rising sun, but even from this distance Lee could tell he was dead. A few minutes passed, and then the rider loosened the rope and the body fell to the ground. Sergeant Howard stood over the Indian, drew his revolver and fired a single shot to his head. The crack of the forty-four caliber colt shattered the morning's silence and even Lee, who had been expecting it, jumped at the report. Lee tried not to feel anything, to think anything, but there was too much anger welling up inside. One of the enlisted men worked the noose back over the Blackfoot's head and coiled the rope, and then the executioners moved back toward the camp, leaving the dead man where he lay.

March gave the order to move out and the men started drifting away. The slow task of packing the camp and loading the horses began. Ouilet led Lee's horse over to where he was sitting.

"Time to go," he said

"Can you loosen these ropes?" Lee asked. "I can't feel my hands."

The scout pushed him roughly by the shoulder and looked at the ropes that tied Lee's wrists behind his back. He shook his head in disgust. The rope had cut deeply into the skin. He signaled to an enlisted man who was working nearby.

"Keep your gun on him," he said.

Ouilet untied the rope and Lee brought his hands forward, shaking his wrists to get the circulation going again. As the blood flowed back into his fingers the pain was almost more than he could bear. The Frenchman waited for a minute but, when he judged that enough time had passed, he signaled for Lee to hold out his hands and tied him up again, but this time, at least, in front, securely but with enough slack so that the hemp did not cut into his flesh. Lee nodded by way of thanks, but the Frenchman refused to look him in the eye. Lee was pushed toward his horse and Ouilet helped him into the saddle.

They moved up the valley, strung out over several hundred yards, with Lee and the other captives securely boxed into the middle of the line. The morning air was cold and their breath, and the breath of their horses, rose up in the air like the steam of a slow and cumbersome locomotive. Those who had thick coats wore them, but as the sun rose into the cloudless sky it began to grow warm. The creek beds they crossed were bone dry and Lee knew they would be looking for water before long. Lee spotted a small herd of antelope in the distance but no one else gave them a glance. The Frenchman rode beside him but did not utter a single word all morning. Finally, after they had been riding for three or four hours, he looked over at the younger man.

"Why don't you just tell him where they are? We will find them anyway."

"I can't. You saw what he did to that Blackfoot back there. Weren't you with him when he wiped out that village?"

"Oui."

"Then you know why I can't tell him. He'd kill them in cold blood."

"That is what soldiers do," Ouilet said with a shrug.

Without waiting for a response, the Frenchman spurred his horse forward and rode to the front of the column. He reined in beside the Lieutenant and Lee could see them speaking for a while. Then the scout rode on ahead, north by northwest, leaving the column behind. March turned in his saddle and looked back. Lee felt his cold dark eyes bore in on him.

Dutch Creek, Montana Territory

Jacob picked up their trail at midday and followed it for most of the afternoon, but they were riding blind now. It was too dark to see the trail, so the old trapper just kept them going in the same direction. The sun was low on the horizion and the shadows of the men on horseback stretched tall across the dry grass. The Colonel knew they should be looking for a place to camp, but they could not afford to stop. They would ride as far as their horses would carry them. If they didn't, they'd have no chance of catching up. Jacob and the Colonel rode side by side at the front of the column. Jacob was hoping he'd be able to pick up the trail again at first light. He was bone tired. He hadn't ridden such a long stretch in a while now. His back ached and the cold wind stiffened his joints. The Colonel was no less exhausted. He'd been on the trail for over a week now and was having trouble keeping his eyes open.

"Jacob," the Colonel said. "You better keep talking or I'm going to fall dead asleep."

"Maybe we should stop?"

"We can ride for another hour, don't you think?"

"Spose so. But we're getting too old for this."

"I know I am," The Colonel said.

More minutes passed with neither man able to think of much to say. Their tired bodies numbed their minds, and even talking seemed like too much trouble.

"How'd you get started in on this?" Cain asked. "What made you come West to begin with?"

"I was a farm boy," Jake started. "My Pa, he was the worst tiller of dirt who ever lived. There were four of us boys and he worked us like slaves. I don't remember much about him, cept him yelling at us and crackin us with a stick if we slacked up."

"Where was this?"

"Western Pennsylvania, I rekon. I don't recall exactly what part. Weren't no towns nearby. The land wasn't no good. You'd plant something in the soil and after a year it'd peter out. I recall moving once or twice, but the tale weren't no different."

"You the oldest?"

"Second. Older brother's name was George. He caught the worst of it. He tried like hell to keep on the old man's good side, but tweren't an easy thing to do. My Ma died somewhere along the way. I couldn't a been more than seven or eight. Don't remember much about her, neither."

"Nothing?"

"Sometimes I think I remember her face. Can almost see it. Then I lose it again. You know what I mean?"

"Yes. "

"I remember sitting on her lap. Hard to imagine an old coot like me ever sitting on his mammy's lap, eh?"

The Colonel laughed. "We were all babes, once."

"Lots of folks were moving down the rivers back then. Rafts and Keel boats down the Ohio. I hated farming, so one day I just took off. Couldn't have been more than twelve years old. Never went back neither. I cain't hardly remember my younger brothers. But I think about Georgie once in a while. I regret our paths never crossed."

"Maybe they did, and you never knew it."

"Maybe. But I imagine I'd a knowed George."

"How'd you start in on trapping?"

"I was working the wharves in St. Louie. Back then, they were rounding up any men who wanted to head west and make a fortune trapping fur. But it was bloody business. You'd lose half the crew to injuns, and a sight more to winter. Most only worked the one season. But I took to it, somehow."

"Money was good?"

"Naw, never panned out the way it was supposed to. But I had what I needed, which weren't much."

Jacob looked down at the grass to make sure he was still tracking, but there was nothing there to see.

"It was the life that kept you in it," he continued. "Being alone. No folks nearby. But the men you did meet; now they were a peculiar breed, bigger'n life and full of beans. And the country, tweren't nothing so grand."

"I can imagine."

"But it ain't for old men, I'll tell you that. I broke near all my fingers, at one time or another, working them traps. Had a couple of toes froze off and part of my ear. A cold wind like this blows in, ain't a part of my body don't start to ache."

"Mine too, and I haven't led half the life you have."

"You had the war," Jacob said. "Thank the Lord I missed it."

Cain nodded his head, but had nothing to say about it.

"This business with March." The Colonel finally ventured. "It isn't good."

"I know it," Jacob answered.

"He could bring the whole Blackfoot nation down on us, and we're not ready, I'll tell you that."

Jacob nodded and the Colonel continued.

"I don't know what he was thinking, going off on his own like that. He was never a likeable fellow, but I never thought him downright unstable."

"I thought the barrel leaked," Jake said. "First time I met him."

"The part about Lee complicates the matter."

"I know it does,"

"You know I like the boy. But I'm a military man; I'm expected to do my duty."

Jacob looked over at the Colonel, but he could only nod.

"There's a certain irony to it. There are men like Lee, who do what they think is right and damn the consequences. And there are men like March, who think only of themselves and who will destroy anything or anybody that gets in their way."

"I seen it all my days." Jake agreed.

"Maybe March is right. Maybe I'm not tough enough to make the hard decisions."

"You're a good man, Colonel," Jacob said. "The road West don't have to be paved in blood."

Lower Huron Valley, Montana Territory

They were in the shadows of the mountains and the foothills rose up before them, the flatness of the prairie broken by creek-beds that cut across the rolling grass. Lieutenant March had been leading them all afternoon and not a soul had been spotted. It was a dangerous time of day. The sun was in their eyes and they could not see what lay ahead, but the column itself stood out in silhouette against the low autumn light. At sunset they found a small creek that ran down from the hills with enough water in it for the horses to drink.

Sergeant Kelly ordered the men to secure the perimeter. They moved slowly, loosening their joints the way men do when they've been riding all day. He positioned them in pairs in a broad circle surrounding the camp. The men were hungry but, once again, the order went out that no fires would be lit. The men grumbled and gnawed at the dried meat and hard tack they carried in their packs. Lee was pulled off his horse and his hands were retied behind his back. He was led to a spot beside the Blackfoot prisoners, who seemed to be holding up better than he was without food or water. A few guards were posted, and they sat on the ground with their backs against their packs, their rifles aimed at the prisoners. Lee could hear March berating the men for not moving quickly enough or for doing a sloppy job setting up camp. His voice had a sharp staccato bite that carried clearly in the still air. It was an unpleasant sound.

An hour passed, and then another. It was a dark night, and the temperature was dropping sharply. Lee lay on his side, trying to stay below the wind. He heard the sound of somebody approaching and looked up. Lieutenant March looked down at him with contempt, signaled for one of the guards to bring a blanket, and sat down on the grass.

"Did you have a pleasant ride," March asked with feigned comradery, lifting a silver flask to his lips. Lee looked him in the eye, but did not answer.

"Are you hungry? Would you'd like something to eat? Maybe a nice cup of tea?

Lee continued to watch him without emotion.

"You've had a chance to think things out. We're way out here in the wilderness. Nobody to save you. If I were you, I'd start thinking of ways to salvage something from all this."

The Lieutenant held the flask out toward Lee, but even if he were inclined to accept it, his hands were tied.

"I have to laugh," March continued. "You really thought you were going to get away with it, deserting your post in the middle of a battle. Then coming out here thinking you'd be a big shot rancher and have everybody look up to you like you were the pride of territory. Even thinking that a girl like Elizabeth Cain would ever be interested in you."

March took another draw from his flask and leaned closer. Lee could smell the whiskey on his sour breath and see the contempt in his eyes.

"Girls like Elizabeth Cain don't marry ignorant vagrants like you. Oh, they may be intrigued for a week or two. But they come to their senses soon enough. Elizabeth is already embarrassed by the likes of you. She told me herself."

"You're a liar," Lee said.

"Am I? What do you think was going on all those months when you were playing cowboy back at the ranch?"

"Leave me be," Jake said.

I saw her every day. I took her riding; we took long walks. We had picnics, made plans. None of them included you, I'm sorry to say."

"I don't believe it. Elizabeth's not fool enough to fall for the likes of you."

The fist lashed out and caught Lee on the cheek and he rolled to the side. March stood and kicked Lee in the head. Lee felt a stab of pain, but March didn't stop there. He continued kicking, over and over until he was so out of breath he couldn't kick anymore. Lee tried to roll into a ball, but with his hands tied behind him he was not able to protect himself. The Lieutenant stood over him, lifted his boot, and stomped down on Lee's head. Lee fought for consciousness. He rolled over onto his stomach, defenseless. March ground Lee's face into the dirt, but he was already out cold. March looked down at the motionless form, then shook his head, straightened his coat, and walked back to his camp.

Lee woke to a buzzing in his ears. Blood had dried on his face and scalp and the deer flies had found him. Every inch of his body cried out in pain and a heavy fog hung in his brain. His vision was blurred and he thought, at first, that a mist had settled over the foothills. His head throbbed so painfully that he had to close his eyes until it subsided. Troopers were packing their gear and loading their horses. Lee, still lying in the dirt, opened his eyes again. He saw Lieutenant March and a group of soldiers approaching. He knew that another beating would probably kill him, but the soldiers ignored him, stopped in front of the Blackfoot and pulled another prisoner from the line.

They cut the bonds from his feet, pushed him toward the edge of the camp and left him standing by himself on the prairie. There were no trees here. No cottonwood or brush alder. This was a firing squad. March ordered the men to bring their rifles to bear. By this time, the prisoner realized what was happening and a look of fear came into his eyes. Lee expected him to turn and flee onto the prairie, but instead he charged, without a weapon of any kind, right at the soldiers, yelling at the top of his lungs. March hurriedly gave the order to fire and the Blackfoot was knocked backward by the force of the blasts, his body turned to pulp by the large caliber bullets. March looked annoyed that the execution had been hurried by such a futile gesture, but he turned on his heels and moved back to camp, shouting orders as he went.

Lee was lifted onto his horse and tied to the saddle. Even so, he wasn't sure he'd be able to keep himself from falling off. Sergeant Howard led the company across the low foothills. Lee was hardly aware of his surroundings. He leaned so low over the horse's neck that all he could see were the rippling muscles of its withers. The Blackfoot prisoners rode in front of him. There was still defiance in the posture of some, but most looked thoroughly beaten. Lee's tongue was swollen and dry and the sour metallic taste of dried blood sat heavy in his mouth. A few of his teeth were loose, and he could move them about with the tip of his tongue. At mid-day the column halted and the horses were allowed to drink from a small spring, but neither Lee nor the Blackfoot were allowed to dismount.

A few hours later a rider was spotted. Sergeant Howard ordered rifles drawn but they soon realized it was the Frenchman, Ouilet, returning from his scout.

"Any luck?" March asked when the rider pulled up beside them.

"Oui. I found them."

"How many?"

"Twenty lodges. They're spread out along a river. A group of young bucks, maybe ten or twelve, are camped off by themselves. The village proper is just up from them."

"How many fighting men?

"Maybe forty," Ouilet replied. "This is Broken Claw's village."

"You know him?"

"Yes. A good man, in my dealings, anyway."

"Well, he shouldn't be harboring murders," March said. "How far ahead?"

"Less than a day's ride."

"Lead the way," March ordered.

Dutch Creek, Montana Territory

Jacob picked up the trail again, right where he'd thought it would be. The trail led straight toward the mountains.

"They're heading for the foothills. The Blackfoot should be camped there this time year. Only place there's reliable water."

"How far ahead?" the Colonel asked.

"Hard to say. The sign seems a little fresher than it was yesterday. Maybe a day or two."

Cain tried not to show his displeasure. They could not ride any harder than they already had. But if they didn't, they'd be too late.

"Maybe I should ride ahead?" he asked.

"Too dangerous," Jacob said.

Cain looked out at the mountains and the low hills in the foreground. His eye searched the horizon for any sign of March and the others, but they were nowhere to be seen.

Huron Creek, Montana Territory

The sun had already set behind high peaks by the time they reached the river. Sergeant Howard set the guard and positioned the men. March ordered the prisoners gagged. He didn't suppose they were close enough that anyone might hear them if they shouted out, but he wasn't taking any chances. Lee was dragged off his horse. He was delirious and his head ached so badly that he simply wanted to pass out. They'd have another cold fireless camp tonight, but Lee wouldn't notice. Lieutenant Almanor had all the horses brought within the circle of the perimeter and set a guard. The other men sat down to eat but it was a silent, cheerless meal. They knew the Blackfoot were close and that took the chit chat right out of them.

After dark, Ouilet made his way over to the prisoner. Lee had not moved. He was still lying in the grass where he'd been dropped and the

Frenchman thought, at first, that he was dead. Ouilet knelt down and rolled Lee onto his back. He was shocked by the swollen purple mass of the young man's face, his hair caked with blood and dirt, his reddened eyes sunk deep within their sockets.

"Oh Mon Dieu," he muttered. "What has that madman done to you?"

He poured water onto his bandana and washed the dirt and dried blood from the young man's face. Lee winced with the pain, so at least the Frenchman knew he was alive.

"Water," Lee whispered in a voice so low the Frenchman had to bend to make it out. He brought the bladder up to his lips and let him drink. When he finished drinking Lee managed to nod thanks and Ouilet was relieved to see he had his senses about him.

"When is the last time you've eaten?" he asked.

"He's crazy," Lee whispered.

"Oui," the old scout answered.

The village lay upstream another day's travel. They would have to ride quietly, staying in the shadows when possible, keeping their dust down.

Lee felt a little better in the morning. Ouilet stayed with him as long as he dared, gave him some food to eat and made him drink. Lee was grateful for the help, though he couldn't figure out why the scout was helping him. When he was lifted back onto his horse the next morning he was still weak, but he could sit upright and hold on.

Late in the afternoon Ouilet told the Colonel that they had better stop. The village was within a mile, and there would be Indians about, hunting and gathering food. March ordered the men back and told Ouilet to show him the village. Huron creek dropped from the side of the mountain in a series of steps, trees lining both banks, deep in shadow now that the sun had dropped below the mountains. They climbed up a low shrub covered hill and looked down on the Piegan encampment. The creek wound out of the trees to the south. It was thirty yards across, but the water was low, no more than a few feet deep at its center. The bank was steep on their side but more gradual on the other, crowning across a field a hundred yards wide. The village was set back at the point where the field leveled out and the lodges were spread apart with plenty of room between them, well back from the bank. The forest rose directly behind and, from this distance, it appeared impenetrable.

"There's no sneaking up on them," Sergeant Howard said. "We'll have to cross open ground, charge straight up the hill."

"They won't be expecting us," March said.

"Do you demand for the surrender, first?" Ouilet asked.

"That would only give them a chance to prepare," March said. "We don't have the numbers. I can't take the chance."

"You told the young man he could negotiate."

"That was before I saw the situation," March said coolly. "Besides, he's in no condition to talk to anybody right now."

"Broken Claw is a reasonable man. Perhaps I can parley."

"Too risky," March looked at Ouilet with displeasure. "And there are the renegades to consider. They might be running the whole show, for all we know. Once we've subdued the hostiles, we can sit down and talk."

"But, Lieutenant," The Frenchman began.

"You don't need to worry. Your job is done. You'll get paid, just the same."

"When do we go in?" Howard asked.

"Sunrise. They'll be looking into the sun. Won't be able to tell how many they're facing or get a clear shot at us."

March pointed to a crossing in the river below them.

"See how the trail splits, just below the village. You and Kelly take half the men and ride in from the south. Stay in the trees until we attack. I'll take the rest and charge right at them. Keep the men moving forward. Don't stop. Meet up with me in the center. If we can keep them from getting to their horses. . ." March let the sentence go unfinished.

"Yes, sir," Sergeant Howard replied.

The main column had moved well back until they found a grove of large trees where they'd be hidden. The men lay scattered about on whatever level patches of bare duff they could find. Lee and the prisoners were led even deeper into the trees so that any shouts of warning would not be heard in the village. Lee was tied in a sitting position to the trunk of a tree. The Blackfoot prisoners were also tied to trees in groups of two and three. The soldiers went about their business without saying a word. Lee recognized the look on their faces, the look of men about to go into battle. Most were young and had never been shot at. Training is one thing but facing the real thing is altogether different. At the Lieutenant's order, the men were told to keep their voices to a whisper, which lent an even more somber mood to the cold dark camp, a mood not alleviated by the fact that fires could not be lit and the darkness in the forest was almost complete. By the time March, Sergeant Howard and Ouilet got back from their reconnaissance, the men were already settled into small groups, checking their rifles and equipment. Sergeant Howard went off to check the perimeter while March grabbed Ouilet by the shirt and faced him.

"It seems as though you're having second thoughts about the campaign, Ouilet?"

"I am not a soldier. I was merely offering my services."

"Just the same. When we head out in the morning you stay back here at camp. You're in charge of guarding the prisoners. If any of them gets away, I guarantee I'll have you shot."

"Oui, Lieutenant. I understand. There is no need to be unpleasant."

Ouilet walked to the rear until he found where the prisoners were being held. A young trooper had his back to the trunk of a tree, his rifle across his lap. The Blackfoot prisoners were securely tied. Some of the trees were so large that three or four were bound to a single trunk. Lee was kept apart and the trooper kept a wary eye on him.

"Have they given you any trouble?" Ouilet asked the trooper.

"No. They're tied up pretty tight."

"Good," The Frenchman said. "I'm going to take a little sleep. Wake me up in a few hours and I'll take the guard."

"OK," he said.

Ouilet could sleep anywhere, a skill developed after many years in the wilderness. He propped his bag against a root bole, spread his legs out in front of him and closed his eyes.

Lee tried to push against the bonds but his hands were tied separately, and then his arms and lastly his torso. He could not so much as wiggle. His head felt clearer than it had earlier, but the sharp throbbing had not gone away, and his body ached with every movement. He was sure a few of his ribs had been broken, but none of this concerned him. He looked over at the sleeping Frenchman. He knew that the water Ouilet gave him had saved his life, but he also knew that his life wasn't worth a whole hell of a lot right now.

A deep despondency overcame him at the knowledge that he was powerless to stop what was happening. Maybe he was cursed. This kind of trouble seemed to follow him, no matter where he went. There was no reasoning with a man like March, especially considering the personal animosity that existed between them. Lee swore to himself that the next time he'd trust his instincts and never let a man like March gain anything over him; but it didn't look like there would be a next time.

The camp grew even quieter, and the evening passed slowly. Only shadows crossed his field of vision, shadows and the still silhouettes of darkened trees rising to the thick canopy above him. He was exhausted from another long day of travel and weak from days of thirst and hunger, but he fought sleep, his mind desperate to find a thread of hope to which he might cling. But eventually his eyes closed and sleep overcame him.

A dream floated up from the depths of his despair. He was on the prairie, and the long green grass rippled in the wind. He was one of the feral mustangs that ran wild over the plains. It seemed so real that it was as if his life as Leopold Stemler was the dream and this was what he truly was. He was running at full gallop across the hills. He felt the pounding of his hooves against the thick grass and the rhythm of his stride ate up great swathes of ground. He was invincible, battling the other stallions for supremacy. But there were no rivals that could beat him, and no animal on the plains that could run him down.

But then, a strange new beast came onto the prairie. At first, he couldn't tell what it was, but it made its presence felt by the visceral wave of fear that swept before it, a raw terror that ate its way into his senses.

Gradually it came into focus, materializing in mid-air, coming straight towards him, death wafting towards him with every beat of its wings. It opened its mouth and screeched with the roar of a tornado. The gigantic eagle opened its cavernous beak and the stench of carrion spewed forth. The eagle cast a shadow across the sun and the beating of its wings shook the earth in rhythmic terror. Lee took all the mustangs that would follow and ran.

At first the ground was firm beneath him and the power in his legs was inexhaustible. But gradually, the land began to rise. The grass grew taller and the earth softer, so that his hooves sank a few inches into the damp soil with every step. He turned to see that it was gaining, and it had grown even larger and its form more terrible as it flew towards him.

Up into the high mountains they ran, and the grass turned white with snow and soon the snow was up to his forelegs, and then his chest and still he fought to break a trail for the others to follow, even though his huge lungs felt like they were on fire and would burst with the strain. He could no longer see the way but pushed blindly onward. A few of the horses fell behind but he could not slow down because the monster was close now.

The noise of the blizzard and the beating of wings was a constant roar, so loud he could hear nothing else, so loud that he shook his head from side to side to make it stop. Finally, with a great surge, he broke out of the clouds onto the very top of the mountain and he drew his family close around him. A sheer cliff dropped thousands of feet to the rocks below. There was no way down. He had no choice but to face the demon. A sudden calm came over him, knowing that all choices had been reduced to one. He turned, looking down at the sea of clouds that floated beneath the summit, knowing that an unknown fate rushed up at him from the depths below. He no longer feared death.

The trooper leaned over and shook Ouilet by the arm. The Frenchman stirred and sat up slowly; cursing the man in a language he didn't understand. Lee heard the noise and lifted his head; his heart was pounding and despite the cold he was slick with sweat. It took a few long minutes before he was able to calm himself and slow his breathing. The trooper moved off to find a flat spot to lay out his blanket, and Ouilet reached into his possibles and pulled out a small tin flask of whiskey. He looked up at Lee, who was watching now, raised the flask in a brief salute and took a snort, then stashed the flask back in the bag.

"I feel asleep," Lee said.

"Good," Ouilet replied.

"Is March going to try to talk to the chief?" Lee asked.

Ouilet shrugged, lifted his rifle to his lap and pulled a pipe out of his bag.

"The Lieutenant isn't interested in talking," he said.

"Did you try to talk him out of it?"" Lee asked.

"How could I? I am only a scout. They don't pay me to plan the strategy."

"You know these Indians. You speak their language."

"Oui. But as I say. I am not responsible for what you Americans do to your Indians. It is inevitable, as I see it. If it is not now, it will be later. Se la vie."

Lee laid his head back against the tree and watched the Frenchman, his features illuminated by the glow emanating from the bowl of the pipe, shrouded in a wreath of smoke that floated on the still air.

"I've seen this before," Lee said in a quiet voice. "In the war, before a big battle, before the shooting started."

Lee looked over at the Frenchman. Something told him that he was watching, listening.

"Men trying to get the hate to rise in them. To get themselves mad enough to kill. The officers would move down the line, trying to stir the fever up, whipping us into a frenzy to fight."

"You ever kill a man?" the Frenchman asked quietly.

Lee ignored the question, sat quietly for a minute, and then continued.

"Once the shooting started you didn't have to think. You moved forward. You fired your rifle; men were dying on all sides of you. Part of you wants to survive and another part doesn't care."

Oiulet didn't respond to this, continuing to smoke his pipe in silence. A few minutes passed.

"I thought it'd be different out here," Lee said. "All this open country. No need for men to be tripping over one another. Then I saw men kill each other over a few grains of gold dust. They'd hang those responsible, or those they thought might be."

"It's rough out here," Ouilet agreed.

"In the war, when the lines clashed, you'd have to fight for your life. Hand to hand. Look a man right in the eye and smell the stink of his breath. And suddenly it'd hit you that you could die, that it might all be over." Lee shook his head.

"Die," he said again, quietly. "It didn't make no sense. So, you'd kill him first. And the whole time you're thinking somebody should just make it stop, give an order or sound the retreat or something, just to make it stop, but no one never did. One side or another would fall back and regroup, then we'd go at it again. And nobody ever had the guts to put an end to it; to call a truce and just go home."

"That's what generaling's all about," Ouilet said.

"But at least back then there weren't women. It weren't children. I suppose it's easier here cause they look different than us. But a man can still recognize a woman when he sees one. Or a child. Do you think there's right in that?" Lee asked.

"No."

"Well, that's what March is aiming to do."

"The Lieutenant is un peu fou," Oiulet said, tapping out his pipe.

"I know one of the Blackfeet," Lee said quietly.

"I know this village myself," Ouilet replied.

"You do?"

"I have traded here. Bought furs from the chief, Broken Claw."

"Did he treat you poorly?"

"No, I have smoked the pipe with him many times."

"Then how can you be part of this?" Lee asked, not loudly, but with a note of quiet incredulity in his voice.

Again, the Frenchman shrugged.

"If things were turned around, I'm sure Broken Claw would not hesitate to kill me."

"That doesn't make it right."

"There is no right, my young friend. You will find that out soon enough, if you live."

The hours passed slowly, but Lee did not fall back to sleep. The darkness was nearly total, but Lee could see that the Frenchman was awake by the occasional glow of the pipe that floated, disembodied, in the blackness before him. Hours passed and Lee noticed a subtle lightening of the sky on the eastern horizon, though the darkness was, as yet, unrelenting in the depths of the forest. Ouilet stood and shook the stiffness out of his knees.

"Merde!" He muttered, crossing over to Lee and pulling a knife from its sheath. "Be very quiet," he whispered. "It is almost dawn."

Ouilet cut the ropes that bound Lee to the tree and then the bonds that tied his hands together. Lee tried to stand but found that he couldn't. A crippling pain shot through his legs and back. He had been absolutely immobile for hours and sensation was slow in reasserting itself.

"I'm sure I'm going to regret this," Ouilet whispered.

"Thank you," Lee whispered.

"Slip off into the hills. The Lieutenant will be too busy to come after you."

"I can't," Lee replied. "Untie the Blackfoot, but tell them to be very quiet."

"I don't know," Ouilet hesitated.

"You've got to trust me. Please, do what I ask. Have them circle around and head to the village. They're unarmed. They'll be massacred if they try to charge the troopers bare handed.

"What are you going to do?" Ouilet asked.

Lee smiled. "I ain't gonna run," he said.

Dawn was breaking, and the soldiers were starting to stir. Lee made his way silently through the trees, ducking out of sight, moving upstream towards the main body of the camp. A few soldiers were already up and attending to their gear. Lee spied Lieutenant March and watched as he checked the load on his double barrel shotgun. The Spencer rifle was leaning against a tree a few yards away. Without hesitating, Lee walked quickly forward, grabbed the rifle and stepped out from the shadows of the trees. It took March a second to realize what was happening, but by then Lee was standing twenty feet in front of him with the rifle aimed at his chest.

"Good Morning," he said.

"What the hell do you think you're doing, Stemler?"

Ouilet walked up beside Lee, his rifle also trained on the Lieutenant.

"I should have known better than to trust you," March said. "You son a French whore."

"I would kill you right now," The Frenchman said, nonchalantly. "But then, I might not get paid."

"So, what are you going to do?" March asked. "Get us all killed."

"No, we're going to turn around and get the hell out of here, before it's too late," Lee said.

"Like hell we are. This is one battle you're not running away from."

The troopers within hearing distance grabbed their rifles and surrounded the three men, but there was nothing they could do as long as Lee and the scout had their rifles leveled at the Lieutenant.

"Tell them to drop their weapons," Lee demanded.

"Don't you dare drop your guns," March ordered the men. "If he makes a move, blow him to pieces."

"Listen," Lee said loudly, so that the troopers could hear him. "Colonel Cain did not order this mission. March went behind his back."

"I'm the acting commander," March said. "I have the right to order an expedition in an emergency."

"What emergency? These Indians haven't done anything."

"Any man that lowers his rifle will be hung as a traitor," March barked out.

The men looked at one another with uncertainty but kept their rifles on Lee and the Frenchman.

"Looks like we have a stalemate," March said with a gloating smile.

Lee looked at Lieutenant with a look of utter contempt and shook his head, then raised his rifle and fired a single shot up into the air.

The sound of the shot echoed off the rocks and lingered in the air for the moment it took March to raise the shotgun to his hip and pull the trigger. Lee was knocked off his feet and Ouilet froze just long enough for Sergeant Howard to step forward and grab the rifle out of his hands.

March took two steps toward Lee, cocking the unfired barrel of the shotgun and it was clear he meant use it, but suddenly the newly freed prisoners jumped out of the darkness and fell upon them. Some were armed with tree limbs; others wielded sharp rocks in the palms of their hands. A few of the troopers went down in the initial assault or were wrestled to the ground. One of the Blackfoot charged the Lieutenant, who managed, at the last second, to turn and fire. The Indian flew backward, his chest ripped open by the force of the blast.

Lee sat up and fought to catch his breath, trying to figure out what was happening. The shot had caught him in the right shoulder and ribs, ripping open the flesh and drenching him in blood, but he could still move. He looked up just in time to see one of the Blackfoot clubbed with the butt of a rifle and fall heavily to the ground, his skull crushed by the blow. Lee tried to stand but could not get his legs beneath him.

He managed to bring his left arm up, pressing his hand against his shoulder to stop the bleeding.

March dropped the empty shotgun and turned back to retrieve the Spencer. Soldiers raced forward to join the fight. Many of the Blackfoot were already dead or being subdued, but Lee could still hear the sounds of struggle in the trees behind him. March lifted the Spencer and calmly shot one of the struggling warriors in the back. Lee saw the shot and heard a grunt as the man collapsed. March turned and saw Lee struggling to his feet and swung the barrel of the Spencer toward him, levering a new round into the chamber. Their eyes met, and Lee knew his luck had run out.

The Lieutenant heard something and turned his eyes away from his victim, looking up to see a large force of Blackfoot warriors ride into the clearing. Mountain Sun looked down from the roan and took in the scene before him. March and the rest of the troopers swung their rifles toward the Indians and, in the half second before another melee broke out, Lee struggled to his feet, stepped forward and lifted his arms.

"No," he yelled to the soldiers. "Don't shoot."

Somehow, nobody on either side opened fire. The soldiers hesitated but did not lower their rifles. Lee turned to Mountain Sun.

"Please, wait," he said, hoping the Blackfoot would understand. Ouilet quickly stepped forward.

"Listen to what the White man has to say," the Frenchman yelled.

Mountain Sun recognized Lee and shook his head in disappointment.

"You brought them here?" he asked.

"No," Ouilet said, not bothering to translate this to Lee. "He was a prisoner. This man," he said, pointing to March, "wanted to bring in the renegades who killed the White hunters. Lee was trying to stop them."

"This is the 'good man' from the fort you told me about?" Mountain Sun asked sarcastically.

Ouilet was about to translate this when there was more commotion to the south and Lee turned to see Colonel Cain and Jacob, with their hastily assembled column, ride into view. One of the Blackfoot raised his rifle at the approaching soldiers but the Frenchman stepped forward to stop him.

It was too late. The bullet pierced Ouilet's skull and knocked him to the ground. Lee ran to his side but the wound was mortal and the Frenchman already dead.

Mountain Sun yelled angrily at the shooter, but at the same time signaled his warriors to spread out and keep their guns ready. Cain and his men reined in their horses. Both parties faced one another over thirty yards of open ground, with March and Lee in the middle of it all.

"What's going on here, Lieutenant?" Cain asked.

"We were getting ready to move into the village. But Grant freed the prisoners and set them on us."

"What were the prisoners doing out here in the first place?" The Colonel asked.

"Insurance," March said. "Hostages."

"Are you alright?" Jacob asked Lee, looking at the blood darkening his shirt.

"I'll be alright," Lee replied.

Cain stood in his saddle and yelled to the men. "Nobody fire unless I give the word."

But despite this, tensions were mounting and both sides were poised to attack. A twitch, a blink, a breath of wind could trigger it, and once the shooting started, there'd be no stopping it. Jacob swung down off his horse, grasping for a way out. By this time Broken Claw had ridden up from the village and had taken his place next to his son. He took in the scene with great distaste; saw the Frenchman lying on the ground with the black of his head blown off, the troopers dead and dying and the slaughtered remains of the Blackfoot prisoners lying among them. Mountain Sun said some words to his father that Jacob could not make out, but Jacob moved forward.

"This is the Chief of the Long Knives," Jacob said in Blackfoot, pointing to Colonel Cain. "He rode here to stop the killing."

Broken Claw looked around again.

"He has not succeeded," Broken Claw said.

"Colonel," March said. "These are the renegades I told you about. They killed those buffalo hunters and they've been raiding up and down the front. I got word of where they were camped. I acted on it. I couldn't wait for you."

"Is this true?" Cain asked Broken Claw.

"We did not kill the White hunters. But I would have, if I had caught them first."

Cain was not sure how to react to such a response. Did the Indians have the right to protect their property within the borders of their own nation, even if it meant killing White men? He felt that he had been backed into the whole issue and knew it would be wise to step away until tempers had cooled.

"I know these Indians," Lee said to Colonel Cain.

Lee walked over to the dead body of the Frenchman.

"Your scout knew them, too. Traded with them. He untied me so that I could prevent this son of a bitch from massacring them."

None of the Indians understood what Lee was saying, but they recognized that a struggle was taking place. They could hear the accusation Lee directed at the Lieutenant, and the look of pure hatred March returned.

"We better get out of here before all hell breaks loose," Cain said. "Jake. Tell the Chief that we are sorry for the misunderstanding. That we will gather our dead and wounded and leave. . ."

Before he could finish the sentence Lieutenant March turned the Spencer on the Colonel and chambered a round, holding the barrel steady on his chest.

"You're no better than he is," March said, indicating Lee. "We're going to finish what we started."

Lee was watching all this in disbelief, and the Blackfoot were also unsure of who was in charge or what was transpiring. The White men are truly crazy, Broken Claw thought to himself.

Lee saw a colt protruding from the belt of the trooper standing beside him and he quickly snatched it out of the holster and turned it on the Lieutenant. March saw the movement out of the corner of his eye and swung on Lee, firing in the same movement. Lee was hit, but even as he fell backward he swung the colt up and pulled the trigger. The shot went through March's left breast pocket and he dropped to his knees. He fell, face first into the dirt. Dead.

Mountain Sun jumped down off his horse and ran over to Lee, with Jacob only a step behind them. The fact that a Blackfoot and the old White man had rushed to young man's aid did much to lower the level of tension. Colonel Cain got down from his horse and walked slowly over to Lieutenant March, turning him over onto his back. There was remarkably little blood, but March's lifeless eyes stared out at him. The Colonel's first instinct was to see if Lee was still alive, but he knew that his duty demanded that he make sure the threat was over. He stood slowly, turned and approached Broken Claw, who had also dismounted. The two men stood face to face.

"There's been too much blood," Cain said.

Broken Claw did not understand the words, but felt their meaning. He nodded his head in agreement and the two men stood together, looking over at the spot where Lee lay in the dirt. The bullet had missed his jugular by half an inch, cutting a furrow in the muscle along the side of his neck as it passed through. There was blood everywhere.

Mountain Sun lifted Lee to a sitting position. Jacob pressed a cloth against the wound to stop the bleeding, shaking his head slowly.

"You are one lucky son of a bitch," he said.

"You call this lucky?" Lee asked weakly.

Mountain Sun looked down at his friend. "I am sorry for doubting you," he said.

"I don't blame you," Lee said, waiting while Jacob translated.

Jacob handed Lee a canteen of water and Mountain Sun held it steady while Lee drank. When Jacob was satisfied that Lee was in good hands, he walked over to Broken Claw and the Colonel.

"How is he?" Cain asked, clearly expecting the worst.

"He'll live." Jacob said.

"Thank God," Cain said.

"Is that the White Brother my son has told me about?" Broken Claw asked.

"Yes." Jacob replied. "He's hurt bad, but he'll live."

"Bring him to the village."

Jacob translated this for the Colonel. Cain looked doubtful and glanced over at Jacob.

"He's too weak to travel," Jake said to the Colonel. "It'll be alright, their medicine's good as our'n,"

"I'd stay," The Colonel said to Jacob. "But I think we better be heading back to the fort. The garrison's bone thin, and with this many guns in one place, the possibility of an incident is too great."

"I spose you're right." Jacob said.

The Colonel walked over to Lee and went down on one knee. Lee tried to smile.

"Sorry for the mess, Colonel."

"Not your fault. How are you feeling?"

"Tired," he said.

"Try not to talk. They're going to get you cleaned up."

Lee looked up at the older man. "March?" he asked.

"Dead."

Lee closed his eyes for a moment and all expression left him.

"You had no choice, son. He would have killed you."

Heron Creek, Piegan Territory

It had been a week since the Long Knives had left. For the first two days Lee fell in and out of consciousness and his fever raged unabated. Raven washed his wounds and packed them with the pulp of a succulent that grew in the sunny spots among the rocks. She made a soup that she forced him to eat and watched him every hour of every day. Gradually his strength began to return. When she felt he was strong enough, she undertook to repair the damage to his shoulder. The shotgun blast had torn the muscle up badly and Raven had to use a small knife to pry the pellets from the flesh. The pain had been intense, but even the Blackfoot had been impressed by how the young White man kept from crying out.

His wounds were starting to heal and on a cool and cloudless afternoon Lee sat on a buffalo skin that had been brought out into the sunshine for him. Mountain Sun sat beside him, sharpening the steel knife that the Colonel had given him. Jacob lay with his back against the lodge, smoking his pipe in the sunshine. Raven brought Lee a cup of tea that tasted so foul it turned his stomach, but he knew better than to refuse it.

"I guess I'm ready to ride some," Lee said to Mountain Sun.

"There is no hurry," Mountain Sun replied. "You are welcome to stay."

"I know," Lee said. "And I'm grateful."

Truth was, he was anxious to get back to the ranch. Chance and Meers had been left there alone and must, by now, have assumed the worst. The next morning Broken Claw had the horses brought up and Jacob strapped on the saddles and packed the bags. They were given enough dried meat and medicine to make the long journey south. Lee reached out his hand and the Piegan stepped forward and grasped it firmly.

"Thank you," Lee said.

Mountain Sun shrugged, but did not release his grip.

"I think the Great Spirit has woven our fates together. Can you see that?" he asked.

"Sure, seems so," Lee answered. "Will you be settling here for a while?"

"I don't think so. This isn't my village anymore, and the men are ready to move on."

"You'll come visit us? At the Ranch?

"I'll come," he said.

"Good," Lee said. "We can hunt again up in the mountains. When the snows melt."

Epilogue

It was the hardest week of my life. I was powerless to do anything but wait. And I made a vow, then and there, that I would not sit by while the men in my Iife made all the decisions and took all the risks. I wanted to partner in things, the good and the bad, for a future that I helped shape, not one whose path I blindly followed.

Elizabeth Cain

Red Creek Ranch, Montana Territory

It was only his second autumn in the valley, but Lee already knew it was his favorite time of year. The mountains were streaked in red, gold and yellow, each ascending to its own elevation. The fragile fabric of the light playing over the meadow seemed to change, to grow softer and more distinct. Mornings were cold, but the sun still had enough strength to warm the valley by midday.

A procession of waterfowl filled the sky, all following the line of the Rocky Mountain Front south for the winter. Geese and ducks were plentiful. The deer and elk came into rut, and the sounds of epic battles carried on the still air till late into the evening.

Lee sat on the porch most afternoons. He could look out over his meadow and see the herd grazing in the distance and keep track of the comings and goings of Jake and the others. They'd wave from a distance, trying to avoid venturing too close because there was always a new chore Lee could come up with. He kept a piece of writing paper nearby in case another project came to mind. He hated being laid up when the weather was still good enough to get some work done. He wouldn't have minded so much if it were winter, when you were indoors anyway.

The days were growing shorter. He was leaning against the porch rail, watching the big clouds float across an ice blue sky. It was cool when the sun ducked behind a cloud and perfectly pleasant when it broke through again. Lee looked down the valley and saw the riders. He called out to Jacob, who came out onto the porch carrying a rifle in the crook of his arm.

"Looks like the Colonel," Jacob said.

"Is she with him?" Lee asked.

"Leastwise somebody is. You know Miss Elizabeth's not one to ride in petticoats."

As they got closer Lee saw that it was the Colonel and his daughter, with an escort of mounted troopers. Lee tucked in his shirt and ran his fingers through his hair. As soon as they rode up, Lee stepped down off the porch to greet them.

"You look a damn sight better than last time I saw you," the Colonel said, extending his hand.

"I feel better. Thanks."

The Colonel turned and shook Jake's hand. "But you're the same sorry old coot you've always been."

"Same, same," Jake said, smiling.

He and the Colonel had developed a friendship of sorts, one that required an insult or two to keep it on an even keel.

Elizabeth swung down off her horse in a single graceful motion, walked up to Lee and gave him a hug, ever so gently, and maybe lasting a second longer than it ought to. Then she walked over to Jacob and gave him one as well.

"Thank you for bringing them back," she said.

"Told you I would," he smiled.

All the men were a little uncomfortable with all this hugging. Lee looked down at his boots and The Colonel looked around at the ranch, the cabin, corrals and barn.

"This is quite impressive." Cain said. "You've put some work in."

"You bet," Jacob said. "I told you. That boy's a slave driver."

"Well, it is something." Cain replied. "Can't remember when I've seen a prettier spot."

"Thanks Colonel," Lee said. "Why don't you come on inside and sit down?"

"Oh, I will. But I've been in the saddle for hours. Just as soon stretch by legs."

"Want me to show you around?" Jacob asked.

"That'd be fine." The Colonel said.

"Why don't you boys take the horses over to the corral and get em settled," Jacob said to the troopers. "Then go on up to the kitchen and Meers will make you something to eat."

The men nodded their thanks, took the horses and led them away. Jake started down the path with the Colonel in tow. Cain turned a questioning look to Elizabeth.

"You go along," she called. "I'll visit here with Lee for a while."

"Alright," her father answered. "Be back shortly."

Jake was already talking up a storm, cursing and pointing things out to the Colonel as they walked toward the barn. They could hear the Colonel laughing as he walked beside the old trapper. Elizabeth turned to face Lee, and her fingers went to the red welt the bullet had carved along the side of his neck.

"That was close," she said.

"Real close," Lee replied.

"My father told me what happened. It's a miracle you weren't killed."

"I would have been, if it hadn't been for him."

"It's awful," Elizabeth said in a tremulous voice.

Lee didn't know what to say to make her feel better. He wanted to tell her that everything was going to be fine, but it wasn't his place to deny her sadness.

I'm real sorry about the Lieutenant," Lee said.

"You got the wrong idea," Elizabeth said, "Back when you saw us."

"I know," he said. "I'm pretty stupid, sometimes."

Lee took Elizabeth by the arm and led her onto the porch and the two chairs he'd positioned there overlooking the valley. But instead of sitting, they leaned against the rail and looked out over the meadow.

"Are you alright, now?" she asked.

"I'll be fine. I mend fast.

"I wanted to come sooner, but it's been a busy time."

"That's alright. I wouldn't have been much company."

Elizabeth looked out over the field of grass towards the creek meandering gently down the valley, and then turned to gaze up at the mountains rising beyond the rock ridge to the west.

"What you've done here, I mean, with the ranch. It's really remarkable.

"I want to show it to you," Lee said.

"I want to see it."

"All the little things. The way the meadow looks in the morning when the sun catches the dew on the grass, or how the horses run full gallop across the valley when we open the corral. I want to take you riding at sunset to watch the way the peaks catch the light, then ride back after dark so you can see the windows of the cabin glowing red in the firelight. I see it every day, Elizabeth, and I ain't never got tired of it."

"It sounds wonderful," she said.

Lee sat down on the handrail and leaned his back against the post, turning to look at her.

"They say peoples coming."

"How's that?" Elizabeth asked.

"Settlers," Lee said. "Jake thinks they'll ruin things, but I think it won't be so bad. A place with a few stores and a restaurant, maybe even a church. Helena's not too far. It might be convenient."

Lee had run out of things to say. He stared out over the meadow, watching as the low angle of the sun cast bands of light and shadow across the valley. Without speaking, he reached out for Elizabeth's hand, and she gave it to him, and then she moved closer beside him and leaned her arm against his and rested her head on his shoulder. Some part of him knew he was happy, that this was what he'd been waiting for, but he didn't trust himself to put words to it, or even acknowledge it, lest the spell be broken. He could hear Jake and the Colonel walking up the path, laughing loudly at some joke, and Lee knew their time, like all time, was borrowed and not their own. But they held on a little longer, reluctant to let go.

"Elizabeth?" Lee asked. But she did not answer, merely squeezed his hand."

"Do you think you could ever be happy? In a place like this? With a man like me?" Lee asked in a quiet voice.

But this time it was Elizabeth who was at a loss for words. She reached up and touched his cheek with the tips of her fingers and, as he turned towards her, he saw a tear welling up in her eye, but only for a moment. A gentle smile brightened her face. And then she was kissing him and nothing else seemed to matter.

About the Author

Gennaro Rosetti is a multidisciplinary creative whose life and work span the landscapes of California and Montana. An accomplished artist, designer, writer, historian, and award-winning furniture maker, his storytelling draws from a rich tapestry of experiences—from the rugged spirit of the American West to the golden glow of 1960s Hollywood, where he came of age. He is a devoted husband, father of two, and proud grandfather of three.